"You've been away from your world too long. When you get back to Seattle you'll realize you have better choices." Reece folded Jordan's hands and placed them on her lap. "In the dark, everyone looks alike."

"In the dark, I can still tell who I love."

"Jordan, please. Don't say that. We are worlds apart." Reece started the truck. "We had a nice camping trip, a couple dates. That's all. You got your story."

"Look at me, Reece. Look me in the eye and tell me you don't feel the same." Jordan turned Reece's face toward her and stared into her eyes. "Tell me you don't care about me the same as I care about you. Tell me you don't love me the same as I love you."

Reece hesitated, wrestling over her response. Her eyes studied Jordan for a long moment, first with adoration then cautious concern. Reece's expression went from love to pain in less than a second. She looked out the windshield and narrowed her eyes as she thought.

"I don't," she said finally, then pulled onto the road.

Visit

Bella Books

at

BellaBooks.com

or call our toll-free number

1-800-729-4992

SKIN DEEP

Kenna White

Bella
BOOKS
2007

Bella Books, Inc.
P.O. Box 10543
Tallahassee, FL 32302

First Edition

Editor: Anna Chinappi
Cover designer: LA Callaghan

ISBN-10: 1-59493-078-3
ISBN-13: 978-1-59493-078-2

Dedicated to Ann,
love of my life, fire in my soul and compass to my journey.

Acknowledgment

Many thanks to all the gals who bring me coffee and offer support as I write for hours in the booth by the window while all the other customers come and go. Sometimes a smiling face is all it takes to brighten a writer's spirit.

And to Cameron and Haley for just being special.

About the Author

Kenna White lives in a small town nestled in southern Missouri where she enjoys her writing, traveling, making dollhouse miniatures and life's simpler pleasures. After living from the Rocky Mountains to New England, she is once again back where bare feet, faded jeans and lazy streams fill her life.

Chapter 1

Jordan Griffin waited impatiently in the rain for the pedestrian light to change. She was already late for the Tuesday morning editorial staff meeting but a morning without a cup of Starbucks to vault her senses into gear was unthinkable. Now she was stuck in the gridlock of downtown Seattle rush hour. As the walk light changed to green and the sea of umbrellas moved across the street, Jordan's cell phone began merrily playing "How Dry I Am." She balanced her umbrella handle between her shoulder and her chin as she fished the phone from her raincoat pocket. With the skill of a circus juggler, she exchanged the telephone for the umbrella while supporting a briefcase strap over her other shoulder and carrying a double latte with a plastic bag hooked over her finger.

"I'm two blocks away, Susan," she said, stepping up on the curb.

"Did you get my biscotti?" the woman on the other end asked.

"Yes," Jordan replied, refraining from saying that was why she was late.

"Come to Mark's office as soon as you get here. We've already started." Susan hung up without waiting for a reply.

Jordan hurried along the sidewalk, dodging slower pedestrians and hoping to make it to the light at the next corner before it changed again. She was sure New York City rush hour traffic and sidewalk congestion had nothing on Seattle. The added extra Seattle did offer was the steep hills and chronic inclement weather that further snarled the downtown commute. It took Jordan six months to be able to hike down Pine Street to Starbucks and back up again to the office building without stopping at least once to catch her breath. She had been a flatlander, a suburban lover, a Colorado native from Fort Collins who wasn't used to six months of nearly constant rain and crowded inner city employment. Her first job after graduating with a master's degree in journalism had been with the *Boulder Gazette*. It was a small newspaper with a narrow readership and an even narrower viewpoint. The job didn't last long but it did teach her to appreciate a good work environment. Her first job with a periodical had been with the *Mountain States Cattlemen's Journal* as an assistant editor. She liked the job in spite of the limited appeal and assignments. She had spent her four years with the magazine driving the backcountry of Colorado and Wyoming, talking with ranchers and taking pictures of cows and sheep. Glamorous, it wasn't. Good experience, maybe. When *Northwest Living Magazine* advertised for an assistant editor, she literally jumped out of her mud boots at the chance to move to Seattle and move toward a more sophisticated style of journalism. It didn't take her long to realize she had finally arrived at a job she enjoyed. She was living the independent lifestyle in a big metropolitan city filled with culture, ambiance, opportunities for travel and great dining and most of all, a fairly well-paying career. Jordan dodged a spray of water sent up by a passing car as it sped through a puddle. She trotted around a group of slow-moving businessmen and rushed into a revolving door, collapsing her umbrella just as the door spun closed.

"Hold the elevator, please," she called as she hurried inside. She stepped to the back of the elevator and leaned against the glass wall, shaking the water from her raincoat and pushing some curl back into her blonde hair. It had been long and flowing from the time she was a third grader in Fort Collins to the time she moved to Seattle. It didn't take her long to see the wisdom of a shorter more manageable style, one more popular with the trendsetters and busy career women in the Northwest.

"Good morning, Lisa," Jordan said to the young woman behind the reception desk as she entered the double glass doors marked *Northwest Living*. The outline of the Seattle Space Needle and Mount Rainier was the magazine's logo and was printed on the door, the wall behind the reception desk and in the carpet of the lobby.

"Morning, Ms. Griffin," Lisa mumbled through a bite of donut. "You are supposed to go right in," she advised, pointing down the hall to the left.

"Thank you," Jordan replied with an understanding smile, but she went down the hall to the right and unlocked her office. After hanging up her coat and checking her looks in the mirror, she grabbed the biscotti bag, her coffee and a stack of folders then went to the meeting.

"Where is my biscotti?" the woman at the far end of the table asked even before Jordan could get in the door. Jordan slid the sack down the table and took her place. A balding man with a dark goatee and a thick pair of glasses sat at the other end. He was reading something and didn't look up but waved at Jordan.

Susan Mackey was the senior editor and had been so since the magazine's inception twelve years ago, mainly because her father was on the board of directors of the consortium that owned it and four other publications as well as a television station. The blind consortium that managed the syndicate of publications agreed to hire Susan, at Franklin Mackey's urging, since she did have a degree in journalism. She didn't have the experience the board would have liked but that is where Mark Bergman came in. He was the managing editor and the best there was. Mark's long work experience brought him kudos that couldn't be ignored by the board. It also allowed a blind eye to the nepotism of hiring Susan. Mark's age was the only factor that kept him from rising to the top of his field. At sixty-five, many of the top magazines considered him too old to handle the rigors of the publishing game. But he had found a home with *Northwest Living*. Mark's job was to keep the train on the tracks and rolling along in spite of Susan's accidental attempts at derailing it. Susan had affixed her job as managerial, something her ego could easily live with.

"Where are the almonds?" Susan asked disgustedly, examining the pastry.

"I have no idea," Jordan replied, hitching in her chair. "You asked for chocolate dipped almond. That's what you got."

"Where did you get it? Starbucks?" Mark asked without looking up. "Truman's Coffee Shop on Eighth is better. Great biscotti."

"The coffee at Truman's is terrible. Tastes like IHOP leftovers," Susan inserted, taking a bite.

"IHOP reuses their coffee grounds," Mark advised.

"No, they don't," Jordan argued with a frown, sorting through her folders.

"Gelfers," Susan stated, covering her mouth as she chewed. "Gelfers reuses their grounds. I saw the manager pouring water back through the machine."

"Gelfers has good pastry," Mark added. "But don't get the cannoli. They store the shells in the refrigerator and they get soggy." Mark had moved on to another page, still reading intently.

"If you want cannoli you have got to go to DeLaurent's at Pikes Place Market. They shave the chocolate into little rolls," Susan said, moaning at the thought. "They are so good."

"Where are Didi and Helen?" Jordan asked, looking at the empty chairs. She was growing tired of Susan and Mark's discussion. Every Tuesday morning they spent twenty minutes playing one-upmanship about some obscure topic. Last week it was where to buy pet food. The week before that it was which recently released movie was worth paying eight dollars to see.

"Helen is in Portland and Didi has the flu. You can e-mail them a rundown of the meeting," Susan advised.

"Swell," Jordan muttered under her breath, knowing something else just got added to her list of tasks today.

They finally got the meeting going. Several story ideas were discussed for future issues and problems were hashed out. Jordan helped decide which of their reporters and contributing writers would be assigned which story. Jordan already had four articles she was working on as well as editing stories from two interns. Mark asked her to look over the cover story on Seattle's microbreweries and the second in a series of articles on junior colleges in the Puget Sound area. It was a heavy load but Jordan knew it was all part of the job. Something else was always added to the plate, even when it was filled to overflowing.

"Did you see the newspaper article on that tanker that went aground by Oak Harbor?" Susan asked, sliding a photograph across the table toward Jordan.

"No, I didn't see it, but I heard about it," Jordan replied, looking through her folders.

"Maybe we should send a photographer out to get some shots and do a story on the danger to the ecosystem and the wildlife."

"As I remember, the tanker was empty. It was an old one and being towed out to sea where it would be sunk and used as a fish reef," Jordan said, still reading. "I don't think it was going to endanger the ecosystem."

"I have a great idea, Jordan. We could cover the building of artificial reefs to help replace a depleting habitat." Susan made the declaration as if she expected some great accolades over it. "Let's get some shots of the rusty tanker. And call research for some stock photos of underwater reefs." Susan spoke eagerly and with purpose.

"We did that story," Jordan said, looking up. "Last November."

"Oh, right," Susan replied then smirked. "I forgot."

"We might take a look at a story on ferry travel, though," Mark said. "The economy is taking a bite out of their business, big time. Oil prices and repair costs are driving the small companies to merge or fold. Might be something there."

"Okay, I'll have Didi check it out, unless you want it, Jordan," Susan said, looking over at her.

Jordan shook her head as she kept reading the contents of a folder.

"I've got one more I want you to check on, Jordan," Mark said, sliding a folder over to her. "Reece McAllister."

"Who is Reece McAllister?" she asked, opening the folder.

"We did an article on her a few years ago. I think it was the year before you were hired," Susan said, looking over at the folder.

Mark opened a back issue of the magazine and slid it over for Jordan to see as well. The article was titled "The Northwest's Ten Best Self-Made Success Stories." The article included two sports figures, a transplanted Japanese couple, three businessmen, a woman who hit the lottery twice, a teenage music prodigy and a female television journalist with dark sultry eyes and a radiant smile. The caption under the photograph read: "Reece 'Race' McAllister embedded with the U.S. Army troops as they roll into Baghdad." She was standing next to an armored Humvee and was wearing an army flak vest and helmet as she interviewed a soldier. In spite of her dusty clothes and the hair-raising environment, her striking beauty was clearly apparent. Jordan studied the woman's eyes and her confident posture. There was a kind and gentle softness in her eyes that even the brutal warfare couldn't diminish.

"She's the one who got the last interview with Yasser Arafat," Jordan said, scanning the article.

"Reece McAllister earned a huge salary as a Global News Network reporter. She was at Ground Zero in Manhattan interviewing the rescue workers. She was on that oil rig in the Gulf of Mexico when Hurricane Katrina roared through the gulf coast. She was in Afghanistan and Iraq several times, bringing live feeds from the battlefields. You name the big story, she was there," Mark explained, cleaning his glasses on his tie.

"I remember her," Jordan said. "Why are we interested in doing another piece about her?"

"Because now she is doing this," he replied, sliding a flyer in her direction.

"Photography?" Jordan asked, reading the flyer.

"She has a showing at a gallery over on Cherry Street. The opening is Thursday evening and runs for several weeks. It seems she has retired from broadcast journalism and has taken up photojournalism instead. She gave up her lucrative job at GNN three years ago and now she travels around Washington taking pictures of mountains and wildlife." He shook his head as if disapproving of the woman's choice.

"And?" Jordan asked, still not convinced this was a story worth her time.

"No one gives up that kind of money without a damn good reason," he replied.

"And we all know you can't make that kind of money taking pictures," Susan offered.

"Some photographers do pretty well if they have built a name for themselves or are taking pictures of famous people," Jordan replied.

"She only takes nature shots. At least that is the kind of things that will be at her showing," Mark said, pointing to the flyer. "There will be thirty-eight pieces on sale and there isn't a human in any of them."

"So you think something fiendish is going on because she now uses a camera instead of a microphone?" Jordan offered.

"Don't you?" he asked, rocking back in his chair and clasping his hands behind his head. "She has turned down an interview with the *Seattle Herald* and a local television station. She was invited to be a keynote speaker at a conference last year in Vancouver and another one in Tacoma just last month. She refused them both. The Oregon Publisher's Conference offered her five grand, but she blew it off. I think it's worth a look. Worse-case scenario, there is no story. Just a loser with a drug addiction or some such thing."

"And best-case scenario?" Jordan asked.

"Best case, maybe five thousand words with a comparative angle and a half-dozen photos," he replied.

"We've heard she had some kind of accident. We're not sure, but it was about the time she and her girlfriend broke up," Susan said.

"Girlfriend?" Jordan asked, assuming this meant Reece McAllister was a lesbian.

"Pella something or other," Susan said. "You know, the model."

"Reece McAllister's girlfriend was Pella Frann?" Jordan asked curiously.

"Yes, Pella Frann."

"There's a big name for you," Mark quipped. "Or at least was. She did the *Sports Illustrated* swimsuit cover two years running." His eyes flashed with a testosterone gleam. Susan and Jordan both had the same image of the voluptuous beauty but refrained from drooling.

"I wonder whatever happened to her," Susan said, her own lesbianism spurring her curiosity onward.

Mark and Jordan shrugged.

"Wasn't she French or Swiss or something?" Susan asked.

"That's something Jordan can ask Reece when she interviews her," Mark offered.

"Assuming she'll give her an interview," Susan scowled.

"I have every confidence in Jordan's ability to get the story," Mark stated. "Turn on the charm, Jordan. Give her that big smile of yours and she'll be telling you anything you want to know."

"You're right. No one can resist Jordan's charm," Susan said then winked at Jordan.

"There may not be a story here," Jordan warned.

"Bring me something before the first of the month and I'll work it in the November issue," Mark said, gathering the folders and heading to his desk. This was the signal that the meeting was over. Jordan collected the information about Reece McAllister and followed Susan out the door.

Chapter 2

Jordan circled the block twice before finding a parking spot. The Rose Hall Gallery was tucked in a corner building. The windows were blocked on the inside by several elaborate enameled Japanese screens. The doors were locked and a handmade sign with artistic calligraphy lettering announced the upcoming opening of the Reece McAllister Photography Collection. Jordan peeked between the screens, trying to see inside, but she could only catch slivers of wall, a leg, a ladder and a stack of frames. She found a spot at the corner of the window where, if she stood on her tiptoes, she could see two women talking. One was a matronly looking woman in her fifties in high heels and a black-and-white checked jacket over a black skirt. She was pointing to one of the walls then at the clipboard she was carrying. The other woman was wearing jeans and a brown turtleneck with the sleeves pushed up to the elbow. Jordan couldn't be sure but the woman in jeans had a profile similar to the photograph she had seen of Reece McAllister.

She had an attractive figure with a well-proportioned body. Her brunette hair was cut just below her ears and was full of restless curls. When she smiled at the other woman, tiny lines lit the corner of her eye and mouth. Jordan wished she would turn around so she could see her entire face so she could be sure if this tall attractive woman was indeed the famous but mysterious television notable, Reece McAllister. Just as Jordan was about to tap on the window to get the women's attention they both strode into the back room and closed the door. She considered waiting for them to return but she was parked in a fifteen-minute loading zone and didn't want a fifty-dollar parking ticket. She waited another five minutes but when no one came out of the closed door, Jordan reluctantly returned to her car. She would just have to wait until Thursday to meet Reece and discover the secrets to her elusive lifestyle.

Jordan returned to the office. She spent the afternoon finishing an article then researched Ms. McAllister's background so she would be well prepared for an interview.

"You're working late," Susan said, sticking her head in Jordan's open office door.

Jordan checked her watch. It was a quarter past six. She was working late for a reason. She had a date at seven and it was easier to stay in town than to drive to her apartment in Kirkland then turn around and come back. She was meeting Mia Eisley for dinner at Christopher's Restaurant, an upscale downtown eatery two miles from Jordan's office. But Jordan knew better than to tell Susan who she was meeting. The last time she admitted she was on her way to meet someone she had to endure a long litany of questions about who it was, how long she had been seeing the woman and what she did for a living. It was easier to keep Susan guessing than to have her questioning who she chose to date.

Jordan hit the save key and shut down her computer.

"The piece on Port Orchard is finished. As soon as Jackie e-mails me the photos I'll crop and send them on to you." Jordan leaned back in her chair, the long hours hunched over the computer stiffening her back. "I have to send Rene back out tomorrow. I can't use one of those photographs she took for the Botanical Society." Jordan stood up and stretched.

"Why not? They looked fine to me."

"Didn't you look closely at the background?" Jordan said, slipping her laptop into its case.

"I guess not. What was in the background?" Susan asked indifferently.

Jordan pressed the start button on her computer and went to put on her jacket while it rebooted. Susan sat down in her desk chair and waited.

"Where are the photos?" she asked as the screen came up.

"Look in Picasa, Botanical Society August shots," Jordan said as she sorted through some folders to take home.

"It won't open," Susan said, tapping the keys. "It wants a password."

"Applesauce."

"I beg your pardon," she said curiously.

"Applesauce," Jordan repeated quietly.

"Oh, okay." Susan typed it in and waited. A screen of photographs opened. They showed two women shaking hands and exchanging a ceremonially large check for the camera. "I don't see anything wrong with them. She got the presentation, didn't cut off their heads and it's in focus. What's the problem?"

Jordan came around behind Susan and reached in over her shoulder. She zoomed in on one of the shots then stood back, waiting for Susan to examine it.

"What do you see?" Jordan asked.

"I don't see anything, unless you mean the incredibly bad taste in clothes those women have. No one wears that color anymore." Susan squinted at the screen.

"Look between them, right under the handshake."

"Oh, my God," Susan said at last. She chuckled then leaned in to get a better look. "Is that what I think it is? Are those two dogs?"

"Yes, they certainly are. And I don't intend on printing a photograph of two stray mutts humping in the park while the Seattle Women's Botanical Society presents the park board with a ten-thousand-dollar check for park beautification."

Susan continued to stare at the screen and laugh.

"We could say it's fertilizer," she said, looking up at Jordan.

Jordan didn't answer. Instead, she gave Susan a disapproving glare.

"Can't the photography department do something with the shots? You know, edit it out somehow," Susan offered.

"There would be a hole in the shot. If it were just grass or pavement it could be done, but there is a section of the mosaic path right there," Jordan said, pointing to the screen.

"Oh, Jordan. For heaven's sake, get over it. Have the photo touched up. Don't worry about the mosaic. No one will notice." Susan gave one more look then closed the file. "You could have them paste a small shot over that, you know, stack something over it."

Jordan rolled her eyes, not happy with Susan's decision but aware she had the final say.

"Suit yourself," Jordan said, turning out the light and heading down the hall. Susan followed, grabbing her jacket as they passed her office. Jordan pushed the elevator button. She knew Susan was going to follow her all the way to her car in the basement parking garage. When the elevator door opened, Jordan was relieved to see several other passengers. Susan waved Jordan in then stepped in and pressed the button to the garage. Jordan found a place by the back glass wall of the elevator, one that offered a spectacular view of Puget Sound with the ferry heading for Bainbridge Island. It wasn't greed over the best view that made her stand at the glass facing the skyline. It was more. It was the only place she felt safe from the confines of the elevator walls. Jordan's claustrophobia engaged as soon as she placed one foot in the elevator and could only be appeased by an unrestricted view out over the city. She had been known to allow half-full elevators go without her if she couldn't conveniently get to the back wall. She found it difficult to carry on a conversation while on the elevator as her mind dealt with the six-foot-square space. She was aware Susan was saying something to her but it wasn't registering. The last two floors of the ride were below ground level and pure torture for her. She clutched the chrome handrail and didn't release her grip until the elevator door opened. She learned to manage her fear for the last two floors of the ride by picturing a double-layer chocolate cake in her mind and counting the calories in French. It was better than grabbing the handrail, closing her eyes and screaming all the way down. She occasionally walked down the twelve floors but the stairwell was no roomier than the elevator and it didn't offer a window to the outside.

The door finally opened and she stepped out, striding purpose-fully toward her car as her heart returned to a normal rate. Susan followed her, seemingly unaware of Jordan's fear.

"Have you tried that cute little nacho bar on Pine? I heard it was nice." Susan hooked her arm through Jordan's and walked along with her in lock-step.

"No, I haven't," Jordan said, fishing in her pocket for her car keys.

"Tonight is margarita night. How about you and I giving them the *Northwest Living* once over? Maybe we could do a piece on downtown ethnic eateries. My treat. I can write it off on my expense account," Susan said with a wink. "I hear the nacho supreme is enough for two or three people. What do you say? We can share a pitcher of margaritas and watch the yuppies."

"Thanks, Susan, but I don't think so. Nachos aren't my favorite food." She tried to be polite in her refusal.

"They've got lots of other things on the menu, I'm sure. I heard they have a cheese fondue that is out of this world. It comes with lots of goodies to dip. And I'm sure they have a great wine list," she added, squeezing Jordan's arm. "How about sharing a bottle of cabernet with me," she said with a sultry voice. "Or two."

"Thanks but I can't," Jordan replied, glad she had reached her car. She popped the locks and reached for the door handle but Susan blocked the door.

"Come on, Jordan. Just one drink." Susan had a devilish grin on her face. She stepped closer, pinning Jordan to the side of her car. "One drink," she repeated in a soft suggestive voice.

"Susan," Jordan began but before she could finish Susan kissed her, trying desperately to push her tongue in Jordan's mouth. Jordan pushed her away and reached for the door handle, frantic to escape her relentless advances.

"Wait, Jordan," she said, grabbing for her. "Don't go. Come have a drink with me. If you don't want to go there, we could go to my place. What do you say?" she persisted.

"No, Susan. Stop it." Jordan again pushed her away, this time holding her at arm's length. "I've told you. I don't date at work. Now let go of my ass and stop that." Jordan gave her a stern glare.

"I could fire you then you could go out with me," Susan teased, one of her hands gliding down Jordan's thigh. "Then I'd hire you back tomorrow."

Jordan grabbed Susan's hand before it slid back up her thigh and into her crotch.

"Goodnight, Susan," Jordan said with a scowl. She opened her car door and climbed inside, tugging against Susan's hold on it. She finally got it closed and drove off, Susan's stare following her as she exited the parking garage.

It had been six weeks since Susan's last advances. Jordan wasn't interested in Susan. It had nothing to do with working for her although that was a convenient excuse. Whether it was her over-stimulated ego or her manipulative personality, Susan just wasn't Jordan's type.

The first time Susan pressed herself against Jordan and suggested they share a quiet date had been only three weeks after she was hired. But Jordan wasn't discouraged by Susan's persistence. She liked her job and she needed the money. She learned to stand up to Susan, say no in a firm but friendly way. Jordan told herself

Susan was like a rash. She was a small inconvenience that only grew into a real nuisance when Jordan forgot to ignore her. Telling Susan she didn't date anyone at work was the salve Jordan applied to the rash to bring it under control until the next flare-up.

Jordan pulled into the parking lot at Christopher's Restaurant, searching for Mia's Lexus SUV. When it wasn't there, she knew she had time to repair her makeup and comb her hair before going inside. Just as she finished, Mia pulled in next to her and tooted her horn. Jordan waved and climbed out of her Civic, dwarfed by Mia's sleek gas-guzzler, something Mia loved to rub in.

"Hi, you sexy thing," Mia said, kissing Jordan on the cheek before walking her inside the restaurant. "I love that sweater on you," she whispered as they waited for a table. She eyed the way it clung to Jordan's body. "It really makes you look good."

"Thank you." Jordan couldn't stop a blush.

"You look really hot tonight, babe. Really hot." Mia's hand slipped down Jordan's back and hesitated at her tight buns.

"This way, ladies," the hostess said, leading them to a table.

"I could use a drink. It has been a tough day," Mia said, waiting for Jordan to choose where she wanted to sit.

"I'm sorry you had a hard day, honey. Tell me what happened," Jordan said.

Mia spent twenty minutes explaining her hectic day, with attention to every detail. Jordan smiled sympathetically and listened intently. Mia sounded like she needed that, she thought. Jordan and Mia were introduced by a mutual friend, one who thought they were the most perfect match she had ever seen. Their relationship started slowly with an occasional drink or coffee meeting. After only two weeks, Mia invited her to go to Victoria, British Columbia with her to a conference at the elegant Empress Hotel. Jordan expected to tour the city while Mia was at the conference, but it became clear as soon as they registered at the front desk that Mia had something else in mind. They spent the entire weekend naked and sweaty. Room service delivery was the only time they spent out of bed.

Mia had been in several relationships, all of them with gorgeous and intelligent women but none of them serious enough to take her out of commission. Jordan didn't plan on doing that either. They were friends, close friends. They enjoyed each other's company but they both knew it wasn't a forever kind of relationship. It was a for-now relationship.

Mia ordered them an expensive bottle of wine and a lavish dinner. After dinner, Mia followed Jordan to her apartment in Kirkland, something Jordan knew meant she planned on spending the night with her. Mia was predictable. She always drank two and a half glasses of wine, ate only half of whatever she ordered, left too much tip even if the service was lousy and she always wanted sex when she followed Jordan home, usually without being invited.

Chapter 3

Jordan folded her arms behind her head and stared at the ceiling fan that lazily stirred the late summer air around the bedroom. Even in the dim light of the muted television she could see how dirty the blades had become. She would have to dust them some day, some day when she didn't have to be at work before seven in the morning and stay well after six in the evening. She needed to catch up on laundry, too. Maybe she would remember to start a load before she left in the morning. No, she couldn't start a load until she stopped at the store for detergent. She scolded herself for forgetting to do that. She had been out since Sunday. She needed milk, peanut butter and apples, too. She wished she had made a list. Life would be easier if she remembered to make a grocery list.

"Are you with me here, Jordy?" Mia asked with a scowl, looking up at her from where she was cradling Jordan's hips in her arms. "I seem to be doing all the work here."

Jordan quickly looked down at her and smiled apologetically.

"I'm sorry, sweetheart. I'm right here." She reached down and stroked Mia's face fondly. "It's wonderful, really. I'm just taking a bit longer to get going tonight. Please, don't stop." Jordan smiled at her, winking and wiggling her butt. She didn't like to fake it but she also didn't want to disappoint Mia.

When Mia started jingling her keys at the restaurant Jordan knew she wanted sex. Mia always wanted sex. They had a polite glass of wine when they got to Jordan's apartment then Mia stepped out of her shoes, kissed the back of Jordan's neck as they sat on the couch before leading Jordan to the bedroom. It took Mia only a few minutes kissing Jordan's naked body before she moved down to her usual position, half on the bed, half off. It usually took somewhere between eight and twelve minutes for Jordan to arrive at an orgasm, depending on the weather, her mood and how tired she was. This evening was no different, at least the foreplay was. Jordan couldn't find the interest this evening. She didn't know why, but her heart and her body weren't into it, not yet. Perhaps it was the long week at work, she told herself. She tried to concentrate on the spot Mia was massaging feverishly with her tongue.

Mia wasn't the only woman Jordan occasionally entertained. J.J., an old college friend who traveled to Seattle on business every other month, had sent Jordan flowers and when J.J. sent two dozen red roses Jordan knew they would be wrinkling the sheets as soon as she came to town. It wasn't that she wouldn't or couldn't commit to just one woman in a monogamous relationship. But Mia and J.J. were just that, women to date. Jordan had told herself she was being too picky. After all, she was a thirty-five-year-old, available, gainfully-employed lesbian. Surely she could find one person who met all her needs. Surely there was one woman in the greater Seattle area who was a good conversationalist, kind, intelligent, attentive and loyal. Someone who didn't use sex as the prime indicator of a quality evening together. Someone who didn't predicate a partnership on how someone looked. Jordan got used to hearing how hot she looked when she wore something low-cut or tight-fitting. She longed for someone to tell her she was hot because she could speak French or because she could paint in watercolors or because she knew all the works of Mary Cassatt.

But Mia was trying. Jordan could feel her hot breath and frantic tongue action feverishly trying to stimulate her womanhood into throbbing ecstasy. Jordan closed her eyes and concentrated. She didn't want Mia to think she couldn't please her. Usually she did. Jordan willed her mind to that spot between her thighs and gave a silent prayer for something to happen and quickly. Like clockwork, Jordan felt the tiny wave roll through her, the wave that meant she was near her peak. It was a small peak but a peak nonetheless. She groaned and allowed it to linger as long as possible. She reached down and grabbed a handful of Mia's thick head of hair, pulling her closer, hoping for the rapture to increase before it drifted away all together. Dutifully, Mia kept up her pace as if she were delivering the orgasm to end all orgasms. Jordan arched her back, reaching for more of the dwindling pleasure. When the last faint throbs subsided, she fell back and opened her eyes. Mia had stopped and crawled up next to her, rubbing her neck and cackling victoriously.

"Now that's how it is done, huh, Jordy?" Mia said triumphantly. She leaned down and kissed one of Jordan's hard nipples then gave it a suck.

"Mmmm," Jordan moaned happily and snuggled against her. Mia pulled the sheet and blanket over them. Within three minutes she was snoring soundly at Jordan's side.

Jordan slipped out of bed and went to take a shower. After her shower, she pulled on a robe and stepped out onto her small balcony that overlooked the valley and Puget Sound. She closed her eyes and enjoyed the soft breeze that stirred her hair and brushed against her face. Jordan leaned against the railing and stared into the bedroom. Mia was spread eagle across the bed, one arm dragging the floor, the gentle sound of snoring wafting through the open door. It was amazing how quickly Mia could fall asleep once the lovemaking was over. Jordan could almost set her watch by it.

Jordan was still breathing heavy and her ears were still red when Mia began to saw logs. A snuggler, Mia was not.

Mia was another of Jordan's friends who liked to experience how the other half lived. She never ate at a restaurant that didn't serve water in a stemmed glass or required less than five minutes to prepare a meal. She considered it totally classless to eat at a place that gave a prize with a meal. In fact, Mia loved to make reservations. Whether it was a busy Saturday night or just an afternoon luncheon, Mia liked the importance a reservation suggested. She was a corporate attorney with a large shipping company so she never looked at the prices. Her best friend was her American Express business card. If she misplaced it, her blood pressure rose uncontrollably, her hands cramped and her upper lip beaded with sweat until she once again located it. Jordan knew Mia would never be a committed partner. She already had one and her name was plastic. Jordan found Mia's obsession with materialistic things a bit much. She was a pleasant conversationalist, at least when she was leading the conversation, she was.

Jordan closed her eyes and breathed deeply. The night air mixed with pine trees, diesel fumes from Highway 5 and the vanilla musk incense Mia had lit on the nightstand. Jordan was chilled by the hollowness of the moment. She suddenly felt the need to wrap her arms around herself as a security blanket against the emptiness that consumed her. She didn't know why. She liked Mia. She liked being with her. She wasn't mean to her or abusive. But there was a wanting in Jordan's heart she couldn't explain.

She turned back to the railing and stared out over the valley, her eyes searching the lights for comfort. She would love for someone to be standing next to her and hold her in their arms. Someone to kiss her and tell her everything would be all right. She gripped the railing until her knuckles turned white. It was several moments before she could let go and move away. She went inside and gently pulled her pillow from under Mia's arm.

"Goodnight, Mia," she whispered as she quietly pulled the bedroom door shut and went to sleep on the couch. The night was long and lonely for Jordan but she had learned to accept it.

"I've got to go, Jordy," Mia said, leaning down to kiss Jordan awake.

"What time is it?" she asked through a yawn.

"Quarter til seven. I'd stay for breakfast but I'm meeting some of the girls at the gym to work out. I'll call you in a couple days. Maybe we can get together to watch the Mariners ballgame this Sunday." She winked and slid her hand under the blanket and down Jordan's abdomen. "Later, cutie." Mia gave her a playful pinch then hurried out the door.

Jordan tossed the blanket over the back of the couch. She climbed to her feet, stiff from sleeping on a too short bed. She dressed and checked her e-mail before heading to work.

Chapter 4

The gallery opened punctually at seven o'clock on Thursday evening to a large and eager crowd. By the time Jordan arrived, the showing was well attended with several dozen admirers, some for the generous reception table covered with wine, cheese and various tidbits that traveled well as the people roamed the rooms. Jordan took a glass of wine and melded into the flow. She noticed a familiar reporter from the Seattle newspaper making notes in a pad. He had a frown on his face. She assumed he was either unhappy with the interview or the event.

"Hi, Grant," Jordan said, striding over to him. "You becoming an art lover?"

"Hell, no," he replied, closing his pad. "I hate this artsy-fartsy shit." Grant rearranged the wad of chew he had tucked inside his lower lip. "And the bitch won't even give me a statement," he grumbled. He nodded back over his shoulder. "You can have her, Jordan. She gives me the creeps." He shivered deliberately. Before

Jordan could ask him why Reece McAllister could give this tall, strapping man the creeps, he had downed a glass of wine in one gulp and headed out the door. Jordan sipped her wine and waited for the crowd around the woman she assumed was Ms. McAllister to dissipate. She could hear congratulations and praise for the photo collection. The group of people blocked Jordan's view but the voice from the center of the circle was crisp, articulate and even cordial as she replied to the well-wishers. The crowd seemed to be transient, the people eagerly moving in and offering a remark then walking away after only a moment. Jordan used this time to stroll the room and examine Ms. McAllister's work. Each photograph was mounted and displayed in a simple but striking black frame. Several were of Seattle's skyline taken from various vantage points around King County. One of a rainstorm caught Jordan's eye. The low-hanging clouds had settled among the tall buildings in the business district, muting the tops of the skyscrapers in a gray mist. Most of the pictures were done in black and white with interesting shadings and asymmetric centering. A group of five shots of the Olympic Mountains showed the harsh contrast between the mountain peaks and the fragile beauty in the mountain valleys. A particular photograph grabbed Jordan so completely she almost dropped her wineglass. It was of a tiny lavender-colored alpine flower growing in the shelter of a huge boulder just above the timberline. The flower was the only color in the photograph. The rest of the setting was black and white, something Jordan found curious. The simple beauty and conquest against adversity touched Jordan deeply. She stood staring at it, frozen by the emotion and strength it portrayed. When she finally looked away, she could see a woman's profile, the same profile she had seen through the window. She was receiving a handshake from an elderly man with white hair who leaned heavily on his cane. This woman had to be Reece McAllister. This was the woman she had come to meet and rob of her life's secrets. The woman was dressed in a pair of black slacks and a black mandarin-style jacket with a gold dragon encircling the sleeve. Jordan noticed she was barefoot. Even with no shoes on, she guessed her to be nearly six feet tall. Jordan watched and read the woman's body language as she shook the man's hand and listened to his compliments. She leaned in to him and smiled with a caring and sensitive posture. She patted his shoulder kindly, thanking him for coming. When he finally turned and walked away, Jordan took the opportunity to meet Reece and shake her hand, something she had been waiting thirty minutes to do.

"How do you do, Ms. McAllister?" Jordan said, striding up to her.

The woman heard her name and instantly turned around. When she did, Jordan gasped and took a step back. The woman's right side profile was all Jordan had seen. The side of Reece's face she hadn't seen was covered with a gruesome, jagged scar that ran from near her temple down her cheek and across her neck, disappearing under the collar of her jacket. It was an angry, nasty scar, raised and pinkish-red ridge. Jordan couldn't take her eyes off the wicked mark even though she willed herself to do so.

Reece watched Jordan's expression as she studied the scar, taking in every inch and crag of it. Reece chuckled sarcastically and unbuttoned the top toggle of her jacket.

"Does this make it easier for you to see?" she asked, pulling the collar open and exposing more of the scar. Her eyes captured Jordan's and held her in a hard gaze. They were soft eyes in spite of the vicious scar, full of emotion and sensitivity.

Jordan stood staring at her, unable to speak or move. As a woman who usually found no difficulty in asking questions and saying the right thing, Jordan found herself speechless for the first time in her life. The disparity between the woman's shocking looks and her sensitive stare caught Jordan completely off-guard.

"My, God. Do you want me to take off my clothes so you can see the rest of it?" Reece asked gruffly.

"No," Jordan replied, finally coming to her senses. "I'm sorry. I didn't mean to stare."

"That's lie number one," Reece muttered.

"I was admiring your jacket. It's lovely."

"Lie number two. Do you want to go for number three? It's usually something like I wasn't staring, I just thought you were someone else." Reece re-buttoned her jacket and pulled the collar up against her neck.

"You're Reece McAllister," Jordan said, extending her hand.

"And you are?" Reece asked reticently before accepting her hand.

"Jordan Griffin."

"Ah, yes, assistant editor for *Northwest Living Magazine*." Reece didn't shake her hand. "And before you ask, no, I won't give you an interview."

"I beg your pardon," Jordan said through a frown. "I'm here to see your work. Is that a crime?"

"Lie number three, Miss Griffin. Mark Bergman sent you to wangle a story out of me, didn't he?"

"Well—" Jordan stammered.

"Did he tell you I turned him down when he called last week? I bet he didn't mention that."

"No, he didn't," Jordan replied, feeling only slightly less than foolish.

"I bet Susan Mackey didn't mention she tried as well."

"You seem to have me at a disadvantage. You are one step ahead of me. I presume you also know what questions I'm supposed to ask." Jordan took a sip of wine, her eyes still watching Reece over the rim of the glass.

"Very good. Get me to offer some nugget of hope," Reece replied.

"May I ask why you wouldn't give Mark or Susan an interview?"

"I don't give interviews, Miss Griffin. I used to get interviews but I don't grant them. It is my experience that the truth is seldom as important as the need for the story."

"If the truth is that important to you why not insure it by granting an interview? That would be one way to make sure we tell the story you want told," Jordan suggested diplomatically.

Reece laughed robustly at Jordan's remark.

"I remember using that old line. Very good. But no thanks. The more ammunition you give a reporter the more chances they have to shoot someone in the foot with it. And most of the time, it is you."

"You didn't like your job as a reporter, did you?" Jordan asked, hoping to sneak in a question.

Reece just smiled at her, her eyes narrowed.

"Don't forget to see the group of photos hanging in the back corner. You'd probably like them," she said, completely ignoring the question. "Try the white wine. It is better than the red."

"Can I get you one, Ms. McAllister," Jordan asked, hoping to extend her conversation.

"No. I don't drink when there are reporters present. Especially when I'm barefoot. I wouldn't want to get shot in the foot." Reece turned and walked away, leaving Jordan to her curiosity. She had to admit, even though she didn't get an interview, she did get an insight into Reece McAllister's personality. She didn't know any of the hows and whys of her sudden metamorphosis from popular and highly touted television reporter to viciously scarred photo-journalist. She did know, whatever the reasons, Reece McAllister was an interesting and mysterious woman. What started as an indifferent assignment was now a compelling challenge for Jordan.

"You may have walked away from me tonight, Ms. McAllister," Jordan muttered to herself. "But I guarantee you haven't seen the last of me. I always get my story, lady." Jordan downed her wine and left, her mind already formulating a plan on how to get inside this woman's head.

The next day Jordan couldn't keep her mind off Reece McAllister or the way their evening had ended. Her journalistic senses couldn't let go. She parked her car in front of the gallery and went inside, her brain busy formulating the first questions she would ask and how she would counter her resistance.

"Hello. May I help you?" the gray-haired woman asked. Jordan remembered her from the day she peeked in the window. She had to be the gallery owner or at least the manager.

"Yes. I was hoping to catch Reece McAllister this evening," Jordan said, looking around the room at the handful of people studying the pieces.

"I'm sorry but Ms. McAllister isn't here. Can I help you with something?"

"When would be a good time to catch her?"

"She was here last night for the opening but I don't know when she'll be back. Maybe not until the end of the showing."

"When will that be?"

"The collection will be on display for four weeks. Were you interested in purchasing something?"

"No. I just wanted to talk with her for a few minutes," Jordan replied, trying to hide her disappointment.

"You and everyone else," the woman said with a smirk. "Let me guess, you are a reporter. Television or newspaper?"

"I beg your pardon," Jordan replied.

"I'm sorry, but I just assumed you were one of the reporters who have been parading in and out of here all day, trying to talk with her."

"I don't work for a television station or a newspaper. I was here last night and was talking with her about some of her work. The ones in the back corner," Jordan offered, looking off in that direction.

"Oh, you mean the doubles," she said brightly. "Aren't they wonderful and so unique." Just then the telephone rang at the counter. "Excuse me a minute," the woman said and stepped away.

Jordan nodded politely then meandered toward the corner to see just what a double was. Two vertical rows of eight by ten photographs were arranged in the corner. Each print was a black-and-white double exposure shot of simple items in nature. One was a rosebud. The result made the rose blurred, hiding the crisp edges of the petals. Another was an eagle in flight, the double exposure also blurring the sharp edges of the eagle's wings. All six framed pieces were unnerving to Jordan, the double exposure masking the purity of the image.

"Aren't they wonderful?" the woman offered, coming to join

27

Jordan in studying them. "The double exposure is so subtle. If you stand to the side and look across the surface of the picture, they don't look double at all. Just sort of three-D."

Jordan tried it and sure enough when she looked at the eagle at a deep angle, it appeared to be just one three-dimensional image.

"How did she do that?" Jordan asked, squinting at each photograph.

"I don't know. She wouldn't tell me but I think it is marvelous. I don't think they would have been nearly as impressive if she had done them in color. The black and white gives them a contrast that jumps right off the paper. The whole set is on hold for a buyer from New York."

"I wish I had come right out and asked her if she double-exposed the shot with time delay or created it under the enlarger," Jordan said, hoping to convince the gallery owner she was indeed there regarding Reece's technique.

"She was talking with one man about the kind of photo paper she used. That might have something to do with it."

"I think you're right. That could definitely affect the exposure." Jordan patted the woman on the arm as if congratulating her idea.

"Honey, I'm sorry, but I don't remember what she said about it. I don't know one photo paper from another," the woman replied apologetically.

"I sure wish I could find out what brand it is and where she got it."

The woman looked to see if anyone was watching then leaned into Jordan.

"You might ask her yourself. I heard her tell someone on the phone she was going to some restaurant Monday night. It sounded like a strange place to me. Why would you want to have dinner at a gas station?" the woman frowned skeptically.

"Gas station?"

"Yes. She said she was going to the 'garage' for a burger and fries about seven."

"Oh. The Garage isn't a gas station. It's a café with pool tables,"

Jordan advised. "A local magazine had it on their top ten places to meet for a date."

"Oh," the woman chuckled. "I guess I don't go to those kinds of places. Anyway, perhaps you could find her there. But please don't tell her I told you. She seems to covet her privacy, poor thing."

"Poor thing?" Jordan asked.

"Well, you have to admit she has a certain . . ." The woman hesitated as she chose her words. "Disadvantage."

"Why do you say that?" Jordan knew what she meant, but she wanted to see how far she would go to explain.

"She was such a pretty girl," the woman replied, shaking her head.

Jordan didn't offer any response.

"It's such a shame," she continued.

"You were probably pretty shocked the first time you met her," Jordan suggested.

"Heavens, yes. No one warned me about her face. I was caught completely by surprise. I think I shrieked so loud I scared Mr. Toms. He's my cat. He sleeps in the office."

"How long have you known Reece?"

"Just a few weeks. Her agent contacted me about the showing. I sure gave that man a piece of my mind," she said, wagging her finger. "I told him he certainly should have warned me. That wasn't a professional way to do business at all. I could have had a heart attack." The woman smirked.

"I'm sure you could have," Jordan agreed, not wanting to upset the woman by telling her she sounded shallow and insensitive. "You know, I never did completely understand what happened to her," Jordan said, leading her into any admission she might make.

"Me, either," the woman replied, touching Jordan's arm. "She absolutely won't talk about it. I came right out and asked her, but she said it was a zit that went bad. Can you believe she was so flippant about it? I was just trying to show some sympathy. She wouldn't even tell me her address so I can send the checks. She said she'd call a couple times a week. If I need to get in touch with her

I leave a message and she returns my call. She is almost cynical about her privacy. I don't think I would put up with it if it wasn't that I feel sorry for her."

"Not to mention your commission for selling her work," Jordan said, growing disgusted with the woman's patronizing attitude.

"Well, yes. That too."

"Thank you for your help," Jordan said, offering her hand. The woman gave a weak handshake and returned to her office. Jordan took a last look at the double exposures then headed out the door. By the time she reached her car, she had placed a call on her cell phone.

"Hey, this is Hope. Leave a message," chirped an answering machine.

"Hey, cousin. Are we still going out Monday evening? I've got a place we might try. Give me a call. Bye."

Monday was Labor Day and Jordan spent her day off doing housework and catching up on mail. She had finished washing her hair and was combing out the tangles when the doorbell rang. Before she could get to it, it rang again then once more for good measure.

"I'm coming. I'm coming," she called as she unlocked the deadbolt and opened the door.

"How's my favorite cousin?" the woman asked, stepping inside and giving Jordan a warm hug.

"How many cousins do you have, Hope?" Jordan asked fondly.

"Let me count. Um, one."

They laughed.

"Did you know you can't get ink out of a silk blouse?" Hope announced as she followed Jordan into the bedroom.

"I didn't know that."

"They say you can put hair spray on ink and it will come right out, but don't believe it. It doesn't work."

"It came out of my tan slacks," Jordan offered.

"Ballpoint ink comes out. But gel pen ink doesn't. I ruined a forty-dollar blouse."

"Take it to the cleaners. Maybe they can get it out."

"I did. They got the hair spray and the mustard out, but the ink is still there," Hope replied, wrinkling her face.

"Is it very noticeable? Maybe no one will see it," Jordan said as she finished combing her hair.

"It's right on the end of my tit. I think they'll notice."

"Wear a vest or something."

"I tossed it," Hope said, looking through Jordan's closet. "I didn't like it anyway. It made me look like a hooker."

"You told me once you thought you'd make a great hooker." Jordan chuckled.

"When was that?"

"You were about eighteen or nineteen. You were worried no one was going to date you once you came out. Remember? You were sure you'd never have sex again," Jordan teased.

"Yeah. I remember that. I asked Belinda Bailey for a date and she told me to dry up. Can I help it if I stutter when I get excited?" Hope replied.

"How long did it take you to get a date?"

"About a week. When Belinda wouldn't go out with me I asked her ex out. She and I went from zero to sixty in one evening. Talk about a ho. I had her in the backseat of dad's Buick before she knew my last name."

"Was it love at first sight?" Jordan asked as she selected a pair of slacks and a dressy blouse from her closet.

"Hell, no. It was more like lust at first sight. You're the one who goes for the love stuff."

"I do not," Jordan argued. "There is no such thing as love at first sight, at least not for me. You can't decide what you feel about a person for at least a month or two. Maybe longer. There are way too many variables."

"My God, Jordy. You make it sound like rocket science. Take it from me. It isn't that tough. You see someone, you buy them a drink, they find a reason to give you their phone number and voila, you've got a new girlfriend." Hope snapped her fingers to show how easy it was.

31

"That isn't how you get a girlfriend. That's how you get a date."

"Same thing. So, where are we going tonight? You said you had someplace in mind."

"Have you ever been to a place called the Garage?" Jordan asked, stepping into a pair of heels.

"You mean the café pub place with the pool tables? Yeah, several times. Why?"

"I thought we'd run by and have a look," Jordan suggested, hooking a pair of gold hoops through her ears.

"You don't know how to play pool, Jordy." Hope gave her a curious stare. "Why are we going there? You're more the bistro and white wine type. The Garage is burgers and beer."

"I know, but it is on our top ten list for places to have a date in Seattle. I thought I ought to see what we are backing this year." Jordan chose a jacket and went into the living room.

"Okay, but you are way overdressed for the Garage."

"What's wrong with what I am wearing?"

"Come with me," Hope said, taking Jordan by the hand and leading her back into bedroom. She took a pair of jeans from her closet and a black V-neck pullover top from the drawer. "Put these on and wear those sneakers you had on the other day."

"You're kidding. I don't wear those shoes out in public. Those are what I wear when I wash the car or go on a picnic," Jordan declared.

"Okay, you can wear these," Hope replied, taking a pair of black ankle-high dress boots from the closet. "Don't you want to blend in?"

"Yes, but I don't want to look like a homeless woman who wandered in off the street."

Hope unbuttoned the top button of Jordan's blouse and pulled it over her head.

"You won't. Homeless women have better taste than this."

"Hope!"

"Shut up and put your arms in this top. Tuck it in your jeans and wear a black belt. Wear a gold chain in that cute little cleavage of yours and you'll be looking good."

By the time Hope was finished with Jordan's wardrobe, she looked twenty-five years old and ready for a night out.

"I feel silly. I haven't dressed like this since I was in college," Jordan muttered as she checked herself in the mirror then followed Hope out the front door.

"You look great. Maybe you can snag a cute one before they realize you aren't twenty-one." Hope winked at her.

"I do not want to *snag* someone," Jordan quipped.

"Speak for yourself."

"What about Barbara?" Jordan asked.

"I knew you would remind me about her."

Hope and Jordan had been as close as sisters since they were toddlers. Their mothers were sisters and each only had one child. They were raised in Fort Collins, Jordan one year older than Hope. Hope had a scholarship to the University of Washington and loved Seattle enough to stay, taking a job as an event planner for the Seattle Convention Center. She was thrilled when Jordan took the job at *Northwest Living Magazine*, their relationship once again as close as ever. Hope's girlfriend of two years, Barbara Curry, was a flight attendant for Alaska Airlines. Hope and Barbara teased each other about dating cute young things, but Hope was faithful to the nth degree. She was sentimental and happily monogamous, even though she wouldn't admit it. Jordan and Hope often scheduled a night out when Barbara was out of town.

Both Jordan and Hope had been out to each other since high school. Jordan was first to announce she had no interest in dating boys. Her attractive, blonde all-American looks made it easy for her to hide her lesbian lifestyle until she chose to come out to the rest of her family and friends. It wasn't until the summer before her senior year in high school that Hope admitted to Jordan she had found the person of her dreams. Jordan assumed it was Mike Smiley, the boy who often gave her a ride to school. But it was Mike's sister, Mindy, that had Hope waiting for his Toyota to pull up in front of her house. When it was clear that Mindy wasn't the slightest bit interested in Hope, Mike was quickly fired as her chauffeur. Jordan and Hope shared many smiles and tears over the years, confessing their innermost secrets and joys, the way sisters would do.

Hope took the interstate to downtown Seattle, circling the block as she searched for a parking spot. The Garage was a popular place. The crowd overflowed onto the sidewalk with everything from teenagers to baby boomers. The parking lot was full and so were all the spaces on the street. Hope had to park three blocks away.

"Busy place," Jordan said as she stepped inside and squinted into the dim lighting.

"You can play pool, bowl, eat or just hang out. There's even a back room with a bar that overlooks the dance floor. It's quite a place."

"Let's find a table," Jordan suggested, pointing to the snack bar area.

The two long rows of pool tables were all in use. The click of the balls could be heard above the jukebox. They found a table and ordered two drafts. Jordan noticed Hope was right. Jeans seemed to be the uniform of the day. Some were dark blue, some were faded and ripped, but everyone was wearing jeans of some kind.

"How about playing a rack with me?" Hope asked.

"Rack?" Jordan asked. "Oh, you mean pool?"

"Yep. I'll teach you. It isn't hard."

"You know me. I've never been very good at sports, Hope. You play. I'll watch."

"I'm not going to play by myself. That looks stupid. You have to at least try."

"Okay. I'll stand there and hold a stick."

"Cue, Jordan. Cue." Hope rolled her eyes.

They waited for a free pool table then Hope helped Jordan select a cue from the rack.

"Pick a shorter one to start with. It won't feel so awkward," Hope advised. She placed the balls in the triangular rack and showed Jordan how to hold the cue. Jordan was right. She wasn't much of an athlete. She wasn't a sissy but sports weren't something she had made time for in high school or college. She was busy as yearbook and newspaper editor, photography club president, secretary of the student council and resident assistant in her college dormitory. There weren't enough hours in the day to be an athlete, not since Jordan only participated in activities she could commit to wholeheartedly.

"Do you want to break?" Hope asked.

"What is that?"

"You hit the white ball into the cluster of colored balls and hope something goes in."

"Why don't you do that," Jordan said, wondering how hard the cluster would have to be hit to sink anything.

"Come on, Jordy. Whack 'em."

"Okay. Here goes."

Jordan lined up the cue ball and gave it a shot. It was a miscue, the ball rolling only a few inches and the cue flying out of her hand across the table. Hope couldn't help but laugh. So did several onlookers. Jordan blushed brightly.

"Maybe I better break," Hope said, handing Jordan her cue.

Hope made two balls on the break and proceeded to sink two more.

"Your turn," she said after a missed shot.

Jordan hadn't been watching. She was scanning the room, hoping to find Reece McAllister.

"Jordy?"

"What?" she said, snapping around.

"It's your turn. See if you can hit the ball this time."

"Which one should I shoot at?"

"I don't think it matters. You'll miss it anyway," Hope teased.

"Thanks for the confidence." Jordan lined up a shot that looked like a sure bet, but true to Hope's prediction, the cue ball hit the red ball at a sharp angle and sent it down the table harmlessly. Hope winked at her. "That's it. I quit," Jordan stated disgustedly.

"No way," Hope argued. "If you don't stay and look like you are playing, one of those hairy guys over there will be asking to play with me." She motioned to a group of college-aged men at a table who were watching them play.

"Okay, but don't miss anymore. Then I won't have to shoot." Jordan sat down on one of the tall stools and sipped her beer while Hope took her time lining up her shots.

"Your turn," she said after cussing at her shot.

"But you just sank one."

"I sank the cue ball."

"Is that bad?" Jordan asked curiously.

"Yes. It means you get to shoot anything you want and put the cue ball anywhere you want."

"Like that will help," Jordan muttered.

"Take your time shooting. I have to go to the bathroom. If you don't stay at the table someone will take it," Hope advised.

"Okay. I'll sink them all." Jordan grinned.

"It's called running the table. Go for it."

Hope headed toward the ladies' room while Jordan wandered around the table, deciding what to shoot. She finally set the cue ball next to a striped ball and lined up a shot. She still wasn't comfortable holding the cue. She tried several grips, hoping to find one she could control. She crouched down over the shot and imitated what Hope had done. Just as she was ready to hit the ball, a hand reached down and picked up the cue ball.

"You're going to miss this one too," a voice said.

Jordan looked up and saw Reece's face staring down at her.

"You're lined up wrong," Reece added, replacing the ball where it was.

"Oh, hello. Fancy meeting you here," Jordan replied with a broad smile.

"Yeah, fancy that," Reece chuckled artificially. "The lady at the gallery told me you were in asking questions. You don't give up easily, do you?"

"Maybe I just wanted to learn to play pool," Jordan said.

"Yeah, right. Then why isn't your friend showing you how to shoot?"

"Friend? Oh, you mean Hope? She's my cousin. She's a better shooter than teacher."

"Okay, Miss Griffin, let's see you shoot." Reece gestured across the table.

"I was about to," Jordan replied, lining up her shot again. She closed one eye and hit the ball. The cue ball missed everything on the table except the rail. It bounced back to her as she blushed bright red.

Reece didn't say anything. She took a swig from her beer then set it on edge of the table. She grabbed a cue and stood next to Jordan, placing her hands on the table.

"Put your left hand on the table like this. Make a little bridge with your index finger and slide the cue along it. Like this," she said, demonstrating how to do it.

Jordan tried the technique. It felt awkward but it was better than what she had been doing.

"Keep your chin right over the stick as you shoot. Now try again," Reece ordered then stepped back.

Jordan did as she was told. This time the cue ball hit what she was aiming at although it didn't go in.

"Hey, I hit one," Jordan said with childish excitement.

"The idea is not to just hit them, but to pocket them," Reece said, grimacing as if she was deciding how much help she wanted to offer.

"But it was better, wasn't it?"

"Line it up again," Reece said, pointing to the cue ball. She waited for Jordan to get set then stood behind her. Jordan suddenly gasped as Reece's arms enfolded her, one hand over each of hers. Reece guided Jordan's aim until she was confident it was lined up correctly. Jordan could feel Reece's body against her back, softly molded to her, her breath warm against the back of her neck.

"Now shoot," Reece said, releasing Jordan's hand, but remaining pressed against her. "Easy."

Jordan made a soft stroke and to her complete surprise, the orange ball dropped cleanly into the pocket.

"Wow. I did it. I actually hit a ball into a pocket," she said, looking back at Reece.

"Will miracles never cease?" Reece went back to her beer.

"Do you want to shoot?" Jordan asked, hoping to break the ice even further.

"No, thanks."

"Are you still afraid of getting shot in the foot?" Jordan asked curiously.

"I see no reason to think I won't be," Reece replied, cocking an eyebrow.

"How did you do?" Hope asked, returning to the table. She hadn't noticed Reece. "Sink anything?"

"One," Jordan replied, still looking over at Reece.

"I'm surprised," Hope scoffed.

"Someone showed me how to shoot," Jordan said, nodding toward Reece.

Hope looked in her direction and gasped as she noticed Reece's scar. She didn't mean to do it but she groaned loud enough to attract attention.

"Hope," Jordan declared loudly, frowning at her.

Reece smirked, the muscles in her jaw rippling, making the scar pulse like an angry snake. She turned and walked away.

"That wasn't nice." Jordan grabbed Hope's arm and squeezed.

"I'm sorry, Jordy. But, shit. What did you expect? The woman looks like she was branded by Zorro," Hope replied defensively.

Jordan fixed her with a fierce stare then tossed the cue on the table and went searching for Reece.

"Wait a minute," Jordan called, hurrying to catch up with her. Reece didn't stop. She walked out the front door and headed up the sidewalk. Jordan grabbed her arm. "Please stop."

"Go back inside, Miss Griffin, and leave me alone," Reece said and pulled away.

"My name is Jordan and I don't want to go back inside. I'm sorry for Hope. She didn't mean to embarrass you."

"She didn't embarrass me," Reece replied, turning around and staring straight into Jordan's eyes. "She embarrassed you. You're the one who reacted." She continued up the sidewalk.

"Then I'm sorry," Jordan called after her. "Please forgive me. Come back inside. Don't let me ruin your evening. And I promise, I won't ask any questions. I won't shoot you in the foot," Jordan added with a reassuring smile.

"I promise you won't either." Reece walked back to Jordan and looked at her with a decisive stare. "I don't want you following me. I don't want to be your friend. And I don't want to give you an interview. I just want to be left alone. Is that clear?" She narrowed her eyes as if to reaffirm her position. "Go back and tell Mark there is no story here. Tell him Reece McAllister still said no. Can you do that, Miss Griffin?"

Jordan didn't like Reece's tone or her condescending attitude. She was doing her job. She was sent to get the story. Why this woman was so opposed to her interest in her past only made Jordan more curious. Reece McAllister had been a very public personality. She was seen on television screens by millions across the country and around the world. Why she now wanted to be so elusive and secretive created a strange mystery, one Jordan couldn't ignore. It had to be more than just the scar.

"I can see something in your eyes, Miss Griffin. I can see that reporter mentality that says never give up on a story. You are trying to figure out how to get something out of me, but I am telling you, there is no story here."

Reece turned on her heels and strode up the sidewalk, leaving Jordan to watch her retreat. She stood watching until Reece disappeared around the corner.

"Maybe, maybe not," Jordan muttered to herself then went back inside.

Chapter 5

"How did the interview with Reece McAllister go last week?" Susan asked as Jordan walked passed her office door.

Jordan stopped in her tracks and stared in at Susan.

"Very funny. You know exactly how it went. Why didn't you and Mark tell me about Reece and her attitude?" Jordan replied.

"Didn't we?"

"No, you conveniently did not."

Susan smiled a coy smile.

"You got the interview, didn't you?" Susan asked in a patronizing voice.

"No, I did not. Reece McAllister doesn't want anything to do with me, the magazine or the entire journalistic world, for that matter." Jordan heaved a disgusted sigh.

"You aren't giving up, are you?"

"Is that a rhetorical question? Are you telling me to try again?"

"This has all the earmarks of a good story, Jordan. We need an insightful story for the November issue. And it would be a real feather in your cap if you could get this interview. Reece McAllister could be a career maker."

"Susan, if you want me to keep trying, just say so. Don't over-inflate this story's worth." Jordan had to admit an interview with Reece McAllister did hold a certain mystique.

"I think it might be worth a second look," Susan said, reaching for her telephone as it rang for the second time.

Jordan went to her office and looked over her schedule. She had two calls to make to fact-check articles then an article to proofread from a freelance contributor. After that, her day was free. The one thing she couldn't get out of her mind was how to establish a line of communication with Reece McAllister. It didn't take long for her to find an address for Ms. McAllister. The Internet revealed she lived in Bellevue just off Northrup. It might be a long shot, but Jordan headed to Bellevue with hopes she could catch Reece at home and in a more casual atmosphere where she would be more open to an interview.

Jordan climbed the steps to the porch at 426 Ziegler. It was a two-story duplex with RM in script letters on the mailbox.

"May I help you?" asked a woman in a straw hat. She was sitting in the middle of her flower bed on a small stool with wheels, pruning and weeding her rhododendrons. Her property was adjacent to Reece's but was filled with gorgeous and aromatic growing things while Reece's yard was covered with a thick stand of grass, nothing more.

"This is where Reece McAllister lives, isn't it?" she replied.

"Yes, but she isn't home." She shaded her eyes from the morning sun and stared at Jordan.

Jordan checked her watch, deciding how long she wanted to wait for her return.

"If you're thinking about waiting for her, she won't be back today," the woman added.

"Did she say when she'd be back?"

"No, but I'm sure it won't be for a month or so. She packed her truck so that usually means she'll be at the cabin awhile."

"She went to the cabin again, huh?" Jordan said, trying to extract as much information as she could. "I thought she wasn't going yet."

"Well, you know Reece. Here one minute, there the next. You'd think she'd get tired of tramping back and forth. Greysome Point is quite a drive."

"No kidding," Jordan agreed. She had heard of Greysome Point. It was on the far northwest corner of the Olympic Peninsula, as remote a town as the state of Washington had to offer. In fact, it wasn't even a town, as Jordan remembered. It was more of a hamlet. She couldn't imagine anyone seeking out Greysome Point as a place to live. "Did she have the mail forwarded in case I decide to just drop her a note?" Jordan asked.

"Yes, but she said she doesn't go pick it up at the post office for a week or so," the woman replied. "Too bad she doesn't have a phone up there. In this day and age, I can't understand why anyone would be without a telephone for a month or two."

"But she has her cell phone," Jordan offered, remembering she had seen one hanging on Reece's waistband.

"That's what I thought, but Reece told me she can't get a signal once you get past Crescent Lake. She doesn't even have television up there."

"Maybe she likes the solitude," Jordan said, finding it curious Reece would live such an inaccessible lifestyle.

"Are you a friend of Reece's or a business associate?" the woman asked.

"Sort of both," Jordan replied cautiously. "We're both journalists."

"I used to love to see Reece on television. She had such a glamorous and exciting life." The woman smiled reflectively. "I wish she'd do that again. She was so good at her job, but—" she shrugged and went back to her pruning.

"You must be a very good friend," Jordan offered kindly. "Have you known her a long time?" Jordan had walked over to where the woman was sitting.

"No. She moved in a few years ago and I kind of keep an eye on the place while she is gone. She likes to take pictures of my flowers."

"She's a very talented photographer."

"You should see the one she gave me of my tulips. They honestly look real enough to touch. I've never seen anything like it before. She's a magician with a camera. She spent a whole afternoon out here lying on her stomach holding this huge lens just waiting for a bee to land on a flower. She caught the bee just as he was about to take off with pollen droplets on his legs. It was incredible. Last winter she took a shot of a drop of dew that had crystallized on a blade of grass. It was in black and white. I wouldn't have the patience or the talent to do what she does."

"I've seen her double exposure work. It is remarkable," Jordan said.

"I have one of those hanging in my living room. I have no idea how she does it but it always attracts attention. Reece gave it to me for watching her house while she was in Europe last summer," the woman reported, smiling proudly. "She hiked all over Tuscany taking pictures of villas. Lord knows what she'll be photographing this month. She said something about going into the mountains in a few days," the woman said, pointing toward the snowcapped Olympic Mountains that grew out of the horizon west of Seattle. "You know how she loves to hike and camp in the wilderness."

"Yes," Jordan agreed, looking toward the muted peaks. "She sure likes the outdoors," she added, coaxing the conversation along. "Did she mention where she was going hiking this time? Did she say if she was going near the Hoh Rain Forest?" Jordan asked, the Hoh being one of the places she knew was a popular hiking spot.

"She didn't say, but I doubt she would go there. Too touristy. She told me the more remote the area, the more she liked it."

Jordan's mind was picturing wild animals, frozen streams and unsanitary conditions. She had never been camping or hiking in her life but the image of it sent a shiver down her back even though it was a warm September day, far from winter's worst.

"Sounds cold," Jordan said, unable to stop the shiver that raced back up her spine.

"Isn't that the truth. Give me a warm bed and indoor plumbing any day," the woman said with a chuckle. "My name is Gloria," she added, taking off her glove and offering her hand to Jordan.

"Nice to meet you, Gloria. I'm Jordan. You have a lovely garden. No wonder Reece likes to photograph it." Jordan shook her hand warmly. She noticed an aluminum tripod cane standing next to Gloria. She could also see the woman had an artificial leg visible beneath her Capri pants. She didn't seem to mind Jordan seeing it or the awkward way she moved through the garden. "I can't grow a weed. I have a brown thumb," Jordan joked.

"Here," Gloria said, cutting several blooms and handing them to Jordan. "You take these flowers home and put them in water. They'll last a long time."

"Thank you, Gloria. They're lovely. Are you sure?"

"Heavens, yes. I have hundreds of blooms in my backyard. Besides, they're almost past their peak. You enjoy them. I tried to get Reece to take some with her to Greysome Point but she didn't have room in the truck."

"I will," Jordan said, taking a sniff. "I know right where I'll put them, too." She took another long whiff.

"Mom," a teenage girl called from the front door. "Grandma is on the phone."

"I'll be right there, Keri," Gloria called back and pulled herself to her feet.

"It was nice to meet you, Gloria," Jordan said, offering a hand as she stepped onto the sidewalk. "Thanks again for the flowers."

"You're welcome. Was there any message you want to leave for Reece?"

"No. I guess not. I'll catch up with her eventually." Jordan waved and returned to her car as Gloria made her way up the steps to the front door. She turned and waved to Jordan then disappeared inside. Jordan found it ironic the one person Reece McAllister seemed to confide in was also scarred. Maybe that was what convinced Reece she was somehow trustworthy. Whatever the reason, Jordan found Gloria's lovely garden a testament to her steadfast work ethic. She knew gardens didn't tend themselves. She took the flowers to her office and found a vase for them, the blooms filling her office with a heavenly sweet aroma. Jordan went into Susan's office.

"You must be losing your edge, Jordan. I can't believe you didn't get that interview with Ms. McAllister." Susan was sipping coffee and sorting through her mail.

"That's what I wanted to talk with you about. I think I know how to get the story you want."

"How's that?"

"I need to get her on her own familiar territory. I need to get her one-on-one."

"Didn't you try that at the showing?"

"It was way too crowded. Besides, that wasn't a comfortable setting for her. She was busy visiting with the guests." Jordan didn't want to admit she tried to ferret out the elusive Ms. McAllister at the Garage, as well.

"Did you call her and ask for a meeting?"

"I found out she has gone to her cabin at Greysome Point," Jordan advised.

"Where is Greysome Point?" Susan asked, wrinkling her forehead.

"Along the coast, way up in the Olympic Peninsula. It is about as remote a place as you'll find. I think if I'm going to get an interview out of her, the best place to do that is someplace like Greysome Point."

"You want to go up there?" Susan leaned back in her chair and chuckled at Jordan. "Why don't you just wait for her to get back then ask her out to lunch?"

"Because she will be gone for a month or two. She is going on a photo shoot into the Olympic Mountains in a few days."

"Two months? Damn, Jordan. I don't have time to wait for that. If we wait for two months for her to come back into town, we won't have it until the January or February issue." Susan stood up and went to fill her coffee cup from the coffeemaker on the bookcase. "Do you know exactly where she lives in Greysome Point?"

"No, but I think I can find it. It is so remote and uninhabited there can't be that many residences. I thought I'd use Google Earth to find her cabin."

"Okay, Jordan. You have a new assignment. Take a few days and find Reece McAllister in Greysome Point. Get that interview. I'll authorize your expenses." Susan stared over at Jordan as if this expedition was her own idea. "Get up there before she goes off into the wilderness. Go tomorrow." Susan sat back down and returned to her mail. "Call me when you get the story," she added as her telephone rang. She answered it, turning her attention elsewhere.

Jordan got what she wanted. She wanted Susan to tell her this story was worth a trip to the secluded reaches of Washington State. Now all she had to do was figure out how to get Reece McAllister to accept her into her private domain. She also had to learn how to become proficient at hiking and camping in the north woods, all in one day. Jordan returned to her office, suddenly aware of what she had gotten herself into. She dialed Hope's number and left a message on her voice mail.

"Hope, this is Jordan. HELP!" she said into the receiver. "What do you know about camping and hiking? I need a course in north woods survival and I need it before tomorrow. Call me."

Jordan left the office early afternoon and went home to pack. She did a load of laundry while waiting for Hope to return her call. She had no idea what to take if Reece was already on her way into the mountains or where she would even go looking for her. She knew campers had to sign in at the ranger stations before heading into the national park but she didn't even know which way Reece was headed. Jordan was tossing clothes on the bed and rummaging through her shoes when her telephone rang.

"Jordy, what is this about you going camping and hiking?"

Hope said, barely able to control her laughter. "You don't know diddly about the outdoors. In fact, you know less than that."

"I am going into the Olympic Mountains to get a story. Are you going to help me or just make fun of me?" Jordan asked.

"Can't I do both?" Hope chuckled.

"Help me first. I don't have much time. I need to know what to take camping? A sleeping bag, right? Then what?"

Hope began laughing hysterically.

"Hope, will you stop that? I'm on assignment here. I have to leave tomorrow morning and catch the Edmonds ferry for Kingston. I need a list of what to buy. Now stop laughing and help me."

"I'm sorry, Jordy, but it is too funny for words. You've never been camping in your life and now you are going into the Olympic Mountains. It's like someone who doesn't know how to swim deciding to learn by swimming the English Channel. You can't do that. You need to work up to it. You need to get your equipment. Learn to use it. Get comfortable with your pack on your back. Break in some hiking boots. Plan your route. Study maps. Collect the essentials. You can't just grab a sleeping bag and go running into the woods." She laughed again. "I'll tell you what. Next summer I'll take you camping somewhere easy. We'll go on flat ground and stay a night or two. You'll get used to it, see if you like camping."

"Hope, I don't have time for that. I have to get an interview and I have to do it this week, tomorrow. This person is going into the woods on a photo shoot and I may have to follow along to get the story. And I have too been camping, sort of." Jordan argued.

"When?"

"Remember that time we camped in grandmother's living room. We made a tent out of two card tables and a blanket. We slept under there for two nights. And as I remember, we ate our meals in the tent, too."

Hope laughed even louder.

"You were nine years old and I was eight," Hope scoffed. "You cried all night the first night because you couldn't find your teddy bear."

"Are you finished making fun of me?"

"Almost." Hope tried to control her laughter.

"Are you going to help me or not?"

"Absolutely. I wouldn't miss this. I can't wait to see you in a camping store. You don't even own a pair of work gloves, let alone a piece of outdoor equipment."

"I do so. I bought a compass last week," Jordan replied.

"That was for your car so you'd stop driving toward Canada when you go to the grocery store. It doesn't count."

"What store do you recommend, smarty pants? Can't I get this stuff at Target or Wal-Mart?"

"Don't do that, Jordy. If you are really serious about this, you want serious camping gear. Cheap stuff won't last long enough to get you through the first night. All you'll have to buy is a pair of hiking boots and your food."

"I may not know much about hiking and camping, but I know I need more than that."

"You are going to borrow my gear. I have everything you'll need. I've got a sleeping bag, a backpack, a tent, everything. I'd lend you my boots but you and I don't wear the same size. Your boots have to fit right or you'll have blisters. And no, you can't buy them at Target or Wal-Mart. I'll meet you at four o'clock at REI. Do you know where it is?"

"The big camping store? Yes."

"Wear heavy socks. If you only have thin ones, wear two pair," Hope advised. "I'll bring my gear and load it in your trunk. I've got a meeting at six thirty but I can show you what you'll need to know before then."

"Thanks honey. See you there." Jordan felt relieved. Hope had been camping and hiking many times and she knew her expertise would be invaluable.

Jordan headed for REI, muttering to herself the entire way,

wondering why she had become so obsessed with getting the truth behind Reece McAllister and her scar. She couldn't decide if it was a personal challenge, not wanting to accept she had failed on two occasions to get any information from her, or if it was something deeper. Whatever it was, she knew hiking and camping across the backwoods of Washington was as bizarre as anything she had ever attempted to get a story. Jordan didn't like coming away empty-handed. There was something about the woman with the sparkling eyes and sensuous voice that spurred her on, more than the woman's freakishly vicious scar.

Jordan pulled into the parking lot and prowled the rows of vehicles, looking for a place to park. Hope was leaning against the side of her car with the trunk up, waving her into a nearby spot.

"Open your trunk. I'll put this stuff in," Hope announced as Jordan stepped out and slammed the car door.

"Are you sure I'll need all this?" Jordan asked as Hope transferred two cardboard boxes to her trunk.

"Yes. And more." She showed Jordan the contents of her backpack and gave advice on how to pack it. As they walked into the store, Hope kept up a steady stream of hiking tips as well as camping dos and don'ts.

"By the way, who is this person you are following into the woods? Is it someone important or just someone you're interested in?" Hope asked then winked at her.

Jordan hesitated, not sure if she should tell her cousin what she was considering.

"Ah-ha. It is. Who is it? Come on, Jordy. Tell me. Some long lost lover? Some cute young thing with Venus-like beauty who has invaded your psyche?" Hope teased.

"Why must everything involve love and beauty?" Jordan snapped defiantly.

"Because most great crusades in life do."

"Couldn't you just accept I am doing my job?" Jordan declared. "Why does it have to be anything else?"

"Jordy, this is your cousin. I know you. You never do anything strange or dangerous or new unless you have a good reason. And if it was just getting a story for your magazine, you'd make a zillion phone calls to get the information then send a flunky to snap some pictures. You'd never get this involved. Come on, let's find you some hiking boots and I'll show you the food you'll need."

Jordan was immediately overwhelmed by the enormity of the store. Everything from clothing and boots to tents and fishing gear lined the aisles, dozens of shoppers handling, trying on, testing and comparing the equipment. Children ran up and down the aisles, playing in the tents like they were clubhouses and chasing each other through the clothing racks. Hope led the way to the food aisle, pointing out the different kinds of prepackaged meals available for the outdoorsman.

"Since you don't have time to plan and individually pack your meals, your best bet is these pouch meals. They are like the military MREs. Ready-to-eat meals," she clarified. "They have a little pouchy thing inside that heats the food. It isn't wonderful but it is better than eating snails and grubs. I also made a list of some snack foods you should take. They offer high protein and are easy to carry. Like trail mix, fruit bars, stuff like that." She handed Jordan a list she had scribbled. "Take a couple bottles of water. I have a water purifier in my pack, but bottled water is easier, at least to start. Most of the meals require just a little water. You can make your own bottled water. Don't drink stream water, if you don't have to."

"What about the idea of pure mountain spring water? I thought the water running down from the melting snow was clean," Jordan asked.

"It is until a deer or a moose pees in the stream or a fish poops in it and a bear . . ."

"Okay, okay. I get the idea," Jordan replied then scowled.

"How many days are you going to be gone?"

"I don't know. Two or three, I guess. It all depends on how well she'll cooperate in giving me the story."

Hope stopped in her tracks and grabbed Jordan's arm.

"Is this the woman from the Garage last night?" she asked.

"Yes," Jordan said, trying to make light of it. She continued down the aisle, picking pouches of food and dropping them in her cart.

"Jordan, not the one with the scar?"

"Yes, and what does her scar have to do with anything?" Jordan scowled back at her.

"Nothing, but I don't think that woman has any intentions of cooperating with you about anything."

"What else do I need? I have the food." Jordan wanted to change the subject. She didn't need Hope to remind her that this assignment was going to be an uphill battle.

"Boots. Ankle high, waterproof and good support." Hope led the way to the boot department and began perusing the styles. Jordan meandered through the stacks, reading the attributes of certain brands.

"Does it matter what brand?" Jordan asked, amazed at how many there were to pick from.

"No, not really. They carry good stuff. You might find something on sale. Maybe a discontinued style or color."

"Here's some pretty blue ones," Jordan said, examining a pair. "How about these?"

"Those are for rocking climbing, Jordy."

"Won't I be climbing over rocks?"

"Those pretty blue boots are for that kind of rock climbing," Hope said, pointing to the climbing wall at the back of the store where several people were strapped into harnesses and making their way up the artificial cliff.

"Oh, my," Jordan gasped as she stared wide-eyed at the climbers. "Then no, I don't need the pretty blue ones." She continued down the aisle. "How about these?" she asked, finding a display of boots on sale. They were chartreuse green with matching laces. "Is this a good brand?" Jordan searched the boxes for a size seven and a half. Hope came to the end of the aisle and frowned at the color.

"Gag. It's a good brand but no wonder they are clearing them out. Those are ugly puppies, Jordy, with a capital ug." Hope went back to searching the stacks of boots.

Jordan pulled the boot from the box and sat down on the stool to try it on.

"May I help you, miss?" one of the employees asked, noticing Jordan struggling with the long laces.

"I need a pair of hiking boots, size seven and a half."

"Do you have these in her size?" Hope called, holding up a pair of navy ones.

"Only whole sizes in that one," the girl replied. She looked down at the pair Jordan was trying on and wrinkled her nose. "I have that brand in black, navy and forest green, but they aren't on sale." She then leaned down to Jordan and whispered. "You don't want that color, miss."

"Why?" Jordan said, continuing to lace the boot.

The girl rolled her lip as if she thought they were disgusting.

"Chartreuse green? I don't know why we even ordered them to begin with. We only sold five pair. They are hideous. They are called mountain sage, but it is more like frosted lime." The girl stuck out her tongue. "You don't want to be seen in those things."

"Actually, they are very comfortable and not nearly as heavy as I thought they'd be." Jordan tried the other one on as well.

"Are you sure about the color, Jordy?" Hope asked, coming to see how they fit.

"They are *very* comfortable, Hope. I've never had shoes fit so well right out of the box." Jordan marched up and down the aisle, testing the fit.

"Stand up on your toes," Hope instructed, watching the way she walked. The employee watched with a sour look on her face.

"It's hard to do that," Jordan replied. "They are too tight around my ankles."

"Good. That's what you want. You want ankle support. Now wiggle your toes."

"That, I can do."

"Then they fit okay," Hope announced.

"Do you want to try on any other pair?" the girl asked indifferently.

"You can't beat the price," Hope said, looking at the box. "Can you live with pea-green, Jordy?"

"I like them," Jordan said, looking at her feet in the mirror. "Unusual, but I like them."

"Wear them around while we shop just to be sure of the fit. Let's go look at the sleeping bags," Hope said. "You are using mine, but I want you to see what you are getting."

"I don't know what the big deal is about sleeping bags. Aren't they all the same?"

"You're kidding, right? There are as many kinds of sleeping bags as there are boots. There's down, combo-kapock, mummy, twinning," Hope stated as she led the way to the camping gear.

"I'm not climbing Mount Everest, Hope. I just need a small, plain sleeping bag."

"For where you are going and the time of year, my three-season bag is what you'll need. It is down, rated to twenty degrees and best of all, it is a twinning bag." Hope grinned coyly.

"What is that?" Jordan asked, scanning the seemingly endless row of sample bags hanging on a rack like winter coats.

"Like this one," Hope said, pointing to a burgundy one. "You can either use it by itself or you can zip two together and have one double-size bag. Very cozy," she replied, raising her eyebrows.

"I certainly don't need to twin it, then."

"Twinning allows for sharing body heat," Hope whispered, giving Jordan a bump. "Maybe this person you're chasing would like to share some body heat."

"Hope, will you stop. I am just trying to get an interview with her. This isn't anything like what you are suggesting."

"Uh-huh. If that's all it was, you'd wait for her to come home to roost instead of chasing her all over the mountains."

Jordan snorted and turned her attention to the sleeping bag.

"Are you going backpacking with all this gear?" Hope asked, smiling to herself at Jordan's evasiveness.

"Does it make a difference?"

"How much weight can you carry? And I don't mean how much you can lift. You'll have to be able to stuff everything in a pack then carry it on your back for several hours. Then set up camp, cook, sleep, break camp, pack it up, hike, then do it all over again. Everything you need will have to be on your back. Food, fuel, utensils, tent, sleeping bag, change of clothes, emergency supplies. Everything. People who hike and camp a lot count every ounce. An extra ten pounds may not sound like much but it can make or break you on the trail."

"Hope, are you trying to scare me off?" Jordan placed a hand on her hip and stared at her defiantly.

"I just want you to realize what you're getting into, Jordy. I don't want you to get hurt. What if you hike in and she isn't there? What if you get lost? You could freeze to death or be attacked by wild animals. This isn't something you should enter into lightly."

"I know. Believe me, I know. I have thought of all that. I am hoping I can get up to her house before she leaves and convince her to let me go with her. That way I'll never be alone. And yes, I'll be careful. I'll have my cell phone with me. I'll check in at the ranger station. I appreciate your concern, honey. But I'll be careful."

"How about you letting me go with you?" Hope suggested hopefully.

"Thank you, but no. I need to do this by myself. Besides, you have a job to do also."

"You must really like her," Hope said, hooking her arm through Jordan's.

"It's business, Hope. Business." She stared at Hope, trying to look professional. Hope watched Jordan's eyes then allowed a slow smile to pull across her face.

"Let's finish getting your stuff. I have a meeting with the committee for the Northern States Gem Society." Hope continued to give Jordan tips and information as she checked out and returned to her car.

"Thank you for your help, honey," Jordan said, hugging Hope warmly.

"You call me if you need anything, anything at all. You hear me?"

"I will. Don't worry about me." Jordan smiled broadly. "I have my new chartreuse boots. I'll be fine." Jordan wiggled her foot, still sporting her new boots.

"Remember, layer your clothes. Several lightweight layers are better than one thick one," Hope added as Jordan climbed in her car. "And don't forget the flexible poles for the tent. You can't set it up without them."

"Yes, I'll remember," she replied, her brain so full of facts she could hardly see straight. She headed home to finish her packing and sort through the gear in her trunk. "I hope I remember to pack a toothbrush," she muttered to herself.

Chapter 6

Jordan slowed as the road wound through the tall pines and fir trees. The thick forest lined both sides of the road like dark green walls. She checked her map and the instructions. According to her directions from the Internet, a dirt road was supposed to be just ahead on the right. It would climb through the forest for nearly a mile, ending on a bluff that looked out over the valley and the Pacific Ocean beyond. That is where she would find Reece McAllister's house, hidden from the world in a wilderness bastion all its own.

Jordan watched for the turn-off for several miles but saw nothing. When she crossed the bridge over Solomon's Creek, she knew she had gone too far and turned around. She started back, scanning the edge of the forest intently for an opening.

"I know I didn't miss it. Where is the freaking road?" She crept along, constantly checking her rearview mirror for other vehicles. "Why am I looking back there? I haven't seen another car in over an hour. Who am I kidding? No one lives way out here." Just then she saw what looked like a gap in the trees. It was a small gap but a space just wide enough for a car to slip through. She stopped on the pavement, eyeing the pair of tire marks that led into the forest. The path was narrow and disappeared around a curve within a few dozen feet.

"You have *got* to be kidding?" She checked her map again. "This is a road?" She put her window down and leaned out, peering into the dark forest. "This isn't a road. It's a deer trail." She checked the map and instructions one more time then eased her car between the trees. She immediately saw a sign nailed to a tree that read NO TRESPASSING in big letters. A few feet farther another sign read TRESPASSERS WILL BE PROSECUTED. The signs looked new. They had been carefully placed so a driver couldn't miss them. Jordan pulled up next to one of the signs and frowned at it. Should she or shouldn't she. She inched forward, the path barely wide enough for her car to miss the sign on one side and a tree branch on the other. She continued to creep along the path, low hanging pine boughs occasionally brushing against the sides of her car. Another sign greeted her as she rounded the curve. It read TRESPASSERS MAY BE SHOT. DO YOU FEEL LUCKY?

Jordan stopped her car and took a deep breath. She checked in her rearview mirror to see if she should heed the warnings and back up but she was already deep in the forest. She looked up at the towering pines, their branches blocking out the afternoon sky. Jordan felt a tightening in her chest, her breath quickening as her eyes scanned the forest that seemed to close in around her. Her claustrophobia had never bothered her while driving her car before but this was different. This was not wide open spaces and blue skies. This was worse than driving through a mountain tunnel. She took a deep breath and wiped the perspiration from her upper lip then eased forward. She wondered how far she had gone and how far she had to go to get to the clearing at the other end. The Internet map showed only a mile or so. Surely she was nearly there. She steered around the trees, keeping her car centered on the path. The forest seemed to thicken and the trees grew taller as she rounded one curve then another. She wished the path was straight so she could see the end or at least drive faster and get out of the darkening forest.

"I don't like this," she muttered. "I *really* don't like this."

She leaned out the window and stared up through the trees for a glimpse of sunlight but there was none to see. The canopy of trees blocked out any hint of sky or open spaces. The confident and self-assured woman felt her hands begin to tremble as she steered onward. Jordan bit down on her lip and narrowed her vision to the path ahead. She was not going to break down and cry. She was not. She was going to dig deep inside her soul and find the courage to overcome this phobia. She absolutely was going to overcome. She squinted at the narrow path, keeping her eyes just above the hood of the car, desperately trying to ignore the menacing crowd of trees that surrounded her. Suddenly she heard something banging on the trunk of her car as if a tree had dropped its branches on top of her. She glimpsed in the rearview mirror and gasped in surprise as Reece scowled at her, her hands banging on the trunk. Jordan slammed on the brakes.

"Can't you read?" Reece yelled angrily. "No trespassing!"

Jordan couldn't open the car door for the row of trees lining the path.

"I thought," Jordan began nervously, still dealing with the trauma of her claustrophobia.

"NO trespassing," Reece repeated, veritably hissing the words. She gave the back of Jordan's car another whack.

"I'm sorry. I didn't mean to upset you. I just wanted to—"

"You just wanted to try again to interview me, that's what you just wanted to do." Reece placed her hands on her hips, creating a larger than life image in Jordan's rearview mirror.

"I said, I'm sorry," Jordan offered, sticking her head out the window. "I'd get out of the car so you could beat the shit out of me but I can't get the door open."

Reece smirked at her, her forehead wrinkled with anger.

"Drive forward about twenty feet," she ordered curtly.

Jordan did as she was told. Sure enough, just around the bend was a wide spot in the path. Jordan stopped and carefully opened the car door, not sure if Reece did indeed plan on accepting her offer to beat the shit out of her for trespassing.

"I thought reporters were supposed to have good reading skills," Reece said, still scowling her displeasure. "What did you think the signs meant, no trespassing for everyone except you?"

"All right, all right." Jordan crossed her arms defensively. "I admit it. I made a mistake. I shouldn't have driven down your precious path. But you are hard to get a hold of, Ms. McAllister. You don't answer your cell phone. How was I supposed to . . . ?"

Reece smirked at her and began walking up the path, ignoring her comments.

"I beg your pardon," Jordan said, furious that she walked away from her in midconversation. "That's rude."

"It's my path. You trespassed," Reece said without looking back.

"Does that give you the right to be rude?"

"I can be rude if I want to, Ms. Griffin. You are a common criminal."

"I am not a common criminal." Jordan realized she was indeed a criminal. She had ignored signs warning against trespassing on private property. "I'm not common. A criminal, maybe, but not common."

"Tell that to the police," Reece said over her shoulder as she kept walking.

"You aren't serious? You are calling the police on me for driving on your road?" Jordan frowned indignantly.

"It's what I pay my taxes for." As Reece rounded the bend in the path and disappeared out of sight, Jordan was left standing next to her car, wedged between the door and a large Douglas fir. Before she could slide by and catch up with Reece, she realized she was again alone in the forest. She stared up at the towering trees, a gentle breeze whistling through the pines. The whistling wind sounded like haunting voices calling back and forth among the treetops. A chill raced through Jordan, a chill she hadn't felt before. She scrambled back into her car and started the engine. She put up her window, hoping to block out the frightening sounds. She couldn't decide if she should try to back all the way out onto the highway or go forward, hoping she could find a place to turn around. Backing all the way to the highway sounded like an impossible task since it was a harrowing drive to get this far going forward. Jordan swallowed hard, peering down the road. Going forward meant dealing with Reece and her anger again. But she certainly couldn't stay there in the forest forever. She had to go one way or the other. Before she could decide, a few rain drops hit her windshield. Then a few more.

"How the hell does rain get down through the trees?" she muttered. The rain continued to fall, the drops large and noisy against the top of her car. The light that had filtered through the trees and dimly lit the forest floor was almost completely blocked out by the heavy clouds and rain. It was late afternoon but it was as dark as midnight in the woods. Jordan turned on her headlights and windshield wipers. She began to creep forward, steering along the path now narrowed by darkness. Shadows seemed to be everywhere, menacing shadows of giant figures and surreal characters animated by the wind and rain. Jordan snapped on the radio, hoping to create a distraction for her mind but she couldn't pull in a station. She hummed to herself as she inched along, her eyes wide and searching through the darkness.

"Hi ho, hi ho, it's through the woods I go," she sang quietly, trying to avoid the panic she felt. "Raindrops keep falling on my head." Jordan changed her tunes, trying to entertain herself as she moved through the darkness. "When you wish upon a star . . ." Just then a flash of lightning and a crack of thunder split the air. Jordan flinched, jerking the steering wheel and narrowly missing a large tree. She slammed on the brakes, digging her wheels into the mud. When she tried to back up and go around, her tires spun their way down through the mud and leaves, creating a rut.

"No, no, no," she gasped. "Not that. Please, not that." She rocked the car forward and back, trying to gently coax it out of the rut but the soft dirt, pine needles and heavy rain had created a quagmire too thick for her small Civic to conquer. She only succeeded in sinking her tires in the mud up to the hubcaps. Jordan gritted her teeth and tried one last time, revving the engine and hoping to explode out of the rut but the car only settled deeper into the mud. She slapped the steering wheel then rested her head against her hands. "I'm a common criminal stuck in the mud. I'm going to be attacked by wild animals and left for dead so the woman up the road can have me hung from the trees as a warning to other wandering reporters." Jordan heaved a deep sigh. "Now what?" She thought about waiting out the rain in the car with the lights on but she knew that would only run the battery down and she would need that later to start the car. Sitting in a small car in a dark forest during a rainstorm didn't sound like something she wanted to do, either. She dug her Windbreaker out of her backpack and pulled it on then climbed out of the car and locked it. She started up the path but stopped after only a few feet.

"That's smart," she muttered. "A flashlight would be good here." She went back for the flashlight from her pack. The rain continued to fall as she moved up the path, her flashlight sweeping along in front of her. She hadn't realized it when she was driving but the path wound up a hill at a slow but steady incline. It suddenly occurred to her, Reece had gone this way. Perhaps she was still in the woods watching her or following her.

"Anyone out there?" she called, hoping Reece was indeed close at hand. The sound of a familiar voice, any familiar voice would be comforting. "Are you there, Ms. McAllister? I was going to leave but I got stuck in the mud. I'm not trespassing. I just need to call Triple A," Jordan said as if she was carrying on a conversation with someone. "Yeah, right. Like Triple A is really coming way out here to never-never land to dig me out of the mud. Who am I kidding?" Jordan pulled her cell phone from her pocket and tried to get a signal but there was none to be had. As she was replacing it in her pocket she took her eyes off the path and tripped over a downed branch. She landed on her knees, skidding across the mud.

"Oh, shit," she grumbled, dropping her flashlight in a puddle. It immediately went out, leaving her in pitch-black darkness. Jordan fished around in the mud, searching for the flashlight, but only came away with a handful of soggy pine needles and something slimy. When a bolt of lightning lit the darkness she looked down at her hand and the four-inch long banana slug crawling down her fingers. She immediately gave a blood-curdling scream and stood up, shaking her hands frantically. "Get off. Get off. Get off," she gasped. "I don't like crawly things on me." She shuddered and shivered, rubbing her hand on her jacket.

With no flashlight to lead the way, she was left to stumble along the path, feeling her way from tree to tree. The downpour was unrelenting, dousing her with a cold, soaking rain that chilled her to the bone. She wished she had retrieved her fleece top from her pack as well. The hood of the jacket refused to stay over her head, sliding back and allowing the rain to drench her hair and the back of her neck. Jordan was cold, wet and most of all, afraid. It was all she could do to keep from clinging to a tree and crying her eyes out. She didn't like the darkness. She didn't like the cold rain. And she certainly didn't like the confined spaces of the forest. But most of all, she didn't like the fear that consumed her. It was unprofessional. It was not like her. She wanted to burst out into a blue sunlit afternoon, a peaceful meadow spread out before her and birds chirping a merry song. But that wasn't happening anytime soon, that she did know. Just as she thought she couldn't take another step up the steep path, the rain eased to a light drizzle and she saw the crest of the hill, a clearing only a few feet ahead. She wrung her hands through her wet hair and stepped into the clearing. She took a deep cleansing breath and smiled up at the sky, glad to see open spaces even if they were filled with storm clouds. "Thank you," she whispered, turning her face up to the heavens and soaking in the relief as her claustrophobia once again went into hiding.

Jordan spent a long moment reveling in the open sky before noticing the cabin set back against the trees. It was a log cabin with all the amenities of a rustic mountain retreat. It had twin chimneys, a wide covered front porch and log walls with a golden hue. Two rocking chairs stood quiet guard on the front porch. Two dormers on the roof made Jordan assume it was a two-story dwelling. The path circled behind the cabin where a pickup truck was parked at the back door.

"So this is where you hide from the world, Ms. McAllister," Jordan muttered as she climbed the steps to the porch. She hesitated a moment, remembering Reece's warning and harsh words, then knocked on the door. When no one answered she knocked again, this time harder and longer.

"Yes, I know. I'm still trespassing. But answer the door, please. I need to call a tow truck. I also need to use your powder room." She knocked again, squinting through the window of the door. "Come on, Ms. McAllister. Have a heart. Nature calls," Jordan added, frowning her disgust.

"You don't listen, do you?" Reece grumbled as she stood next to a tree, her arms crossed in a defiant stance. Her hair was wet and matted to her head, advertising she too had been caught in the rain.

Jordan snapped a look at her, her hand in mid-knock.

"I'm sorry but I couldn't help it. My car is stuck in the mud and I can't get a cell signal to call a tow truck."

"And you need to use the powder room," Reece added with a smirk.

"Yes, I do," Jordan replied hopefully.

"Weren't you a Girl Scout?" Reece asked, waving her arm toward the thick forest. "There are lots of trees. Pick one, any one."

"You have *got* to be kidding," she scowled.

"First you trespass and want me to ignore it then you waltz up here and want to use my bathroom facilities. Pushy, aren't you, Ms. Griffin?"

"I'm not pushy. I just need to use the ladies' room. Is that a crime? And if you don't plan on allowing me to use it, please tell me soon so I can make other arrangements." Jordan wanted desperately to cross her legs, but refrained from giving Reece the satisfaction of knowing how urgently she needed to use her facilities.

Reece heaved a sigh then disappeared around the back of the cabin. Within a minute she opened the front door and waved Jordan in. With a smirk on her face, she pointed to the bathroom.

"Through the bedroom, second door on the left."

"Thank you," Jordan replied, using every muscle in her body to control her urge to run. Even if it meant her teeth were going to float, she was going to demonstrate dignity in front of this woman.

When Jordan came out of the bathroom she noticed the bedroom was neat and orderly. The bed was made with what looked like a handmade quilt. There were no clothes tossed on the chair or floor, no piles of laundry waiting to be folded or put away, no stacks of books or newspapers on the bedside table. She noticed there were no photographs, either. Just a plain, orderly bedroom. A bedroom that could belong to anyone for there was nothing personal or intimate in it. No bits of memorabilia, no snapshots tucked in the corner of a mirror, no wilted flowers waiting to be pressed, no half-burned candles from a long night of passion, no comfy sleepers left by the bed, nothing to indicate someone lived and loved in this room. Perhaps it was the guest bedroom, Jordan thought. Maybe Reece used another bedroom, littered with clothes and stuff, too messy to allow an intruder to see. Jordan ran her finger along the dresser, a knotty pine, rustic-looking piece of furniture right out of the 1950s. It was a small dresser with just three shallow drawers, not much room for a wardrobe. Jordan's unending curiosity wanted to open one of the drawers and see what was stored inside. She wanted to see if there was a clue to what made Reece tick. Did she hide her mementoes in a drawer? Was there a stack of love letters hinting of cologne and tied with a satin ribbon? Does Reece wear silk pajamas or lacy nightshirts? Does she use a dildo or has she remained celibate since she and Pella parted ways? If Reece thought Jordan wouldn't continue to scratch and dig for the story behind the scar and her secrecy about it, she had another think coming.

"All set?" Reece asked, leaning on the bedroom doorjamb, her arms folded tightly.

"Yes, thank you. I appreciate your generosity. Is this your bedroom or is this the guest bedroom?"

"Guest bedroom?" Reece scoffed. "This is a mountain cabin not a hotel."

"I noticed there was no mirror in here. I wanted to do something with my hair. I'm sure it looks terrible, all wet and matted down like this."

"It looks fine. Besides, it's supposed to rain all evening, maybe all night. You'll just get wet again."

"I didn't know I was going back out in the rain."

"Where did you say your car was stuck?" Reece asked sarcastically.

"On the path near where you saw me."

Reece raised her eyebrows as if to say that meant Jordan would have to walk in the rain to get back to her car.

"You don't mean you're sending me back out there in the woods, do you?"

"You just don't get it, do you?" Reece declared with a frown. "I don't want people around. I don't want to be interviewed. I don't want trespassers infringing on my privacy. I don't like you hounding me or stalking me or following me. I just want to be left alone." She unfolded her arms and headed for the front door. "Now if you'll excuse me, I have things to do." She opened the door and motioned for Jordan to leave.

Jordan hesitated then walked out onto the front porch, fuming with disgust that this woman would indeed send her back into the dark forest in a rainstorm to a car stuck in six inches of mud. Where was her sense of humanity, her compassion, her fair play? The rain had again begun to fall, the raindrops fluttering through the trees and making puddles.

"Can you at least call a tow truck for me?" Jordan asked, swallowing back her anger and fear over returning to the dark and imposing forest.

"I don't have a landline. My cell phone gets the same signal yours does. Besides, there aren't any tow trucks within thirty miles. You'd be lucky to get one up here by the weekend."

"Then how am I supposed to get my car out of the mud and back on the highway?" Jordan asked, her hand perched on her hip defiantly.

"I have absolutely *no* idea, Ms. Griffin. Maybe you should have thought of that before you passed the six signs that said no trespassing." Reece stared back at her.

The wind suddenly changed and the rain pelted against Jordan's back, soaking her hair and chilling her back as it ran down the inside her jacket. She didn't move. She stood her ground, her eyes riveted on Reece's. They exchanged dueling stares, their eyes narrowed and cold like razor-sharp swords ready to draw blood at a moment's notice. The wind whistled through the trees as the rain fell heavier, soaking Jordan to the bone. Reece's jaw muscles rippled as she returned Jordan's stare. Jordan could feel a lump rise in her throat, a childish fearful lump of intimidation. The last thing she wanted to do was show Reece McAllister weakness. She didn't want to let her see fear or even the slightest tear. She wanted to remain strong and independent. How else could she command respect from this woman?

Just as Jordan was about to shout out her disgust over Reece's rude behavior, a crack of lightning and a blast of thunder split the darkening sky, a treetop exploding with a flash of light. Jordan screamed and jumped, falling off the porch and into a mud puddle. It wasn't a far drop, but enough to stun her. She lay sprawled in the mud, too shocked to move, staring up at the rain as it washed over her face.

"Shit! Are you all right?" Reece asked, jumping down from the porch and kneeling next to her.

"What happened?" Jordan asked weakly, staring at the sky.

"You fell backward off the porch," Reece said, helping her to a sitting position.

Jordan's eyes were as big as saucers. She sat staring blankly, a dazed look on her face.

"Are you all right?" Reece asked, holding her up.

Jordan sat in the middle of the puddle, assessing the damage from the fall. It didn't take her long to realize she was startled but uninjured by the fall. She noticed Reece had changed. The fall had transformed her from a fuming, angry landowner to a concerned, caring woman. Jordan also realized, as sneaky as it seemed, she might be able to use this to her advantage. Reece was now kneeling next to her, her eyes full of concern and worry, her hand gently supporting Jordan's back.

"Was I hit by lightning?"

"No. I think it just scared you and you stepped back. Although, that one was close. Fried a treetop over there," Reece said, pointing to the woods beyond the cabin.

"I saw my life flash before me and it wasn't pretty," Jordan said, trying to get to her feet. She leaned on Reece as if her legs were still rubbery and weak. Reece helped her up the steps to the porch, leaving a muddy trail across the cedar planks. She eased Jordan down into one of the rockers and pulled a log stool up next to her to sit on.

"Are you dizzy? Are you having trouble seeing?" Reece looked deep into Jordan's eyes, studying her pupils for telltale signs of concussion or worse.

"I think I will be okay if I can sit here a minute or two before I head back into the woods. I need to catch my breath and get my bearings," Jordan said with a sigh, playing on Reece's sympathy.

"Wait here. I'll get you a drink of water." Reece raced into the cabin and returned in less than a minute, splashing and spilling water from a glass as she returned to Jordan's side. "Here," she said, thrusting it into her hand. "Drink it slow." Reece stood and watched nervously as Jordan obliged, sipping slowly. She leaned her head back, playing the distressed damsel to the hilt. "Do you need more? I can get more," Reece said.

"No, thank you. That was plenty. I don't think I should drink too much all at once." Jordan closed her eyes and sighed heavily. She peeked out of one eye to see if Reece was reaping the benefits from her performance. She was. Her forehead was furrowed and her eyes showed a pained expression.

"I should have heated the water. I should have made coffee or tea. That would have been better, huh?"

"No. I'm fine. If I'm going back into the forest to my car, I better not drink anything hot. It would be too much of a shock, what with the cold rain and all."

"You aren't going back into the woods. When you are strong enough to walk, you are coming inside. You need to change out of those wet clothes and get warmed up."

"I didn't realize it was getting chilly. I guess my body is still in shock." Jordan was giving an award winning performance and Reece was completely captured by it. Jordan wished her high school drama teacher could see her now.

"Come on. Let me help you inside." Reece gently hooked an arm under Jordan's and eased her to her feet. "Go slow. Lean on me."

"I don't want to track in on your clean floors. I'm all wet and muddy."

"Don't worry about it. They'll wash." Reece helped Jordan into the bedroom. "My jeans will be too big for you, but I'll get you some clean sweats." Reece helped Jordan into the bathroom and placed a sweatshirt and sweatpants on the counter for her. "Call me if you need anything else," she said then closed the door.

Jordan listened for Reece's footsteps to leave the bedroom but there were none. She knew the surly Ms. McAllister was standing right outside the bathroom door, ready to jump through hoops if she acted the least bit injured. Jordan leaned against the door, a smug smile on her face.

"Are you doing all right?" Reece called through the door.

"Yes," Jordan replied with a thin voice. "I'm sorry for interrupting your day."

"That's okay. If you feel faint, sit down on the toilet," Reece offered. "I don't want you to fall."

"All right. I will," Jordan said, sighing dramatically. "Shame on you, Jordan," she whispered to herself. "Shame, shame, shame." She closed her eyes and grinned broadly at her victory.

Chapter 7

"How are you feeling? Has the room stopped spinning?" Reece asked, handing Jordan a cup of coffee.

"Yes, thank you," Jordan replied, settling on the couch and pulling her feet up under her legs. "And thanks for the dry clothes."

"They aren't very fancy but I don't keep ball gowns out here in the woods." Reece eyed Jordan over the rim of her cup as she took a swallow.

"They're great, really." Jordan rubbed the arm of the soft sweatshirt. "I'll have to get a pair of these."

"You don't own any sweats?"

"Sure, but mine aren't this kind of material. Mine are nylon."

"You mean those thin ones with the white stripe down the side?" Reece scoffed. "Those aren't sweats. They're jogging suits. Real sweats get softer with age. They have thin spots and holes from years of wear. Those things just get runs in them like panty-hose."

"No, they don't. I've got a set of Donna Karan's that I've had for three years. They haven't run," Jordan argued defensively.

"Have you ever put them on when you just wanted to curl up on the couch and read a book or when you have a cold and want to sip a cup of tea?" Reece replied.

"Well, no."

"What do you grab to put on when you want to spend a rainy day on the couch?"

Jordan wrinkled her forehead as she thought.

"I didn't know there was specific attire for that?" she said.

Reece chuckled and turned to stir the fireplace. When her back was turned, Jordan rubbed her hand up and down the sweatpants, admiring the well-washed comfort of the fleece and wondering why she didn't own any. When Reece finished stoking the fire, she pulled on her jacket and slipped a nylon poncho over her head. She stepped into a pair of tall rubber boots and retrieved a flashlight from the closet.

"Where are you going?" Jordan asked, watching her gear up.

"I'll be right back. You stay here." Reece opened the front door.

"Are you going after firewood? Can I help?"

"No. If you need more wood in the fire, there's plenty in the wood box behind that door," Reece said, pointing to the cabinet next to the hearth.

Jordan came onto the front porch and watched as Reece trotted across the yard and disappeared into the forest, a flash of lightning illuminating the path where she had gone.

"Where are you going?" Jordan called into the darkness. The only reply was a rumble of thunder. "Reece?" The wind blew a cold mist across her face, chilling her deeply. "Reece?" she called again, even louder.

Jordan went back inside and sat down on the hearth, warming her back and enjoying the last of her coffee. Her eyes slowly scanned the room, studying the tidbits of Reece's life. A section of moose antler hung on the wall, decorated with bits of bark and pine needles. Several walking sticks stood in a tall basket, each with unique wood character or bent design. A thick wool afghan in a red and brown plaid was neatly folded over the back of a large leather chair, a chair with aged character and comfortable charm. A wooden bowl of apples sat on the table surrounded by three ladder-back chairs. Jordan wondered why three instead of two or four chairs? She remembered the dormers she had seen and wondered where the stairs were that led to the second floor. Perhaps that was where Reece kept her mementos and personal items. Or was it more house than she was able to take care of and closed it off? The cabin was modest and quaint but it was also perfectly comfortable.

Jordan's curiosity got the best of her. She wandered around the cabin, studying the few simple decorations and making judgments about Reece's personality. The well-burnished woods and warm leather upholstery gave the cabin a rich rustic charm. The stone fireplace provided warmth as well as a cozy amber light perfect for reading, dining or just escaping the rigors of work. Jordan wondered how often Reece had come here to rid herself of the stress of her busy world. A burgundy, brown and tan braided rug covered most of the wide plank flooring and was thick enough to invite bare feet even in the coldest weather. The wrought iron lamps were topped with stretched parchment lampshades. The far end of the main room had three doors. Jordan opened the center door and found a neatly appointed kitchen, small but efficient. There were no dirty dishes in the sink. The only thing out of place was the coffeemaker that stood at the end of the counter with a half-full carafe. Jordan refilled her cup and stirred in a teaspoon of sugar with the tiny wooden spoon. She peeked in the cabinet.

"I see you like green beans, Cheerios and tomato soup, Ms. McAllister," she muttered, reading Reece's stock of canned goods. She opened the refrigerator and poured a bit of milk into her coffee. The refrigerator was sparsely stocked with only the bare essentials, milk, jelly, catsup, mustard, a jar of sweet pickles, a tub of butter, one hydrator full of vegetables and the other full of fruit. "Vegetarian, I bet."

Jordan finished examining the kitchen and went to check the other two doors. The one on the right led to a vestibule and then out a back door of the cabin. The door on the left was locked. Jordan jiggled the handle but it wouldn't budge. This simple locked door piqued her curiosity more than the secrecy about Reece's scar or her absolute refusal to being interviewed. Jordan had become single-minded in her determination to get Reece McAllister's story and this locked door only added to the list of prime questions she had for the elusive woman. She rattled the doorknob again then went back to the couch to enjoy her coffee. The warmth of the fireplace folded around her, her eyes growing heavy as she sat waiting for Reece's return. As much as Jordan tried to fight the urge, she slowly slid down on the couch, rested her head on the arm and closed her eyes. She would only allow herself a five-minute nap, that was all. Then she would be up and pacing the front porch, waiting for Reece's return. But a short rest wouldn't hurt anything.

Jordan drifted off to sleep as the rain continued to fall, sending torrents of water down the roof, across the yard and filling the creek. The rain created a soothing melody against the windows. Jordan pulled the afghan down from the back of the couch and snuggled it around her shoulders then drifted back asleep.

Sometime after the rain eased to a gentle drizzle, Reece came back onto the porch, shaking and stomping the mud from her boots and poncho. She hung the poncho on a peg outside the front door and stepped out of her boots. She looked like a drowned rat as she stood by the fire, shivering with cold. She didn't wake Jordan. Instead, Reece stoked the fire then went to take a shower and put on dry clothes.

"I didn't hear you come back," Jordan said, yawning and stretching. "Why didn't you wake me up?"

"I saw no reason to wake you up while I took a shower," Reece replied, standing with her back to the roaring fire. Her hair was wet but combed back, a few curls dangling over her forehead. There was an innocent look to Reece McAllister as she stood in the amber glow of the fireplace, her face scrubbed and clean. Jordan noticed Reece's scar looked pink and soft like the skin of a baby's bottom. She wondered if it felt that way as well.

"What time is it?" Jordan asked, folding the afghan over the back of the couch.

"Little after eight," Reece replied, turning back the cuffs of her corduroy shirt.

Jordan sat up with a start.

"After eight?" she gasped in surprise. "How long were you gone?"

"You sure ask a lot of questions, Ms. Griffin. Are you always so nosy?"

"I didn't know I was being nosy. I was just asking what time it was and where you went."

Reece smirked and tossed a log on the fire.

"I'm going to make some dinner," Reece said, heading for the kitchen.

Jordan hopped off the couch and followed her.

"I'm *not* nosy," Jordan proclaimed righteously.

Reece chuckled.

"Yeah, right. As a reporter, you wouldn't be worth your salt if you weren't."

"That's just being curious. There's a difference." Jordan followed her into the kitchen and leaned against the sink as Reece squatted in front of the refrigerator and collected an armload of vegetables from the hydrator. She dumped the produce in the sink and ran water on them. She took a bowl from the cabinet and filled it with lettuce, tomato, feta cheese and anything else that looked like a salad ingredient. Jordan watched intently, wondering if she was making just one salad for them to share or if Reece McAllister, true to her word, didn't want to be bothered and was conducting her evening as if she was alone. Jordan certainly didn't want to assume Reece was going to feed her but she did invite her inside and trusted her enough to leave her alone in her cabin while she left for a few hours.

Jordan remembered the prepackaged meals she had packed for the camping trip. She wished she had dug them out and brought them with her instead of leaving them in the car. She certainly couldn't go trekking off into the night to find her car and retrieve them. Jordan told herself she wasn't that hungry, anyway. She could wait until the first light of day to go in search of her car and its contents. Of course, that is assuming Reece would allow her to spend the night on the couch and not out in the cold rainy forest.

Reece continued to wash, slice, chop and prepare a skillet full of vegetables to sauté, dropping in a handful of almonds and fresh parsley. She defrosted a baggie of sliced chicken breast and added it to the skillet. By the time she shook a liberal splash of white wine over the stir-fry, Jordan was licking her lips and swallowing back her interest in the heavenly aroma. Jordan finally could stand the culinary torture no longer and excused herself.

"I think I'll sit by the fire a while. You enjoy your dinner," Jordan said, taking a last long whiff.

"Did you want any more coffee?" Reece asked as she gave the skillet a flip, artfully tossing the vegetables and catching them without losing a single piece.

"No, thank you. I've had plenty." Jordan said, heading for the door. She went to the fireplace, stuffed in another log and sat down on the hearth, feeling a bit abandoned and intimidated. Her grumbling stomach didn't help.

A few minutes later Reece came through the door carrying two plates, silverware and napkins sticking out of her shirt pockets. She crossed the room and handed Jordan a plate artistically arranged with golden fried vegetables and chicken, salad with oil and vinegar dressing, a half peach with a dollop of whipped cream on top and a crusty breadstick across the edge. Jordan's eyes widened, genuinely surprised at Reece's generosity.

"Did you really think I wasn't going to feed you, Ms. Griffin?" she asked, seemingly reading Jordan's thoughts. She handed her a set of silverware and a napkin then sat down next to her on the hearth. She looked over at Jordan then moved to the other side so her scar was hidden from her view. "You may be a common criminal but the sheriff likes us to feed the trespassers before turning them in. Cuts down on the expenses at the jail," she added dryly.

"Ah, I see," Jordan said, restraining a smile. "I'll remember that. Thank you though. It looks wonderful."

"By the way, what's the pack for?" Reece asked as she settled in.

"What pack?" Jordan replied as she savored a bite of chicken.

"The one in the backseat of your car."

"How did you know I have a pack in my car?"

Reece laughed out loud and shook her head.

"What?" Jordan asked, tasting the salad.

"Do you always answer a question with a question?"

Jordan thought a moment, fixing Reece with a curious stare. "Do you?"

"Touché," Reece said, studying Jordan's defiant stare.

"So, how did you know I have a pack in my car?" Jordan asked after another bite.

"I saw it when I moved your car," Reece replied.

"When did you move my car?"

"While you were sleeping," she replied nonchalantly. "And before you ask, I found the keys where you dropped them in the puddle outside. I parked it behind the cabin. You wouldn't want it to be hit by some roving reporter ignoring the signs to keep out and sneaking up my private drive."

"How did you get it out of the mud by yourself?" Jordan asked, her forehead wrinkled with curiosity.

"Instead of asking a question, why not just say thank you," Reece admonished.

Jordan blushed, realizing she was indeed being rude.

"Thank you," she said quietly. "I appreciate your kind gesture." She still was dying to know how Reece moved it by herself since the wheels seemed to be completely impacted in the mud when she left the car in the forest.

Reece finished her dinner and tossed the paper napkin in the fire.

"In case you are still wondering, I used a couple of planks of wood under the wheels to get it out," she said, heading for the kitchen. "Next time, don't spin your tires and you won't get stuck. Easy does it."

"I'll remember that, thank you." Jordan smiled at her. She took her plate to the kitchen and went to work washing dishes.

"I can do the dishes," Reece argued, reaching for the sponge.

"I know you can. But so can I." Jordan refused to give up her place at the sink.

"Have it your way."

When Reece finished in the kitchen, she left Jordan rinsing the dishes and went into the bedroom. She collected a pillow and sleeping bag from the closet shelf and went about making a bed on the couch.

"That looks warm and comfy," Jordan said, coming into the living room.

"I don't have overnight guests very often, but it'll do."

"How often is not very often?" Jordan asked coyly.

Reece raised an eyebrow at the question as if to warn Jordan she was once again being nosy.

"Okay, okay. I know I should have respected your privacy but thank you for not turning me out into the cold or calling the sheriff on me. I appreciate your letting me spend the night and for getting my car out of the mud," Jordan added genuinely.

Reece didn't reply. Instead, she continued nest-making. Jordan leaned down, trying to see her expression.

"Is that a smile, Ms. McAllister? I think your crusty exterior is cracking. I see a twinkle in your eye."

"The hell you do," Reece grumbled, shooting a feisty stare at Jordan. "Don't sleep in too late in the morning. The sheriff usually comes around early collecting the riffraff."

"Now which is it? Am I a common criminal or am I riffraff?" Jordan asked in a saucy voice, her hands leaning on the back of the couch as Reece moved the coffee table out of the way.

"Both. I'm sure there'll be more. I'll let you know when I think of them."

"How about dedicated reporter, trustworthy journalist, compassionate, kind?" Jordan offered. "And above all, a great driver."

With that, Reece burst out laughing.

"One that reads signs with complete comprehension, right?" Reece added with a glare.

"That, too."

"I thought I left all the cocky self-assured journalists at GNN."

"Don't equate me with those snobby television reporters who are more concerned with their hairdos and makeup than in getting the story right," Jordan replied, crossing her arms over her chest.

"A reporter is a reporter. You have the same hang-ups as any other news hunter," Reece retorted.

"I do not," Jordan scowled. "I tell the truth. I give the readers an honest unbiased look at the issue."

"Yeah, right," Reece muttered. "You slant the story with your own viewpoint. Every reporter does it. It's second nature."

"I do not," she argued.

"Sure you do. You may not do it intentionally, but you do it. It's in your body language or in the way you word the questions for an interview. For print media journalists, it's in the way you compose your pictures or in the way you arrange the paragraphs of the story."

Jordan frowned, ready to take exception to Reece's statement.

"You may not even be aware you do it, Ms. Griffin, but you do it. Like that story you did a few months ago on Seattle mass transit. Your lead was about the deteriorating condition of the city's buses. You smacked the reader with your opinion before you got out of the first paragraph. There wasn't anything about the budget cuts or the need for mass transit for the elderly until the bottom of the second page. And the pictures showed one of the new buses flying down the interstate and another being serviced. Where were the photos of the little old lady trying to get her grocery bags onto the bus without dropping her cane? That's where the human interest story was, not with the out-of-date buses. Every city has deteriorating buses. That's a given. You've got to find the small thread in the story to make it important to the reader. Have you ever ridden a city bus?"

"Of course I have."

"I don't mean once when your car was in the shop or because you were slumming to get the story. I mean every day, several times a day, for a month or two, carrying grocery sacks and library books and a sack lunch, waiting in the rain and in the snow and when you don't feel good, sitting between the smelly men getting off work and the runny-nose kids?"

"I'm sure that is important too but that wasn't the story I was after."

"It should have been. There are a lot of people in Seattle who can barely afford the cost of a bus ride. If they need to go across town to the doctor or the social security office, they may have to give up eating that day. They couldn't care less if there's a new six-foot bronze statue in front of the transit offices."

"You are quite passionate about some things," Jordan said, studying Reece's face, the muscles in her jaw rippling.

"Someone has to be," Reece muttered then tossed a log in the fire, squinting at the flames.

"Maybe you'd like to talk about something else." Jordan smiled at her.

"I don't want to talk about anything," Reece replied and opened the cabinet next to the fireplace. She took out a decanter and poured a small amount into two glasses. She swirled it in her glass and took a sip. "Here. This will ward off the night chill," she said, handing the other glass to Jordan.

"What is it?" Jordan asked, taking a whiff.

"Burnt wine," Reece replied sarcastically.

Jordan took a sip, holding it in her mouth, reluctant to swallow.

"Brandy." Reece took another sip. "It won't kill you."

Jordan swallowed, her eyes widening as she did.

"That is smooth. You're right. That will certainly take away the chill."

"It's Remy Martin cognac. But then all cognac is brandy."

"I didn't know that," Jordan said taking another small sip, allowing the liquid to slowly flow down her throat.

"Haven't you had cognac before?" Reece asked, perching a foot on the hearth.

"No, I don't think so. My knowledge of alcohol is limited to white wine and an occasional margarita when I go out with my cousin, Hope. You met her."

"Oh, yes. The one with the big eyes."

"I'm really sorry about that," Jordan began, but Reece held up her hand to stop her before she could say any more.

"You never said why you have a backpack in your car. Are you going camping once you finish trespassing on my property?" Reece asked, moving past the subject of Hope.

"I hope so," Jordan replied, careful not to give away her intentions of convincing Reece to let her go along on her camping trip.

"I must admit I'm surprised. You don't strike me as the outdoorsy type. I had you figured for the indoor sports type."

"Indoor sports?"

"Yeah, you know. Walking the mall, going to the theater, reading," Reece offered in a patronizing voice.

"Those aren't sports. Indoor sports would be basketball, volleyball or bowling."

"Do you play basketball, volleyball or bowl?" Reece asked.

"Well, no," Jordan replied with hesitation. "Pool. Pool is an indoor sport," she added with wide-eyed revelation.

"Yeah, I saw how well you play pool," Reece scoffed.

"It was only the second time I played."

"Second time? My God, what did you do the first time? Rip the felt with your cue?" Reece asked with a surly attitude then took a sip of cognac.

"No," Jordan replied smugly. "Did you know that pool balls don't bounce?"

Reece immediately choked and spit the cognac into the fire, igniting a small fireball.

"Yes, I knew that." Reece couldn't help smiling at the thought.

Jordan giggled, knowing she had brought a smile to her face.

"Maybe next time you can give me a few tips so I can become a fish," Jordan said happily.

"What the hell is a fish?"

"You know. Really good pool players are called fish."

Reece threw her head back and laughed robustly.

"You mean shark. Pool shark."

"Yeah, that."

"Why doesn't your cousin Hope teach you?"

"She's too busy trying to impress."

"Who?"

"Anybody who is watching. She often forgets she is in a committed relationship."

"Ah, a committed relationship. That expression smacks of gaiety," Reece announced as she downed the last of her drink and set the glass on the mantel.

"If by gaiety you mean Hope is gay, yes. She is. That's her backpack and camping gear in my car. I borrowed it."

"Is she going to meet you?"

"No."

"You know you shouldn't go camping alone," Reece advised with a motherly tone. "Even veteran campers need to be cautious."

"I don't plan on going camping alone," Jordan offered carefully.

"I didn't think you had much experience in the deep woods."

"How about you? I noticed you have a backpack in the corner. Do you go camping and hiking alone, Ms. McAllister?"

Reece narrowed her eyes and turned her attention to the fire.

"That's where I keep my pack when it's not in use," she replied.

"Well, do you go alone? Even veteran campers need to be cautious," Jordan said in a mocking tone.

"Sometimes it's better to go alone, especially if you have work to do."

"When there's work to do, that's all the more reason to take someone with you. You can share the load." Jordan had begun laying the groundwork for what she hoped would be Reece's consent that she go along. She knew she would have to be careful, weaving a web so tight even Reece couldn't find a hole to escape.

"My cameras aren't that heavy. I can carry them just fine without help."

"I didn't mean things like that. I meant sharing little jobs like pitching the tent or carrying water or building the fire. Those jobs could be shared, making it easier to camp with a partner than alone."

"Have you ever pitched a tent in the woods?"

"Well, no, but how much harder can it be than pitching it in your living room?"

"You pitched a tent in your living room?" Reece asked with a frown.

"Well, sort of. I spread it out," Jordan replied.

"I feel sorry for your camping partner."

"Are you saying it is more difficult to set up a campsite in the forest than it is in your own backyard?"

"A dozen times more difficult, a hundred times. You have to find a flat place that won't flood if there is rain. You need a good water source. You have to consider if there are wild animals in the area. You need a supply of wood unless you plan on packing in a half dozen fuel tanks."

"You make it sound like it is a serious business just to camp out for a couple days," Jordan suggested.

"It is serious. It can be dangerous if you aren't constantly aware of your surroundings."

"Hope told me that," Jordan added.

"You should have listened to her. I hope whoever you are going camping with knows what they are doing."

"I think she does. At least, I trust that she does."

"Where are you camping? Do you have a reservation for a spot in the park?"

"I don't know. She hasn't told me yet," Jordan replied, looking cautiously optimistic. "Where do you camp?"

"Lots of places."

"And this time?"

"What makes you think *I'm* going camping?" Reece asked, scowling at the question.

"Your next-door neighbor said you were. She said you were on your way into Olympic National Park on a photo shoot."

"I'm going to Seven Lakes Basin and across Appleton Pass," Reece said nonchalantly, not realizing she was telling Jordan exactly what she wanted to know.

"I saw signs for that just past Port Angeles," Jordan acknowledged. "You turn on the road to Sol Duc Hot Springs Resort. There's a campsite at Eagle. Is that where you are going?"

"Not necessarily," Reece replied, suddenly aware she was giving more information than she wanted to give. She grabbed her glass and took it to the kitchen, anxious to change the subject. When she returned, Jordan was still sipping at her drink, her eyes watching Reece intently.

"You better get some sleep if you are going camping tomorrow," Reece said, sitting down on the couch.

"But you are sitting on my bed," Jordan said, taking the last sip.

"The hell I am. I'm sleeping here. You get the bedroom. The sheets are clean." Reece fluffed the pillow then stretched out on top of the sleeping bag with her hands behind her head.

"I'm not putting you out of your bed, Ms. McAllister. That is for sure," Jordan argued. "I can sleep very nicely right here on the couch. So you go get in bed. You have a full day of camping tomorrow yourself." Jordan stood in front of the couch and waved for Reece to get off.

"Don't tell me what to do, Ms. Griffin. This is my cabin. I'll sleep where I want." She crossed her feet and wiggled in to get comfortable.

"I am *not* taking your bedroom. Remember, I'm the common criminal, the riffraff. I have earned the right to sleep on the couch. You go get in your own bed." Jordan crossed her arms and scowled down at her.

"You're like gum stuck on my shoe. Are you always this much trouble?" Reece asked, staring up at her.

"Yes, usually more."

"Damn," Reece groaned. Suddenly Reece's eyes got wide and she took a deep breath, fixing Jordan with a suspicious look.

"You don't think you are going camping with me, do you?" Reece asked caustically.

Jordan looked down at her, but didn't say anything. Reece leapt to her feet and glowered at her.

"Oh, no, you are not. Don't even think about it, lady. You aren't going anywhere near where I'm going." She waved a finger at her. "Do you hear me, Ms. Griffin?"

"I was thinking about camping in the Seven Lakes Basin then maybe hiking over Appleton Pass," Jordan announced nonchalantly.

"The hell you are," Reece yelled. "You'll do no such thing. You stay away from there, you hear me?"

"If I'm not mistaken, it's open to the public. I won't be trespassing. I can camp anywhere I want."

"Now look here," Reece said, her blood pressure rising by the second. "You are not going with me. I don't want a buddy to share the load. I hike and camp alone. Do you hear me? *Alone!*"

"Don't tell me where I can go, Ms. McAllister. I have every right to camp anywhere I want. It is government land. Not yours." Jordan stood nose to nose with Reece, their eyes flaming at each other. "I don't need to go with you. I can go alone."

Reece turned away, frustration growing by leaps and bounds. She ran her hand through her hair and groaned loudly.

"You can't go camping up there by yourself. It's dangerous wilderness. You're a novice, a greenhorn. It's not like camping in your backyard. You'll fall off a mountain or freeze to death. You'll break a fingernail and bleed to death."

"What do you take me for? I'm not a child, you know," Jordan scoffed.

"You aren't an experienced camper either."

"If you won't let me join you," Jordan said, walking into the bedroom. "Then I'll follow you." Jordan looked over her shoulder, smiled a cheeky grin and closed the bedroom door behind her. She no sooner stretched out on the bed, her hands folded behind her head, than the bedroom door burst open and Reece filled the doorway with an angry look.

"Goddamn it," she grumbled, staring over at Jordan's naive expression.

"What time are we leaving?" Jordan asked coyly.

Reece mashed her teeth in disgust, her eyes narrowed with anger. "Early. You better be ready. I'm not waiting around."

"Goodnight," Jordan said, pulling the covers up around her shoulders and turning to face the wall. Reece couldn't see the smile growing across Jordan's face.

Jordan had won round one. She had weaseled her way into Reece McAllister's camping trip. Now she just had to extract a story from her. It wouldn't be easy, but every task started somewhere. Jordan could hear Reece grumbling and muttering to herself as she went about closing up the cabin and turning out the lights. She could hear doors and cupboards being opened and closed as Reece rummaged around the living room, collecting and packing her gear. She occasionally came into the bedroom, opening and closing the dresser and closet as she assembled her camping supplies. She continued muttering and slamming drawers. But Jordan didn't move. She listened to the noise, using every bit of self-control not to chuckle at her victory.

Chapter 8

The cognac had worked miracles. Jordan had slept soundly, waking only as the smell of coffee wafted under the bedroom door.

"Good morning," she said, going into the living room and finding Reece stuffing the last few bits of gear into her pack. Reece didn't answer at first. A narrowed glance was all she offered. "How did you sleep?" Jordan asked, ignoring her surly expression.

"Fine," Reece muttered.

"Is that coffee I smell?" Jordan took a long whiff. "I love the smell of coffee in the morning. Having it at home is better than Starbucks."

"There's probably a cup left in the pot. You can have it. I'll be ready to go in ten minutes."

"Ten minutes?" Jordan scowled. "I wanted to take a shower and wash my hair. And I need to get some clean clothes from my car."

"I brought your stuff in already. I put your pack over there." Reece pointed to the backpack Jordan had borrowed from Hope along with her tote bag. "No time for a shower. I want to make it to Bottleneck Point this afternoon. I want to get some shots of Bridal Pass at sunset. Grab some coffee and the banana on the counter. We need to get going." She left Jordan with a disappointed expression as she headed out the back door with her pack. "Of course, if you've changed your mind about going," Reece said, sticking her head back in the door.

"No, I'll be ready in ten minutes," Jordan replied, knowing Reece would love for her to back out. She gulped down the coffee, peeled the banana and stuck it in her mouth as she hurried into the bathroom, her clean clothes under one arm and her toiletry bag under the other. She rushed through her morning routine, choking down the banana as she washed and brushed herself awake.

"Are you ready?" Reece called, banging on the bathroom door. "The morning is running."

"One minute," she replied, taking a last look in the mirror and wondering what happened to her hair.

"Don't put on any perfume or anything smelly," Reece added, yelling through the door.

"Why not?" Jordan asked, opening the door and looking out.

"Attracts bugs and makes it easier for the mountain lions to track us." Reece gave Jordan's hair a serious look.

Jordan noticed Reece's stare and immediately ran her hands through her unmanageable hair.

"I know, I know. I can't do anything with it this morning. If you'd give me thirty minutes I could wash it and try to look like something," Jordan pleaded.

"No time for that. Wait here," Reece announced and went into the living room. She returned a minute later with a wide rubberband. "Turn around and hold still," she ordered. Reece gathered up Jordan's hair and applied the band, pulling it against her head in a tight ponytail. "There. All done. Let's go."

"I'm coming," Jordan said, fluffing out a few curls for bangs.

"Those won't show when you put a hat on," Reece admonished.

"I hadn't planned on wearing a hat."

"Suit yourself but don't complain to me about sunburn or eye strain." Reece went to the back door and held it, waiting for Jordan.

"Okay, I guess I'm ready." Jordan grabbed her jacket and headed out the door.

"Aren't you forgetting something?" Reece asked, motioning toward Jordan's pack still standing in the corner.

"Oh," Jordan replied, surprised it wasn't already in the truck. "Yeah, I guess I'll need that." She went to pick it up, expecting it to fly up to her shoulders. Instead, the weight of it pulled back like a boat anchor. "Gosh, I don't remember this being so heavy." She used both hands and hoisted it up then carried it out the door. Reece followed and watched as Jordan fought the cumbersome pack into the back of the truck. Jordan knew Reece was testing her, testing her strength and her resolve to complete this task. She suspected Reece would love for her to give in and go home, taking her backpack and curiosity with her. But that wasn't happening. She was going camping and she was getting the story on Reece McAllister, even if it killed her. After all, surely the pack would be easier to carry once she got used to it.

"I assume you checked your pack and have everything you'll need," Reece said, climbing into the cab and starting the engine.

"I'm sure I have everything I'll need," Jordan replied, climbing in the cab as well. "I have a sleeping bag and a tent. I have food, bottled water, matches. Lots of stuff. Hope is an experienced camper. She loaned me all her gear. The only thing I had to get was my hiking boots. What do you think?" Jordan tapped her new green boots together.

"At least you won't lose them in the woods. Are they fluorescent? Do they glow in the dark?"

"No. The color is called bright mountain sage," Jordan argued defensively.

"Let me guess, they were on sale. Half price?"

"I happen to like the color."

"I assume you wore them around the house for a couple weeks to break them in?"

"No. I didn't have time. I just bought them two days ago."

Reece frowned at her.

"Buckle up. This is going to be a bumpy ride," Reece said, pulling out with a lurch.

"You have no idea how bumpy, lady," Jordan muttered to herself as she tightened her seatbelt.

Reece followed the narrow path through the woods toward the highway, tree branches brushing against the side of the truck as she maneuvered the rut-riddled drive. Jordan grabbed the handle as the truck rocked back and forth, lumbering over a downed log. Reece didn't slow down as the path narrowed, threatening to close in completely. Jordan's knuckles whitened as the forest darkened. She took in a deep breath and averted her eyes, a twinge of claustrophobia tickling at her stomach. Suddenly the truck skidded to a stop.

"Why are we stopping?" Jordan asked.

"Didn't you see the tree? The storm must have brought it down." Reece shut off the engine and climbed out.

"Do you need my help?" Jordan asked as she too climbed out.

"I got it." Reece picked up the small tree that had fallen across the path and swung it out of the way. She then began collecting the broken branches and tossing them aside.

Jordan couldn't help but look up at the dense canopy of trees. She squinted up through the branches, straining to see bits of sunlight. She felt perspiration forming on her upper lip and her palms growing sweaty. The air in the woods had stopped moving. An eerie silence was all around them. The only sound was Reece's footsteps crunching over the pine needles. Jordan walked around the truck and helped Reece clear the path, feeling the need to keep busy and be near someone.

"Okay, let's go," Reece announced, tossing the last of the branches aside.

Jordan climbed in the truck, glad to be moving again.

"Are you all right?" Reece asked, noticing Jordan's pale complexion and wide-eyed stare.

"I'm fine." Jordan took a deep, cleansing breath and focused on the path ahead. "The woods sure are thick, aren't they?"

"I like it that way. No one can see in. Natural privacy." Reece cocked an eyebrow as if sending a message to Jordan.

"How far is this campsite?" Jordan asked, changing the subject.

"It'll take us about two hours to get to the cut-off of the highway then another hour to where we leave the truck. We'll hike about two miles this afternoon before we set up camp."

"Two miles? That isn't very far."

"If you say so," Reece replied, hiding a smile.

Jordan used the ride to formulate the questions she would ask Reece and how she would ease into the interview. She knew, as an experienced journalist, Reece would be wary of anything she asked. Gaining her trust would be the first task. Getting Reece to confide in her would come later. Jordan wished she could make notes on her voice activated recorder or in a notebook but that would be too obvious. She would have to be discreet. She would have to be cunning and sly to get this story.

"You sure are quiet," Reece said, hanging her arm out the window as the mid-morning sun warmed the air. "You are usually chatting up a storm. What's the matter? Still working on your questions?"

Jordan looked over at her, smiling coyly at her insight.

"I promise I won't shoot you in the foot, Ms. McAllister."

Reece looked over at her with a cautious stare.

"You bet you won't, Ms. Griffin. This is *my* camping trip. I have work to do. The only reason I am allowing you to come along is to save the park rangers from having to search for you. If I let you wander through the woods alone you'd be lost in twenty minutes. I'm doing park service a favor. I'm doing the wildlife a favor, too. You're too thin to be bear meat. Just remember, I didn't force you to come. You made this decision on your own." She shot a cold stare at Jordan.

"I remember. But don't treat me like a child, Ms. McAllister. I can take care of myself." Jordan didn't like being patronized. She was a big girl. She may never have been camping before but she was still a strong, independent and intelligent woman. In spite of her inexperience, she had every intention of surviving in the woods and returning to Seattle with a five-thousand-word story about Reece McAllister's failed relationship, retirement from television broadcasting and the history behind the menacing-looking scar that seemed to have marked far more than just her exterior.

"Fine with me. I won't have time to babysit." Reece hung her wrist over the steering wheel. Jordan sat quietly, watching the mountain splendor fly by, the thick forests and valleys seemingly unending. Occasionally they would pass a hillside laid bare by loggers, the stumps of fallen trees all that remained on the devastated land. The logging company posted signs advertising the year the land was replanted and the year the tiny saplings would be ready to harvest.

"I hate to see the forest cut down and looking so bleak like that," Jordan said, staring at the colorless hillside.

"Yep," Reece said, her eyes never leaving the road.

"Seems like there could be a better way," Jordan added.

"Is your magazine printed on paper?" Reece asked.

Jordan looked over at her. "I know. We use paper and wood. It's just a shame to scar the land like that."

"You'd rather have the logging done away from the highway?"

"Maybe," Jordan replied, looking up the hill, the cleared land extending well over the top of the ridge.

"Keep the scars out of sight?" Reece suggested.

Jordan didn't answer. She read the innuendo in the question and refused to agree. No, she didn't think the scarred land or Reece's scar, for that matter, needed to be kept out of sight. They were part of life, part of the cycle of existence. Reece was not going to goad her into saying she didn't like to see her scar. She never thought herself that shallow as to think that.

Reece studied Jordan as she stared out the window, her eyes sympathetically scanning the hillside as if trying to heal the scarred land.

"How about a donut and a cup of coffee?" Reece asked, pulling into the graveled parking lot next to a gas station and convenience store. "I need some gas." She eased up to the pump behind another pickup.

"I could use something. That banana didn't stay with me very long." Jordan climbed out and went inside. "Can I get you something?"

"I'll be in shortly." Reece went about fueling the truck and washing the windshield.

Jordan strolled the aisles, drooling over the donut case and fresh brewed coffee. Before making her decision, she made a trip to the ladies' room. While in the stall, she could hear two women enter the restroom.

"Can you believe that?" one woman said, her voice husky.

"I wonder what happened to her. Maybe she had a bad car accident," the other woman said.

"She was probably attacked by a rabid dog," the husky one said then laughed loudly.

"Can you imagine having sex with that scar hanging over her head?" They both chuckled again. "I bet she's gay. She must have to do herself."

Jordan heard them dry their hands and leave the restroom. She stood behind the stall door, stunned by what she had heard. How could anyone be so insensitive? At least Reece hadn't heard them and their rude remarks. When Jordan came out of the restroom she assumed they were the two dyke-ish looking women standing by the coffee machine. Jordan couldn't decide if she wanted to say anything to them or not. She was afraid her contempt for their offensive remarks would only open a can of worms she couldn't contain.

"Hi, cutie," one of the women said in Jordan's direction, the remark identifying her as the woman with the husky voice. Her eyes moved down over Jordan's body and back up again.

Jordan didn't reply, already thoroughly disgusted with their behavior.

"I'm sure she doesn't have sex," the other woman said, motioning toward Reece as she stepped into the convenience store, her voice loud enough for Jordan to hear. "No one would want to be with her." Reece had heard that as well. Jordan stared daggers at the two women, her nostrils flaring with contempt. She didn't say anything, her resentment for the pair so strong she couldn't speak. Instead, she walked over to Reece and smiled lovingly at her.

"I'll wait for you outside, sweetheart," Jordan said then looked back at the two women and smiled smugly. She stroked Reece's face tenderly, her fingertips tracing the scar down to her chin. "The air is a little stale in here," she added in the women's direction. Jordan walked outside and didn't stop until she was in the truck, slamming the door to cool her anger.

A few minutes later Reece came out, carrying a sack and two cups of coffee. She climbed in the truck then handed Jordan a cup and a donut.

"What was that sweetheart thing all about?" Reece asked through a scowl as she started the engine.

"Nothing," Jordan replied, taking a bite of her donut. "Nothing at all."

Reece grinned curiously then pulled onto the highway.

Jordan smiled to herself. She was happy with her actions and pleased that Reece had allowed her to touch her face. The scar was surprisingly soft to the touch. Jordan had answered one of her questions. The scar tissue wasn't hard and leathery. It was tender and soft, like the look in Reece's big brown eyes when Jordan touched her. Jordan sighed deeply, wishing she had had the gumption to kiss her instead of just touch her. That would surely have sent an unmistakable message to the rude women. But Jordan was satisfied she had done the right thing.

They stopped for hamburgers in a small town outside the entrance to Olympic National Park. It took another hour to get to the ranger station. Reece pulled into the parking lot just after one in the afternoon. They checked in with the park rangers and locked the truck, ready for a two-mile hike before setting up camp. Reece hoisted her pack into position and buckled the waist strap. She wore nylon cargo pants, a T-shirt with a fleece top tied around her waist, a tan ball cap with a rainbow sunburst on the front, sunglasses and well-worn brown hiking boots. She looked like a seasoned hiker, one with experience and confidence to handle any problem that arose.

Jordan struggled her way into her pack, grunting and groaning as she settled it into a comfortable position. She was wearing a bright blue sweater over a white turtleneck, tan jogging pants, designer sunglasses and her new green hiking boots. She looked like a fish out of water. She grimaced and fought the straps of her backpack like it weighed a hundred pounds. She leaned forward, trying to adjust the weight of the pack more evenly.

Reece hung a bottle of water from her waist strap and checked her compass against her map. She opened her aluminum walking stick and headed for the trailhead at the edge of the parking lot.

"You ready?" she said, looking back at Jordan, who was still wrestling with her pack.

"I'm coming," she called, hurrying to catch up.

"We should be in camp by five if we shake a leg," Reece announced, taking long strides on the well-worn trail.

"I thought you said it was only two miles," Jordan asked, following along behind, occasionally adjusting the straps.

"It is."

"Oh," Jordan replied, frowning curiously.

Jordan's curiosity about why it would take so long to go such a short distance was quickly answered as the trail changed from well-worn flat ground to a narrow trail of steep inclines and abrupt switchbacks. Exposed roots and downed limbs littered the trail, making footing perilous in spots. Jordan was surprised how quickly the parking lot and the ranger station had disappeared, leaving them deep into the mountainous terrain. But the heady smell of pine trees and open air was invigorating. Jordan took deep breaths, enjoying the wide-open spaces and fresh innocence of the outdoors. The long valleys and thickly covered mountains whistled and called to her in calming voices. The beauty of hiking the north woods was apparent in vistas Jordan had never imagined. She suddenly was furious with Hope for not insisting she go camping with her. But camping with Hope couldn't hold the mystery or fantasy that camping and hiking with Reece McAllister held.

"You didn't tell me how beautiful it was," Jordan said, stopping at the ridge to look out over the valley beyond.

"It's Washington. Everybody knows it has a lot of natural beauty." Reece didn't stop. She kept an even pace, her walking stick clicking every stride.

"Shh, did you hear that?" Jordan whispered.

"What?" Reece asked, looking over her shoulder.

"The way the wind sings in the treetops." Jordan stood silently listening.

"It's the chief's daughter," Reece replied, continuing up the trail.

"What chief's daughter?"

"Supposedly an Indian chief lived up here in the forest. According to the legend he had a daughter, Surianna. She was very young, beautiful and innocent. He kept her safe in the woods, away from the dangers of the world. He wanted her to marry a handsome warrior, have many children and be happy. The chief spent many years searching for a worthy warrior to be her husband. He would bring them into the forest to meet her. But she never found one she liked. They were either too old or too fat or too poor. There was always some reason not to like them. And, of course, the chief only wanted Surianna to have the very best and to be happy so he kept searching. One day an Indian princess from another tribe was passing through the forest and became lost. She came upon Surianna by a stream, bathing in the mountain water.

Her body glistened in the sunlight. The Indian princess was so captivated by Surianna's beauty she sat on a rock and watched her, wishing she had the courage to talk to her. Finally, Surianna noticed the Indian princess sitting on the rock and called to her. She told her to come into the water and bathe with her. She did. They stood together in the mountain stream, their bodies gleaming in the waning light of sunset. They touched each other, caressing each other's young and gorgeous bodies. Surianna and the Indian princess instantly fell in love, both knowing they had found their life's partner. They slept together in the woods, away from the troubles of the world and their families. But when Surianna's father found out, he didn't approve. He wanted Surianna to have a husband and many children. So he demanded Surianna marry the next warrior he found, regardless of who it was. Surianna was so upset she ran away. According to the legend, she spent the rest of her life searching for the Indian princess but never found her again. The whistling wind through the trees is Surianna calling to her lover. At least, that's how the story goes." Reece said, continuing her metered pace up the trail.

"That's a beautiful story, but so sad. Surianna never found love."

"Sure she did. She found the Indian princess."

"But it was such a fleeting love," Jordan added.

"It's just a fairy tale."

"It's a lovely story. Whatever happened to the Indian princess?"

"She went hiking in the woods alone and was never heard from again," Reece said, looking over her shoulder at Jordan as if mocking her intentions.

"I don't think so. I think she was so in love with Surianna she spent her life looking for her lost love until she finally found her. True love is often tragic like that." Jordan sighed at the romantic thought. "I think the whistling wind is their sighs as they make love."

Reece scowled back at her.

"My God, you are a romantic, aren't you?"

"Don't you believe in love everlasting?" Jordan asked.

"No. I don't believe in love at first sight, either."

"I have to agree with you there. Love at first sight is just love with blinders on. True love is a long process, one that takes months and years to develop."

"If ever," Reece muttered, stopping to check her map.

"Are we there yet?" Jordan asked, knowing it sounded childish. Her pack had begun digging into her shoulders and lower back.

"No." Reece took a drink from her water bottle then continued up the trail.

Jordan dug her water bottle from the side pocket of her pack, wishing she too had thought of hanging it in a more convenient spot. She also wished she could reach the baggie of trail mix she had packed, but at that moment she couldn't remember where she packed it. Hope was right. Experience is a good camping companion. Next time she would plan better. She also would dress for the exercise. Her turtleneck and sweater were too much clothing for strenuous hiking. No wonder Reece was wearing a T-shirt. She looked perfectly comfortable and relaxed in her attire. Each of the pockets on the legs of her pants had a function. Each one had an important piece of equipment within easy reach. The compass, map, trail snack, water bottle, handkerchief all were mere inches away.

Jordan wished she had given the hike and the equipment more thought. As she followed Reece up the trail, gasping for breath as the grade steepened, Jordan couldn't remember what she had packed. She knew she had stuffed the sleeping bag in the bottom of the backpack. And there was a small stuff sack that was marked tent but the rest of the contents of what she was lugging up the mountain was anybody's guess. She groaned and pushed her way past a boulder that jutted out, partially obstructing the trail. A small lizard scurried across it, disappearing between the cracks in the rock.

"Eeewww," Jordan said, snatching her hand back and rubbing it on her pants.

"What did you say?" Reece called, well up the trail.

"Nothing," Jordan replied, adjusting her shoulder straps. "Just enjoying nature."

"Don't touch this bush," Reece warned, pointing her walking stick toward a scraggly looking plant with big leaves.

"Is it poison ivy?"

"No, worse. It's devil's club and it has tiny thorns on the stems and under the leaves. If you fall over a cliff and this is all there is to grab on to, it'd be better to just drop."

"That bad, huh?" Jordan replied, catching up to the plant in question and giving it a careful study.

"Yep. Even bear steer away from this one."

"There is another one over there," Jordan announced, pointing to the other side of the trail.

"They'll be all along here. Some grow as big as trees."

"If they are that bad, why don't they kill them?"

Reece looked back at her and frowned.

"They have beautiful leaves and provide vegetation as well as protection for some of nature's creatures. You can't just kill what you don't like."

"If you say so," Jordan said, being overly careful not to touch the menacing bush.

Reece twirled her walking stick like a baton as she reached the top of a rise then started down the other side. It was a short decline, ending at a small footbridge that crossed a stream.

"Almost there," she announced, looking back at Jordan as she began the descent, her pack pushing her into a trot.

"Good. How much further?"

"Over that hill, around the next one and to the river beyond," Reece said, pointing to the vast valley visible between the ridges of the mountains.

"You're kidding," Jordan gasped in horror.

Reece chuckled and unbuckled her waist strap. She pulled her pack from her back and leaned it against a tree. Jordan hooked her hands through her shoulder straps and hung on, waiting to regain her breath. She leaned back against a tree, resting her weight on it as she flexed and shook out her feet.

"Don't you want to take off your pack?" Reece asked, looking none the worse for the hike.

"No. I'd never get it back on," she groaned, closing her eyes and taking a deep breath. "How much farther is it, honestly?"

"Twelve feet," Reece replied, motioning up the hill to a flat spot near a grove of trees.

"Really? This is where we are camping?" Jordan looked up at the spot then at Reece for confirmation.

"Yep." Reece had begun unpacking her tent and supplies. She found a flat spot suitable for her needs and cleared away the twigs and rocks. She then spread her drop cloth before opening out her small tent. It took her no time at all to affix the tent poles and pegs, creating a cozy nest just right for one.

Jordan watched intently, going to school on Reece's technique. Jordan couldn't imagine there was much to this tent pitching—after all, it was small and relatively lightweight. How hard could it be to convert the little sack of nylon and flexible poles into a sleeping quarter? She pulled her tent from its protective nylon sack and unrolled it. It was neatly folded and ready to be erected. Jordan spread the plastic drop cloth, just like she had seen Reece do, then situated the tent on top. That was the last thing that came easy for her. The tent poles were lightweight aluminum alloy with an elastic band threaded through the middle, allowing a flick of the wrist to turn the cluster of connected short poles into two long ones. Jordan turned the tent sack inside out searching for the instructions on what to do with the poles. She wasn't going to ask Reece and offer her fodder for her sarcasm.

"Do you need some help?" Reece asked, swallowing back a chuckle.

"I can do it," Jordan replied just as one of the flexible rods whacked her on the nose. "Ouch," she said instinctively, rubbing her nose.

"I assume you are going to turn your tent right side up," Reece suggested, watching Jordan wrestle with the poles.

"Of course, I am." She quickly flipped it over with one hand, creating a wadded mess. She tried to straighten it out with one hand while waving the tent poles with the other. The stubborn tent refused to cooperate. Jordan tried standing on one corner while pulling the others out flat, but it wasn't to be. The swirling wind played fanciful games with the thin nylon material. After two failed attempts at attaching the poles, she heaved a disgusted gasp and tossed the poles aside. She would unpack the rest of her gear then come back to the tent later. But first, she needed to find the little girl's room or at least the little girl's tree. She dug in her pack for her baggie of toilet paper and discreetly disappeared into the thick forest, making sure she was far enough away to ensure privacy. Just as she found a suitable spot to call her own, she heard footsteps coming toward her through the brush.

"Who is there?" she called, a twinge of fear in her voice.

"The potty police," Reece said, walking toward her, waving a plastic garden trowel. "Use this, Ms. Griffin. It means less damage to the environment and leaves the area more acceptable to the next camper." She stabbed the trowel into the ground like plunging an ice pick into a block of ice.

"Thank you, I think," Jordan muttered to herself as Reece walked away, leaving her to her personal business.

When Jordan returned to the campsite her tent was pitched, the poles perfectly threaded through the tent loops and the pegs secured at the corners. Even the front canopy had been stretched and tied to a tree, offering a small but useful protection from the elements. Reece was collecting dry twigs around the edge of the clearing.

"Thank you for setting up my tent, but I could have done it," Jordan called, studying how it was done.

"We didn't have that kind of time." Reece piled the wood next to the metal fire ring then picked up her camera bag and checked her equipment. "I'll be back," she announced.

"Can I go with you?" Jordan asked hopefully.

"No," Reece said adamantly. "I'll just be gone thirty minutes or so. You stay here and see if you can start a small fire in the ring.

Maybe you could boil some water or something." Reece started off toward the top of the hill.

"What if I didn't want to stay here? What if I wanted to see the sunset, too?" Jordan muttered to herself disgustedly as Reece disappeared over the crest of the hill. "Who died and made you boss?" she called, stomping her foot.

Jordan busied herself around the campsite. She started a tiny fire, large enough to heat one marshmallow, spread her sleeping bag in her tent, carried a pan of water from the stream and stacked the twigs in neat piles next to the fire ring. She noticed the scarlet glow from beyond the hills and assumed the sun had performed its magic. Reece would surely be back shortly, but by the time it was completely dark she began to worry. Jordan kept the fire small, just as Reece had told her, but she wished it was bigger and brighter. Being stranded in the forest alone was new to Jordan. She didn't like it. It felt strange and unnerving, to say the least. She rolled a large rock closer to the fire and sat down, keeping her back to the hill and her eyes riveted toward the trail. Even though she couldn't see anything, she strained toward every sound and movement.

"Is anyone there?" she called as a branch snapped in the distance. "Is that you, Reece?"

"No," Reece said from directly behind her, scaring Jordan and making her jump.

"Don't ever do that again," she scolded, grabbing her throat. "You scared me."

"Sorry. Why didn't you build a fire?"

"I did. See," she replied, pointing to the tiny amber glow.

"That isn't a fire. I get more heat from my Bic lighter." Reece tossed several twigs on the fire and coaxed it into a full-blown blaze. "There. Now you have a fire to keep you warm and ward off the animals."

"What animals?"

"The ones who want your dinner. We'll have to suspend our food from the trees before we go to bed."

Reece wasted no time in heating a small pan of water and adding various dried ingredients to make a hearty soup. Jordan found one of the dehydrated meals Hope insisted she buy and sat next to the fire to open it.

"What the hell is that?" Reece asked, frowning at the aluminum pouch.

"It's beef tips with gravy over brown rice with mushrooms," Jordan read. "And I'm starving." She licked her lips, ready to enjoy the long anticipated meal. "You're not supposed to have to heat it. It heats itself."

"You have to massage that lower section of the bag first," Reece said, stirring her soup.

"Are you sure?" Jordan asked, examining the pouch. She tilted it toward the light of the fire to read the instructions. "Oh." She rubbed the lower pouch between her hands, creating a chemical heating action. "Oh, ouch," she said, setting it down on a rock. "I didn't know how it works. How long do I wait?"

"Few minutes should do it," Reece sat back on her heels, waiting for her soup to finish simmering.

Jordan anxiously opened the pouch and emptied the contents onto her aluminum plate. To her surprise, it looked more like dog food than an epicurean delight. The aroma was also less than appetizing. She stared down at her dinner, poking at it with her fork. She carefully took a small bite, too hungry to respect her nose's opinion. She could hear Reece's restrained chuckle.

"Good stuff, huh?" Reece teased.

"It isn't bad," she replied, swallowing hard to get it down.

Reece took her pan of soup from the fire and sat down cross-legged to enjoy it. She went out of her way to moan and slurp her approval. She ate slowly, enjoying each and every bite. She even drank the last drops of broth from the pan. Jordan couldn't help but watch Reece finish her dinner, her own leaving a sour taste in her mouth. Reece ate an apple as she washed her pan and utensils. She dropped another log on the fire, smugly satisfied with her dinner.

Chapter 9

"I'm turning in," Reece said. She tossed the last of her cup into the fire, raising a tiny plume of ash and steam. "I want to be up early to get some shots of the sunrise."

"How early is early?" Jordan asked, trying to see her watch in the dim light.

"You don't live by a watch while you're in the woods. You live by nature and by your internal clock. I'll be up and gone before you open your eyes," Reece replied, banking the fire for the night.

"If I'm up, may I go with you?"

"If you are awake, dressed and ready to head out when I am, sure." Reece looked over at her with a half smile. "But I won't hold my breath."

"Maybe I'd like to see the sunrise, too."

"Suit yourself." Reece headed for her tent.

Reece was an experienced camper and was settled into her sleeping bag and nearly asleep before Jordan decided what to wear and what to remove before wiggling her way into her insulated cocoon. The night sky was full of brilliant stars and the sounds of the forest. Jordan stretched out on her back with her head outside the flap of her tent, watching and listening to the chirping and croaking of the night. The sounds were foreign to her but she found them soothing and restful. She preferred not to think about the woodland creatures just beyond their campsite that were probably watching her. She snuggled the top of the sleeping bag around her shoulders. It took only a few minutes before she was toasty warm and nestled in for the night. She closed her eyes and heaved a contented sigh. She knew she would sleep well tonight.

When she opened her eyes, the sun was streaming onto her face from over the rim of the hill and the birds were singing from the treetops. She quickly scrambled out of the sleeping bag, stumbling over the tent pegs as she rushed out of her tent.

"Reece?" she called, noticing her tent and sleeping bag were empty. "Ms. McAllister," she yelled, her hands cupped to her mouth. She listened to the echo. "Damn," she muttered then stomped her foot in disgust at oversleeping.

"I told you I get up early," Reece said, striding back into camp with her camera bag over her shoulder.

"You could have woken me up," Jordan suggested, placing her hands on her hips.

"I told you, you had to be ready if you wanted to go." Reece set her camera bag on a stump and went about packing her sleeping bag and tent.

"What are you doing?"

"Breaking camp. I want to be on that ridge by sunset," she replied, nodding toward the next hilltop over. "We've got to go down that valley and up the other side."

"You mean I set up this tent and unpacked all this stuff for just one night?" Jordan's eyes scanned the mess she had made while searching for her gear.

"That's why it's called hiking. You walk, camp, walk, camp." Reece had a condescending tone.

"I know, but how about breakfast?"

"Didn't you bring trail mix, granola bars, Pop Tarts, any of that easy stuff?"

"I think so," Jordan replied, her mind conjuring up the image of fresh squeezed orange juice, scrambled eggs, rye toast with peach marmalade and hot steaming coffee. She would settle for restaurant coffee. It didn't even have to be Starbucks.

"Break camp first. You can eat something once we get moving."

Reece dumped the water pan into the fire and stirred it to make sure it was completely out. She was packed and ready in half the time it took Jordan to dismantle her tent. Jordan couldn't remember how the tent was folded so she wadded it up and shoveled it down into the bottom of her backpack. She wrestled the tent poles and pegs into one of the larger pockets. Jordan didn't know how she had packed all this equipment while sitting in her living room, but it sure didn't fit as neatly now as it did then. Her pack was full to overflowing and she still had her jacket, her sleeping bag pad and two baggies of food to fit in.

Reece had her pack on and was leaning against a tree, waiting for her to finish.

"Roll that pad up and tie it to the top. Tie your jacket around your waist by the sleeves." Reece crossed her arms and watched.

Jordan finally struggled to get her pack onto her shoulders with a grunt and gave a determined grin.

"Okay, I'm ready."

Reece shook her head and started up the trail with long strides.

"Is this going to be another race to the finish line?" Jordan called, as she chewed on her cold strawberry Pop Tart.

Reece only nodded and continued her pace. Jordan groaned and lengthened her stride, determined to keep up.

"Watch your step here," Reece warned, taking the stone steps carefully. The trail had narrowed as it passed along the rim of a stone outcropping. The rocks were stained with moss and lichens, making them slick. "I don't think anyone has been along here in weeks. These steps are like glazed ice."

Jordan maneuvered the long stone treads gingerly, like a child taking stairs for the first time.

"I didn't know moss was so slippery," she acknowledged, falling behind Reece's pace.

As soon as she was clear of the steps and back on firm ground, she hurried to catch up, her backpack jostling with every step. Just as she was about to close the gap between them, Jordan caught her toe on a root and stumbled, falling off the side of the trail and perilously close to the edge of a cliff. She screamed and grabbed for a tree to stop her roll toward the edge. Reece looked back just as Jordan came to rest, her legs hanging over the side. It wasn't a long drop, only a few feet to a ledge below, but it was far enough to scare Jordan completely white.

"Help," she yelled, her feet flailing wildly. "Reece, please. Help me!" Jordan wrapped her arms around the tree and kicked at the air, trying to pull herself back onto solid ground. Reece immediately dropped her pack and ran to Jordan's side. Reece sat down and dug her heels into the dirt as she grabbed onto Jordan's shoulder straps and pulled with all her strength, easing Jordan away from the cliff.

"Are you okay?" Reece asked, still holding onto Jordan's pack.

"Yes, but that was scary," Jordan replied, pulling herself to her feet and dusting off her clothes. "Thank you."

"I told you to be careful," Reece said with a frown, going to put her pack on again.

"I was careful on the mossy part," Jordan replied, surprised at Reece's concern. "But I had to run to catch up."

"Don't run," Reece quipped as she started up the trail again. "Running only causes problems."

"No kidding," Jordan muttered as she adjusted her pack.

Reece didn't stop until she had descended the slope and crossed the footbridge over the creek. Jordan was able to keep up since her pack pushed her along the downhill grade. Reece used her walking stick like a pro, assisting her stride and exploring foreign objects along the trail. She didn't need to look back to see if Jordan was keeping up since her gasps and groans could be heard loud and clear. Jordan felt a cramp biting at the back of her leg and the straps of her pack digging into her shoulders, but she never complained or stopped. She knew Reece was still testing her and she was not giving in.

"Are we stopping to rest?" Jordan asked breathlessly as she caught up with Reece, who was checking her compass and map. Jordan leaned over and rested her hands on her knees as she gulped in breaths.

"No, just checking how far we have to go." Reece took a swig from her water bottle and popped a handful of nuts into her mouth. "You ready?" she asked, looking back at Jordan.

"Oh, sure," Jordan gasped, swallowing hard and breathing through her mouth.

"Watch out," Reece said, noticing something behind Jordan. "Don't step back."

"Why?" Jordan asked, still grabbing her knees for support. "Will I fall over and die?" she quipped. She tried to stand up but her pack pulled her backward.

Reece grabbed for Jordan as she began to fall backward, stumbling over the ball of roots of a devil's club. Jordan couldn't stop herself. Her center of gravity was already off-center as she hung in midair over the dangerous thorn-covered bush. She waved her arms, trying to stop her fall, the huge leaves with their thousands of hidden thorns waiting to catch her. Reece hooked her fingers through one of Jordan's shoulder straps and gave a frantic yank just as she was ready to topple into the bush. It wasn't a graceful move but it was strong enough to pull Jordan out of the way. Reece, however, was hopelessly headed for the thorns herself. Unable to stop her fall, she fell sideways into the bush, her shoulder and back taking the brunt of the damage. She stiffened as the tiny thorns pierced her shirt, holding her like glue against the dinner-plate-size leaves.

"Reece!" Jordan screamed, reaching for her. "Give me your hand. I'll pull you up." Jordan tried to step into the mashed bush and help Reece to her feet.

"No, get back. You'll get caught, too," Reece yelled, the pain visible on her face.

Jordan instantly dropped her pack and looked for something she could use to push the thorny branches out of the way. She found Reece's walking stick and carefully held back the thorn-covered branches as she reached in, offering Reece a hand.

"I told you to stay back," she argued, grimacing from the pain.

"Shut up and give me your hand," Jordan said with a frown. "Easy does it."

Reece begrudgingly took Jordan's hand and climbed to her feet, every move pure torture. Jordan helped her to a safe clearing and removed her pack. It had taken many of the thorns but Reece's shoulder, neck and side were covered with tiny nearly transparent thorns, some so small they looked like little more than lint.

"We've got to take your shirt off," Jordan said, choking back a lump in her throat at what had to be excruciating pain.

"I can't," Reece said through a gasp, her eyes closed tight.

"I can't see how bad it is until we get that fleece shirt off. I'll help. We'll do it real slow."

"I think you'll have to cut it off," Reece said after the first attempt at pulling off a sleeve. "There's a knife in the outside pocket of my pack."

"Are you sure?" Jordan said, desperately wishing she could do something to help relieve Reece's agony.

"Yes," she replied, her eyes still closed and her body rigid.

Jordan retrieved the knife and began cutting away the shirt. Some of the thorns came off with the shirt but many still stuck to her skin, some surrounded by a drop of blood.

"I think we'll have to take off the T-shirt, too," Jordan said, pulling up one of the sleeves to see how many thorns covered her shoulder.

"Cut it," Reece ordered, the pain making decisions difficult.

Jordan did as she was told, carefully cutting away sections of the gray T-shirt.

"It's okay to cry, you know." Jordan wanted to touch Reece's shoulder to console her, but there was no place without a thorn.

"Just cut it off," she replied in a whisper.

Jordan cut away the last section around her neck and let it drop. This was the first time she had seen the extent of Reece's scar and it took her breath away. The scar started at Reece's left temple and ran down her cheek, over her jaw, across her neck and shoulder then disappeared under her bra. There was a shorter scar that started at her shoulder and went part way down her back. Both were pink, puffy and irregular in shape. Several of the larger thorns were deeply embedded in the scar tissue. Jordan held up Reece's hair and examined the thorns stuck in the side of her neck. Reece's body was lean, her shoulder and back muscles sculpted and toned. Her breasts were round and firm, supported by a sports bra.

"Did you bring a first aid kit?" Jordan asked, studying the damage.

"Yes, in the left pocket. It's a little red zipper pouch."

"Come sit over here on this big rock." Jordan guided her to the flat rock and eased her down then went to get the first aid kit. She took out a tube of antiseptic, tweezers and cotton swabs. Just as Jordan was about to pull the first thorn from her shoulder, Reece raised her hand and stopped her.

"There's something you should know about these thorns," Reece said, her jaw muscles rippling.

"I don't care if they are dangerous. I'll be careful. Just sit still and let me do this." Jordan was determined to take care of Reece, regardless of the danger to herself.

"Remember I told you if you fell over a cliff it would be better to fall than grab devil's club? It's because the thorns are like fish hooks. They have a barb on the end so they don't come out very easy." Reece looked back at Jordan, her eyes expressing her pain.

Jordan gasped, her hands trembling at the news.

"How do I get them out?" she asked cautiously.

"Pull. Or if they are in far enough, feed them on through and come out a new hole."

"Oh my God, Reece," she said painfully. "There are dozens of them. Maybe we should try to get you to a hospital."

"I can't walk out of here with those things in me. I'll be okay once you get them out. Just do it. I trust you."

"Okay, but tell me if you need to stop."

"Don't put antiseptic on each one. Wait until you are finished and do it all at once," Reece said.

"Here goes," Jordan said, taking a deep breath and gritted her teeth. She griped the first thorn and pulled but it didn't come out. It clung tightly to Reece's skin, expelling a drop of blood at being tugged. Reece stiffened and groaned.

"Did you get it?" she asked.

"No," Jordan replied apologetically. "It is stuck in there pretty good."

"Jordan, you have to pull hard," Reece said, fixing her with a hard stare. "It will hurt more if you have to do each one several times. Just yank them."

Jordan took another deep breath and tried again, giving a strong pull. This time the stubborn thorn came out, leaving a tiny jagged hole in Reece's skin. Jordan could hear Reece gasp but she didn't move.

"Are you okay?" Jordan asked carefully.

"Keep going."

Jordan pulled another out and again Reece gasped.

"Okay?" Jordan asked again.

"Don't ask. Just pull them out. I don't want to be here all day," she replied through a lump in her throat.

Jordan did as she was told, methodically extracting the thorns. She worked in sections. First her neck, her shoulder, her side then her back. With each thorn, came a small gasp from Reece, but she never said anything. She never cursed or screamed out in agony. Instead she sat quietly, her body taut, fighting the pain and the tears. Several of the thorns were so embedded in Reece's skin, the tip was barely visible. Jordan was sure the pain of removing the thorns was enough to make Reece collapse under the torture, but she didn't flinch. Jordan did her best to make each extraction as brief as possible.

"I have to ask," Jordan said, trying to find something to take their minds off the terrible work. "Why do you wear a sports bra? Is backpacking a sport?"

"Is this your idea of a diversion?"

"Maybe. Maybe I just want to know why you wear a sports bra."

"I wear a sports bra to keep the straps on my backpack from digging into my shoulders. My regular bra straps get in the way of my pack."

"I never thought of that. Hope didn't tell me. No wonder my shoulders get sore."

"That and because you don't have the weight distributed correctly."

Jordan kept plucking the thorns as they talked. Reece gave small gasps and groans, but kept her eyes straight ahead.

"I guess I should have done a bit of research on hiking and camping, but your neighbor said you were leaving in a few days so there just wasn't time."

"I wondered how you found out," Reece replied then sucked air through her teeth as a deeply embedded thorn was coaxed out.

"She is very nice and she has the most gorgeous flowers. I was jealous."

"She does that every year."

"It is amazing she gets around so well," Jordan said.

"Why? Because of her leg? I don't think she lets it bother her."

"What happened to her?"

"Cancer," Reece replied.

"What a shame. How long have you lived next door to her?"

"Three years. I bought that duplex as an investment. I needed a place in Seattle. Greysome Point is too far away for business purposes."

"But the cabin is so cozy and the view is so gorgeous. I see why you love it so."

"Solitude."

111

"That too, but it is so serene and beautiful the way it sits into the hillside overlooking the valley and the ocean." Jordan yanked at a stubborn thorn, ripping a hole in Reece's back just above the scar. "Oh gees. I'm sorry, Reece. That one left a hole."

Reece winced but said nothing.

Jordan placed her hand on Reece's leg gently.

"Should I stop for awhile?" she asked softly.

"No," Reece replied as one tear slowly rolled down her cheek.

Jordan patted her leg and continued. It took thirty minutes for Jordan to extract the thorns she could see. Reece never moved.

"That is all I can see but I think there are some under the back of your bra. I can't get to them unless you take it off."

Reece heaved a deep sigh and thought a moment.

"Are you sure you can't pull it up to get them?"

Jordan tried but she only succeeded in pressing the tiny thorns deeper into Reece's back.

"Wait, stop," Reece groaned. "I'll have to take it off."

"Can I help?" Jordan offered.

"No, let me do it." Reece took a deep breath then pulled the sports bra over her head in one quick motion. A few of the thorns came with it but several more remained firmly stuck to her skin. She folded her arms over her chest to afford herself a measure of modesty as Jordan once again began plucking the thorns from her back, but it was obvious she was more embarrassed at exposing her scar than her breasts.

Jordan couldn't help but notice Reece's round and toned left breast as well as the jagged mark across her right one. Her nipples were dark and erect, something Jordan assumed was brought on by the cool breeze and the excruciating pain.

"Just a few more," Jordan said, glad to be finished with the job. She couldn't imagine how difficult it had been for Reece to sit there and allow the thorns to be ripped from her skin one at a time. And the humiliation of having to expose herself like that seemed to only compound the misery. "There. All finished," Jordan said, rubbing Reece's arm reassuringly.

"Check and make sure," Reece ordered without moving. "Rub your hand over the skin carefully. I don't want to have to do this again."

Jordan did as she asked. She gently floated her hand over Reece's back, shoulder and neck, searching for any missed thorns.

"Ouch," Reece yelled as Jordan passed over one, scraping it against her palm.

"I've got it. Hold still." Jordan removed it and returned to scanning her skin. "How does it feel? Any more?" Jordan wanted to say how soft her skin was, how delicate it felt and how sorry she was to have caused so much suffering, but she knew she would end up in tears if she said anything. The tiny droplets of Reece's blood dotted her skin like badges of courage. Jordan swallowed back the urge to cry over Reece's pain. She didn't want to allow her emotions to overwhelm her.

"I guess that's all," Reece said, finally sighing and relaxing her stiff posture.

"Should I put the antiseptic on now?"

"No, not yet." Reece stood up and walked to the edge of the stream that followed the trail through the woods. It was a fast running stream of icy mountain waters, splashing and spilling its way over boulders and downed trees on its way to the Pacific Ocean. Reece walked stiffly, her body still throbbing from the torture of removing the thorns. She sat down on a rock and removed her boots and stuffed her socks inside. She then pulled off her pants and panties, shaking them out before tossing them over a tree branch. She took a deep breath then stepped into the icy water. She yelled out in shock as she sat down in the current up to the neck, the crystal clear water rushing around her body and cleansing away the pain and blood. Her face turned white and her eyes closed tightly as she remained in the water for several seconds, bobbing up and down. She turned to Jordan and pointed to her pack.

"Could you find my extra shirt? It's in a blue nylon stuff sack near the top of my pack." Reece's words came through shudders and shivers as she remained in the mountain stream up to her chin.

"How can you stand that cold water?" Jordan asked in horror, stunned at her actions. "Aren't you freezing?"

"Yes, I am. But it is actually better than the pain from the thorns. It will reduce the swelling, too." Reece took a deep breath and went under the water. She came up, her eyes wide and her teeth clenched. "There's a small towel in there also."

Jordan hadn't moved. She stood at the edge of the stream, staring at Reece.

"Are you going to get my shirt and the towel or do I have to get them myself?" Reece asked, her chin quivering frantically.

"Yes, I'm sorry. I'll get them. But will you get out of there before you catch pneumonia? That can't be good for you." She went to Reece's pack and pulled out the blue stuff sack and the towel. Reece finally stepped out of the stream. She clutched her arms over her chest as she stood on the bank, shaking the water from her hair. She didn't seem to mind she was naked in front of Jordan.

"Here's your towel," Jordan said, handing it to her and trying to keep her eyes above Reece's neck. It was difficult. Reece McAllister's body was beautiful. She had long lean legs, a flat toned abdomen and the darkest patch of pubic hair Jordan had ever seen. It was thick and dripping with icy mountain water. Reece quickly dried herself and stepped into her clothes. She sat down on the rock and pulled on her socks and hiking boots.

"God, that was cold," she muttered, shaking her head again, flipping Jordan with cold droplets.

"Wait a minute. Shouldn't I put this antiseptic on now?"

Reece looked at her, suddenly remembering they hadn't done that yet.

"I guess so," she replied, removing her shirt. Her nipples were standing at complete erection like two plump raisins. "Just make it fast. I'm freezing."

Jordan spread the cream over her back and rubbed it in. She applied a generous amount to her shoulder and neck as well. The dip in the cold mountain stream had indeed reduced the swelling and removed the blood from the tiny pits that covered her skin. Jordan stroked Reece's skin gently, massaging the antiseptic evenly. She allowed her hands to continue flowing over her soft skin long after the cream had disappeared. Jordan traced her fingertips along the scar that draped across Reece's shoulder. It wasn't a curious touch but one filled with tenderness and sympathy. Jordan wondered if Reece had accepted the pain her scar surely caused as quietly as she had accepted the pain of removing the tiny thorns. Or did she scream out in terror as her skin was ripped and gashed by some unforeseen predator. Jordan's fingertips lingered over the scar as if trying to understand the cause of it.

Reece sat quietly as Jordan massaged her back. She seemed to know Jordan was staring at her scar but she didn't move. Instead she allowed it, as if a gift for her assistance in removing the thorns. When Jordan's fingers moved up her back and began exploring the path the scar took up the side of her neck, Reece tipped her head to the side, allowing a full view of it. Reece closed her eyes as Jordan's hands moved over her cheek to the end of the scar and back down again.

Jordan couldn't speak. The fact that Reece was allowing her to touch this so personal part of her existence was enough to make the moment intimate. She trusted her and that was enough to take Jordan's breath away. Jordan's fingertips were as soft as velvet as they floated over Reece's shoulder. She closed her eyes, drinking in the heavenly scent of pine mixed with the minty smell of the antiseptic. It was natural and pure, like the innocence they shared at that moment.

When Jordan opened her eyes again, Reece was looking at her. It was a look Jordan hadn't seen before. They sat motionless, staring into each other's eyes. Jordan could barely breathe. Reece had completely captured her in a tender gaze. Jordan's mind was working overtime and she couldn't stop it. She imagined Reece's arms around her, pulling her into a warm yet gentle embrace, Reece's lips soft against her own. In her mind, it was a passionate, tender moment, Jordan falling into Reece's arms and giving herself to the kiss. She imagined her arms around Reece's neck, her lips parting and her tongue delving deep inside Reece's mouth. She could almost feel Reece drawing her across her lap, cradling her in her arms. Jordan gasped, her heart pounding in her chest.

"Are you finished?" Reece asked, frowning back at Jordan's absent minded gaze.

"Yes, I think so," Jordan replied, returning to reality.

"We have to be going or we'll never reach our campsite before dark," Reece said, going to collect her equipment and don her back. "Come on, if you're coming." She started up the trail, gingerly adjusting the straps over her tender shoulders.

"Wait for me, Reece," Jordan called, scrambling into her pack. "I'm coming. Wait."

Jordan rushed to catch up, her pack bouncing from side to side as she trotted up the trail. Reece was taking long strides, her sunglasses hiding her narrowed focus.

"Will you slow down?" Jordan asked.

"No time to slow down. We've got several miles to cover and only a few hours of daylight left. Come on." Reece took longer strides, widening the gap between her and Jordan. She kept a healthy distance between them, never out of sight, but far enough ahead so Jordan couldn't see her face or ask her questions. She occasionally stopped to check her compass and her map, but never long enough for Jordan to come within reach. It wasn't hard for Jordan to realize she was doing it intentionally. It gave Jordan a whole new list of questions she was dying to ask Reece.

Chapter 10

Jordan followed, her ankles, feet, shoulders and back all screaming at her to slow down or stop. When Reece disappeared over the crest of a hill, Jordan felt a chill settle over her as she trudged along the trail alone, a chill that didn't end until she reached the top of the hill and could see Reece again. The memory of the imaginary kiss so captivated Jordan, she found herself pursing her lips as she walked along the path. She finally shook her head, disgusted with herself for giving in to such a childish and unprofessional fantasy. She tried to concentrate on formulating the questions she hoped she would get to ask Reece.

"Are you back there?" Reece called.

"Yes. I'm dropping bread crumbs like Hansel and Gretel."

"Good. The grizzly bears can have a nice snack before they eat us."

"There are no grizzly bears in Washington," Jordan replied, catching up.

"Want to bet," Reece scowled.

"Only in the northern Cascades. Not the Olympic Peninsula. I do remember that from an article we did on ecosystems. So there." Jordan stuck her tongue out at Reece then smiled.

"Then what's that?" Reece pointed into the forest.

"Oh my God," Jordan gasped, grabbing Reece's arm. "Is there a grizzly bear in there?" She peered into the woods.

Reece chuckled and tossed a rock at the trees. A chipmunk scampered down one tree and up the next then disappeared through the forest.

"It's a chipmunk. Isn't he cute?"

"Timber tiger," Reece corrected then started up the path again.

"I thought they were chipmunks," Jordan said, giving a last look at the animal then following Reece.

"Same thing," Reece announced as she poked her walking stick at a clump of toadstools.

"Timber tiger, huh? I like that name better. By the way, how are your wounds? Aren't you in terrible pain from the thorns?"

"No. The cold water and antiseptic took care of it. I suggest we pick up the pace or you will be pitching your tent in the rain," Reece declared, looking at the gray clouds on the horizon.

"Oh, no. Not rain," Jordan sighed.

"Yep." She pointed to the clouds. "Come on. Long strides, Ms. Griffin."

"Don't you think you could call me Jordan? After all, we did—"

"Come on." Reece cut her off before she could finish her sentence.

Jordan took a deep breath and used every ounce of energy she had to keep up with Reece's pace. They crossed a creek and found a flat spot on high ground just as the wind began to pull at the tree branches.

"Better hurry. Get your tent up first then put your pack in it while you get the pegs sets," Reece said, immediately clearing a spot big enough for both their tents. She had hers pitched, her gear stowed, her rain suit on and was off collecting firewood while Jordan wrestled with her tent poles.

The rain started slowly. Jordan continued to fight the wind and the poles as a light mist filled the air with humidity. By the time she had one side of the tent supported, the mist became light rain. Jordan was near tears as she fought the last pole into place, the rain growing heavier. She quickly tossed her pack inside and crawled in. She stuck her head out the flap and pounded the front pegs into the ground.

"Screw the other pegs," she scoffed, wiping the rain from her face. She sat cross-legged in her tent with her head out the flap, looking at the rain pelting the ground. She held the front canopy up like an umbrella, shielding herself from the wind-driven rain. Along with the rain came a drop in temperature. Her damp clothing was now chilling her. She rummaged in her pack and pulled out a jacket and an extra pair of socks. She used the socks as mittens and wrapped the jacket over her lap. She contemplated getting out her sleeping bag but she didn't want to wrestle with it just now.

"Why are you in there?" Reece asked, stacking another load of wood. "It isn't raining that bad. Put on your rain suit and come help."

"What rain suit? Should I have one of those?" Jordan asked, sitting in the open tent flap.

"Didn't Hope give you one? How can you go camping in Washington state without a rain suit?"

"I have no idea. Let me look." Jordan began pulling things from her pack, hoping something looked like a rain suit. "I have a big square plastic thing," she said, finding it hard to see what she had in the confines of the tent.

"Is there a hole in the middle of it?"

"Yes, I think so," Jordan replied, struggling with it.

"It's a poncho, then. Put your head through the hole, pull up the hood and get your ass out here." Reece had begun laying a fire in a sheltered area under an outcropping of rocks. "There's no room service out here in the woods."

"Ah, heck. I wanted eggs Benedict on a tray with one of those silver domey things over it," Jordan said as she crawled out of the tent and pulled the poncho over her head. It was backward, the hood crowded up around her face. She quickly turned it around before Reece noticed.

"Bring some of the pine needles from under the trees. They make good fire starters. Dig down for the dry ones."

Jordan grabbed two handfuls and brought them to the fire ring.

"Ouch, ouch, ouch, ouch, ouch," she muttered as she dropped them next to Reece.

"What?"

"I poked myself." She pulled the socks from her hands and examined the tiny hole in her finger. "It sure is hard work having fun in the woods, isn't it?"

"Only when you bring a rookie with you," Reece replied, coaxing the fire to start.

"I didn't know *you* were a rookie," Jordan said with a straight face.

"Do you need me to remove something?" Reece asked, looking at Jordan's finger.

"No, I don't think so. How about you? How are you feeling? I can't image how sore you must be."

"I'm all right."

"I'm really sorry if I hurt you when I pulled the thorns out. Some of them were really embedded."

"Don't worry about it."

"I'm grateful you took that fall for me." Jordan rubbed up and down on her own arms as she thought about the dozens of thorns she had removed from Reece's body.

"Yeah, I was the logical choice," Reece said, starting the fire.

"Why do you say logical choice?"

"I already have the scars. A few more wouldn't matter." Reece's tone was sarcastic at best.

"I didn't say that." Jordan scowled at her. "I never said anything of the kind."

"It's true, right?"

"No! It most certainly is not. Why would you say that?"

Reece shrugged then looked up at the sky, noticing a small patch of lighter clouds moving overhead. "The rain is letting up. You stay under the cliff and heat some water. You'll be dry here. I'll be back in a few minutes."

Reece unpacked her camera bag and headed over the hill. Jordan didn't argue about going with her. She was too tired, wet and sore to do anything but sit by the fire and warm up. She would finish setting up her tent in a few minutes.

Jordan had just finished shaking out her sleeping bag when her cell phone jingled from inside the pocket of her pack.

"Finally, I get a signal," she said, frantically digging it out. "Hello, Susan," she said, glad to be once again in touch with the outside world.

"I've been trying to call you for two days. Don't you ever answer your phone?"

"I'm in the Olympic National Park. I haven't been able to get a signal. This is the first time I've had one since I got off the ferry at Kingston."

"What are you doing in the National Park?" Susan asked, sipping her coffee loud enough for Jordan to hear.

"Is that Starbucks?" Jordan asked with a moan.

"Double mocha latte," Susan gloated, taking a long slow slurp.

"You could have said it was stale office coffee."

"Starbucks. And the froth is nice and tall, just the way I like it."

Jordan sighed at the image, remembering the small aluminum cup of boiled beans Reece had called coffee.

"Well, what are you doing up there?" Susan repeated.

"Trying to get the story you sent me on."

"Reece McAllister?"

"Yes. She is hiking and camping her way to Seven Lakes and I'm hoping somewhere along the way I can convince her to give me an interview."

"You mean you don't have it yet?" Susan sounded disgusted.

"Not yet."

"What are you waiting for?"

"Reece McAllister covets her privacy like no one I have ever met."

"You better turn on the charm or something, Jordan. If you don't get this story you can bet another magazine will. Promise her the moon but get that story. Do you hear me? I'm not paying for you to just go camping." Susan enjoyed exercising her authority. "I can slide the story in next month's issue if you get going. I have a spot saved for it. We can stretch it with several stock photos but you'll need to get some recent shots. Try to get some close-ups. If you can't get close-ups, take long shots. We can crop."

"Yes, yes. I know exactly what you want. You want some shots of her scar," Jordan acknowledged, uncomfortable with the idea.

"This issue is going to fly off the shelves. You watch. Keep in touch." The call ended with the sound of Susan slurping her coffee.

Jordan immediately tried to make a call but her cell had lost its signal as quickly as it found it.

"Damn mountain range." She went back to straightening her tent.

"Who are you talking to?" Reece asking, coming down the trail.

"My cell phone. Why can't you get a signal out here?"

"Because bears and mountain lions don't know how to use cell phones."

"Very funny." Jordan stuffed the phone in her pocket and went to find something for her dinner.

Reece once again added a bit of dried this and a bit of dried that to her small aluminum pan and created a hearty stew. Jordan set her foil pouch next to her on a rock waiting for the ambition to massage the heating element into action. Her memory of the dog food from the night before didn't conjure up great expectations for this meal, either. She sat eating an apple and a package of crackers while Reece stirred her stew. Jordan tried not to watch, the rich aroma only making her drool all the more.

"Here," Reece said, stabbing a spoon into the stew and handing it to Jordan. "Give me your pouch."

"That's okay. I'll eat it in a few minutes. I'm going to let my apple settle first." Jordan stared at the stew longingly.

"Take this and give me the damn pouch," Reece demanded, giving her a harsh glance.

"Reece, no. You eat your meal. I'll eat mine."

"Either you eat this stew or I'll dump it in the dirt. Then you can eat your pouch and I will go hungry. Your choice." Reece held the pan out, poised to be dumped.

Jordan stared at Reece, trying to decide if she would indeed dump the delicious looking stew in the dirt and go hungry. From what she had seen of this woman, Jordan had no doubt she would do it in a heartbeat.

"I'd love to have the stew. Thanks." Jordan accepted the pan and took a bite, the heavenly taste better than anything she had ever eaten in her life. She didn't realize she was so hungry. "Mmmm," she moaned. "This is so good." Jordan closed her eyes and chewed slowly, savoring every morsel. "Are you sure about this?" she asked.

"Sure," Reece replied, activating the heat packet on the meal pouch. "I've never tried chicken tetrazzini in a pouch before."

"I hope it is okay."

Reece opened the pouch and poured it out on the plate. There were three tiny pieces of chicken and four pieces of tomato swimming in a sea of cheesy broth. They both stared at it, watching the bits of fat floating on the surface as if they were doing the backstroke across the plate.

"Bon appétit," Reece said, swallowing hard. She stabbed one of the pieces of chicken with her fork and put it in her mouth. She closed her eyes and chewed. It wasn't a contented, satisfying look like Jordan's, but a tortured, painful expression. She swallowed then took another piece, forcing a smile between bites.

"Here. Have a cracker with it," Jordan said, handing her the package.

Reece took one and popped it in her mouth whole, obviously trying to camouflage the taste of the chicken.

"Mmm," Reece said, mimicking Jordan's moan. "Great cracker."

"I'm sorry, Reece," Jordan said, shoving the last of the stew back at her. "Here, eat your dinner."

"No. You eat it. I'm fine," she chuckled. "Actually, it isn't too bad. Looks disgusting but it tastes okay."

"Are you sure?"

"Yes, I'm sure." Reece ate the last of the bites then drank the broth. By the time they cleaned the utensils and straightened the campsite, it was dark, cold and late.

"Aren't you going to bed?" Reece asked as she unzipped her tent and prepared to crawl inside. "We've got a long hike tomorrow."

"Yes, in a few minutes," Jordan replied, huddling closer to the fire. "You don't mind if I put another log on the fire, do you?"

"Suit yourself." Reece stepped out of her camp slippers and crawled inside.

"Good night," Jordan said. "Thanks for the wonderful stew."

"You're welcome. Good night," Reece said then zipped the tent flap.

Within a moment Jordan was alone with the sounds of the forest. The darkness was all around her. The moonlight was blotted out by the heavy layer of clouds and drizzle. She arranged two logs on the fire, poking the ashes into a full blaze. Jordan knew she should go to bed. She was tired and there would be another day of hiking tomorrow, but she couldn't bring herself to face the cramped confines of her tent. The night before was beautiful. The skies were clean, the air fresh and warm. She had slept with her head outside the tent flap. But tonight was different. The mountain air was cold. The chilly mist threatened to intensify into a full-blown rainstorm at any minute. There was no way she could sleep hanging out the front of the tent tonight. She would freeze to death and be soaking wet. But she broke out into a cold sweat at the thought of being closed up inside that tiny tent. She didn't want to admit her fears to Reece, either. Jordan knew she would tease her unmercifully if she knew she was afraid of her own tent. She placed another log on the fire and moved further under the rock cliff as the rain once again began to fall. She leaned back against the rocks and closed her eyes, her arms crossed over her chest. She fidgeted on the flat rock, trying to find a comfortable position.

The rain blew through the trees, a cold dampness stinging her cheeks. Jordan alternated between feeding the fire and napping against the rocks. It was a poor substitute for a warm night's sleep. She had just tossed another stick of wood on the fire and fallen back to sleep when she was shocked awake by a hand on her shoulder.

"Aren't you going to bed?" Reece said with a scowl.

"I thought I'd sit up awhile, if you don't mind."

"I don't mind but you are about out of wood," Reece replied, shining her flashlight on the nearly depleted pile of firewood.

"I'll be fine. You go on to bed."

"Are you sick or something?" Reece asked, pointing her flashlight at Jordan. Her light caught a tear glistening in Jordan's eye.

Jordan shook her head and folded the collar of her jacket up around her neck.

"No, I'm all right." Jordan diverted her eyes, afraid her face would give away her fear.

"If you're all right, why are you sitting by a dwindling fire at midnight during a cold rain?" Reece asked.

Jordan shrugged.

"There has to be a reason," Reece said persistently.

"I don't like tight places," she replied. She stared at the ground, too embarrassed to look Reece in the eye.

"Claustrophobia?"

Jordan nodded and shoved her hands in her jacket pockets,

expecting Reece to laugh or toss out a string of jokes at her expense.

"But you slept in your tent last night," Reece justified.

"I slept with my head outside the zipper. Just my body was in the tent. I could see the sky and the stars so it was okay."

"I guess you can't do that tonight," Reece said, shining her flashlight toward Jordan's tent, the rain pelting it relentlessly.

"I thought I could sit here by the fire a bit. You go on to bed. I'll be all right."

Reece gave a grunt and headed for the tents, but instead of crawling back into her own, she reached in Jordan's tent and pulled out her sleeping bag. She took it to her tent and spread it out next to her own sleeping bag. She then went back to the fire where Jordan was again trying to get comfortable against a rock.

"Come on, Ms. Griffin. Let's go." Reece took Jordan by the hand and pulled her to her feet.

"Go where?"

"You are sleeping in my tent with me. Come on."

"With you?"

"You'll have to. I already moved your sleeping bag into my tent. It's bigger and it has more head room." Reece gave a half smile. "Besides, if you are in my tent worried about me taking advantage of you in your sleep, you won't be thinking about your claustrophobia." She pulled Jordan along, taking long determined strides. "We've got a long day tomorrow and we need some sleep."

Jordan hesitated, the idea of sleeping with Reece bringing on a fresh round of fear. She hadn't considered sleeping with her. Interviewing, yes. Sharing a tent, no. How could she keep an objective point of view if she was thinking about this woman lying only a few inches away from her? But Reece could be right. Her claustrophobia might not stand a chance if her mind was on Reece McAllister's lithe body just a breath away. She could only worry about one thing at a time.

"By the way, I snore," Reece added.

"Loudly?" Jordan asked, allowing her to lead the way.

"Like a freight train on rusty rails," Reece replied, opening the flap to her tent. "Take your boots off and get in before the rain gets heavier."

Reece allowed Jordan to pull off her boots and crawl in first. She waited for her to get snuggled in her bag before taking her place next to her. Reece didn't close the tent flap but pulled it back and tied it open. The front canopy provided protection from the rain but the opening gave Jordan a sense of relief.

"Zip up your sleeping bag around your shoulders and you should be warm enough," Reece said, digging in her bag for a knit stocking cap. She pulled it out and perched it on Jordan's head. "This will keep your head warm."

"Thank you, Ms. McAllister," Jordan replied, adjusting the cap down over her ears.

"You better call me Reece. After all, we are sleeping together." Reece snuggled down into her sleeping bag, pulling it up around her face so only her eyes and nose were visible.

"Good night, Reece," Jordan said, her eyes straining to see out the tent flap and the open spaces beyond.

The two sleeping bags completely filled the small tent, one overlapping the over. It was a tight fit but one that gave Jordan a sense of protection and reassurance. She felt no threat from the woman in the next sleeping bag. Within five minutes both women were asleep. Jordan woke once, Reece's leg heavy against her own. She gently pushed it away, Reece moaning softly as she turned on her side and returned to snoring. When Jordan woke in the morning, she was warm and cozy in her cocoon, the sounds of chirping birds serenading her awake. Sometime during the night Jordan had snuggled against Reece's side, her body molded against her. Jordan looked up at Reece, her arm propped under her head. She was looking down at Jordan, watching her sleep.

"Good morning," Jordan said, smiling up at her. She didn't realize she had crowded Reece up against the wall of the tent.

"Morning," she replied. "Did you sleep all right?"

"Yes, I did. It was wonderful. I haven't slept so soundly in months." Jordan looked over at the tent flap. It was closed, zipped tight. Jordan's eyes widened and she took a deep, nearly frantic breath.

"Relax," Reece said, reaching over and unzipping it. She pulled the flap back so Jordan could see the blue skies. "It's open."

Jordan scooted closer to the tent opening and breathed in the fresh air.

"I'm sorry. I know it is silly but I can't help it. I've had trouble with tight spaces ever since I was little. I got stuck in a pillowcase once, head first. I was about four. I appreciate you offering to share your tent."

"You can give Hope back her tent. Get yourself one with a higher peak and a larger canopy."

"I like this one. Maybe you can help me pick one out for my next adventure."

"Don't tell me you actually like camping?" Reece chuckled.

"Parts of it." Jordan tried to unzip her sleeping bag. It was stuck, her hands and arms inside. She continued fighting with it, tugging at the heavy metal zipper. When the top of the bag flopped over her head, Jordan gasped, frantically clawing at it. The more she wrestled with the obstinate zipper and unyielding sleeping bag, the more hysterical she became.

"Wait a minute. I'll get it for you," Reece said, trying to help.

Jordan couldn't help it. She was too consumed to stop. She had to get out of the restricting bag at any cost. She kicked and flailed, trying to free herself.

"Get it off of me. Get it off," Jordan screamed, tears rolling down her cheek.

"STOP!" Reece sat up and grabbed Jordan by the shoulders and shook her. "Jordan. Stop," she yelled. "I'll get it." Reece climbed out of her sleeping bag and straddled Jordan to keep her from kicking herself into a frenzy. She pulled the zipper from Jordan's grip and worked the teeth free, inching it down until it was open enough for Jordan to crawl out. Jordan scrambled out of the tent, gulping deep breaths like a swimmer just saved from drowning. She rushed out into the open where she had a clear view of the blue skies. She turned her face upward to feel the sun's rays on her face, the last tears trailing down her cheeks. She closed her eyes and drank in the clean air.

"You okay?" Reece asked, coming to stand next to her.

"Yes," Jordan replied, her voice trembling. She wiped the tears from her face.

"The zipper just got stuck," Reece offered, reaching over and awkwardly patting Jordan on the shoulder.

Jordan nodded, trying to find composure.

"They make sleeping bags with no-fail zippers, you know," Reece added, trying to help. Before she could say anything else, Jordan threw her arms around Reece's neck and hugged her tightly, sobbing against her shoulder. Reece folded her arms around her, holding Jordan as she cleansed her need to cry.

"Maybe they make sleeping bags with snaps," Reece said, as Jordan finished and wiped away the tears.

"Maybe so," Jordan replied with a chuckle as she pulled a tissue from her pocket and blew her nose. "Am I now officially an outdoor sissy?" Jordan asked, too embarrassed to look her in the eye.

"I don't think so," Reece replied, brushing back stray locks of hair from Jordan's face. "We just know what kind of equipment you prefer." She smiled down at her. Jordan joined her in laughing. "Are you ready for some coffee and maybe some breakfast?"

"I would love some coffee. But would you mind if I make it?" Jordan had remembered Reece's attempt at coffee and decided she couldn't possibly do any worse.

"Sure. You can be the official coffee maker. I'll build a fire."

"I'll be right there as soon as I brush my teeth and wash my face," Jordan said, finally once again herself.

"Me too," Reece said, grabbing her toiletry baggie.

Jordan was surprised Reece didn't break camp immediately to send them on up the trail. They enjoyed coffee, a cup of instant oatmeal with raisins and brown sugar and an orange before starting the job of repacking their gear.

"Put your tent in the bottom of your pack," Reece said as she rolled her tent into a tight roll. "You won't need it tonight. You can sleep in mine." Jordan didn't argue with her.

"Thanks," Jordan replied, a relieved smile on her face. "I won't zip my sleeping bag closed, either."

They sat next to the fire and finished their coffee as they enjoyed the fresh brilliance of a morning in the forest.

"Why are you so secretive?" Jordan asked nonchalantly, hoping to catch her off guard.

Reece looked at her but didn't answer. She grabbed her camera and went to the edge of the cliff to snap a picture.

"Did you ever think by telling your story you might inspire someone else to deal with life's problems? Life's challenges?" Jordan added, following her.

"Challenges? You mean my scar? You think this is a challenge?" Reece asked, focusing for another shot.

"Well, isn't it?" Jordan replied. "Isn't that the real issue? If you don't think it is, then tell me what Reece McAllister thinks is her greatest challenge, her greatest accomplishment, her greatest fear. Tell me what you want your viewers and readers to know about you. Tell me why you are standing on a cliff, taking pictures of a sunrise with a magazine reporter who doesn't know squat about camping or hiking. Let me tell your story the way you want it told."

"I'm standing here with you because you prostituted yourself to get the story."

"I beg your pardon. I do not prostitute myself," Jordan said indignantly.

"Sure you did. You bought a pair of ugly hiking boots and some gross dehydrated meals then borrowed your cousin's camping gear so you could con me into taking you into the woods and confessing my story to you. You hate camping and hiking yet you were willing to sell out for the sake of a story."

"I don't hate camping and hiking. I love the outdoors. The mountains are beautiful and the air smells so fresh and pure."

"Give me a break. You've never been camping in your life and you'd rather be strolling up Third Avenue shopping for a sweater than sitting on a log next to a roaring fire."

Jordan crossed her arms defensively.

"I beg your pardon. Don't tell me what I like or don't like. Just because I've never gone camping before doesn't mean I don't like doing it. You weren't born with a backpack on your back or a camera in your hand. You had to experience it for the first time and learn to like it. I deserve the same chance. So back off, Ms. McAllister." Jordan leered at her, her feathers in full ruffle.

"How bad do you want this story, Ms. Griffin?"

"Not bad enough to sleep with you," Jordan said.

"I didn't ask you that, now did I?"

Jordan didn't know how it happened, but once again Reece McAllister had maneuvered her into a corner and once again she goaded Jordan into saying the wrong thing. She had no idea why she said that. It just slipped out.

"If the tables were turned, you'd move heaven and earth to get the scoop. You wouldn't give up until you knew every detail. Why should I be any different?" Jordan said, composing herself. "You have a chance to tell your story the way you want it told. I promise I'll treat you fairly. How many reporters would give you that assurance? I want to write your story, Reece. And I want you to tell me what you want in it. That is the long and the short of it."

Reece looked over at her, the camera still in front of her face. She stared at Jordan skeptically, trying to decide if she could believe her.

"Are you about to shoot me in the foot, Ms. Griffin?"

"Only if you refuse to call me Jordan." She smiled and raised her hand for Reece to accept a handshake.

Reece took two more pictures then scanned the long valley, heaving a deep sigh as she contemplated her choices.

"Okay," she said finally then looked over and accepted Jordan's handshake. "Don't make me sorry I trusted you."

"I won't. I promise," Jordan said, shaking her hand firmly. She knew Reece held huge reservations about this agreement. Whatever doubts she had and whatever pain lurked in her past, Jordan knew she had to reassure Reece she could be trusted if she was to get the whole story, including the smallest details and secrets.

"Wow! Look at that," Jordan gasped as the sun burst through the clouds, showering spokes of light across the valley. "Quick, take that shot."

Reece had already begun snapping pictures. Jordan shoved her hands in her jacket pockets and stood next to Reece. They watched in silence as the morning splendor marked the beginning of a new day. Both were consumed with their own thoughts, Jordan with the questions she would finally get to ask and Reece with the answers she would allow Jordan to hear.

Chapter 11

"Tell me about yourself. Where you were born? How many brothers and sisters you have? What your parents do? Background stuff like that." Jordan waited for Reece to sit down so she could place her small pocket recorder next to her.

"Wow, you are thorough, aren't you?" Reece replied, sitting on a flat rock next to the fire.

"We have to start somewhere," she offered compassionately.

"I was born in Port Angeles, Washington. My father was Byron McAllister. My mother was Rachel McAllister. They were both killed when I was about three." Reece said it so matter-of-factly it took Jordan by surprise.

"Oh, Reece, I'm so sorry." Jordan reached over and touched Reece's hand softly.

"That's okay. I don't even remember them. I have a couple of pictures but I don't have any independent memory of them. I look like my father. He had curly brown hair and was tall. My mother was a small, frail looking woman. She liked to cook. She made and sold cakes to the local restaurants. My father was a mechanic." Reece swirled her coffee, watching it ripple in the tin cup.

"What happened to them?" Jordan asked carefully.

"Car accident. Nothing special. Nothing dramatic. Just two people in the wrong place at the wrong time." Reece climbed to her feet and went to bring an armload of wood to the fire.

"Who raised you? Grandparents?"

"An aunt for a couple years but she died, too. Then I was in foster homes until I was old enough to drive. Five or six different ones. Most of them were overcrowded. I was in one home with twelve other kids. The father drank. The mother bitched and watched soap operas. So the kids raised themselves. I was in the last home for only about two weeks. When my bedroom door opened in the middle of the night with a man standing in the doorway in his underwear and a bottle of beer in his hand, I knew it was time for me to take my life into my own hands. I knew I couldn't do any worse."

"Did he—?" Jordan asked with a horrified look on her face.

"Rape me? No. He tried, but he was too drunk. I took a Polaroid snapshot of him passed out across my bed and sent it to child services." Reece chuckled. "That was my first journalistic photograph. I was reporting child abuse at the grass roots level. I was sixteen. I left the next day and never looked back. A friend let me live with her until I graduated from high school and earned a scholarship to Washington State."

"When did you know you wanted to be a television journalist?"

"That isn't something anyone plans. It just happens. Like any job, you work up through the ranks as a journalist, doing anything and everything they tell you to do. You make coffee for the boss. You drive all night in a rainstorm to deliver a videotape. You wait hours in the cold for someone to drive up so you can snap a picture of them. You write and rewrite a two-paragraph blurb only to have it cut at the last minute. You come in early and stay late. You promise you can do anything and do it better and faster than they need it done. You give up vacations so you can be there when something big happens. And if you are lucky, very lucky, you get a break, a small break. A teeny tiny break that means you might, if the angels smile down on you, get a six-second spot pointing to where a truck went through a fence and killed someone's cow. That's how you know it is right for you. And maybe not even then. Maybe not until you have done a thousand spots and traveled a million miles in a hundred countries. Maybe not until you have seen dead bodies and angry crowds and crying homeless children." Reece looked away as if she had become so caught up in her response she couldn't think clearly. "I'm sorry. I got carried away."

"No, I liked it. Don't stop." Jordan smiled over at her, pleased Reece felt at ease with her enough to talk so frankly.

"You expected me to say something like I knew I wanted to be a TV reporter right after I graduated from college with a master's in journalism or when I had some great epiphany about a reporter bringing a heart-wrenching story to the screen. Well, it just doesn't happen like that. You work your way up until there is no place to go but on the air."

"Did you ever set your sights on being a prime-time network anchor?" Jordan asked, checking her notes.

"No," Reece replied instantly. "That wasn't something I wanted any part of. They are stuck behind a desk. I much preferred to travel and see the stories unfold, not just report them."

"How hard was it?"

"Hard? Physically, mentally or emotionally?" Reece asked, leaning back against a log and stretching her legs.

"Yes, all those?"

"Physically, very hard. I had chronic and permanent jet lag for years. My body got so used to sleeping in a plane seat, it rebelled when I got into a bed. My digestive system never got used to eating monkey, beetles or weasel. My skin was perpetually dry and scaly. My voice changed an entire octave one year from breathing in so much desert dust. I had to spend two weeks at a hydrating spa to get my voice back."

135

"Sounds grueling," Jordan replied sympathetically.

"Mentally, it was up and down. I hated being gone for long periods of time. Pella and I had busy schedules. She often was doing a spread in one exotic corner of the world while I was in another. We had a hard time getting our schedules to dovetail." Reece smiled at the ground, as if reflecting on their time together. "Later on, it became easier. But the first few years it was almost impossible to find more than a few days we could spend together. It was a month apart, two days together, a month apart, two days together," she explained. "And of course, there was dealing with the assignments. I guess adjustments were part of the game."

"How did you deal with seeing so much horror in the world?" Jordan asked, trying to visualize how she might deal with it.

"You mean bombs and war?" Reece heaved a deep sigh as the images crystallized in her mind. She stared into the campfire, her eyes fixed and unyielding. "You don't deal with it. You just report it and go on. You stand in front of a bombed out school with the blood of children forever staining the walls behind you and hope what you say brings the cold reality of it to the couch potatoes back home. Reporting natural disasters are even harder."

"Why?" Jordan asked seriously.

"There is no one to blame. It is human nature to blame some-one for a disaster. A terrorist bomb, a mortar shell, a landmine, a shooting, poor architecture, bad design, aging buildings. Even a plane crash. People want to know who was at fault. It makes it easier to accept if we can point a finger. But natural disasters mean no one is to blame. It means we have to accept that it happened without a cause. No one wants to blame God. Did you ever notice after a tornado, people stumble around the remnants of their homes with a dazed look on their face? They are left with no answers as to why they have nothing left. But after a bomb blast people have hatred in their eyes so deep it stains their soul. Even if the person who set the bomb is killed in the blast, there is still someone to hate. It doesn't change the outcome, but it is strange how fulfilling it is to have someone to blame. I have seen mothers carrying dead babies from a mudslide with an empty look in their eyes. They hug the babies to their breasts and ask why. Mothers carrying their babies killed in a terrorist attack would rip the heart from the person responsible without giving it a second thought." Reece got up and went to her backpack for a snack. Jordan suspected she needed a diversion.

"Take a wild guess for me," Jordan asked, deciding it was time for a lighter topic.

"Guess what?"

"How many miles do you think you have traveled while on assignment?"

"Damn, that is a hard one." Reece settled back on the ground and tossed a log on the fire. "How many miles?" She thought a long minute, squinting off into space. "It would be just a guess but probably to the moon and back. My business manager once told me I have enough frequent flyer miles to fill an entire plane with friends and take it to Europe, if I wanted to."

"Wow, I thought I traveled a lot," Jordan joked.

"I was on a first name basis with several of the crews that flew from New York to London." Reece laughed at the memory.

"Speaking of names, I found a reference to a nickname." Jordan hadn't finished her question before Reece was laughing out loud.

"You are referring to people calling me Race McAllister, right?" she joked, still chuckling to herself.

"Yes. Where did that come from?"

"I was always chasing the sunset, trying to extract every moment out of the day. That's how I got the nickname. GNN started using Race McAllister across the bottom of the screen when I was doing a story," she added lightheartedly. "But I didn't mind. My agent thought it was cute."

"Are you still Race McAllister?" Jordan asked cautiously.

"No. Just Reece. I'm not in that much of a hurry anymore. I'd rather take life slow and easy."

"How have you been changed by what you have seen? Is that part of it?"

"Changed?" Reece looked at Jordan, her eyes staring right through her as if she wasn't there. There was a long pause Jordan didn't want to fill. She wanted Reece to decide what and when she would answer. "Change is an elusive subject. We all change. We change from day to day, minute to minute. It can be so slight it is almost unnoticeable, like suddenly liking mustard on ham instead of mayonnaise. Or it can be a life-altering evolution. Have I changed? Sure. So have you." Reece heaved a deep sigh as if expelling the evils she had witnessed that caused her metamorphosis.

"How did your years in war zones and disasters, if you'll excuse the expression, scar you inside?" Jordan asked, hoping she didn't offend Reece by her reference to scarring.

Reece gave a small smile, understanding Jordan's need for the question.

"Do you think you would have been scarred if you had seen your world changed so drastically you weren't sure you would feel safe anywhere ever again?" Reece looked at Jordan with a soft but plaintive smile. "We are all scarred and changed by what we see and experience."

"Did you consider yourself good at what you did?"

Reece shrugged. "That wasn't for me to say. I just tried to give the viewers the information so they could make informed decisions on who to vote for or where to spend their consumer dollars."

"What did Pella think of what you did?" Jordan asked, easing into the subject of Pella Frann. Reece looked up at her, not really surprised at the direction the interview was taking.

"Pella liked what I did, I guess. She was a very staunch liberal. She was way over the edge about some things. But she liked my work, I think. She was always telling me what to wear and how to stand to get the best use of the limited camera time I had." Reece chuckled. "Like I needed gradient eye shadow and wet-look lipstick when I was standing in the middle of the desert."

"So she was trying to help you look your best in spite of the setting?"

"Yeah, you could say that." Reece knelt at the fire and

rearranged the logs so they would burn evenly. "Do you want more coffee?" she asked, swirling the last of it in the pot.

"No, thank you. I bet it is like diesel fuel," Jordan teased.

"Probably," Reece replied, dumping it in the fire.

"When and where did you meet Pella?" Jordan asked softly.

Reece took a deep thoughtful sigh as she sat back down on her log and got comfortable.

"December twenty-third at the Banff Springs Hotel in Banff, Canada. She was there doing a shoot for ski wear. She was standing in the snow with nothing on but a pair of high-heeled black boots and a thigh-length ski parka," Reece said, smiling a reflective smile. "She was thirty-eight, twenty-four, thirty-five. She was six-feet-two in heels. She had a pair of eyes that would melt butter in Alaska. I saw her out the window of my room. She had a crowd of cameramen, grips and makeup girls drooling all over her. When she flipped her hair and wet her lips, I thought the cameraman was going to bust his zipper." Reece's eyes flashed as she remembered the moment.

"Did you run out into the snow and introduce yourself?"

"No," Reece chuckled. "I didn't actually meet her until later that night. She was eating a late dinner in the dining room with several crew members. I was at a corner table and I guess I was staring a little too long. She got up and walked over to me, leaned down and planted a kiss on me that curled my toes. Then she asked, is that what you were wondering?" Reece blushed slightly.

"And what did you say to her?" Jordan asked.

"I said yes, thank you for clearing that up for me. Then I asked if she wanted to have dessert with me," Reece replied, a smile visible behind her eyes.

"Sounds very dramatic," Jordan offered, watching Reece enjoy her memory.

"That was twelve years ago."

"What caused the breakup?" Jordan asked cautiously, not sure how the question would be received.

"The same thing that causes most breakups. Time and change." Reece acted like her answer was all she wanted to offer.

"Like what?" Jordan asked, undeterred by Reece's short answer.

"Pella is older than I am by several years. We had some differences that time only exacerbated. It took a while to come to a head, but let's just say my retirement and our separation found common ground." Reece chose her words carefully, as if making sure she divulged only generalities and nothing incriminating.

"Was there someone else?" Jordan asked softly.

"No. Not for me. I can't speak for Pella but I doubt it." Reece began brushing dirt from her shirt as if it needed tending at that moment.

"I have to ask, did you get the scar before or after your separation?"

"Before," Reece replied quietly.

"How did it happen, Reece?" Jordan asked the question with compassion, knowing this would be the hardest admission Reece would have to make.

"It was an accident. Just an accident. No big deal. I went through a plate glass window at the house. Clumsy, I guess." Reece went to her pack again and took out a jacket against the chilly night air then returned to the fire.

"How many stitches did it take to close the wound? Do you know?" Jordan asked.

"As I remember, the doctor said three-hundred-sixteen, from temple to tit. Then another eighty-eight for the second part that goes down the back of my shoulder." Reece subconsciously rubbed her hand against her cheek and down her neck. "Scars that are going to be visible are done a little differently."

"Did you ever consider a plastic surgeon to repair the tissue damage?"

"Four different ones. They all said the same thing. My skin type and the depth of the cut, as well as the width of the cut, make it impossible to correct. Two of the doctors even told me I could be worse off than I already am. I don't remember the exact medical term for it, but I was encouraged to leave well enough alone. I was only a few millimeters away from losing an eye." Reece stared off into space. She finally lowered her eyes and sighed.

"How long did it take you to recover?"

"Almost a year. I had several infections and lots of swelling." Reece shifted her position. "The section down my neck took the longest. I guess because you are always moving it."

"How long after the accident did you and Pella separate?"

Reece scrunched her mouth and chewed on the corner of her lip a moment as if thinking about her reply.

"I have something I want to tell you, Ms. Griffin, and I want it perfectly clear." Reece kept her gaze down, not wanting to be confrontational. "The subject of Pella Frann is going to be limited. This story you are doing isn't about her. She isn't part of my life anymore. We had some wonderful years together but our private life is just that—private. I won't tell you about our sex life or what happened between us to cause our separation. It is enough for you to know I loved her and she loved me. That is all. She is living her life now and I am living mine." Reece finally looked up at Jordan, her eyes reaffirming what she had said. "I haven't seen Pella in nearly three years. The end." She gave Jordan a long, purposeful gaze. "Is that clear enough?"

"Clear enough," Jordan replied after reading the look on Reece's face. As a reporter, it was killing her not to ask more questions about Pella but she respected the barrier Reece had erected around the subject.

Jordan asked a few more questions about Reece's career, enjoying her tales of travel and excitement. Reece told about her award-winning stories and the humorous times she spent in embarrassing moments. It was after ten when they both agreed it was late and they were exhausted.

Chapter 12

Jordan couldn't keep her eyes open another moment. She set her cup on a rock and climbed to her feet, ready for a good night's sleep.

"Would you mind if I turned in?" she asked through a yawn.

"I've been waiting for you to say something. Go ahead and get comfortable. I'll be along shortly. I'm going to count the leaves." Reece said, heading into the forest.

"Why are you going to count the leaves?" Jordan asked curiously.

"You're kidding. You really don't know?" Reece asked, looking back at her with a smirk.

"Oh," Jordan said with a chuckle, finally realizing what she meant. "I never heard it called that."

"Camp expression."

Reece disappeared into the darkness carrying toilet paper and the plastic garden trowel. As soon as she was out of sight Jordan realized she too was in need of counting leaves. She considered heading off in the opposite direction, but remembering what Reece had said about getting lost in the endless forest kept her near the campfire.

"Are you about finished counting those leaves?" she called into the darkness. There was no answer. "Reece? I think I could count a little myself," she said, cupping her hands to her mouth. There was still no answer. The more she stood waiting, the more she needed to count. "Reece, are you about finished," she yelled, biting down on her lip as the urge increased. Jordan couldn't wait. She grabbed a tissue and hurried into the underbrush. She stumbled over a rock and racked a branch through her hair as she searched for a suitable place to relieve herself. As much as she disliked the crudeness of going to the bathroom in the woods, she had adapted well. When she finished, she used a stick to bury the unmentionables then headed back to camp, she thought. But the darkness and the pine trees all looked alike. Reece was right. Within ten paces she knew she was lost.

"Shit," she muttered. "I know I passed a tree with a broken branch. Where the heck is it?" She circled through the woods, the moon occasionally beaming through the clouds and treetops. "Okay," she declared, placing her hands on her hips disgustedly. "Reece, you were right. I took a wrong turn." Jordan spoke as if camp was only a few feet away and Reece would pop out from behind a tree to lead her back to the warm fire and the awaiting tent. "Come on. You can tease me about this too." She stood, staring up through the treetops, waiting to be rescued. But no one came. Reece didn't jump out and surprise her. She didn't trot in and retrieve her like a knight in shining armor. "Reece?" she yelled at the top of her lungs. When only the mellow hoot of an owl replied, it dawned on her she was indeed lost and alone in the vast forest. "No," she said, stomping her foot angrily. "No, no, no. I didn't do this again. I didn't make a stupid, juvenile mistake. PLEASE!" she called into the night. She knew she could do one of three things. She could continue roaming the woods, hoping to

143

stumble onto the camp by sheer accident. Or she could stay where she was, waiting for Reece to come find her. Or she could do the obvious third choice, scream and cry from panic at being lost. She straightened her posture, crossed her arms over her chest and took a deep breath. She was not going to succumb to the third choice. She was going to be mature about it. She was going to sit quietly on a rock, if she could find one in the darkness, and wait. She knew Reece would eventually wonder where she was and come searching for her. At least she had her jacket and heavy socks on to keep her warm.

Jordan found a flat rock in what seemed to be a clearing and sat down, disgusted with herself, but resigned to wait out her rescue. She hummed quietly to herself, trying to pass the time. She couldn't see her watch but she guessed she had been waiting for twenty minutes. She occasionally called out, hoping to direct Reece's search to her.

"Reece, I'm over here. Reece!" She blew her breath onto her hands to warm them, the night air turning cold. "Reece McAllister. I'm over here. I'm ready to be rescued. I'm tired and I'm cold. You can come find me now." She refused to give in to her fear that she wouldn't be found. Reece surely was experienced enough to search the woods for her. She had all the modern doodads and equipment a hiker would need to search for a lost camper, Jordan assumed. She pulled her knees up to her chest and locked her arms around them, rocking back and forth. "Come and find me, please," she said quietly, her voice cracking. "I want to go back to the tent now."

From the darkness, Jordan could hear footsteps coming toward her. She leaped to her feet and strained to see into the woods.

"Reece, I'm over here. Boy, am I glad to see you." Jordan felt a deep sense of relief warm her down to her toes. A branch snapped, cutting the silence like a knife. A deep growl rumbled in the distance. Jordan's eyes widened and she gasped, scrambling onto the rock. The growl came closer. A pair of green cat's eyes pierced the darkness. They were large eyes, not the eyes of a neighborhood tabby, but the eyes of a mountain lion. She stood on the rock, motionless. She couldn't see the big cat but she could hear it moving toward her, its steps slow and methodical as if it was stalking her. The green eyes moved through the underbrush like a pair of evil fires burning their gaze upon her. She remained perfectly still, too afraid to scream. She swallowed carefully, certain any movement would spring the cat into an attack. She wanted to run, but in the darkness she knew she wouldn't make it ten feet before she fell over something, rendering herself helpless before the animal. She had always heard not to show fear before a wild animal, but she couldn't help it. Tears welled up in her eyes and her chin quivered. The cat stood just out of sight behind a tree, the sound of its breathing the only sound in the forest. Jordan knew it was sizing her up and ready to spring.

"Nice kitty," she said, a lump rising in her throat. "Pretty kitty."

The mountain lion screamed out a growl that rattled through her. She screamed and hugged her arms tightly around herself.

"Don't move," a voice whispered. It was Reece. She stepped out of the woods and shone two flashlights at the big cat. The animal was frozen by the bright lights, its lean body poised as if it was only moments away from an attack. Reece kept the lights trained on the cat's face as she moved closer to Jordan, taking up a post directly in front of her. The women and the cat stood like statues, staring at each other for a long moment, dead silence between them. Finally, the cat looked into the woods from where it had come and leaped out of sight, the sound of its footsteps fading into the darkness.

Jordan closed her eyes and sighed, her body trembling with relief. Reece turned the flashlight onto Jordan.

"I suppose you have a reason to be out here on the edge of the cliff in the dark," Reece asked, frowning at her.

"What cliff?"

Reece took Jordan by the arm and led her to a pile of jagged rocks and shone the light over the edge. Jordan's eyes widened as she peered over the edge at the long drop to the valley below. She could see the tops of trees growing up out of the darkness. Jordan felt faint. As if the mountain lion wasn't enough, the thought of stepping off a several-hundred-foot cliff turned her stomach into knots and instantly drained the blood from her head. Her face was completely white and her hands shook uncontrollably.

"Next time you want to go for a stroll in the woods, take a flashlight and let me know where you are going." Reece pulled her away from the cliff and gave her an angry scowl.

"I was just going to the bathroom. Then I got lost." Jordan was never happier to see anyone in her life.

"I figured as much." Reece headed through the woods, the light from her flashlight leading the way. Jordan reached out and grabbed for Reece's shirt. She wasn't going to be stranded again. Reece reached back and took her hand, holding it tightly. She eased her up next to her side then wrapped an arm around her shoulder. "Are you finished having adventures for tonight?" she asked jovially.

"I hope so," Jordan replied, leaning into Reece. "I certainly hope so."

Reece ruffled her hair and chuckled.

"I'm not sure I can let you out of my sight," Reece declared.

Jordan wrapped her arm around Reece's waist and rested her head on her shoulder. Reece hugged her close as they walked along the route back to camp. She stood guard as Jordan took off her boots and crawled in the tent.

"What is this? What happened to my sleeping bag?"

"I twinned them," Reece replied, shining the flashlight into the tent. "Yours is on the bottom. Mine is on the top. It's like one jumbo sleeping bag. That way you won't zip yourself in again."

"When did you do this?" Jordan asked as she slid inside and took her place.

"While you were playing Lewis and Clark with the mountain lion."

Jordan snuggled in and waited for Reece to slide in next to her.

"And no more questions tonight, Ms. Griffin," Reece said, getting settled.

"I wasn't going to," Jordan replied, sighing deeply, her mind on anything but being a reporter. She closed her eyes and took in the sweet aroma of pine, fresh air and Reece lying next to her. A warmth took hold of her all the way down to her toes. It was more than just the security of being safe and sound in the tent. Much more. She tried to ignore it but her body wouldn't let her. It tingled in all the wrong places if Jordan planned on ignoring Reece McAllister tonight.

The next morning Jordan woke first. She was warm and cozy in the double sleeping bag. Reece was sleeping soundly on her side, her arm draped over Jordan's waist. It was a secure feeling for Jordan, unlike Mia's heavy arm flopped over her. Jordan eased over on her side, facing Reece but making sure she didn't disrupt her arm. Jordan watched Reece sleep, her slow, measured breaths a comforting meter. She carefully reached up and picked a lock of hair from Reece's face, gently placing it behind her ear. Reece didn't move. Jordan studied her eyelashes. They were long and had a natural curl to them that any mascara-wearer would be envious of. Jordan carefully moved another lock of hair so she could see the top of the scar. It was microscopically close to the edge of her left eye. She wanted to touch it. She wanted to allow her fingers to explore the boundaries of the pink ridge of tissue and follow it down Reece's cheek. She wanted to know if the scar was warm to the touch or cold. She wanted to know if it had a pulse. She wanted to know if it hurt. She wanted to know if Reece had to endure pain with every waking moment or was the scar tissue numb and unfeeling. Jordan studied Reece's mouth. Her lips were pleasantly full. They looked moist and tender. Jordan wondered what it would be like to touch them, or better yet, kiss them. She wondered if Reece was a good kisser, one with a passionate yet gentle touch. She wondered if Reece was a French kisser or if she gave short, dry pecks. Jordan sighed softly at the thought of Reece's lips against her own.

Suddenly Reece's eyes popped open. Jordan gasped in surprise, knowing she had been caught staring. Reece didn't say anything. She just stared at Jordan then closed her eyes again.

"Are you watching me sleep?"

"Yes," Jordan replied, knowing she had no choice but to confess.

"Am I doing it correctly?"

"Does it bother you?" Jordan asked softly.

"It doesn't bother me. When you are in a remote place like this you have to find entertainment where you can, I guess." Reece opened her eyes.

"I'm having a lovely time in the outdoors," Jordan said, snuggling under the sleeping bag. She looked out the open tent flap at the clouds billowing over head. "It's going to be a wonderful day. How far are we hiking today? Five miles? Ten?"

"Just two. You'll be out of the woods and on your way home by dinnertime." Reece stretched and yawned herself awake.

"Really?"

"We made a big circle. The ranger station is just over that hill," Reece replied, pointing out the tent flap.

"But I thought you were going to Seven Lakes to take pictures."

"I'll get them next time."

"I didn't mean to interrupt your trip," Jordan said apologetically.

Reece chuckled. "Yes you did. But that's okay. I've taken shots of the lakes region before. Besides, it's going to rain all afternoon and most of tomorrow, too."

Jordan began to smile unconsciously.

"What are you so happy about?" Reece asked.

"I don't mean to sound ungrateful but I am looking forward to a long hot bath. I may soak for a week."

Reece laughed.

"Don't you want a nice refreshing dip in the creek?" she asked jokingly.

"No. I'll leave that to you." Jordan shivered and groaned at the thought.

"I'll start a fire. You stay in here until I get it going," Reece said, crawling out of the tent and stepping into her camp slippers.

Jordan enjoyed her last day in the woods. She made them coffee and straightened the campsite, leaving it cleaner than they had found it. Reece packed her own gear then showed Jordan a few tips in packing hers. They started out just after ten for a leisurely trek down the hill to the ranger station. Reece pointed out some interesting wildflowers and unique sites along the way. Once they were back at Reece's cabin, Jordan loaded her gear into her trunk, ready to return home.

"Thank you, Ms. McAllister," she said, extending her hand to Reece. "I appreciate your allowing me to go along on the hike and for granting me an interview."

Reece took her hand and shook it warmly. Their hands remained locked together for a long moment after the shake was completed.

"You're welcome, Ms. Griffin," she said, her eyes deep and soft as they studied Jordan.

Jordan climbed in her car and started the engine.

"I have some videotapes if you need them for background but I doubt they would be much use to you," Reece offered, looking in the driver's side door then closing it for her.

"I'll remember that," Jordan said. She was tired, dirty, hungry and sore from the trip into the mountains but she still wished she could find a reason to stay. When Reece didn't invite her in, she knew it meant she too was tired and ready for a quiet, restful evening alone. Jordan waved and pulled away, weaving her way back out the path to the highway and the drive to the ferry in Kingston.

Chapter 13

Jordan had been back to the city and to work for two days when she stood at the corner and waited for the pedestrian light to change. She punched Reece's number into her cell phone. If she remembered correctly, Reece had a meeting at the gallery today so she should be in the city, not at Greysome Point. The light changed and Jordan stepped off the curb, joining the morning rush of people on their way to work. She sipped her latte while she moved in and out of the crowd, trying to find an open space.

"Hello, Ms. Griffin." Reece's voice was bright and fresh.

"You sound chipper this morning, Ms. McAllister. I was worried I might wake you up."

"I've been up since six. Did you see the sunrise this morning? It looked spectacular rising over Mount Rainier."

"No, I didn't see it. My apartment faces the city, not the east."

"Too bad. Maybe you should move across the street."

"Then I'd miss the sunsets," Jordan mused.

"True. You would."

"But I'll try to get up to see it tomorrow."

"Don't bother. It's supposed to be rainy. Stay in bed and keep warm."

"Okay." Jordan laughed. She suddenly remembered the way Reece looked lying next to her in the sleeping bag.

"Was there something else?" Reece asked after Jordan's long silence.

"Oh, yes. You said something about some videotapes of your television reports."

"Yeah."

"I was wondering if I could see them. I thought I might find something to use. You know, how television reporting has changed, how women have had an impact on prime-time journalism, the dangers of in-depth reporting, high demand subject matters. That kind of thing."

"Shit. That sounds like a half-dozen articles, Ms. Griffin. Not just one on an ex-reporter. That's a lot to expect from a bunch of thirty-second bits."

"Would you mind if I take a look at them?"

"Help yourself. I'll bring them by your office. How about tomorrow afternoon? I've got a meeting and a doctor's appointment this afternoon."

"Are you sick?" Jordan asked instantly.

"No. Just a checkup. I'll be waiting on the exam table in a paper dress for two hours, I'm sure. They have to make sure the instruments are properly refrigerated first."

"Oh, one of *those* checkups," Jordan mused. "It's hard to remain dignified with your feet in stirrups."

"No kidding and I love the conversation. The doctor always asks some stupid question, like did you see the exit ramp on Michigan Avenue is closed, just as she shoves those salad tongs up inside you. Your voice goes up two octaves as you try to reply, making you sound like you were just goosed by a moose."

Jordan was nodding and laughing as she hurried along the sidewalk.

151

"So if it's all right with you, I'll bring the tapes by tomorrow afternoon," Reece added.

"I'll look forward to it," Jordan replied.

"Knock, knock," Reece said, standing at Jordan's office door. She was carrying a box of videotapes.

Jordan looked up and smiled warmly.

"Hello there," she replied, her eyes falling gently on Reece.

"Why you want to see these is beyond me. It's old news, kid." Reece set the box on her desk.

"I don't want to see them for the news," Jordan replied, looking through the titles on the tapes. "I want to see the famous Reece McAllister taming the wild media."

"I don't know if there is much wild media taming in here," Reece muttered, reading one of the titles. "It is more rambling than anything else. I can't remember how many times I had dead air while waiting for someone to come through a door or make a speech." She tossed the tape back in the box.

"I appreciate your letting me borrow them. I'll return them in a few days, if that is okay with you."

"Sure. No problem. I can always get copies from the network. The tapes are marked chronologically. The older stuff is my days with Channel Fourteen here in Seattle. I warn you, you'll be bored inside of ten minutes with this stuff. If you are having trouble sleeping, pop one of these tapes in the VCR and you'll be asleep in no time. Works better than hot milk."

"Oh, stop that. It will not. I will love to see them. If I had known I was going to meet a famous television newsperson I would have watched you more closely." Jordan placed a hand on Reece's arm. "I'll love watching them—and you. I plan on watching them all weekend. I'll put on a big pot of coffee, wear my faded jeans and veg-out on GNN tapes."

"Do you want me to carry them down to your car? I assume it is in the parking garage. That's where mine is."

"My car is in the shop today. Broken something or other to do with the starter. I rode the bus. But I can manage. Thank you. And by the way, I thought the parking garage was for building employees only."

"And guests," Reece corrected.

"Oh, I didn't know that."

Reece checked her watch.

"How about letting me give you a ride home? You don't want to be lugging that box of tapes all over creation."

"That's okay. But thank you for the offer. I live way out in Kirkland."

"Kirkland isn't way out. Everett is way out. Or Auburn. That is way out. But not Kirkland. Kirkland is just a camel spit away," Reece said as she took Jordan's jacket from the coatrack and held it open for her. "And Tacoma, that's way out." She rambled on while Jordan watched her, a smile growing across her face. "Bellevue, not so much. Gig Harbor, yes. Definitely way out. Now Edmonds is a toss-up."

"Will you stop?" Jordan finally said, shutting down her computer and slipping into her jacket. "Yes, I accept your offer of a ride."

"Tell you what, I'll set the trip meter in my truck and you can establish a fair distance to represent *way out*. You could do a story on it. Title it 'Living Way Out in Seattle's Environs and Liking It.'" Reece snapped off the lights and waited in the hall for Jordan to lock her office.

"You're sure chipper this evening."

"It's the smell of news." Reece took a deep breath and closed her eyes. "Don't you smell it? It's like an aphrodisiac, a stimulant to the psyche. As a reporter, you should know that. It gets under your skin as soon as you write your first freelance clip, your first sidebar. It's addictive." Reece was rambling again.

Jordan smiled at her, wondering why the talkative nature.

"What is up with you?" Jordan asked, taking a long look.

"Dinner."

"Dinner is up with you?"

"Yes. I should have thought of it sooner. Would you like to have dinner with me on the way home? And don't tell me you aren't eating these days," Reece said. "Besides, we can talk about the story you are doing on me. Call it a working dinner."

"I would love to have dinner with you," Jordan replied happily.

"Seafood or steaks?" Reece asked as she followed Jordan to the elevator.

"You pick," Jordan replied, her mind already doing summersaults over the invitation.

"I know a place," she said and pressed the button.

"Where are we going?" Jordan asked, straightening Reece's collar.

"Hagen's."

"Great place. Lovely view, too."

When the elevator door opened, Reece waited for Jordan to step in then followed. She pushed the button for the parking garage. Jordan moved to the back wall and held the railing, her eyes riveted on the bustling city streets below. Reece stood next to her. She seemed to sense the elevator ride was difficult for her.

"You okay?" Reece asked quietly. She discreetly placed a hand on one of Jordan's and squeezed gently.

Jordan looked down at Reece's hand covering hers and nodded then looked into Reece's eyes.

"Thank God for glass elevators," she replied with a smile.

"I'm right here," Reece whispered. She remained at Jordan's side until the elevator opened in the garage. "We're here. Come on. Dinner is waiting."

Reece pulled out of the garage and headed north on the interstate. The traffic was its normal four lanes of rush hour gridlock. It took twenty minutes to go two miles.

"I should have taken the ferry to Bainbridge Island for dinner," Reece muttered to herself as she sat behind a semi-truck belching diesel fumes.

"Who goes to Bainbridge Island for dinner?" Jordan asked.

"Haven't you eaten at Harry's Crab Shack? It overlooks the harbor."

"No. I've been over there to interview people but not to eat. Seems like a long way to go just for crabs."

Reece stared over at her curiously.

"You have *got* to be kidding." She checked her rearview mirror and eased over three lanes then took the first exit off the highway.

"Where are you going? This isn't the right exit for Hagen's."

Reece zigzagged her way through the streets. She drove like a woman on a mission, darting in and out of traffic, taking corners like she was a race car driver. Jordan held onto the oh-shit handle as they careened down the steep hills and around corners.

"Reece, could you tell me where you are going in such a hurry?" Jordan asked, gasping as they slid between two delivery trucks.

"I've changed my mind. We're having seafood for dinner." Reece pulled into the parking lot to the Bainbridge Island ferry. She paid the attendant and pulled into the line in the holding area. The ferry had just begun loading the vehicles for the 6:20 crossing.

"Where are we going, Reece?" Jordan asked curiously.

"You aren't much of a reporter if you can't figure that out," she teased.

"Harry's Crab Shack?"

Reece nodded, draping her arm over the back of the seat while they waited their turn to load.

"I should have thought of this when I was on the ferry earlier."

"You were on the Bainbridge Island ferry today?" Jordan asked.

"No. The Edmonds to Kingston ferry. I was coming back from Greysome Point."

"I thought you were in the city last night."

"I was. But I had to get the tapes you wanted to see," Reece explained, pulling ahead as the attendant waved her onto the ferry.

"Do you mean the tapes were at Greysome Point and you drove all the way out there today just to get them?" Jordan frowned at her.

"I went out last night and came back this morning. You said you wanted to see them for background on your story. How else was I supposed to get them?"

"Reece McAllister, why didn't you tell me the tapes weren't here in Seattle?" Jordan grabbed Reece's sleeve and shook it. "I could have waited. But thank you. That was sweet of you to do that. Now I know I will have to watch each and every one of them."

"No. Don't do that. You'll die of boredom." Reece eased into her parking spot behind a car with a backseat full of kids. "Come on. Let's go upstairs." Reece turned off the engine and led the way to the stairs to the passenger deck. She took Jordan by the wrist and led her through the bustling crowd to the upper deck and a pair of seats by the window. She sat down next to Jordan so her scarred side was away from her. The ferry was completely full when the whistle sounded and the boat lumbered away from the pier. Most of the passengers were businesspeople going home after a long day in the city.

"Tell me about this Harry's Crab Shack," Jordan asked, turning in her seat to face Reece. "What kind of place is it?"

"You'll see."

"Is it the kind of place I may want to do a story about? I'm always looking for special eateries I can cover for the cuisine section." Jordan noticed a woman staring at them from across the aisle. She had a pained look in her eyes, one full of pity and horror. It was the same look Jordan had seen on the face of the two dykes at the gas station. Reece couldn't see the woman's gaze but Jordan could. The woman looked at Jordan as if questioning why she chose to be with this disfigured woman. Jordan stared back at her with unyielding defiance. She slipped her arm through Reece's and leaned into her. It was the clearest statement she could make.

"Let me guess," Reece asked in hushed voice. "Someone is looking at me."

"What makes you say that?"

"Just a hunch." Reece didn't look at the woman. Instead, she kept her eyes out the window.

Jordan desperately wanted to get up and smack the woman for her cruel stare. Instead, she turned away, trying to put it out of her mind.

"Well, tell me about this place we are going. Is it very far from the ferry landing?"

"Look at it this way, you won't have to hike over a mountain to get there," Reece said then laughed.

"You aren't going to let me live down that camping trip, are you?"

"I hadn't planned on it. Now, tell me the slant you plan on taking in the story."

"Actually, I'm not sure. I have to check with Mark and see what he had in mind. If it were up to me, it would be Greysome Point hometown girl has had enough of the bright lights and has come home. Something like that."

"Gag me," Reece scoffed.

"What's wrong with that?"

"Where's the drama, the excitement, the hook?"

"I plan on including your long list of achievements and awards as well as your popularity that you left behind," Jordan replied.

"Hell, no. You know what the hook is as well as I do. If you want your readers to read the story, not just look at the pictures, you have to tell them what the photographs don't tell them."

"Such as?"

"Jordan, you know what you have to say and so do I. I knew it when I agreed to give you the story."

Jordan just looked at her.

"You know the story about the farmer and the donkey?" Reece asked.

"I'm not sure."

"A farmer had a donkey he was very proud of. He was always bragging on the donkey, telling his friends how smart he was and how he could do any job around the farm. So a group of his friends, the doubting ones, decided to go out to his farm and see this amazing donkey for themselves. The farmer was glad to show off his prized donkey. He led them into the barn where the donkey was calmly eating hay. The farmer picked up a shovel and whacked that donkey right over the head with it. The donkey dropped the mouthful of hay and immediately trotted out of the barn and began plowing the field. The men stared at the farmer. They had never seen anything like it. One of the men said that is great, but why did you hit the donkey over the head with the shovel? The farmer said the donkey would do anything, but first you have to get his attention.'"

Jordan laughed out loud at the story as did several people within earshot of Reece's story-telling.

"Jordan, you have to lead with it. Smack the reader over the head with it." Reece thought a moment then gestured with her hand as if she was proclaiming banner news. "Reece McAllister, one-time Peabody Award-winning GNN reporter, is forced to retire from broadcasting after a tragic accident causes facial disfigurement."

"Reece, NO!" Jordan looked at her, her forehead furrowed. "I'll do no such thing."

"That's the story, Jordan, and you know it. You can put in all that other crap you want to but lead with your strong suit. Hell, tell them I'm a crotchety hermit who goes off into the wilderness for days at a time. Tell them I take black-and-white photographs of nature because it is a pure form of expression. Tell them I live in a two-room cabin deep in the woods. Tell them I live alone and like it."

"Reece, stop it." Jordan put her hand on Reece's mouth to stop her tirade. "There is more to Reece McAllister's story than all that. Let me decide, okay?" Jordan spoke softly, as if appeasing an angry child. "I can write this story myself. I don't need you to go into martyrdom for me."

Reece sat quietly looking out the window, concentrating on the lights from the Bainbridge Island landing.

"We better head back downstairs. We'll be landing soon," Reece said finally.

Jordan hated to admit it but Reece was probably right. The

inherent high point to the story would be her scar. As an experienced journalist, Reece certainly knew what would draw the reader's interest. But Jordan didn't want to make it sound like that was all there was to this wonderfully charismatic woman. Yes, she was scarred but she was also warm, funny, caring and very intelligent. She also had more journalistic insight than anyone Jordan had ever met. If it were up to her, Reece McAllister would still be on television in spite of her scar. She had so much to offer.

Reece pulled off the ferry and followed the street until it dead-ended in front of a small parking lot next to a flat-roofed house with a small sign, partially obscured by a wisteria bush that read Harry's Crab Shack and Bar.

"Here we are," Reece said, pulling in next to a row of motorcycles. Inside was a dimly-lit dining room decorated with cast-off fishing equipment and buoys. Three long rows of highly polished wooden tables stretched across the room with short benches on either side as chairs. The customers shared the long tables with other diners, crowding into any available spot. Rolls of paper towels, bottles of catsup and jugs of vinegar dotted the tables. Baskets of discarded shells marked those customers who were eating crab legs. Reece pointed to an open spot near the window and Jordan snaked her way through the cramped aisle to it. A waitress followed them, snatching up the last customer's empty baskets.

"What'll it be to drink?" she asked, giving the table a half-hearted wipe.

"Jordan?" Reece asked.

"Iced tea, please," she replied, scanning the menu. "Do you have decaf iced tea or maybe chai tea?"

The waitress wrinkled her forehead at her.

"Chai what?" she asked.

"Bring us two Heinekens," Reece advised. "You can't drink that crap while you're eating seafood," she said in Jordan's direction. "It'll give me indigestion."

Jordan chuckled.

"Okay, beer is fine."

"Will you bring us a basket of droppings, too?" Reece said as the waitress turned to leave.

"What kind of sauce would you like? Mustard, horseradish, dill or mild?"

Reece looked over at Jordan and thought.

"How about a little of each one?"

"Sure," the waitress replied then left them to read the menu.

"What are droppings or don't I really want to know?" Jordan asked, looking at what the other diners were eating.

"Shrimp and clam pieces deep fried. They are the broken little pieces that they used to feed to the seagulls. Someone told Harry he was tossing out a fortune to the smelly birds so he started frying them. He adds some kind of spice to the batter. I don't know what it is but it sure as hell makes them tasty."

"What is good?" Jordan asked, scanning the menu.

"Everything. Crab legs, clams, oysters on the half shell, shrimp, clam chowder."

"What are you having?" Jordan asked, trying to see what the lady behind her was eating.

"Fish and chips," Reece replied, replacing her menu in the holder without looking at it.

"I didn't see that on here."

"Down at the bottom. It is the most popular with the locals. It is always fresh from the dock."

"Then I will have that, too."

"Are you sure you don't want crab legs or jumbo shrimp?" Reece asked.

"I trust your judgment."

"Two fish and chips," Reece ordered when the waitress set the beer bottles on table along with a plastic basket of fried nuggets and several small bowls of dipping sauce. "What is the catch today?"

"Tilapia, marlin, swordfish and halibut." The waitress rattled off the choices as if she could do it in her sleep.

"Halibut," Reece replied without hesitation.

"Cole slaw?" she asked.

"No."

The waitress jotted down the order as she walked away, replacing her pencil in her hair as she finished.

"Cole slaw might be good with the fish," Jordan suggested, surprised Reece didn't ask her.

"Not here, it wouldn't. They don't make it fresh. They buy it at Costco."

"Oh," Jordan replied, looking at the dish of cole slaw down the table from them. "And in case you are wondering, I ordered halibut because it isn't always available. Harry won't offer it on the menu when it is over five bucks a pound at the dock."

"How do you know this stuff?"

"I ask," Reece said, taking a long draw from her beer.

"Did you ever bring Pella here for dinner?" Jordan asked, surprised at herself for asking.

"I don't remember. Possibly, but she liked eating in the city. Toppers was her favorite place."

"Where is that?"

"On Capital Hill about halfway down. It was one of those trendy places with white tablecloths. They serve stuff like artichokes and salmon or spinach and crab soufflé. If it's weird, Toppers serves it. They had shark brains on the menu for a while."

"Oh, gross."

"Pella was a vegetarian, at least most of the time. For some reason, she didn't think seafood counted as meat."

"You are teasing me."

"I am not. Pella liked poached white fish with lemon and steamed asparagus. No salt, no pepper, no nothing on it." Reece made a ghastly face.

"Is this when she was modeling and had to keep her weight down?"

Reece nodded as she sampled the various sauces.

"Try this one," Reece said, dipping a shrimp piece into the dill sauce and handing it to Jordan. Jordan had her hands full, breaking apart two bits of fried shrimp. "Open up," she ordered and popped it in Jordan's mouth.

"That's good. Try this one," Jordan said, dipping a piece into the mustard sauce and holding it up to Reece. She opened her mouth and Jordan popped it in.

"Yes, that is definitely mustard. But I like it."

"Spicy brown mustard, I think," Jordan replied, trying another one herself. They sat feeding each other bites as they sampled all the sauces, combining some for extra flavor. Reece got some dill sauce on Jordan's nose, laughing as she wiped it off. Jordan responded by dipping a bite in the horseradish sauce then touching it to Reece's chin before putting it in her mouth. They giggled at the fun, looking at each other with long gazes and warm smiles. The story about Reece, her scar, Pella and the past weren't mentioned again. Instead, they joked and laughed, sipping their beer and eating fish by the sea.

"I love this fish," Jordan said, licking her fingers. "You'll have to bring me here again," she added, as she wiped her mouth with her napkin and pushed the basket back. "I'm stuffed. I can't remember when I last ate so much. And yes, Harry's Crab Shack will be in the cuisine section one of these days. It is definitely worth a mention."

"I will," Reece replied, tossing her napkin in her basket and stacking it on top of Jordan's.

"You will what?"

"Bring you here again," Reece said, smiling over at her.

"I didn't mean you had to—"

"I would love to bring you here again for fish, Ms. Griffin," Reece interrupted, looking deep into Jordan's eyes.

Jordan felt her heart skip a beat.

"I would like that," she replied. "I would like that very much."

"Maybe next time we can have oysters on the half shell," Reece said softly, her eyes never leaving Jordan's. "You know what they say about oysters." There was the slightest curl at the corner of her mouth.

"I hear it doesn't take very many," Jordan replied, their eyes swimming together.

"Probably not." Reece allowed her fingers to touch Jordan's hand. "Some things don't have to be taken in great quantities to be good. Sometimes just a taste is enough." She raised her other hand and let it rest on her cheek, covering her scar.

"I hear that is true," Jordan added with a whisper, her heart pounding in her throat at Reece's sensuous gaze.

"Would you like dessert?" Reece asked with a low voice.

"Yes," Jordan replied in a hushed tone, her brain overriding her logic as she imagined what kind of dessert Reece had in mind.

"What would you like? Cheesecake, pie?"

"I beg your pardon," she replied, blinking herself back to reality.

"Dessert. They have ice cream, cheesecake, pie," Reece said, reading the menu.

"Oh, no. Nothing for me. I'm full."

Reece gave a curious smile then went to pay the check. Jordan hurried outside, in need of fresh air. She had no idea why her heart was racing. She strolled over to the edge of the parking lot and watched the seagulls squawking at each other. The waves from passing boats lapped at the rocks, the pungent smell of fish and seaweed in the air. Jordan took a deep breath, trying to calm herself and get her bearings after Reece's long and suggestive glance. She knew she was reading way more into her stare than she should have. Reece was just being polite. But Jordan found Reece's eyes burning into her soul, screaming silent words of passion that she couldn't ignore. She closed her eyes and listened to the sound of the waves and the seagulls.

"Are you praying to the gods for a safe crossing?" Reece asked as she came up behind her.

"No, I was just listening. The waves have the most innocent yet mysterious sound when they roll ashore." Jordan looked out over Puget Sound, watching the lights of Seattle twinkling on the horizon.

"I never noticed that." Reece stood next to her and watched Jordan as she again closed her eyes to listen.

Jordan sensed Reece was staring at her. She slowly opened her eyes and looked over at her.

"Thank you for dinner," she said softly.

"You're most welcome, Ms. Griffin."

"Why won't you call me Jordan?"

Reece chuckled.

"I don't know. I guess because that means we would be on a first-name basis."

"And aren't we? After all, I slept in your tent, twice."

Reece smiled and looked out over the water.

"And I did take care of you after you fell into the thorns. I applied the antiseptic to your back and shoulder. I think touching your skin like that deserves a first-name basis," Jordan justified. "After all—"

Before she could finish what she was saying, Reece pulled Jordan to her and kissed her. It was a surprise but a pleasant one. Jordan pulled herself tightly against Reece and the embrace. She slipped her arms around her neck and parted her lips to take in Reece's inquisitive tongue. It was a long kiss, full of expression. It didn't stop until giggling interrupted them. Several customers had stepped out of Harry's and were watching the women. Reece quickly stepped back and led the way to the truck. She seemed more embarrassed for Jordan than for herself. She started the engine and pulled out of the parking lot.

"Sorry about that," Reece said as she sped down the street on the way back to the ferry. She seemed almost angry with herself for having kissed Jordan.

"Why are you sorry?" she asked. "I thought it was nice."

"That's a great way to ruin a perfectly good evening."

"Maybe it is a great way to start a perfect evening," Jordan suggested softly.

Reece narrowed her eyes but kept them straight ahead. Jordan smiled coyly, knowing it was difficult for Reece to keep her attention on the road.

Chapter 14

The ferry was just docking as Reece paid for their ride back to Seattle. The return ferry was little more than half full. A mass of twinkling city lights in the night skies reflected off the water as they strolled the observation deck. Jordan slipped her arm through Reece's as they stood at the railing, watching a tanker slide up Puget Sound, bound for the open waters of the Pacific Ocean.

"Will that ship pass Greysome Point on its way out to sea?" Jordan asked.

"Yes, probably. I get a lot of ships gliding along the horizon on their way to Japan, China, Alaska, even down to California."

"Could you see them from the upstairs windows of the cabin?" Jordan asked cautiously.

"Yeah," Reece replied, keeping her eyes on the passing ship.

"What's up there on the second floor?"

"Another bedroom and bathroom."

"Was it the master bedroom?" Jordan asked carefully.

Reece nodded.

"Tell me about it," Jordan asked, as they moved on down the railing.

Reece took a deep preparatory breath deciding if she wanted to answer.

"I had a darkroom put in right off the master bedroom. I used to get these wild ideas in the middle of the night. I stayed up all night one time trying to enlarge a photograph on pink photo paper." She shook her head and laughed.

"Do you still go up there?"

"Just to the darkroom."

"Is that where you had the accident?"

Reece swallowed hard and squinted out over the water.

"No," she replied, lost in thought. Jordan squeezed her hand, watching her eyes narrow as she seemed to relive the moment. "That was at our house in Redmond. I sold it. It was too big."

A blast from the ferry whistle brought them both back to reality.

Reece took Jordan's hand as they walked down the stairs to the car deck. The rows of traffic filed off and dissipated into the city streets. Reece headed for Jordan's apartment in Kirkland.

"I had a lovely time," Jordan said. "I'm glad you came to the office today."

"Me too," Reece said.

"Will you come by again soon?"

"Probably," Reece replied, smiling coyly at her.

"When?" Jordan asked.

"I don't know. Do I need an appointment?"

"No," she replied softly. "Oh, turn here, on Allison. Last building on the left." She dug in her pocket for her keys. Reece pulled into the driveway and turned off the engine. They sat staring at one another for an awkwardly long moment. Jordan fidgeted nervously with her keys, feeling like a teenager on her first date, wondering if she should expect a good night kiss. She lowered her eyes and unbuckled her seatbelt. As she reached for the door handle, Reece placed a hand on her arm to stop her.

"I had the most fantastic time tonight," Reece said, still holding Jordan's arm.

Jordan looked up at her, fully aware of an undercurrent of passion growing within her. She could feel her chest tighten and her breath quicken as Reece touched her.

"The most fantastic time," Reece repeated softly, looking deep into Jordan's eyes.

Jordan was about to give in to her inner urges and kiss Reece, but just as their lips were about to meet, the headlights from a car pulled into the drive next to Reece's truck.

"Damn," Jordan muttered. "That's my neighbor."

They sat silently watching as the middle-aged woman got out and began carrying sacks of groceries into her apartment. It was a slow methodical process. The woman seemed to have bought out the entire store but could only carry two plastic sacks at a time. After she left with the third load, Jordan looked over at Reece and laughed.

"Come on, let's go inside," she said. Reece followed, holding the storm door as Jordan fumbled with the keys. Knowing Reece was right behind her made it all the more difficult for Jordan to find the right key and unlock the door. She couldn't concentrate with Reece's body just inches away. Finally, she unlocked the door and turned to Reece, half wishing they could end the evening with a smile and a kiss and half praying it would be more.

"Thank you for dinner and for the ride home," Jordan said, extending her hand to Reece. "It was wonderful. I'll have to remember Harry's Crab Shack."

Reece took her hand and shook it firmly, her eyes lost in Jordan's.

"You're welcome, Ms. Griffin. We'll have to make plans to go there again." Reece stood with Jordan in the doorway, the moonlight gleaming down around them. Reece had a confident self-assured look about her. Jordan, on the other hand, felt like a nervous schoolgirl.

"I really think you should call me Jordan," she whispered.

"Jordan."

"See how easy that was?"

"Jordan," Reece repeated, bringing her lips closer.

Jordan couldn't speak. Her heart was pounding so hard she was sure Reece could hear it. She tried to pull her hand away but Reece refused to release it.

"Don't you want to hold my hand?" Reece asked.

"My hand is sweaty," Jordan said after clearing her throat. She couldn't catch her breath as Reece moved closer.

"I don't mind." Reece pulled their hands against her chest, pulling Jordan to her as well. "I like the feel of your hand. It's soft." She placed a kiss on the back of Jordan's hand. "And you smell so good."

"I smell like Harry's Crab Shack. I smell like fish."

"No. You smell like lavender and vanilla," Reece said barely audible.

"That's my hand lotion." Jordan could feel Reece's fingers massaging her hand. "Do you like it? I can use something else if you don't."

"Yes, I like it. Don't change a thing. That is your smell. I have put that scent in my memory bank next to your name. I will always associate you with that scent. It is lovely. And so are you." Reece said, kissing her hand again, letting her lips linger on Jordan's skin.

The storm of passion that was raging just below the surface was growing faster than Jordan could contain. She leaned into Reece and smiled up at her, her lips parting slightly as she gazed into Reece's eyes. She raised her face, ready for Reece to take control and kiss her. She didn't have to wait long. Reece took Jordan's face in her hand and kissed her full on the mouth. Jordan pulled her hand free of Reece's hold and slipped her arms around her neck, pressing herself into the kiss. Reece's arms enfolded her in a strong, commanding embrace. As their tongues delved deeper into each other's mouths, Reece allowed her hands to float down over Jordan's back. With a soft yet deliberate move, one of Reece's hands slid up under Jordan's blouse and released her bra hook. It was like unleashing a caged tiger. Jordan laced her hands through

Reece's hair and pulled herself tighter to Reece's body. Jordan wasn't sure when it happened but Reece's hand had found one of her breasts and was holding it, the nipple hardening at the touch.

Reece grabbed her and turned her around, kissing her wildly as they stumbled in the door, their hands and mouths frantically groping the other. Jordan's keys were still dangling in the lock as she pulled Reece down on the floor. Jordan coiled a leg around Reece's body as she rolled on top of her. Jordan pulled at Reece's jacket and sweater as she painted kisses down her neck, her hands fumbling to find their way inside her clothing.

Reece unzipped Jordan's slacks. Her hand plunged inside as she continued to cover Jordan's neck and breasts with kisses. Jordan's body arched as Reece's fingers found her moistening folds and massaged them. Jordan pulled at Reece's bra with both hands, gasping and groaning, her mouth ready to take in her awaiting nipples. They wrestled the clothes off each other's bodies like they were on fire, in a race where the finish line was an ecstasy beyond their wildest dreams, an ecstasy neither one could wait another moment to find. Reece nipped and licked at Jordan's skin as her hand slid inside Jordan's yearning. Jordan closed her eyes, moaning as the hot passion consumed her. She cupped her hand over Reece's and pressed down, urging her on to harder and deeper exploration.

"Yes, Reece. Yes, yes," Jordan gasped, her nails digging into Reece's back. She rolled her hips upward, straining for more. Reece grabbed the back of Jordan's hair and directed her mouth to hers. Their tongues dueled and danced together as Jordan rode the waves of her orgasm to a frenzied climax.

Jordan's body glistened with sweat as Reece pulled herself against her, their bodies gliding and floating over each other. They both gasped and breathed heavily from the frantic lovemaking. Reece finally pulled herself up next to Jordan, holding her in her arms as they caught their breath. Jordan smiled over at her contentedly, brushing the hair from Reece's face. A shaft of light from the window struck Reece's scar as if pointing to it. She seemed to know the scar was clearly visible and she raised a hand to cover it. Jordan pushed her hand away and touched the top of the scar, trailing her fingertip down the ridge of pink skin. She followed the scar down Reece's face, across her neck and shoulder then across her breast to where it ended just above her right nipple. Jordan cupped her hand over Reece's breast like a protective barrier against the pain she surely had felt when the skin was so brutally ripped and slashed.

"I guess you did want dessert," Reece whispered.

"All that was missing is the whipped cream," Jordan replied, snuggling against her. She closed her eyes and sighed as a deep sense of satisfaction flowed over her. Jordan had never done such a crazy and impulsive thing before in her life but pulling Reece down on the floor at that moment was exactly the right thing to do. Her heart told her so. Reece's body next to hers on the living room floor of her apartment couldn't seem more sensual if they were together in a king-size bed surrounded by a thousand flickering candles. This was as good as it could possibly get, she thought. She hooked a leg over Reece's and hugged her side.

"Should I close the front door?" Reece asked, noticing it was still standing open.

"No," Jordan replied, holding onto Reece, refusing to let her go. "I may never close it again." She nuzzled Reece's neck.

"What are you going to tell the postman when he comes to the door tomorrow?"

"Tell him to leave the mail and go away. I'm busy."

Reece laughed, brushing her hand across Jordan's face tenderly.

"Will you stay the night with me?" Jordan asked softly. "I do have a bed, you know."

Reece smiled at her, playing with a lock of Jordan's hair.

"Not this time," she replied in a whisper.

Jordan propped herself up on an elbow and looked down at Reece.

"Why not? I've got you undressed. I did all the work for you," she said with a grin. "Besides, I want you to." She leaned down and kissed her tenderly.

"I can't," Reece replied, kissing her cheek then climbing to her feet. She went about dressing while Jordan watched. Reece held out a hand to Jordan and helped her to her feet. She wrapped her arms around her and looked into Jordan's eyes, smiling at her. "Thank you for the lovely evening, Ms. Griffin." Reece chuckled. "Jordan."

Jordan pressed her naked body against Reece.

"Thank you for dessert, Ms. McAllister," she replied with a devilish grin. "Reece."

Reece kissed her then swatted her bare bottom.

"Will you call me?" Jordan asked, walking her to the door, the moonlight streaming in the open door.

"Yes," Reece replied, stroking Jordan's face before heading for her truck.

Jordan watched from behind the door as Reece slowly pulled away, honking once as she turned the corner.

"Oh, Ms. McAllister, what have you done?" she muttered, a dreamy look in her eyes. "I'm going to have to rethink love at first sight," she whispered as she slowly closed the door and leaned her forehead against it.

Chapter 15

"Hello," Jordan said as Reece picked up the telephone.

"Hey, it's the ace reporter," Reece mused.

"I wish," Jordan chuckled. "Did I interrupt something?"

"Yes. I was doing one of those peasant jobs."

"Which one? There are several. Vacuuming, ironing, mending?"

"Laundry. I decided to take out the trash, too, while I was in the mood."

"I need to do some of that," Jordan replied, remembering her full hamper.

"I figured you for the efficient type. You know, anal retentive about housework."

"Only in my mind." They laughed. "But I do try to keep up with it. If I worked a regular nine-to-five job I might stand a better chance."

"Journalists don't get a nine-to-five job unless they have their head stuck in the sand. Life goes on twenty-four hours a day which means news goes on twenty-four hours a day. You should know that by now, Jordan," Reece explained kindly.

"Actually, that is why I called. How would you like a home cooked meal tonight while I pry some additional information out of you? I want to go over some of the notes I took when we were on the camping trip. I want to be sure I got everything down right."

"Like what?" Reece asked. "Which note are you talking about?"

"Oh no. You can't answer any questions before dinner. I want you fat and happy so you'll tell me everything I want to know," Jordan teased.

"Okay, I'll take you to dinner at Hagen's. We never did make it there."

"No, no. My place, Ms. McAllister. I want to cook dinner for you. I have a brand new grill and I want to try it out. How would you feel about blackened salmon steaks grilled to perfection? I can make a salad too."

"It sounds wonderful but I don't want to put you out."

"You'd only put me out if you said no. It's Saturday and I already shopped for the dinner. I don't do this very often so please don't disappoint me."

"In that case, dinner would be great. What can I bring?" Reece asked.

"Nothing, unless you'd like something special to drink. I have iced tea, coffee, Coke and I think I have a couple Perrier waters in the fridge."

"What time do you want me to come?"

Jordan smiled to herself at Reece's question. She may not have meant it to sound suggestive but Jordan certainly took it that way.

"How about six thirty? That gives me time to hide the dirty laundry," Jordan replied.

"Six thirty it is." She hung up.

Jordan grinned broadly. Reece was coming to dinner. She suddenly realized she had a mountain of chores to do before six thirty. She had put off housework for a week and it was screaming at her from every room. She put on some music and hummed along as she cleaned the apartment. She changed the bed, putting on the satin sheets Hope had given her for her birthday. She arranged candles on the nightstand and fluffed the pillows for all they were worth. She opened her jar of lavender potpourri and allowed the aroma to float through the room. When she was finished, she gave one last look then went to shower before starting dinner. Jordan wore a pair of tight-fitting jeans, ones she thought Reece would like, a deep V-cut blouse and no shoes. She remembered Reece was barefoot when she first met her at the gallery and if it was good enough for Reece, it was good enough for her. Jordan selected a stack of CDs for the changer. She chose a light and eclectic mix of vocals for the first hour then soft and sensual instrumentals for later in the evening. She wasn't sure if Reece liked that kind of music but she was willing to try. She dimmed the lights in the living room, a feature the landlord had pointed out, but one Jordan had never used before. She adjusted the lights up and down then sat on the couch, trying out each setting for ambiance and allure.

"Screw it," she finally said, disgusted with the triviality. "Dim is dim." She went to make the salad.

Reece arrived right on time. She was so punctual Jordan suspected she was sitting at the corner waiting for six thirty on her watch.

"Come in," Jordan said, opening the front door as Reece started up the steps. Reece was wearing a pair of jeans that made her legs look long and lean. She had a white turtleneck under a navy blazer. She had her small camera bag over her shoulder. Jordan knew Reece didn't go anywhere without her camera. But it was Reece's bright smile that caught Jordan's eye.

"Did you get all the laundry hidden?" Reece asked, stepping inside.

"I hope so," Jordan replied. "If you see anything sticking out from under the furniture just kick it back under."

Reece handed Jordan a bottle of wine.

"Thank you. That was sweet," Jordan said fondly. "Maybe we can have it for dessert. I forgot to get anything for dessert but I could whip something up. I'm sorry."

"Nope, no dessert for me," Reece said, looking around. "Can I put my camera bag someplace?"

"Sure. Anywhere is fine. Bedroom, couch," Jordan replied. The timer went off in the kitchen and she hurried to check it. "Make yourself at home."

Reece took the camera bag into the bedroom. She was gone several minutes. Jordan assumed she was looking around, getting the lay of the land since she only saw the living room floor last time she was there.

"Something smells good," Reece said, coming into the kitchen. She had taken off her blazer and pushed up the sleeves of her white turtleneck. It hugged her neck and covered as much of the scar as a collar could be coaxed into covering. Jordan noticed Reece tried to keep her scarred side away from her.

"I'm trying a new recipe for salmon. Since we printed it in the cuisine section, I thought I should try it," Jordan said.

"Can I do something? Set the table?" Reece asked, noticing there didn't seem to be a table set yet.

"Nope. It's all done. We will eat in about four minutes." Jordan turned the salmon steaks on the electric tabletop grill.

"When you said you had a new grill I thought you meant one of those outdoor gas things or maybe something that uses charcoal."

"Those things are too much hassle. I never have the coals hot enough when I'm ready to cook. And the gas tanks are always running on empty when I want to make something. I won this one. Hope put my name in for a drawing at the home show last month. She works at the convention center. She's an event planner."

"Event planner. That sounds like an interesting job."

"She says it is extremely hectic right before an opening. Like coming up on deadline at the magazine."

"So you and Hope are pretty close, as cousins go?"

"She's more like a sister than a cousin. I know I can always count on her." Jordan took up the plates. "Are you ready to eat?"

"Yes. Where are we eating? Catch as catch can on the couch?"

"No. Follow me." Jordan pushed back the curtain and stepped out onto the balcony outside the dining room. She had set the small bistro table with a tablecloth and matching napkins, a single candle inside a glass hurricane shade and a basket of fresh flowers, ones Jordan had made a special trip to the Pike's Place Market to buy. The balcony was small but the candle, the flowers, the fresh scent of the open air and the view made it an intimate and romantic setting. Jordan had always wished she had more occasions to use the balcony, something she paid dearly to have but seldom used. This was the night and she wanted it to be perfect. The sun had just settled into the distance, a brilliant and breathtaking orange glow over the horizon. Jordan took Reece's hand and led her to her place.

"Wow," Reece exclaimed, impressed with both the gracious table setting and the spectacular view. "Look at this. You went to a lot of work. And you did a great job, Jordan."

"I checked with the newspaper and this is supposed to be the peak moment for the sunset. I ordered it just for you." Jordan smiled at her warmly. "I know how much you like settings like this. Have a seat and enjoy it."

Reece sat down, her eyes reveling in the golden sunset.

"I'll have you know I am showing great restraint," Reece said, smiling at the spectacular view.

"I know you are," Jordan replied, walking behind her and touching her shoulder. "You want to go get your camera and take a dozen shots of it, don't you?"

"How did you know?"

"When you've been around photojournalists as long as I have, you get to know them," Jordan said with a wink as she took her place. "I won't mind if you want to take some shots."

"No. Not this time. This time I can sit and enjoy it." Reece smiled over at Jordan.

Jordan's salmon was a big success. So was the ambiance. They ate dinner as the last faint glow disappeared behind the Olympic Mountains. They talked about Reece's awards and her television assignments. It was completely dark and the candle had burned down to a short nub when the chilly night air sent them inside.

"What was the assignment you disliked covering the most?" Jordan asked as she filled the dishwasher.

"Disliked? Gosh, I'd have to say covering the overcrowding at the humane society. I did that one back when I was working for the local television station," Reece replied, handing her the plates.

"That must have been a terrible one."

"Smelly, noisy, filthy, understaffed. Take your pick. It was all of those and more. The thing I hated most was the animals that had to be euthanized. But I guess it was better than letting them starve to death on the streets or spreading disease." She shook her head as if that was enough on that subject.

"Okay, top three favorite people you got to meet through your work?" Jordan asked, wiping the counter.

"Three is tough. I've met many I considered interesting. I'd say Fergie, for one. She doesn't take crap from anyone, even the Queen. Maybe Hillary because I didn't agree with her politics and she knew it. She and I had quite a discussion. She wouldn't let me air most of it but it was interesting. Number one would definitely have to be Sally Smithfield." Reece nodded decisively. "Yep, Sally Smithfield has to be top of the list."

"Who is Sally Smithfield?"

"Was. Sally died in two thousand."

"Ah, that's too bad. Who was she?"

"She wasn't anyone famous. She didn't have any money. I don't think she ever rode on an airplane or stayed in a fancy hotel. She was a very athletic girl when she was young. She could run like the wind. She had blue ribbons for winning races in elementary school. I interviewed her the day she graduated from Mississippi State University with a bachelor's degree in physical education. She wanted to be a gym teacher. It had taken her a bit longer than the normal student but she had a few small delays. She dropped out of school when she was fourteen and got married. She was pregnant and her family refused to support her so she married the kid who got her pregnant. He was fifteen. They lived in a run-down farmhouse in a hick town in Mississippi. She wanted to go back to school but every time she thought she might do it, she turned up pregnant."

"How many children did Sally have?"

Reece laughed.

"Sally and Arthur Smithfield had fourteen children. She told me she would probably have had more but Arthur died in a farming accident when he was thirty-two."

"So she decided to go back to school after her husband died?"

"Well, almost. She had to raise the kids first. And a couple of her daughters had kids out of wedlock so that added to the clan. She worked as a maid for a local family. She finally decided it was her turn so she enrolled in a GED program in the Greenwood, Mississippi school system. Then she got a Pell Grant and qualified for a scholarship to MSU. It took her a few extra years to finish but she did it. She graduated with honors. Her family gave her a brand new pair of Nike sneakers for a graduation present."

"That is great. Did she receive any offers to be a PE teacher after she graduated?"

"Actually, she did. But Sally had a heart attack and died three days after she graduated. She was ninety-six years old when she passed away." Reece smiled at the memory.

"Ninety-six?" Jordan's eyes widened.

"Yep. But she didn't look it. She didn't look a day over eighty." She winked at Jordan.

"I can't even imagine how hard that must have been for her to finish college."

"Sally said when she was a little girl she could do cartwheels all the way around the block without stopping. And she could run from Cold Creek Crossing to Gilbertville in less than an hour. She said it was about ten miles. I was teasing her and asked if she could still do it. She gave me a scowl and said heavens, no. But she could still walk it. She walked that road from Cold Creek Crossing to Gilbertville on her seventy-fifth birthday with her twenty-four grandkids and forty-one great grandkids. She said only two of them finished the walk with her." Reece shook her head in disbelief.

"What a woman!" Jordan gasped.

"Do you want to know the kicker?"

"There's more?" Jordan asked curiously.

"You bet. Sally told me she discovered she was gay when she was about forty years old. She told me she knew she didn't like men coming at her with that thing. She much preferred the soft skin of a dainty woman. Sally had a lesbian partner for over fifty years. She survived her. She was younger than Sally. I think she was only eighty-two when she died a couple years ago. I wanted to interview her but she wouldn't allow it. She said Sally was the one with the glamorous life."

"What a beautiful story," Jordan said, touching Reece's arm. "I can see why you would put her on the top of your list. You must have come away from that interview with a sense of accomplishment and pride."

"Not for me. I just asked the questions. Sally was the hero in that one."

"When I am old, I want you to interview me. I bet you made her feel so comfortable and relaxed." Jordan smiled at her.

"Are you going back to college when you are old?" Reece mused.

"Maybe not college. But I might find something to do to attract your attention if you promise to interview me."

"Like what?" Reece rearranged a lock of Jordan's hair.

"I don't know. Maybe I'll go hang-gliding or mountain climbing or something."

"When you are old, maybe you should find something to do inside that is less hazardous to your health. We know how you are in the great outdoors," Reece chuckled.

"Hey, I survived the camping trip. You're the one with the thorn wounds," Jordan replied, turning out the lights in the kitchen. The lights in the living room shed a dim light on them as they stood looking at each other. "Would you like to come in the living room and sit down? You might be more comfortable than standing in my cramped kitchen."

Reece didn't move. She leaned against the counter and gazed over at Jordan.

"What?" Jordan asked, noticing her invading stare.

"I am so glad you didn't fall into the thorn bush. You are so beautiful, Jordan. It would have been a real shame if you had been the one with the thorns." Reece's soft eyes captured Jordan's. "A real shame," she added softly.

"I wish I could have saved you from falling too. I know it was very painful for you. I hope I didn't make it any worse."

"You didn't," Reece said, reaching out and touching Jordan's face. She slid her hand down Jordan's neck and shoulder then took her hand and drew her closer. Jordan leaned against Reece, her eyes lowered as Reece ran her hands through her hair, lacing her fingers through the soft curls. The touch sent a thrilling shiver up Jordan's back.

"I hated it that I had to hurt you like that," Jordan whispered, leaning her forehead against Reece's lips.

"If I ever fall into a devil's club again, I want you to be the one to take out the thorns."

"Don't even say that. I hope you never do that again."

"I don't plan on it but you never know what's going to happen." Reece slipped her arms around Jordan's waist. "You have to be ready for every eventuality. You have to be ready to accept whatever comes your way." Reece kissed Jordan's forehead then one cheek. She moved to the other side, kissing her cheek and trailing kisses down her neck.

"True. You never know when something is going to happen. Some things come along that surprise you," Jordan whispered as she closed her eyes, enjoying Reece's lips against her skin. "Some things come along and take your breath away."

"Some things are like a breath of fresh air in a stale, cold world," Reece said, her kisses lingering over Jordan's neck. She unbuttoned the top button of Jordan's blouse and kissed the soft skin in her cleavage. "Some things are like a prize you never thought you could ever win."

The curtains gently floated on the breeze. The candles flickered, barely lighting the bedroom with an amber hue. Two half-empty glasses of wine sat on the bedside table. A white satin sheet covered Reece and Jordan from the waist down as they lay in each other's arms sharing a kiss. The faint sounds of piano music floated around them as they clung to each other. They had shared the passion of slow and tender lovemaking. The rain had started again, softly pattering on the deck outside the window.

"Close your eyes," Reece whispered. Jordan did as she was told, sighing softly as Reece touched her face. Reece then reached down and retrieved the red rose she had hidden under the edge of the bed. She held it under Jordan's nose then drew the rose down between her breasts, the petals stroking her skin. Reece carefully drew circles around Jordan's nipples with the tip of the rose then placed it on Jordan's lips.

"That feels incredible. And it smells so sweet." Jordan drew in a deep breath.

"This rose is as soft as you are." Reece traced a line down Jordan's stomach with her fingertip, stopping just above her pubic hair. "As soft as you are inside, too."

"You have the most sensuous touch, Reece. You make me shiver just by touching my hand. Did you know that?" Jordan looked at her lovingly, tracing the outline of Reece's lips. "And I love the way your scar gets real pink when you have an orgasm. You'll never be able to hide it from me. Or fake it," she teased, playfully biting her earlobe.

"Don't be silly. My scar doesn't change colors. It's just hideously puckered skin. You can't make anything glamorous out of it."

"Oh yes, I can. And if you don't believe me, let me demonstrate," she advised, moving down Reece's body, nipping and licking her way toward the thighs.

"Stop that," Reece scoffed, trying to act mad.

"No, I won't and you can't make me," Jordan said with a childish giggle, looking up at her. She wiggled her way down under the sheet. It didn't take long before Reece was gasping and tugging at the pillow as she felt another peak rising up from deep inside her core. Jordan's tongue skillfully and tenderly brought Reece to a screaming climax. As she finished, her body glistening with sweat, Jordan pulled herself up next to her. She kissed her then slid out of bed and scurried into the bathroom. She returned with a small mirror.

"See," she said, sliding back under the sheet and holding it up to Reece's face.

Reece looked then tossed the mirror on the floor and rolled over on top of Jordan.

"Think you're pretty smart, don't you?" she said, holding Jordan's face between her hands.

"Yes, I do. After all, look what I have in bed with me," Jordan replied, a soft loving look in her eyes.

Reece smiled down at her. She slowly lowered her lips to Jordan's, taunting and teasing her with her tongue. Finally she took Jordan's lips in hers, devouring her in a long, passionate kiss. Jordan folded her arms over Reece and pulled her down tight against her, their bodies molded together like one.

"You'll stay with me tonight, won't you?" Jordan asked in a whisper. "Last time you didn't."

Reece didn't reply at first.

"Yes," she said finally. "If you want me to."

"There is nothing I want more," Jordan replied tenderly.

Reece climbed out of bed and went to the window to watch the rain. Her lean and sculpted body shimmered in the candlelight as she stood watching the glow of city lights in the distance. Jordan came to stand next to her, her body against Reece's. She placed her arms around Reece's waist, hugging her warmly.

"Are you all right, sweetheart? Is there something on your mind?" Jordan asked, pressing a kiss into Reece's shoulder.

"No. I was just checking the rain." Reece heaved a heavy sigh as if she wanted to say something but didn't know how to start.

"We can always count on rain in Seattle," Jordan replied, looking up at her, trying to read her strange mood.

Chapter 16

"Hello, Reece. Are you there? Pick up if you are screening your calls from irritating reporters with nagging questions," Jordan joked. "Okay, I'll call you later. I just wanted to see if I could bring the videotapes back. Bye." Before she could end the call, Reece answered.

"Are you finished with them already?" Reece asked.

"Hello there. Yes. Actually, I had the media department copy them onto a DVD. I can have shots copied to the layout that way."

"Sounds like copyright infringements."

"No, I didn't plan on doing anything with them but watch them. I'll have the legal department check with the network before we use any shot," Jordan quickly clarified.

Reece laughed.

"I was kidding. Help yourself. I have the copyright to any of my pieces. I can allow usage of the shots." She continued to laugh.

"Shame on you, Reece. You scared me."

"Can you wait until the weekend for me to come get them?"

"I could bring them to your apartment," Jordan offered.

"I'm not at the apartment. I'm on the ferry on my way to Kingston. I'm going to work in the darkroom for a few days. But I should be back by Sunday."

"You're going to Greysome Point today?" Jordan's voice was heavy with disappointment.

"Yes. I have some ideas for some enlargements."

Jordan didn't say anything.

"I don't suppose you would like to bring the tapes out to Greysome Point and spend the night with me, would you?" Reece asked.

"When?" Jordan replied without hesitation.

"Wow, I guess you would," Reece chuckled. "How about tomorrow? Can you get away in the afternoon?"

"I have a piece to get proofed in the morning then I'll have the whole weekend to myself. I could be there by mid-afternoon." There was a childish excitement in her voice.

"Okay. I'll see you then. And Jordan, watch out for mud puddles." Reece laughed then hung up, the sound of the ferry whistle blaring in the background.

"Bye," Jordan said to the dial tone, a bright smile on her face. She sat looking at the receiver as she thought about spending the weekend with Reece. She began planning what she would take. She wanted to look her very best for Reece. She knew they would be deep in the woods in her cabin but she wanted to look perfect for her.

"Jordan?" Susan asked, bringing her back to her senses. She was standing in the doorway, scowling at her. "Jordan, what are you daydreaming about?" she asked stiffly.

"Hi Susan. Nothing." Jordan hung up the receiver and tried to look busy.

"We are five hundred words short on that story Francine submitted on the new Boeing contract."

"So?"

"Francine is in Hawaii on her honeymoon. She won't be back until the fifteenth." Susan placed a hand on her hip and smirked. "I should have never allowed her to go until we went to press on that."

"Can't you add something? Maybe a picture? Slap a shot of the Boeing logo across the page."

"I already did that. We have more artwork in the article than copy as it is."

"Susan, no one is going to know it is five hundred words short but you. Drop in an ad on the corner of the page and forget it."

"Couldn't you—" Susan began carefully.

"No," Jordan said, instantly raising a hand and shaking her head. "I will not. I'm not going to rewrite it and add five hundred words."

"Jordan, it wouldn't take you fifteen minutes to knock it out." Susan came to the desk and looked down at her plaintively. "It can be anything. Background, sidebar, I don't care."

"Susan," Jordan said through a heavy sigh.

"Maybe we have something you can use in archives." Susan wasn't going to take no for an answer.

"Susan, you do it," Jordan said, going to a file cabinet and trying to look busy. "You're the senior editor. Check Francine's file and see if she left something out. She always leaves a copy in her completed folder. Do a search for the date she submitted it. That's the way she stores stuff. I can't imagine she would intentionally short the article."

"Didn't you do something on Boeing last year? Maybe you've got a blurb we can use."

"I did an article on the museum at Boeing Field. And I used everything I had. Remember, you wanted six pages instead of four." Jordan sat down in her desk chair with a folder and began leafing through it.

"Please, Jordan. I have to have it ready tomorrow afternoon." Susan placed both hands on the desk and leaned into Jordan. "I'll give you a day off next week if you'll do it for me. What do you say?"

"I don't need a day off. I already have one coming and it's tomorrow."

"Says who?" Susan asked. She straightened her posture and scowled down at Jordan.

"You. That's who. I asked for Friday off a month ago. I'll have my copy off to layout by nine thirty then I am out of here. This will be my first vacation day in months and I am looking forward to it."

"I never said you could take Friday off. We've got a staff meeting and I have some assignments I want to go over with you."

"Susan," Jordan exclaimed, frowning up at her. "You told me it was all right. I've made plans. We even talked about it on Monday. You said have a great weekend. Remember?"

Susan slowly shook her head, the power of her authority racing to her head. Jordan knew exactly what she was doing and it was called blackmail, pure and simple. It became perfectly clear that unless she agreed to fix Francine's article, Susan wasn't going to give her Friday off. It wouldn't be the first time Jordan's plans had to be changed for one of Susan's last-minute schemes or harebrained ideas, but this was different. This time Jordan had plans that mattered. Canceling a luncheon with Mia or a shopping date with Hope was unfortunate, but not dire. She had learned to apologize with enough finesse to keep them happy. But she didn't want to cancel the date with Reece. She didn't want to tell her she couldn't come to Greysome Point Friday afternoon and spend the night with her. More than anything, Jordan wanted to keep this date. She wanted the weekend to be special, perfect, memorable. Susan was not going to ruin it for her. Jordan tossed the folder on her desk and leaned back in her chair.

"Okay, five hundred words," she said, through clenched teeth.

"Thank you, babe. I knew you'd do it for me. I can always count on you," Susan replied, giving a wink and turning to leave. "By the way, check the layout and make sure five hundred is enough. It might be a bit more. You know, give or take." Susan strode out of the office and disappeared down the hall.

"Five hundred, my ass. I bet it is more like a thousand," Jordan muttered, logging into the story. She scanned the layout, her eyes growing wide. "Damn you, Susan. It hasn't even been edited yet." Jordan knew that she would be working late tonight. Dinner would be a candy bar from the vending machine and a cup of reheated coffee. If she wanted to be finished and ready to head for Greysome Point by mid-morning, she was going to be burning the midnight oil at her desk tonight.

Jordan was exhausted when she unlocked her front door. It was almost ten o'clock and she hadn't eaten anything since lunch. Her stomach was growling but her body was so tired she couldn't bring herself to fix anything. She dropped her briefcase, jacket and purse on the couch, stepped out of her shoes and pressed the answering machine button.

"Hi, Jordie. It's Hope. How about a movie or dinner or something this weekend. Give me a call if you are free. I'll be baching it. Barbara is going to San Diego for her grandmother's birthday and I do *not* want to go watch a bunch of old people drool into their slippers. Later."

The machine beeped again.

"Jordan, this is Susan. I forgot to tell you, I think it would be great if you took tomorrow afternoon off. Have a great weekend if I don't see you in the morning. And thanks for taking care of that little detail for me."

Jordan flipped the bird in the direction of the answering machine as it beeped.

"Jordan, this is Reece." Jordan instantly came to stand by the machine to listen. "I hope I'm not calling too late. I didn't want to disturb you, but I wanted to tell you, if you get here in time and aren't too tired," she said, rambling a bit. "I thought we might go to the Landing tomorrow night. It's a little place down by Forks. They have pretty good food. They also have pool tables." Reece chuckled. "And we know how well you play pool. And they have a band on Friday night. Country-western but at least it's live. I didn't know if you like country-western music or not. No big thing, but I thought if you wanted to go, I'd take you out to dinner. It's no Harry's Crab Shack but then again, what is?" Reece laughed nervously, sounding like a teenager asking for a date to the prom. Jordan sat on the arm of the couch and listened, a smile growing across her face. She thought Reece's message was cute. The answering machine beeped the end of the message and started the next one.

"Also, it's not a fancy place," Reece added. "Jeans. Nothing special. But the steaks are good. If you get here in time, we can head on down about five. It takes an hour to get there." There was another pause. "I guess that's all." The machine beeped again.

"I would love to go to dinner with you, Ms. McAllister. And breakfast and lunch and tea and anything else you can think of," Jordan muttered as she sashayed down the hall to the bedroom. Jordan suddenly felt refreshed, invigorated. She changed into pajamas. It was almost one in the morning before she could close her eyes and sleep.

Jordan was in her office and churning out the article to be proofread before anyone else arrived. She skipped her morning stop for a latte, her mind clearly fixed on her goal. She wanted to be finished and on the highway to Edmonds and the ferry by nine o'clock. Her suitcase was in the trunk of her car. There was a happy tune in her morning hum and a grin on her face as she punched out the story and sent it to layout. Without a wasted motion, she turned out the desk lamp, slipped her key in the office door and hurried down the hall, her hair flowing out behind her as she rushed into the elevator.

"Jordan," Susan said, greeting her and taking her arm. "I'm glad I caught you." The elevator door closed and they rode it down. Jordan moved to the back wall, trying to ignore Susan's persistent hold on her. "I think we're going to have to put a hold on the Boeing story. I know, I know. You worked late on it but I heard there is a snag in the contract. Something to do with congressional appropriations. Maybe we can do something with it next month. I was thinking, you could dash out a little two-page piece on government contracts and how they affect the Seattle business industry."

Jordan just smiled at her, hoping the elevator would hurry up and open in the parking garage.

"Of course, if you wanted to call Boeing and find out how the contract stands, maybe we could go ahead and use it but you know how silly we would look if it isn't a done deal and we print that big story." Susan still had Jordan's arm in a death grip. "Jordan, are you listening to me?"

"Yes, Susan. I heard you." She watched the elevator lights count down, anguish on her face every time it hesitated at a floor. It was clear Susan planned on ruining her weekend. It wasn't the first time. But not this time. Not this weekend, Jordan thought. She kept a placid expression on her face so Susan wouldn't know how much she was looking forward to her time off.

"I know you had plans today, but—" Susan started.

The elevator door opened and Jordan pulled away. She stood in the doorway and looked back at Susan.

"Yes, I have plans today. You can throw that story in the trash for all I care, Susan. Have a nice weekend. Bye," Jordan gave an artificial smile and pressed the button to the tenth floor, sending the elevator and Susan back upstairs. She then ran to her car and roared out of the parking garage. She put a CD on the car stereo and headed for Edmonds. She arrived at the loading area just as the last car was pulling onboard. She gave the attendant one of her most alluring smiles and conned him into allowing her to load as well. The thirty-minute crossing seemed like forever. Jordan paced the deck, watching the shore at Kingston grow out of the horizon. She stopped at Sequim for gas and a Coke, but even though it was past lunchtime, she wasn't hungry. Her mind was fixed on her goal—Greysome Point and Reece McAllister. Nothing else mattered. She roared past Reece's driveway entrance once, and had to turn around, her mind so consumed with their plans together she had forgotten to look for it. She pulled onto the path and stopped at the first NO TRESPASSING sign. There was a yellow sticky note taped to it that read EXCEPT JORDAN GRIFFIN. She took the note and held it in her hand, her fingers tracing the words like they were gold.

"Thank you, Reece," she muttered. She stuck it to her dashboard and pulled ahead, winding her way along the narrow path. The overhanging trees were no match for her determination. Reece was standing on the front porch of the cabin when she pulled up, a bright smile welcoming Jordan back.

"Hello," Jordan said, climbing out and looking up the steps at her.

"You made good time," Reece said, her hands in the back pockets of her jeans.

"There wasn't much traffic." Jordan climbed the steps, her heart pounding as she moved closer. "It was an easy trip."

Reece stared down at her, her eyes twinkling with emotion.

"How are you?" Jordan said, placing a hand on Reece's sweater.

"Fine." Reece took a deep breath, as if to stifle her own feelings of relief at having Jordan once again at Greysome Point. "I'm glad you could get away. No pressing stories you had to cover?"

"No. It was pretty quiet." Jordan leaned in to her.

Reece's hands remained in her pockets as she looked at Jordan fondly. Her eyes did a slow deliberate scan down Jordan's body and back up again. She seemed to approve of the way Jordan looked, her smile growing wider as she took in her every detail.

"What are you grinning at?" Jordan teased.

"Don't interrupt me. I'm working," Reece replied then looked her up and down again. "You look very nice, Ms. Griffin. Very nice indeed."

"Thank you," Jordan said quietly as she blushed.

"Would you like to come inside?" Reece still hadn't moved.

"Yes, as a matter of fact, I would love to come inside," Jordan replied, her hand stroking Reece's face softly. "Are you inviting me inside?" she asked in a whisper.

"Yes, I am." Reece leaned down and kissed Jordan, her hands still in her pockets.

Jordan put her arms around Reece's neck and kissed her back.

"I missed you," Jordan said, holding on to her.

"Why the hell did you miss me?" Reece asked, looking down at her.

"Because I did. I like being with you. I like doing things with you. I like the way you look at me," Jordan replied, ruffling her hands through the back of Reece's hair.

"You're just trying to get a story out of me," Reece joked.

"I already did that," Jordan replied, kissing Reece's nose playfully. "I'm after something else from you now." There was a seductive lilt to Jordan's voice.

"And that would be?"

"You aren't much of a reporter if you can't figure that out for yourself," Jordan declared, one hand sliding down Reece's back.

"I've been retired for a long time. I may need some help."

"I'll be glad to help you," Jordan said, walking them backward toward the cabin door.

Finally Reece took her hands out of her pockets and wrapped them around Jordan, kissing her passionately as they crossed the threshold. Reece picked up Jordan and carried her into the bedroom and placed her on the bed, their kisses soft and tender. Jordan closed her eyes and sighed softly as Reece's mouth traced kisses down her neck and up the other side. Reece's hand had slid down over Jordan's slacks, cupping at her crotch and pressing tightly against her. A sudden involuntary shiver shot up Jordan's body as Reece's fingers found her tender nub.

"I thought I was supposed to help you," Jordan muttered, between kisses.

"Shh," Reece whispered. "I'm busy."

Reece unzipped Jordan's slacks and gently pushed them down, her hands sliding her panties out of the way. She pulled Jordan's sweater over her head and released her bra with one quick flick.

"How am I doing?" Reece asked as she floated kisses down Jordan's body.

"Shh," Jordan replied through a groan. "I'm busy." She spread her legs and arched to Reece's touch, a fire growing from deep inside that was too hot to contain. Reece took Jordan in her mouth, feeling her passion as it grew. With the softest touch and careful artistry, Reece created a web of ecstasy Jordan couldn't resist. Her mouth and hands were like the instruments of angels, fluttering in and around Jordan's soft womanhood. Jordan had never had such complete and all-consuming sex before. She couldn't remember when lovemaking had been so carefully orchestrated and so thoroughly satisfying. Jordan's body was Reece's to do with as she wanted. As Reece moved over her, caressing her and igniting one fire after another, Jordan gasped and moaned at the touch until she could contain her emotions no longer. Tiny tears rolled down her face and dropped onto the pillow, her eyes closed tight as one orgasm after the next washed over her.

"Are you all right? Am I hurting you?" Reece asked, noticing Jordan's tears. She wiped away a tear as it rolled down Jordan's cheek.

"No," Jordan replied in a whisper, touching Reece's face tenderly. "No, you are definitely not hurting me." She drew Reece to her and kissed her, her tongue invading Reece's mouth.

Reece rolled Jordan on top of her, Jordan's smooth skin covering her like a silken comforter. Reece stroked Jordan's back as they kissed. The heavenly mix of Jordan's perfume and their lovemaking filled the air. Reece held her tight in an enveloping embrace, one that took Jordan's breath away for its passion and sensitivity.

"You have the most wonderful kiss," Jordan said, snuggling against her. "Your lips on mine are like a thousand butterfly wings invading my soul, so soft yet so thrilling. I don't think I have ever kissed anyone who sends me to heaven like you do."

"It is my pleasure, I assure you." Reece sighed heavily. "And, I might add, I have never kissed a natural blonde before," she said in a lusty voice, patting Jordan's bottom.

Jordan laughed.

"A natural redhead, but never a blonde," Reece added.

"Who was the redhead?" Jordan snickered. "Tell me, tell me, tell me."

"You don't want to hear this, do you?"

"Yes, I do," Jordan replied, wiggling herself against Reece. "Tell me who the redhead was."

"Lucinda Alvarado."

"And who is Lucinda Alvarado?" Jordan asked, propping herself up on Reece's chest.

"New Year's Eve, two years ago. I met her at a lesbian bar in Seattle."

"You mean you *picked her up* in a lesbian bar in Seattle," Jordan corrected, smiling a cockeyed smile at her.

"No, I didn't pick her up. Lucinda came in to the bar in a pair of black leather pants and a halter top, one of those kind that are cinched up in the middle to accentuate the cleavage. Well, take it from me, Lucinda didn't need any help accentuating the cleavage. She had plenty of it and she knew how to show it off. I was minding my own business, sitting at the end of the bar ringing in my own new year when she sent me this look across the room. She slowly ran her tongue over her upper lip then winked at me like she knew me from someplace."

"Did you know her?"

"No. Never met her before. And believe me, I would have remembered. I tried to ignore her but when I got up to go to the ladies' room, she followed me. When I opened the door to come out of the stall, there she was in all her glory. She was holding up her halter top. She asked me which tit I liked best. She kind of bounced them a little to give me a chance to decide."

Jordan laughed. "Was one better than the other?" she asked.

"If you'll pardon the pun, it was a toss up." Reece smiled reflectively.

"Are you telling me you had sex with Lucinda Alvarado in the ladies' room of the bar?"

"Hell no." Reece scowled up at her. "We did it in the men's room. It was a lesbian bar. No one was using the men's room." Reece gave a husky laugh.

"You didn't," Jordan scoffed. "In the men's room?"

"Oh yes I did. Of course, I was feeling no pain so I have no idea what I really did to her."

"Did you ever see Lucinda again? For a date, I mean."

"Nope. I heard a couple of weeks later that Lucinda picked me on a dare. She won a hundred bucks that night," Reece reported, trying to sound proud of her dubious selection.

"No, Reece. She didn't?" Jordan looked down into her eyes critically.

"Yes. I'm a hundred-dollar fucker." She laughed robustly. "Actually, I was chosen as the woman most likely to go home without a date on New Year's."

"Oh, Reece, baby. What a cruel thing to do." Jordan's eyes were full of compassion.

"Hey, not that many people can say they won a hundred-dollar bet for someone. Besides, it was no big deal. It didn't mean anything to me." Reece became defensive about her experience with Lucinda, as if she was sorry she brought it up. She eased Jordan off of her and climbed out of bed.

"Where are you going?" Jordan asked, noticing a change in Reece's demeanor.

"I thought we'd get ready to go to dinner," she said then went into the bathroom.

Jordan lay on the bed, staring at the ceiling and wondering what had happened. Reece seemed to have changed as quickly as a chameleon. She was happy and loving one moment, defensive and standoffish the next. Jordan went about dressing, making a special effort to look nice for Reece. It took her thirty minutes in front of the mirror before she was satisfied.

"Are we going today or tomorrow?" Reece called as she sat on the couch with her feet up on the coffee table.

"Today," Jordan said, stepping out of the bedroom. She was dressed in a pair of gray slacks and a silver sweater that clung in all the right places. It shimmered in the light as she walked across the room. She had tiny diamond earrings in her ears that sparkled through the soft cascades of her blonde hair. "I'm ready."

Reece looked over her shoulder and raised her eyebrows at Jordan's attire.

"Wow. Yes, you are," she declared, standing up. "And very nice, indeed." She looked Jordan up and down.

"Am I worth a hundred dollars?" she joked as she turned slowly for Reece to see.

Reece scowled at her but didn't answer.

"Reece?" Jordan said, following her out the door. "I didn't mean anything by it. I was just kidding." She reached out and took Reece's arm. "I'm sorry."

"You're not a hundred-dollar fuck. Never tell yourself that. I don't think it is a joke." Reece fixed Jordan with a determined stare then opened the door for her.

"I didn't mean—" Jordan began as Reece climbed in and started the engine, but thought better of it. She realized Reece was sensitive about her looks and the joke was taken wrong. She didn't want to hurt her feelings. It was the last thing she wanted to do. Jordan decided it was better left alone, at least for now.

Chapter 17

They made amusing conversation all the way to the restaurant. They stopped twice, once to watch a pair of eagles gliding over the treetops, then to admire the majestic, unrelenting waves crashing against the shore. Reece carried a digital camera with her and took several shots along the way.

The Landing, an older wood-framed restaurant, sat on a bluff overlooking the harbor. It had green siding worn bare by the onshore wind. The parking area was little more than a sandy lot with the perimeter marked by driftwood logs burnished to a white luster from years of exposure to the elements. The restaurant was partially filled with an eclectic mix of gay and straight couples, young singles and families. An elderly couple celebrated with a family gathering in the side room, an anniversary cake being shared by the guests at the long banquet table. Several people were sitting at the bar watching the large screened television, cheering an imminent Seattle Mariners victory. A pair of women played pool in the back room that contained a small dance floor and tiny stage. The ambiance was casual and friendly. Several people waved at Reece and shouted hellos. She shook hands with the owner, the bartender and several of the patrons.

"This looks like a fun place," Jordan said, taking off her jacket and getting comfortable at the table. "I can hardly wait. I can shoot pool again," Jordan teased, looking into the back room. "Will you teach me?"

"Maybe. Is it safe?"

"Sure it is. I'm a good student. I pick up things fast." Jordan winked.

"What would you like to eat?" Reece asked, studying the menu.

Jordan grinned broadly, a suggestive innuendo in her eyes. She giggled softly, succeeding in bringing a blush to Reece's face.

"For dinner, Ms. Griffin," Reece declared, tapping the menu.

"In that case, surprise me," Jordan replied. She propped her elbows on the table and leaned on her hands, watching Reece. "You didn't disappoint at Harry's Crab Shack so I trust you again."

"Can I help you?" a waitress asked. "Do you know what you would like?"

"Two filet mignon, medium-well, baked potatoes, Caesar salad. And a bottle of Sager's merlot. Anything else?" she asked, looking at Jordan for confirmation.

"That sounds wonderful. I haven't had a good steak in months and months."

"You'll like them here," Reece replied, handing the menu to the waitress.

"I'm sure if you like it, I will too." Jordan couldn't help it. She was flirting with Reece for all she was worth. It just felt like the right thing to do.

"You really do look nice this evening," Reece said, leaning back and enjoying the view across the table. "Thank you."

"Thank you for what?" Jordan asked, blushing a bit herself.

"For that extra thirty minutes you had me wait. It was well worth it. Do you always take that long to get ready?"

"Only for special occasions."

"I didn't think this place was considered that special," Reece advised.

"It isn't the place you go. It's the people you are with that make it special," Jordan replied softly.

"I'll remember that," Reece said, smiling over at her.

They sat staring at each other, both doing their best to send silent messages to the other in their gaze. They ate dinner, sipped wine and talked about their pasts. Jordan told about her childhood days in Colorado, growing up a college professor's daughter. She related how she and Hope shared sibling mothers. Reece confessed she was a brat as a child, constantly getting in trouble at school for asking too many questions and ignoring instructions. Reece was a good conversationalist, something Jordan couldn't say about all the women she dated. Many of them rattled on about themselves and their interests, ignoring Jordan completely. Jordan hated for the meal to come to an end. They had spent a lovely evening laughing, eating and smiling at one another, comparing the days of their youth and the obstacles to becoming a reporter.

"Okay, now it is time to work off your dinner," Reece said, standing up and holding the back of Jordan's chair.

"How are we doing that?" Jordan asked, looking up at her. "Jog down the beach?"

"Lord, help me, but we are going to play pool."

"Oh, goody," she replied, following her into the back room. "I'm sure I can do it this time."

Reece selected a cue for Jordan and one for herself. She racked the balls then broke, scattering them around the table and sinking two.

"Okay, your turn, Ms. Griffin." Reece stepped back.

"I thought if you got some in on your first hit, you got to go again."

"It's called the break. Not in this game," Reece replied. "You get to shoot."

Jordan circled the table, studying the choices. She had no idea which one she should choose.

"Any suggestions?" Jordan asked, circling again.

"The red one. It is right in front of the pocket, practically hanging on the lip. I don't think you can miss it."

"Okay," she replied, leaning over the shot. She lined it up, closed one eye, and stuck her tongue out the corner of her mouth as she struck the cue ball. It missed.

"I guess I was wrong," Reece muttered.

"Are you going to help me do this or just let me make a fool of myself?" Jordan asked with a scowl.

Reece gave a chuckle and stepped to the table.

"Okay, first of all, you have to get down over the shot. You are standing up too straight. You can't line it up that way. And next, you have to let the cue slide right under your chin. That is the only way you can tell where it is going. Like this," Reece said, demonstrating the technique. Jordan tried.

"Like this?"

"Here, put this hand back here." Reece slid her hand to the end of the cue. "And make a little bridge with the other hand. I thought I showed you this before." She formed Jordan's fingers into a gentle curve and rested the cue on it. "Now, slide slowly. Keep your chin right over the cue."

Jordan did as she was told. It still felt awkward but she was determined to do it correctly. Reece's touch made it all the more difficult to concentrate. Her smooth skin was like velvet. Jordan fought the urge to drop the cue and throw her arms around Reece, kissing her wildly and begging her to take her, right there on the pool table.

"Go ahead. Line it up and shoot again," Reece declared, watching as Jordan crouched over the shot.

Jordan closed one eye, held her breath and gave the ball a firm stroke. The cue ball struck the red ball forcefully, sending both balls skipping off the table and rolling across the floor. A waitress stopped one of the balls and scowled over at Jordan as she blushed with embarrassment.

"That's a little too hard, honey." The waitress set the ball on the table.

"I'll get the other one," Reece said, following the red ball as it rolled behind the bar and lodged under the ice machine.

The women at the next pool table chuckled at the errant shot, making the humiliation even worse for Jordan. She covered her face with her hands, groaning at the shot. Reece returned with the other ball and gently rolled it across the table.

"I know. I know. I can't play pool. And I can't hike or camp to save my life. I can't drive in the mud either." Jordan heaved a disgusted sigh.

Reece took the cue from Jordan's hand and returned it to the rack.

"Let's try something else," Reece offered. She took Jordan by the hand and led her toward the dance floor. A mirrored disco ball was spinning and several couples were dancing to something country. "How are you at dancing?" she asked, stepping onto the floor.

"Reece," Jordan complained, her face growing pale.

"Don't tell me you can't dance either," Reece frowned.

"Well, not to country-western music," she said hesitantly, taking a step back. "I can dance to other music but I've never been to a country-western bar before."

"No," Reece replied, pulling Jordan onto the floor with her. "I'm not taking no for an answer on this one."

She took Jordan in her arms and spun her around. Jordan didn't have a chance to decline as Reece maneuvered them across the floor, gliding effortlessly as the music played. In spite of her lack of experience, Jordan felt her movements totally controlled by Reece's commanding presence. They circled the floor, locked together in a perfect western two-step. Reece was light on her feet. Jordan relaxed in her arms and gave herself to the dance, surprised at how easy it was to follow. When the music stopped, several couples applauded their graceful style. Jordan blushed and walked off the floor, assuming Reece would follow. When she looked back, Reece was still on the dance floor. The music began again. This time it was a slow song dripping with country emotions. The other couples returned to dancing while Reece stood in the middle of the floor holding out a hand as if to call Jordan back to dance. Jordan moved into Reece's arms, their eyes greeting each other with a loving gaze. Finally Reece began to dance, gliding them easily around the floor. She pulled Jordan tighter to her, one hand drifting down Jordan's back, coming to rest just below her waist. Jordan closed her eyes and melted into her embrace. They drifted around the floor, not a word spoken between them.

At the end of the dance, Jordan looked up into Reece's eyes.

"I thought you said you couldn't dance," Reece whispered.

"Have we found something I can do?"

"Perhaps we have."

The music began again, another slow dance.

"Maybe we should try another one, just to make sure," Jordan said, remaining in Reece's arms. Reece swayed them into motion, once again guiding them in graceful arcs and turns. The other couples left the floor one by one, returning to their tables or the bar. Reece and Jordan were alone on the dance floor, moving in perfect unison to the music. Jordan closed her eyes and placed her head on Reece's shoulder, her fingers hooked through the belt loops on the side of Reece's jeans. She could feel Reece's heart pounding through her shirt. It was a comforting sensation, one that brought a small contented smile to Jordan's face.

"Hey, Reece," a woman's voice interrupted. "Who you got there?"

Jordan opened her eyes and saw a tall woman with a long graying ponytail standing on the dance floor, looking her up and down. Reece stopped dancing and released her hold on Jordan.

"Brandy, how are you?" Reece said, shaking the woman's hand. "I haven't seen you in months."

"I've been down south scoping a rag for the boss." Brandy carried on a conversation with Reece but kept her eyes on Jordan. "Aren't you going to introduce me?"

"Brandy, this is Jordan. Jordan, this is an old friend from my days with GNN. She and I covered several stories together back in the nineties."

Brandy offered Jordan a hand, smiling broadly at her. Jordan assumed she wanted to shake her hand so she accepted it. But Brandy had something else in mind. She took Jordan's hand and immediately spun her across the floor.

"You don't mind, do you sport?" Brandy said in Reece's direction, her arms tight around Jordan. "Jordan needs to dance with someone who knows how." She laughed and spun again. Jordan hung on to keep from falling as they moved wildly around the dance floor. Reece stepped back off the floor and watched as Brandy danced Jordan over every inch of the wood flooring, occasionally dipping and twirling her like a ballroom dancer. It was all Jordan could do to keep up with her. Reece went to the end of the bar to watch. She narrowed her eyes and studied them intently whenever Brandy's hand wandered too far down Jordan's back and onto her rear. Jordan couldn't see Reece's expression but she could feel her eyes watching them. When the music stopped, Jordan pulled away from Brandy's embrace and headed off the dance floor. Before she could get off the floor, the music started again with a faster song. Brandy grabbed Jordan and pulled her back into her arms.

"Come on, Jordan. Reece won't mind. One more dance for an old friend," Brandy grinned, awkwardly rubbing herself against her in a crude two-step. Jordan pushed her back, trying to get away but Brandy was a tall woman with a firm grip.

"We are not old friends, Brandy," Jordan said coldly.

Brandy laughed and spun her around, pressing herself against Jordan.

"We could be," she whispered, sticking her tongue in Jordan's ear. "Besides, I'm much better to look at in bed. Hell, I'm better to look at all the time."

Jordan felt herself instantly fill with rage. The remark struck a chord that ignited something deep inside. She glared up at Brandy, her blood pressure rising beyond anything normal.

"Let go of me," she said through her teeth. Brandy didn't. Jordan couldn't contain herself. She slapped Brandy across the face with all the force she could muster, the sound of it clearly heard above the music. Brandy instantly let go of her. Before Jordan could get away, Brandy slapped her back, knocking her down. Reece was on the dance floor like a shot, ready to defend Jordan's honor.

"You little slut," Brandy said, holding her cheek and scowling down at Jordan. Reece grabbed Brandy's arm and spun her around, her eyes flaming at Brandy's words and actions.

"What the hell are you doing?" Reece shoved Brandy into a table and went to help Jordan up. Brandy scrambled back to her feet and rushed Reece from behind, sending the two of them sprawling across the dance floor. Reece pushed her off and climbed to her feet, grabbing Brandy by the shirt collar.

"You're lucky I don't beat the ever-loving shit out of you," Reece said with clear and cold tones. She pushed her back then went to Jordan. "Come on. Let's go," she declared, leading her toward the door.

"Scarface," Brandy called after them. "Fucking scarface," she yelled even louder.

Reece didn't look back. She hustled Jordan out into the parking lot and opened the truck door for her. Jordan could see how incensed she was. Reece's jaw rippled with anger. She climbed in and started the truck, revving the engine wildly.

"Are you all right?" Reece asked finally, her words barely restrained.

"She didn't hurt me," Jordan said, touching Reece's arm gently.

"I should never have let her dance with you," she muttered, pulling out of the parking lot, slinging a plume of gravel behind the truck. "She was drunk."

"Why did you?" Jordan asked, studying Reece's face.

"I have no idea." Reece roared down the road, grinding through the gears.

"I shouldn't have slapped her."

"Why the hell not? She had her hands all over you." Reece looked over at her, her eyes still angry.

"That isn't why I slapped her."

"Why did you then?"

"Because of what she said," Jordan replied.

"What did she say?"

"She said she was better to look at." Jordan was ashamed to repeat it.

Reece shrugged and stared out the windshield.

"She's right," she muttered.

"Stop the truck," Jordan demanded, gripping Reece's arm tightly. Reece pulled onto the shoulder and skidded to a stop.

"What's wrong?"

"I have something to say and I don't want you to argue with me. Agreed?" Jordan stated.

"Okay," Reece replied skeptically.

"I don't think anyone is better looking than you." Jordan unhooked her seatbelt and slid over to Reece's side. "I love the way you look at me. I love the way your eyes tell me what you think. And I love the way you look. I don't see the scar," she said, her hand stroking Reece's cheek. "I see Reece McAllister."

"No, Jordan. The scar is there. It will always be there. It is part of me now. It marks me and who I am."

"Your scar is only skin deep, Reece. Don't let it go deeper." Jordan looked tenderly into her eyes.

"I see how people look at me. I see how disgusted they look."

Jordan pressed her fingers against Reece's lips.

"You don't see that in my eyes, do you?" Jordan whispered.

"No," Reece replied, diverting her gaze. "But that isn't the point."

"What is the point?"

"I don't want people to judge you by my looks." Reece looked at Jordan and placed a hand on her cheek. "You are so beautiful. And I am this hideous monster. You deserve better. You deserve someone as gorgeous as you are."

Jordan shook her head and pulled a slow smile.

"I've had that kind of woman. I've had the trophy dates. And they have had me. I've had the cover girl dates and the red carpet affairs. I've been wined and dined by women with large expense accounts and gorgeous hairdos. I've gone on ski trips to Aspen with women who looked like a movie star in their ski pants and tight sweaters. I've gone to the opera with women in thousand-dollar dresses and diamonds around their neck. I've ridden in convertibles to five-hundred-dollar-a-night getaways with women so rich they can't count it all. I've even been chased by women willing to spend a small fortune just to sit across the table from me and sip champagne. And do you know when I had the most fun?"

"Probably drinking champagne in a ski lodge," Reece replied.

"No. Sitting by the campfire with you and sipping your terrible coffee. My hair was a mess, my clothes were filthy, my feet hurt and I was scared to death a wild animal would attack me in the night. But I was with you. That is all that mattered. You were there and I was on cloud nine. My feet didn't hurt anymore. My heart was pounding in my chest and I didn't care what I looked like. I knew you would take care of me. Your eyes told me so."

"You've been away from your world too long. When you get back to Seattle you'll realize you have better choices." Reece folded Jordan's hands and placed them on her lap. "In the dark, everyone looks alike."

"In the dark, I can still tell who I love."

"Jordan, please. Don't say that. We are worlds apart." Reece started the truck. "We had a nice camping trip, a couple of dates. That's all. You got your story."

"Look at me, Reece. Look me in the eye and tell me you don't feel the same." Jordan turned Reece's face toward her and stared into her eyes. "Tell me you don't care about me the same as I care about you. Tell me you don't love me the same as I love you."

Reece hesitated, wrestling over her response. Her eyes studied Jordan for a long moment, first with adoration then cautious concern. Reece's expression went from love to pain in less than a second. She looked out the windshield and narrowed her eyes as she thought.

"I don't," she said finally, then pulled onto the road.

Jordan didn't reply. She didn't know what to say. She sat quietly, staring out the window as they drove along the winding road back to Greysome Point and Reece's cabin, the headlights carving out a path in the inky darkness. Jordan's mind was a jumble of emotion. Reece had been so caring and kind until she was confronted with Jordan's declaration of love. The evening had gone from passionate to lonely and Jordan didn't know how to fix it. A tear slowly rolled down her cheek. She could feel her heart breaking, but she didn't know what to say.

When Reece pulled off the road and followed the drive to her cabin, Jordan closed her eyes, not wanting to see the tight path carved through the woods. All she could think of was collecting her belongings and getting out of there as soon as possible. It didn't matter how late it was or how dark it had become, she wanted to go home. She wanted to throw herself onto her bed and cry her eyes out. She had fallen in love with Reece McAllister and she didn't love her back. She had confessed her feelings and came away with only heartache. How could she have misread this woman so badly? How could she have given herself so easily to her touch and embrace only to be brushed aside like so much garbage?

Reece parked next to Jordan's Civic. She turned off the engine but before she could say anything, Jordan had climbed out and slammed the door. She rushed inside the cabin and gathered her things, stuffing it all in her tote bag. She loaded it into the trunk of the car without saying a word. Reece stood watching, speechless. Jordan climbed in the driver's seat and started the car, fighting the tears that threatened to consume her.

"Where are you going?" Reece asked, opening the driver's door and looking in.

"I'm going home," she said, her voice trembling.

"Jordan, I didn't mean to hurt your feelings. I'm sorry. Please, wait. Spend the night. It's too late for a long drive. The ferry doesn't run at night."

"I'm going home," she repeated, keeping her eyes straight ahead.

"It's almost midnight," Reece said, scowling at her. "Don't be foolish."

Jordan snapped a look at her.

"That's my style. Admit it. You think everything I do is foolish," Jordan said, stiffening her posture. "I do the wrong thing and say the wrong thing."

"I never said anything of the kind," Reece declared, reaching in and turning off the engine. "Stay the night with me, Jordan. Please."

"Why would I want to do that?"

Reece squatted down and looked Jordan square in the eye.

"Ask yourself why."

Jordan stared back at her. She was fighting with herself over what to do and Reece knew it. She wanted desperately to stay, to sleep in Reece's arms all through the night and the next day and the next. But it would only be a temporary stay. Reece had made it clear she didn't share the same feelings. She didn't love her. Spending the night with her would be just for the fun of it, like a fleeting passion. Nothing more. It would be just like Reece had said, prostituting herself for the moment, sex for the sake of sex. That wasn't what Jordan wanted. She didn't want to sleep with Reece, to make love to her and then drive off in the morning like nothing had happened. She didn't want to extend their time together knowing it would still end with no promise of a future. She had been through those pointless relationships and she thought this one would be different. She thought this one would last. But she was wrong and it was killing her.

"I can't," she said. "I can't stay with you. There's a ferry leaving Kingston at five tomorrow morning and I'll be on it." She started the car again and pushed Reece back so she could close the door. She pulled away, searching for the entrance to the path.

Reece didn't offer any help. She stood on the back steps to the cabin, watching Jordan inch along the driveway. She finally found the opening and headed into the forest, her headlights piercing the darkness. Jordan accelerated, the sides of her car scraping the branches and bushes along the path as tears rolled down her cheeks. She pulled out onto the highway and headed for Port

Angeles, speeding around the curves and down the hills. Jordan's professional maturity was overwhelmed by her emotions. She felt the little girl in her emerge. Jordan had never fallen in love before. Not completely, totally in love. Not so deeply in love it hurt her all the way down to her soul to know she was in love alone.

Chapter 18

Jordan closed her office door and turned on the desk lamp, hoping to remain unnoticed, at least for a while. She didn't feel like visiting with anyone. She didn't want the copy girl to poke her smiling face in the office and offer to bring Jordan a donut from the break room. And she didn't want Mark's morning jokes or Susan's morning flirt. She wanted to be left alone to think. It was a work day but Jordan's mind was on anything but work. It was on Reece McAllister and the casual, almost indifferent way she cast off their growing relationship. Jordan couldn't believe she had read her so wrong. Something in Reece's kiss and the way she looked at Jordan made her think she too shared an attachment, a deep, loving attachment. Jordan leaned back in the chair and sipped her coffee, staring blankly at the poster of Mount Rainier hanging on the wall. It was the closest thing she had to a window to stare out of but it only reminded her of their camping trip. Jordan smiled as she remembered the rainy night they shared in Reece's tent.

Jordan closed her eyes and took a deep breath as if it could resurrect the sweet aroma of the pine forest in a gentle rain. She could almost see the way Reece had carefully arranged their two sleeping bags together and propped the tent flap open so Jordan could see outside, diminishing her claustrophobia. She could hear the rain in the trees, the heavenly sounds of nature in the woods. It brought a smile to Jordan's face. Waking in the morning to Reece's warm smile upon her brought on a soft sigh. Just then the telephone rang, making Jordan jump, spilling her coffee on her pant leg.

"Hello," she said, angry with herself for making a mess. She grabbed a tissue and began blotting the wet spot.

"Hey, Jordy. This is Hope. How's my cuz?"

"Hi, Hope. I'm fine. I just spilled my coffee all over my pants, but I'm fine. How are you? How was Denver?"

"Great. Mom says hi. Dad says don't take any wooden nickels, whatever that means. And your folks say why haven't you called this week."

"Is everyone okay? Did they all get off for their trip?" Jordan asked, dabbing some water on the spot.

"Yeah. Venice and Rome, look out. The four of them are on their way. By the way, did you know there is a new country-western gay bar in Denver? It's on Colfax. Way cool." Hope advised with a chuckle.

"No, I didn't know that."

"Oh, yeah. I forgot. Jordan Griffin doesn't frequent the country-western establishments, do you, Jordy?" She laughed robustly.

"I'll have you know I've been to one."

"Yeah? When?"

"Recently," she admitted.

"Did you wear cowboy boots and do the electric slide?" Hope teased.

"I didn't wear cowboy boots because I don't own any. And I don't know if I did that slide thing or not but I did dance."

"I don't believe it. My cousin, Jordan Griffin, danced at a country-western bar. Did you break a nail?"

"Do you need something, Hope, or did you just call to tease me about my dancing?"

"I called to ask if you wanted to go to lunch with me today. I'll be downtown and I thought we could go to that restaurant in Pike's Place Market, the one with the view over the bay. I can never remember the name of that place. You know, the one with the balcony."

"Athenian?" Jordan supplied.

"Yep, the one from 'Sleepless in Seattle'."

"Athenian."

"Can you meet me about one?" Hope asked. "I have a meeting and I don't think I can be there before that."

Jordan thought a moment. She didn't feel much like company today but she had to eat and maybe she would feel better after she got some work done.

"Sure, I can meet you at one o'clock. I'll look forward to it, hon. Thanks for asking me."

"Is everything all right, Jordy?" Hope asked cautiously. "You sound like something is bothering you."

"No," Jordan sighed. "I'm fine. I have a coffee stain on my tan slacks but I am fine. See you at one."

"Later," Hope said and hung up.

Jordan went to the ladies' room to do some damage control on the stain.

"This is going to look great when I go to lunch," she muttered to herself.

"What is?" Susan asked, coming out of a stall.

"Oh, hi, Susan. I spilled coffee all down my pants and I am meeting my cousin for lunch today."

"Coffee should come out," Susan said, studying the spill. "Cold water should float it right out."

Jordan dabbed water over it, creating a larger wet spot, but the stain was still visible.

"I don't think so. I am just making it worse."

"Take them off and let me try," Susan said, holding out her hand.

"What?" Jordan scowled.

"Oh, for heaven's sake, Jordan. This is the ladies' room. We are both women. Take off those nasty things and let me fix them for you. You don't want to wear that stain all day."

Jordan hesitantly unzipped her slacks and slipped them off. She felt an embarrassing blush rise over her face as Susan's eyes moved over her bare legs and lacy string bikinis. She pulled at her blouse, but it did little to cover her exposed panties. Susan's stare lingered over Jordan's crotch as if her clothing was transparent, making her uncomfortable. Finally, Susan turned her attention to scrubbing the stain from Jordan's slacks, rubbing them together under the faucet. After several minutes of effort, the soaking wet slacks were free of coffee. Susan wrung them out and held them up to the blower to dry.

"It's a good thing they are polyester or it would take years to dry under this thing," Susan joked, her eyes again scanning Jordan's body.

"Here, I can do that," Jordan insisted, reaching for her slacks and hoping they would offer cover from what Susan couldn't keep her eyes off of.

"Are you sure?" Susan asked, taking one long last look.

"Thank you, though. I'll tell Hope you saved the day," Jordan mused, trying to ignore Susan's stare.

"Anytime, Jordan." Susan smiled at her and patted her hip. "Anytime at all."

She finally left Jordan to dry her pants. It wasn't until she had left the ladies' room that Jordan relaxed her jaw. Whether it was Hope's invitation to lunch, the coffee stain or Susan's irreverent stare, Jordan found the will to work. She finished two stories and sent them off to layout. But the interest to work on Reece McAllister's story wouldn't come. She knew she should decide on how to do the story but she couldn't bring herself to do it. Not yet.

Jordan left the office and rode the bus down the hill to Pike's Place Market. She was early so she strolled the market, admiring the fresh flowers and watching the fish mongers tossing salmon to entertain the tourists.

"Hey, Jordy," Hope called over the crowd. She rushed up to Jordan and gave her a hug.

"Hi, cousin. You look chipper today. How was your meeting?" Jordan asked as they strolled back to the restaurant arm in arm.

"Damn thing was canceled. I waited a half hour before the secretary got around to telling me Matt was out of town."

"I'm sorry."

"Hey, I didn't mind. He's a schmuck anyway. So, tell me what you have been up to. What is this crap about you going to a country-western bar?"

"Let's find a table," Jordan said, pointing for her to follow the hostess as they went up the stairs and found a window table that looked out over Puget Sound. They ordered the luncheon specials and fawned over what kind of dessert they would have, if they had room. Jordan noticed the ferry leaving the dock, the ferry bound for Bainbridge Island. She stared at it blankly, her mind remembering the evening Reece took her to Harry's Crab Shack. It was also the night they returned to Jordan's apartment and barely got inside the door before they couldn't wait another moment to have each other.

"Jordan," Hope said, studying the small smile that curled her lip. "What are you thinking about, honey? You have the strangest look on your face."

"Nothing," she replied, lowering her eyes. "It was nothing."

"Uh-huh." Hope grinned at her. "Jordan, what went on last week while I was gone?"

Jordan heaved a deep sigh, stirring her fork through her salad. Hope reached over and touched her hand.

"Jordan, what is it, honey? Tell me."

"I have no idea what happened, Hope." She looked up at her with a pained expression.

"Does it have something to do with that woman you were trying to interview, the one with the scar across her face?"

"That isn't all there is to her, Hope," Jordan said defensively. "She was a television journalist, a very intelligent woman, an award-winning reporter. That scar isn't all there is to her." Jordan's voice had risen to an accusatory level.

"I'm sorry, Jordy. I didn't mean anything by it." Hope frowned at her, as if the tirade came out of the blue.

Jordan heaved a sigh and closed her eyes.

"I'm sorry, honey. I didn't mean to yell at you like that."

"Okay, now tell me what happened between you and this wonderful, award-winning, intelligent, journalistic woman." Hope placed her fork on her plate and folded her hands in her lap to listen.

Jordan looked at her a long moment, trying to read how receptive Hope would be for her explanation. Hope leaned forward and nodded support.

"I'm listening," Hope added with an understanding nod.

"Well," Jordan began cautiously.

"You are in love with her, aren't you?" Hope asked, touching Jordan's hand.

Jordan didn't know what to say. She hadn't mentioned one word of her adventures with Reece McAllister, yet Hope had read her completely.

"How did you guess that?"

"It's in your eyes. The moment I said anything against her, you sprang on me like a cat with your claws out. It is the same reaction you had at the club that night when I first saw her and gasped. You could have strangled me that night too. But this is stronger. Now you have put a personality behind your defensive zeal. You love her so much you can't see straight, if you'll pardon the pun," Hope teased. "It's okay, Jordy. Really. If you think she is wonderful, then so do I. Now tell me why you are so upset," Hope added, leaning back.

"The only thing I know for sure is that she has me completely confused. We went camping and don't even ask what kind of disaster that was. You loaned me the equipment, but you couldn't loan me the experience I needed to know what to do. I looked like an idiot out there."

"Is that what this is all about, your making a fool of yourself on a camping trip?"

"No, that is just where it began. I wanted to get an interview with her and finally she agreed. It took a fall in the thorns and sleeping in her tent but I got it." Hope opened her mouth when she mentioned sleeping in Reece's tent but Jordan stopped her before she could ask what that meant. "And no, I didn't sleep with her, just slept in her tent, Hope. I know good and well where your mind was going."

Hope gave a mischievous grin.

"Anyway, I thought we were getting along so well. It was a rocky start but she finally seemed to accept me and my questions. She even acted friendly toward me. She told me about her career, her challenges and awards, her various relationships and even her last partner, Pella Frann."

"The supermodel from the Eighties Pella Frann?" Hope asked, her eyes wide with envy.

Jordan nodded.

"My God, Jordy. That woman had the most gorgeous—" Hope started then stammered as if she couldn't decide what to say. "The most gorgeous everything." She laughed. "I had this fantasy about her." Hope leaned forward and whispered. "It had to do with her, a feather and a hammock." She winked at Jordan.

"I don't think I want to hear that," Jordan replied.

"Okay, so Reece told you all about her life. Then what?"

"She came by the office to deliver some videotapes of her work. She took me to dinner on Bainbridge Island. We had a wonderful time," Jordan related, a dreamy far-away look in eyes.

"And?" Hope said, waiting for her to come back from her dream world.

"Oh, where was I?"

"You and Reece were on Bainbridge Island, fucking your brains out."

"Hope!" Jordan chided, looking around to see if anyone had heard her comment.

"Well, did you?"

Jordan couldn't stop the blush that shot up over her face.

"You did," Hope declared. "Good for you, Jordy."

"We did not fuck our brains out on Bainbridge Island," Jordan whispered, leaning in and scowling at her.

"Where then? On the ferry in the backseat of her car?"

"NO! Besides, she has a pickup truck."

"What kind?" Hope asked playfully.

"I have no idea. A Toyota Tundra, I think. And before you ask, it is black."

"Wow. Nice truck. Now, where is it you and this woman—" Hope started.

"Hope!" Jordan interrupted. Another blush reddened her face. She lowered her eyes as she remembered the tender moment on her living room floor.

"Come on, Jordy. Tell me," Hope pleaded, leaning in.

"My apartment," she said softly.

"Where?"

Jordan looked around then allowed a slow grin to crawl across her face.

"Just inside the front door on the living room floor," she added.

"I knew it," Hope said, laughing and slapping the table. "You were hot for her. You couldn't keep your hands off of her. It is only twenty feet from your front door to your bedroom and you couldn't even wait that long. I love it." Hope smiled broadly.

"Will you stop that," Jordan said, frowning at her and the attention she had attracted.

"I'm sorry, Jordy, but I think it is great. How long has it been since you couldn't wait to have someone? Who have you ever been so totally consumed with that you couldn't wait fifteen seconds to get into the bedroom? There is hope for you yet, cousin." Hope beamed broadly at her.

"Yes, well, she doesn't feel the same about me," Jordan said, looking away.

"What do you mean?"

"I told you about going to a country-western bar?"

Hope nodded.

"She and I were dancing and one of her friends was there. She was this tall woman with hands like an octopus and an evil sense of humor. She made some crack about being better looking than Reece. Well, I slapped her. She slapped me back and that's when Reece came to my rescue. Later I told her what her friend said and she agreed. She thought I would be better off with someone else. I told her I cared deeply about her but she didn't feel the same about me."

"You told her you loved her, right?"

Jordan nodded.

"And she said she didn't love you?"

"Yes," Jordan admitted solemnly. She looked up at Hope, tears glistening in her eyes.

"Oh, honey. I'm so sorry."

"I've never been so wrong about someone in my life."

"First things first. Are you sure about your feelings for this Reece what's her name?"

"McAllister," Jordan said. "And yes. I'm sure. At least I thought I was. It was a beginning, a good beginning, I thought."

"Is it possible she has someone else?" Hope asked carefully.

"No, I don't think so. She said she lives alone and she likes it."

"Do you think she has any feelings for you at all?"

"I thought so. I truly thought so."

"Is this Pella Frann person still around?"

"No. Reece said they broke up and she hasn't seen her in three years."

Hope wrinkled her brow in thought.

"And Reece is definitely gay?" Hope asked softly.

Jordan smiled slightly.

"Oh, yes, definitely gay."

"What do you plan to do about Ms. McAllister?"

"I have no idea." Jordan replied, pushing her salad back, her appetite waning.

"Do you want her, Jordan?" Hope asked seriously.

"Not if she doesn't want me," she replied.

"That is not what I asked."

"Hope, I can't answer that. I just know I felt like we were developing a relationship and not simply because I was interviewing her. I felt it was more. I felt it was much deeper than that."

"I see only one answer for you, Jordy."

"What is that?"

"Go get her."

"Don't be silly. You don't *go get* Reece McAllister. She is a strong-willed independent woman. She is totally in control of her destiny. She doesn't need me or anyone else in her life."

"I don't know about that. I can't believe she isn't the slightest bit self-conscious about her looks. You can't tell me she doesn't worry about what people think of her when they see her. And don't jump down my throat but you have to admit she does turn heads."

"I told her it doesn't bother me. And it truly doesn't. Yes, it was a shock the first time I saw it. I didn't expect it. But it isn't who she is. She is so much more than that scar."

"It may not bother you but it might bother her."

"She seems to handle it all right. She just ignores those stares she gets. She seems very strong when it comes to the looks and stares she gets."

"How did it happen?"

"She fell through a plate glass window. It was an accident."

"And plastic surgeons couldn't help?"

Jordan shook her head.

"They tried but her skin tone and the depth of the scarring made it impossible to cover. It might have even made it worse," Jordan replied.

"Jordan, cousin, sweetheart. You have a problem. I don't know what to tell you other than to say if you want her and love her, your path is set. And remember, you are a strong-willed woman yourself. Hell, I've never seen anyone so focused when it came to getting what you want." Hope looked at her watch. "Shit. I have to

219

go. But call me, Jordy, day or night. I want to help. I'm here for you if you need to talk."

"Thanks, honey." Jordan followed Hope down the stairs and hugged her good-bye. She couldn't decide if her admission to Hope helped or made it worse. She knew the afternoon would be filled with thoughts of Reece and what had gone wrong. She caught the bus and went back to work. Somewhere in the back of her mind she was arguing with herself over whether she should do what Hope had said, go after her. But the fact remained—Reece didn't love her.

Chapter 19

"Jordan, I have a message for you from Susan," one of the interns said, sticking her head in Jordan's office. "She wants to know when you will have the McAllister story ready or at least a rough draft. She said you are supposed to get on with it. At least that is the gist of what she said." The girl raised her eyebrows as if Susan's message was frivolous, to say the least. "Any reply?"

"I'm heading home," Jordan said, filling her briefcase with folders and notes. "Tell Susan I'll have something on the McAllister story maybe tomorrow. If she doesn't like it, tell her—" Jordan stopped herself before saying something she might regret.

"Tell her what?"

"Tell her I have a headache and I'll work on it at home."

"Okay, but if you ask me—"

"Kim, if you want a word of advice from someone who has been around a bit longer than you have—"

"Don't say it, Ms. Griffin. I know. Keep my mouth shut and do my job. Right?"

Jordan smiled coyly at her.

"See you tomorrow, Ms. Griffin," Kim said, heading up the hall.

"Thanks for delivering the message, Kim," Jordan called as she followed her down the hall on her way to the elevator.

Jordan drove home, fixed herself a cup of herbal tea, turned on the television and popped one of the DVDs into the player. It was a scratchy copy of Reece's early days as a reporter for a Seattle television station. She was dressed in an oversized ski parka with a fur-trimmed hood circling her face. She was reporting on a record snowfall and the booming ski industry while standing knee deep in fresh powder at the Summit at Snoqualmie Pass. Her face looked pink and chapped as the wind whipped around her, blowing the snow against her cheeks.

"Oh, Reece, you look so young," Jordan mused, sipping her tea and smiling at the television.

The next clip was from the top of the Space Needle. Reece was covering the newly redecorated restaurant and the newly raised prices. Reece was dressed smartly, looking very much like a professional woman. The clips of her first two years included everything from covering house fires and traffic accidents to interviewing public officials and visiting dignitaries. Jordan noticed how articulate she was, even when her subject was hesitant. Reece had a camera presence even in her early years when she was limited to a few precious seconds of air time. Her questions were thought-provoking and probing but an empathy came across on the screen. Jordan noticed Reece's hairstyle had changed over the years from long, straight and fly-away to a shorter cut with soft bouncy curls that stayed out of her face when the wind blew. Jordan knew reporters, men and women, wore makeup while on camera to mask that washed-out anemic look but it was hard to tell if Reece was wearing much—she looked so natural.

Jordan changed the disc and settled back on the couch as Reece began her career with GNN. Her first assignment was just as Reece had said, covering hurricane preparations in the Florida

Keys. She was standing on a beach, holding a ball cap on her head and reporting the size of the ocean swells. Rain had begun to dampen her shirt and the wind was blowing it back and forth, occasionally exposing a patch of stomach.

The next clip was from Homestead, Florida. Reece was interviewing one of the civil defense workers on storm shelters and supplies available to the evacuees. Jordan studied Reece's face as she interviewed the official. She had a look of deep concern as she repeatedly asked the worker what he needed and if he was all right. Jordan replayed a section of the clip, trying to listen to Reece's voice. She couldn't be sure, but it sounded like her voice cracked as she asked about injuries to the local residents.

Jordan continued watching the clips, making notes on types of coverage and assignments. As Reece's experience grew, so did the importance of her assignments. Jordan watched her interview several members of European royalty, Hollywood celebrities and government notables. She was always respectful yet inquisitive in her interviews. She had learned the art of rephrasing a question so she could extract an answer from even the most resistant public figure.

"She's not going to tell you that," Jordan said out loud as Reece asked a film star if she was planning on marrying her present boyfriend. "Oh, my God. She told you that?" she gasped as the woman admitted she was. "Don't believe her, Reece. Everyone knows she's gay."

Reece's next question hit the topic right on the head. She asked the young beauty if she ever had fantasies that involved women. The celebrity blushed bright red and laughed robustly then signaled for the interview to end.

"Told you," Jordan muttered, going to change the disc.

She turned up the volume and went into the kitchen to make a sandwich for dinner. She craned her head around the corner when an interesting segment came on.

"Miss Frann, can you tell me when you knew you wanted to become a model?" Reece's voice asked. Jordan came flying out of the kitchen, holding a knife full of mayonnaise.

"I was very young." Pella's voice was heavy with a French accent. Her eyes were sky blue and her makeup was impeccable. She was wearing a low-cut spaghetti strapped dress with a diamond necklace nestled into her ample cleavage. She seemed to know how to work the camera to her best advantage. She tossed her long brunette hair so that soft cascades floated sensuously over her shoulders. She moistened her lips so the light glistened on them when she spoke. When she smiled there were no telltale wrinkles at the corners of her mouth or eyes like most people have. She had the smoothest skin Jordan had ever seen. "I don't remember when I first knew I wanted to be a model but I know it is all I ever wanted to do." The words dripped off her tongue like French champagne.

"My God, no wonder you fell for her, Reece," Jordan muttered. "She's gorgeous."

Jordan sat on the arm of the couch watching intently. She studied Pella's face and the way she played to the camera, flirting with Reece as well as the viewers. She would occasionally flip her long hair then lean into Reece, her breast rubbing Reece's arm. Pella occasionally stumbled over her words, substituting a French word when she couldn't think of the English word she wanted to use. Reece asked her about modeling, current fashions, traveling the world and the sudden financial success she enjoyed. Pella answered each question dutifully. She seemed to prefer the questions about her rise to success, the ones that referred to her sparkling beauty and her discovery by a top Paris modeling agency when she was only nineteen. Jordan heard no reference to Pella's age. That was something she would have to research, she thought. Jordan noticed Reece's eyes. She seemed lost in Pella's beauty, watching her every move and gesture in pure devotion.

"Watch out, Reece. You're going to start drooling on her," Jordan mused. She pushed the pause button and went to finish making her sandwich. She set her plate on the coffee table and sat cross-legged on the floor then restarted the DVD.

When Reece asked how many years she had been modeling, Pella didn't answer the question. Instead she quickly changed the subject, lavishing compliments on Reece's hairstyle, her big brown eyes and her shoes.

"*Où avez-vous acheté vos chaussures?*" Pella asked, pointing at Reece's loafers.

Reece stammered a moment, blushing at the compliments.

"Thank you. But I don't understand that much French," she replied.

"I'm sorry," Pella said with a giggle. "I asked where you bought your shoes."

"Yes, you did," Jordan said with a frown. "But you didn't say it right." She dropped the sandwich on the plate and grabbed the remote. She pushed the rewind button and played it again, turning up the volume.

"*Où avez-vous acheté vos chaussures?*" Pella asked.

Jordan replayed the clip several times, listening carefully to Pella's words and pronunciation.

"Your structure is all wrong, lady. A Frenchman wouldn't say that. That isn't street talk. That is book language. You should have said *vous avez acheté vos chaussures où*," Jordan said, playing it one more time. "I don't think you are as French as you want us to believe, Ms. Frann."

Jordan listened to the rest of the clip, hoping to catch another mistake but Pella didn't use more than a French word here and there. Jordan continued watching clips, skipping ahead through repetitious war stories and interviews with foreign dignitaries, hoping to find more interviews with Pella but there were none. On the last DVD, Jordan watched Reece accompany U.S. troops into Kuwait, Afghanistan and Iraq. She wore an army helmet and flak vest while she interviewed a soldier. He was eighteen years old from a small town in Iowa with a death grip on his weapon and a terrified look in his eyes. His voice was shaking as he told Reece his name and rank. She tried to calm him by asking what kind of truck he drove back home and if he rooted for Iowa or Iowa State. By the end of the interview, the boy was relaxed enough to wave to his family back home and tell his high school sweetheart he loved her.

He showed Reece the picture of her he had taped to the inside of his helmet.

The last clip on the DVD was one with a senator from Washington State. They were discussing the gay civil rights amendment that had slowly growing support in the state legislature. Jordan studied Reece's face. The clip was before the accident since both of her cheeks were smooth and clear.

"You were a gorgeous woman yourself, Reece," Jordan muttered, pressing the pause button at a moment when Reece was smiling at the camera. "What a shame. What a terrible shame, Reece." Jordan sat staring at Reece's smile, her face frozen on the screen. Jordan got up and went to the television. She held her hand over Reece's left cheek where the scar cut across. "You're still a gorgeous woman, sweetheart," she whispered. "I don't know what is going on with Pella Frann but she has nothing on you." Jordan let her fingers linger over Reece's lips, remembering their softness. The memory of Reece's words telling her she didn't love her was the only thing that came between Jordan and a smile.

The telephone rang and drew Jordan back from the memory.

"Hello," she said.

"Hey, Jordy," Hope said, chewing a bite of something crunchy.

"How's the world's best event planner?" Jordan asked, flopping down on the couch, ready to be distracted from her melancholy mood.

"I don't know. Give me her phone number and I'll call and ask her."

They laughed.

"Hey, Jordy. Are you busy Monday night?" Hope asked.

"I don't think so. What's up?"

"It's Stephanie's birthday, Barbara's sister. And yes, I know you and Stephanie don't get along real well, but we are taking her out to dinner at the Garage, that place you and I went to a few weeks ago. Remember? They had the pool tables."

"I remember." Jordan instantly remembered the moment Reece came to help her shoot the ball.

"Jordy, are you there?" Hope asked, listening to the silence on Jordan's end of the telephone.

"I'm here. You are taking Stephanie to the Garage for her birthday."

"It isn't very glamorous but we asked her where she wanted to go and that is what she picked. She likes to go places where she can wear jeans. How about coming along with us?"

"Thanks anyway but I don't think so." Jordan's mind was still remembering Reece and the way she stormed out of the establishment the night she and Hope had found her there.

"Oh, come on, Jordan. I bet you need to get out and socialize. It will do you good, honey. Really. Come have a great hamburger, a drink, maybe dance a little. It'll take your mind off of her."

"Off who?" Jordan asked.

"Jordan," Hope scoffed. "You know exactly who I mean. Reece McAllister, that's who."

Jordan heaved a heavy sigh. She didn't realize how transparent she was.

"You can laugh a little, maybe get a little drunk. It's the perfect prescription for what ails you, cousin," Hope insisted.

"I didn't know there was anything ailing me."

"Come on. Go with us," Hope whined.

Jordan thought a moment.

"Okay," she said. "I'll go. But I'm not getting drunk, Hope. So don't push it."

"Fine with me. You want us to pick you up?"

"No. I'll meet you there. What time?"

"About seven. How's that?" Hope asked.

"I'll see you there. And thanks for asking me, honey."

"And don't get all dressed up for this, Jordy. Don't wear one of your business suits. Go casual, okay?"

"All right. Casual," Jordan chuckled.

"See you, honey." Hope hung up before Jordan could act on her second thoughts. Her palms became sweaty at the thought she would go back to where she and Reece had first touched.

Chapter 20

Jordan found herself fixated with Pella's interview. At first she thought it was just jealousy that made her unable to ignore it but the more she thought about it, the more she knew something was strange about this French model. It wasn't much to go on, but Jordan knew her language wasn't that of a native Parisian. A real Frenchwoman she was not. Jordan felt it.

She arrived at work early, rolled up her sleeves and began to dig through the archives for anything she could find on Pella Frann—her age, her work history, anything. She found an old layout for a swimsuit company with some tiny words printed along the margin of the photograph. It took a magnifying glass but she could read Mitchell, Prine & Shultz. That was all she needed. Mitchell, Prine & Shultz was one of the largest modeling agencies in New York City. It had offices in London, Paris and Los Angeles.

"Mitchell, Prine & Shultz," a receptionist said in a clear and professional telephone voice. "May I help you?"

"Hello. My name is Jordan Griffin and I am assistant editor for *Northwest Living Magazine*. I am interested in talking with an agent about one of your models," Jordan said, studying her computer screen at the list of agents in their New York office. "Is Richard Holcomb in his office?"

"No, I'm sorry he is in a meeting. Can I take a message?" she said in a voice Jordan knew meant he didn't take calls, he returned them if he wanted to talk to you.

"Is there anyone I could speak with," Jordan asked, deciding if she should create an elaborate scenario about how the magazine needed a model with all of Pella Frann's attributes, her age being the key factor or if she should just come clean about her interest in her.

"Could you hold for one moment, please?" she said then clicked Jordan to music. A minute later she returned. "I am going to connect you with Patrice Fowler. She is one of our assistant coordinators. She will be able to help you, I'm sure."

Jordan knew that the translation for "assistant coordinator" meant someone's secretary, usually one who had been there a while and knew as much as the agent, if not more.

"Hello, this is Patrice Fowler. May I help you?" the woman said in a slow but polite voice.

"Hello, Miss Fowler. I'm Jordan Griffin with *Northwest Living Magazine*. I was hoping to talk with an agent about one of your models."

"Who would that be, Miss Griffin?"

"Pella Frann." Jordan decided it was better to say as little as possible, allowing Miss Fowler to guess why a magazine was interested in the model. She hoped less would be more when it came to getting information.

Patrice laughed.

"Did I say something funny, Miss Fowler?" Jordan asked.

"No. I am sorry, but I thought we had heard the last on that subject, Miss Griffin."

"What do you mean last? And please, call me Jordan."

"We no longer have Pella Frann under contract. She hasn't worked for us in almost five years," Miss Fowler explained, almost proudly.

"I thought she was with you. Do you know if she changed agencies?" Jordan asked.

"Ms. Frann retired. I heard she worked for a short time on her own but she is fully retired now, I'm sure," Patrice replied. "And good riddance to her," she muttered.

"I beg your pardon."

"Nothing. I'm sorry, Jordan. But Pella Frann isn't available. If you need a model, I am sure we can find the perfect match for your needs."

"No, I don't need a model. I was just interested in talking to Pella or her agent. Do you have any idea which agency she went with after she left yours?" Jordan asked, not satisfied with the information she had gotten so far.

"I have no idea," Patrice replied, becoming indifferent with the conversation.

"So you don't know where I can get a hold of her?"

"No, I do not." There was a pause then Miss Fowler continued as if she was cupping her hand against the receiver. "A word of advice, even though she sounds French, don't bother looking overseas for her. Even if you could find Pella Frann you'll wish you hadn't," she said quietly then hung up.

"Hello, Miss Fowler. Hello." Jordan sighed and hung up the receiver. She redialed the number, but when she asked the receptionist if she could talk with Patrice Fowler she was told Miss Fowler was in a meeting and couldn't be disturbed. The subject of Pella Frann was closed.

Jordan leaned back in her chair and stared at the ceiling.

"Don't look overseas," she muttered to herself. "Where do I look?" Jordan Googled Pella Frann but found only publicity shots from years ago and ads with her gorgeous body plastered across the screen. "Nice belly button, Pella," she declared as she scanned the shots. "But where are you now?" Jordan did a chronological search starting with when she was a new face in the modeling industry. She changed her hairstyle over the years but her face and her body stayed young and fresh. She modeled for everything from swimwear to motorcycles, athletic apparel to cruise travel. She often wore little more than a string bikini and a smile, her long seductive hair blown by artificial wind and sand strategically stuck on her golden tanned legs.

Jordan dialed her archive department.

"Jerry, this is Jordan again. Tell me, how far back can you go? Do you have anything before the magazine changed owners and names?"

"Sure. Actually, I can go back about thirty years. I have all of the issues of *Tidewater* and most of the issues of *The Puget Sound Magazine*. I've transferred most of them on disk. What do you need, Jordan?"

"Can you see how far back you have anything on Pella Frann?" she asked.

"I thought we already did a search on her," he replied.

"We only went back through our issues. I need earlier than that."

"Exactly what am I looking for?" Jerry asked.

"A name, a city, anything that tells me something about her past. I am hoping to find a date of birth and a birth city."

"Okay, but it may take a while," he groaned.

"Give me a call if you find anything, Jerry. And thanks," Jordan said. Within a minute her telephone rang.

"Hello," she said, still scrolling through her computer search.

"I forgot to tell you something I did find this morning," Jerry said. "Did you see the ad in our January issue of ninety-eight? There was an ad for jeans with her in it. I remember that ad," he chuckled. "She was wearing a pair of tight jeans and a bikini top made out of a red bandana. That is all she was wearing. I remember it because it was taken on Mercer Island. You can see the Space Needle in the background and the only place that has that view is the bridge to Mercer Island. I don't know if it is any help but I thought I would let you know. I'll let you know if I find anything else," he said then hung up.

"Mercer Island, eh?" she muttered, bringing up the issue on her screen and zooming in on the ad. "Who took the shots?" She squinted at the photo credits. "You're kidding? Rene?" Jordan grabbed for her telephone. "Is Rene down there?" she asked the man who answered the call.

"Yeah, somewhere," he replied.

"Don't let her leave. This is Jordan and I will be right down." Jordan said, jumping to her feet as she hung up the telephone. She hurried down the elevator to the photography department.

"Rene, can I talk with you a minute?" Jordan asked, waiting for her to look up.

"Hey, Jordan," she said, continuing to work over the photographs. "Did you see the shots of the Botanical Society presentation? I can't believe I didn't see those dogs."

"Yeah, I saw them. Susan said block it out and forget it."

"I know. She told me that too."

"That isn't why I came down. I need to ask you about a shoot you did with Pella Frann several years ago."

"Who?" Rene asked, looking up with a frown.

"Pella Frann. It was an ad for jeans back before you came to work for the magazine," Jordan offered.

"Oh, yeah. I was working freelance."

"You did the shoot on Mercer Island, right?"

"Yeah, I think so. That was a long time ago," Rene replied, furrowing her forehead as she tried to remember.

"Do you remember anything about Pella Frann?"

"Gosh, you are asking me to remember one of hundreds of subjects I have photographed. Maybe thousands." Rene looked at the ceiling as she tried to find a memory of Pella and the assignment. "Could you give me a hint of what I am supposed to be remembering?"

"Pella Frann was a tall, gorgeous brunette."

"Most models are, Jordan." Rene chuckled.

"She had a French accent."

"French? Oh, yeah. I remember. The one with the ego."

"Ego?" Jordan asked.

"She was the one obsessed with her looks. She never lifted a finger to help do anything. On these freelance shoots, everybody carries something down to the site. She wouldn't even carry the makeup case."

"So she was difficult to work with?" Jordan suggested.

"Difficult? Hell, Jordan, she was a pain in the ass. That shoot should have taken an hour, tops. All I needed was one view. It was all researched. I had the spot all worked up and the angles all set. I was going to bracket the shots for exposure and be done with it." Rene shook her head and frowned disgustedly. "It took four hours. Four freaking hours. All because her majesty wanted her makeup checked and retouched after every shot. The poor makeup girl worked harder than anyone else on the shoot. By the time I had the shots I needed, the sun was going down and I had to change my settings. It worked out okay but I would never work with her again."

"Sounds like a pretty high-strung model, even for the French," Jordan teased.

"I'll tell you, I wasn't so sure she was French. I know, she's got an accent but I asked her about some places I worked in France and she had no idea where they were."

"I've lived in Seattle several years and I have never been to the top of the Space Needle. Maybe she just wasn't well-traveled," Jordan argued.

"If you are an international model, French or not, you have worked a photo shoot in Nice or Cannes. It's on the French Riviera, for God's sake. Most models have shots taken along the coast in their portfolios. Also, when I mentioned the Cote d'Azur, she didn't know where it was," Rene said.

"The Blue Coast," Jordan supplied.

"Yes, that's what Europeans call the French Riviera."

"Do you remember any reference to her age? You know, for

thirty, you look good, Ms. Frann. Something like that?" Jordan asked.

"No, I don't remember anything like that. I know she had to be old enough to have a smallpox vaccination. She had the little circle on her arm. She insisted the makeup girl cover it completely. That or she refused to expose that arm to the camera."

"Did she say anything about where she was born or where she called home?"

"Sorry, Jordan. I don't remember. Besides, she didn't talk much. I was the lowly photographer there to capture her essence on film, that's all. She didn't have much use for me. And I didn't have much use for her, either."

"Who was she working for at the time? What agency? Mitchell, Prine and Shultz?"

"Yeah, I think that's who it was."

"Anything else you remember?" Jordan asked, hoping for a tidbit of information that would lead to the mysterious Pella Frann.

"Sorry. I think my brain blotted out most of my work with her. It was a perfectly forgettable experience." Rene chuckled.

"Thanks, Rene. You were a big help." Jordan smiled at her and patted her back.

"Are you working on a story about her?"

"No, just reference on another story," Jordan replied, turning to leave.

"Have fun," Rene said then went back to her layout.

Jordan returned to her office and spent the rest of the day following every lead she could find to track down Pella Frann. She ignored work on two other stories as she became immersed in her search. Her journalistic curiosity morphed into an obsession that wouldn't be satisfied until she had the complete story, even though Reece had asked her to ignore Pella's history.

It was after six when she turned out the desk lamp and headed to the Garage and Hope for a night out with the girls. As Jordan drove across town, she wished she had called to cancel the dinner.

She wasn't in the mood for a birthday party. Her brain was a tangled web of facts and curiosity about the elusive Ms. Frann. There may not be anything unusual, but something nagged at Jordan about the woman. She wondered if it was no more than her connection to Reece that made her obsess over the model. Somewhere in the back of her mind, she knew Reece and Pella had been partners, lovers. Jordan believed that Reece knew every detail about the woman. But Reece gave Jordan limited information. Maybe Reece didn't believe in kiss and tell, Jordan thought, but she wanted to know more. She wanted to know why they were no longer together. Why was Reece alone?

Chapter 21

Hope, Barbara and Stephanie were already on their first drinks when Jordan arrived at the Garage. Even for a Monday night, the club was crowded. Some were eating dinner, some playing pool, some mingling around the bar. The back room bowling lanes were full as well. The dance floor was crowded with both straight and gay couples dancing to something rock.

"Jordan, over here," Hope called, standing at the railing. Jordan weaved her way through the crowd and joined them at a table in the dining area.

"Hi Barbara. Hi Stephanie," Jordan said, giving everyone a hug. "Happy Birthday, Stephanie."

"Thanks, hon. I'm glad Hope talked you into coming along. Four is a much better number than three." Stephanie was a thirty-something woman with dishwater blonde hair and wire-framed glasses. Her earrings looked like Christmas tree ornaments with beads and sparkles whipping her neck whenever she turned her head. She was wearing the tightest jeans Jordan had ever seen and a long sleeve T-shirt with a picture of a race car on it. She didn't look anything like Barbara. They resembled sisters in no way, whatsoever. Barbara was a tall brunette with huge brown eyes and a large bustline.

"What are you drinking, Jordy?" Hope asked, leaning in and yelling over the the music and noise.

"I have no idea," Jordan replied. "How about a glass of water with lemon?"

"I don't think so," Hope smirked. "How about a strawberry daiquiri or maybe a margarita? You look stressed. Come on. Loosen up."

"I am not stressed. I'm pensive over what to order," Jordan replied, looking at what everyone was drinking.

"I'm having a Hurricane," Stephanie announced. "It has rum and grenadine in it." The drink was served in a tall hurricane shaped glass with streaks of red running through the orange colored fruit juice. She twirled the umbrella as she took a long sip.

"Too much fruit juice," Hope advised and shook her head, discouraging that choice.

"Get a double something, Jordan," Barbara said, holding up her glass that looked like a double bourbon on the rocks. "No pain, no gain."

"I don't need any pain," she frowned.

Hope stood up and waved the waitress over.

"I'll have a margarita, frozen, no salt," Jordan said.

"Anyone else?" the waitress asked.

"Are we ordering or what," Stephanie asked, making a large dent in her drink then ordering another.

"Let's get a pizza. One of those jumbo jobs they serve on the little cake stand," Barbara said brightly.

"Anything is fine with me, but no anchovy on it, please." Jordan wrinkled her nose at the thought.

"Gag me with a spoon," Stephanie quipped. "And no onions."

"Why no onions?" Hope asked sternly. "I like onions."

"Yeah, but they don't like you," Barbara teased.

"Okay, jumbo supreme, no fish and no farters," Hope announced. The waitress took the order and returned to the kitchen. "Come on Barb. Let's dance. I like this song. You can apologize to me for saying I smell."

"I didn't say you smell. I said onions didn't agree with you," Barbara argued.

Hope took Barbara by the hand and pulled her onto the dance floor.

"I heard you are working on a story about that GNN reporter," Stephanie said, yelling above the noise.

"Yes," Jordan replied.

"I also heard she retired because she got some horrendous scar across her face."

Jordan didn't want to discuss Reece's life with this soon-to-be intoxicated woman.

"I haven't got the whole story yet," Jordan advised and shrugged her shoulders, hoping it would discourage further questions on the subject.

"Tell me, is she as tall as she looked on television?"

Jordan nodded and sipped her drink.

"Cool," Stephanie said, slurping the bottom of her drink.

"How old are you this year, Stephanie?" Jordan asked, hoping to divert the conversation.

"God, don't even mention it. Thirty-five. Can you believe it? Thirty-fucking-five. My life is practically over the hill and I don't have a girlfriend or a boyfriend or anything."

Jordan hoped the pizza arrived soon or the birthday girl was going to be crying in her Hurricane. Stephanie seemed to be headed for one of her poor-pitiful-me moods and Jordan didn't want to hear it. She was young, attractive, healthy and gainfully employed as medical transcriber at a large Seattle hospital. She had no reason to be unhappy unless she chose to be. Stephanie was openly bisexual and had dated dozens of people, trying to find the right one. Jordan suspected Stephanie's problem was in her attitude and the bottom of a drink.

Stephanie waved the waitress over and ordered another Hurricane.

"Come on, Steph," Jordan said, standing up. "Let's dance before you get yourself drunk." Jordan was willing to sacrifice herself to keep Stephanie from getting soused in the first hour of her birthday party. Stephanie weaved her way through the tables, dancing with herself all the way to the dance floor.

Jordan danced discreetly to the rock music, trying to stay at the edge of the dance floor where she wouldn't feel confined. Stephanie quickly became lost in the music, gyrating like a go-go dancer. She seemed oblivious to anyone around her, occasionally bumping into fellow dancers. There was no gap between the songs. Before Jordan knew it, they had danced to three songs, her forehead moist from the exercise and crowded spaces.

"Pizza," Hope yelled at them, noticing the waitress delivering the pizza to their table. They filed off the dance floor, Hope leading the way. Stephanie followed her sister, still dancing in the aisle as she made her way to the table.

"I love to dance," Stephanie said, flopping down in her chair and flipping her hair dramatically. "But only the fast songs. I don't dance to the slow stuff."

"Why not the slow songs?" Jordan asked, curious why anyone wouldn't want to dance to sensuous and intimate slow music. She tore off a piece of pizza and fought with the cheese strings that followed the slice to her plate.

"Slow music is nothing but a disaster. Guys can't dance slow. They just use it for an excuse to feel you up. Girls are no better. They always want to lead and then they want you to follow them to their car in the parking lot. Sometimes I just want to dance. No expectations of sex. You can't do that when you slow dance. Sooner or later, they always want to get in your pants." Stephanie rolled her slice of pizza into a tube and took a big bite.

"You can slow dance without expecting to have sex," Jordan replied. "Slow dancing can be very soft and relaxing. Touching someone like that can be very fulfilling. It stimulates the endorphins, makes you feel connected. And no, it doesn't have to end up in someone's bed."

"Give me a break. What rock are you living under?" Stephanie teased. "No one puts their hand on your ass unless they want a piece of it."

"Stephanie," Barbara scolded. "That's enough," she said with a disciplinary stare.

"I, for one, like slow dancing," Hope inserted, winking at Barbara.

"I know you do," Barbara replied, kissing her cheek softly.

"See what I mean," Stephanie said with a cocky smirk.

After the pizza and another round of drinks, Hope and Barbara signaled the waitress to bring out the cake they had left with the bartender. A parade of waitresses filed through the aisle, singing happy birthday and clapping. Adjacent diners joined in, singing and applauding. Stephanie blushed bright red, giving her sister a punch in the arm for the embarrassment. Hope and Barbara gave her a Palm Pilot for her birthday. Jordan gave her an envelope with a gift card from Amazon.com. She had purchased it last month and planned on using it as a retirement gift for one of the employees at work but on such short notice, she didn't have time to get anything else for Stephanie.

"Now there is a walking advertisement for birth control," Stephanie said, staring at a woman sitting at a table across the room. She was alone and was reading a book while working on a glass of white wine. She was well-dressed but not attractive. Her hair was thinning and her glasses were large, making her look like an insect. She was thirty pounds overweight with no makeup to hide her wrinkles. "Can you believe she isn't wearing some Cover Girl to hide that face?" Stephanie chuckled then slurped her drink, still staring rudely at the woman.

"That isn't nice," Hope said, trying not to look.

"My God, Hope. You can't miss her. She needs to be on that show where they do the makeover. No, she needs to be on the show where they do the cosmetic surgery." Stephanie wasn't whispering and it was beginning to bother Jordan. "She's probably a ho," Stephanie added indignantly.

"Stephanie, that is rude." Jordan pushed her arm to get her to stop staring at the woman. "How can you judge someone like that? Just because someone isn't a Miss America doesn't mean they aren't a wonderful person."

"I'm just saying, she is definitely not a ravishing beauty."

"And we are?" Jordan argued. "Who's to say who is beautiful? It is only skin deep. Many people are gorgeous, once you get to know them. And many beautiful people are downright monsters inside. It's all subjective."

"What the hell does that mean?"

"Beauty is in the eye of the beholder, that's what it means." Jordan scowled at her.

"Right. And I am a beholder. I say she is ugly."

"Steph, will you stop it." Barbara was doing her best to control her obstinate sibling.

"I hope you never get a wrinkle or a zit," Jordan said, disgustedly. Stephanie had never been someone Jordan admired and this evening was only reinforcing that fact, birthday or not.

"Is anyone interested in playing pool with me?" Stephanie asked, noticing an empty table.

"No, thank you," Barbara said adamantly. "I hate pool. There is no way my ass looks good when I bend over like that."

"Jordan will play with you, won't you Jordy?" Hope teased, remembering the last time they came to the Garage.

"No, I will not. I can't play pool and you know it." She instantly remembered the night she and Reece played pool at the Landing. "Why do I always end up at places with pool tables?"

"Because bars don't have computers, that's why," Hope said, bumping her shoulder into Jordan's.

"Come on, Jordan. Come play with me. I can't play worth shit either. But people are always watching women who play pool." Stephanie stood up and grabbed her drink. "I think they are just looking to see if you have a panty line," she added, whispering in Jordan's ear. "Bring your drink. I promise not to say anything else to make you mad."

Jordan heaved a sigh, but reluctantly followed her to the pool table, sending an unhappy glare in Hope's direction. She sat on a stool along the wall and watched, her mind on anything but playing pool. Stephanie racked the balls, making sure she was getting all the attention her tight jeans could afford. She sauntered around the table several times before taking the first shot.

"Jordan, it's your turn," Stephanie called, catching Jordan lost in a daydream.

"Why don't you go ahead and shoot again?" Jordan offered, contented to sit and watch.

"Okay." Stephanie wasn't very good, but she was having fun wiggling and leaning over, giving a show to anyone watching.

Jordan leaned back against the wall and stared at the ceiling, her mind lost in memories of the evening she and Reece spent together on her satin sheets by candlelight. A slow smile formed across her face as she enjoyed the memory. It was hard not to end at the same place every time she remembered Reece, the place where they parted ways knowing they didn't share the same feelings. Jordan sighed and drew her eyes down. As she focused on the bustling crowd, she suddenly gasped and sat up straight. Reece was sitting at the end of the bar, looking back at her with a frozen stare. Their eyes met for a long moment. Finally Reece spun on her stool and faced the bar, leaving Jordan staring across the room with her heart in her throat.

"Hey, Jordy," Hope said, hurrying up to her. "Did you see who's here?"

"Yes, I saw," she muttered, still staring at Reece's back.

"Aren't you going to go talk with her?" Hope asked, pulling at Jordan's arm.

"No," Jordan declared decisively.

Hope frowned at her.

"Jordan, go ask her to dance. Talk with her. Something. You know you want to. Swallow that stubborn pride of yours and go over there."

"Hope, I appreciate your concern, but please don't push. I realized I was wrong. I was just infatuated with her. I'm sure it was because she was a celebrity and all. I'll get over it."

"Then you have nothing to worry about. Go talk with her and buy her a drink. Thank her for giving you the interview." Hope nodded as if to encourage the idea.

Jordan had to admit she would love to have an excuse to go talk with Reece. Hope took her cue and pulled her off the stool.

"Go on," Hope whispered in her ear.

"Hope, will you stop," Jordan argued, but it was a weak defense for her desire to cross the room and be at Reece's side. "This is not the time or the place. I'm not going to mix business with my social life."

"Would you like to dance?" a woman asked, coming up to Jordan with a soft smile. She was well-dressed and attractive. She had a quiet voice behind big blue eyes.

"Sure, she would," Hope said, pushing her toward the woman. "She isn't doing anything else, are you Jordan?"

Jordan glared daggers at Hope.

"If you aren't going over there to talk with her, why not?"

"Don't you have someone else to bother?" Jordan asked sarcastically.

"Just you, cousin." She grinned at her.

The woman held out her hand and Hope placed Jordan's in it.

"My name is Kelly. And your name is Jordan, right?" she said, pulling her toward the floor. "I've never seen you in here before."

Kelly led as they moved across the floor, blending in with the crowd of dancers. Jordan followed, their steps graceful and artistic. Kelly made small talk as they circled the dance floor, trapped in the flow like horses on a carousel. Jordan stared through the crowd to where Reece had been sitting at the bar but the stool was empty. A sinking feeling came over her, thinking Reece had left and she didn't get to talk to her. She turned her attention back to Kelly and their dance, trying to accept Reece's indifference to seeing her.

"Do you work in the city?" Kelly asked politely.

"Yes. You?" Jordan asked.

"No. I work in Redmond. But I guess that is sort of in the city." She smiled. "I work for a *big* computer company . . ." Kelly gave a knowing wink.

"That sounds interesting." Jordan was trying to be polite and attentive, after all, Kelly was attractive and seemingly intelligent. So far she had done nothing objectionable. She didn't let her hand slide down to Jordan's rear. She didn't smell or sound drunk. She didn't step on her toes. She didn't talk on and on about herself. She was the perfect dance partner. And for all Jordan knew, perhaps the perfect date. But Jordan wasn't interested. She had enough women in her life. Enough egos and emotions to soothe. And now there was one that simply wouldn't go away. One that haunted her even when she wished it wouldn't. One that had been watching her from the bar but had disappeared into the faceless crowd.

Jordan felt someone tapping her on the shoulder.

"How are you this evening, Ms. Griffin?" Reece asked. "Do you mind if I cut in?" she asked Kelly. For an instant, Jordan wished Kelly would say no. It would be easier. It would mean Jordan could continue to heal the wound Reece had caused when she said she didn't love her. But before Jordan knew it, Kelly had smiled discreetly and backed away. Reece took Jordan in her arms and continued the dance, floating them around the floor. Jordan couldn't say a word. She felt her heart pounding in her throat as Reece's body pressed against hers, her arms holding her in an embrace that sent a shiver down Jordan's body, making her knees weak.

Reece didn't say anything. Instead, she held Jordan tight, letting the dance take them where it would. Jordan closed her eyes and leaned her head on Reece's shoulder, drinking in the sweet aroma of her. Jordan could hear occasional gasps and murmurs from fellow dancers, whispering about Reece's scar. She resisted the urge to scowl at them. She much preferred to stay in Reece's arms, ignoring the world around them.

"How have you been?" Reece asked finally, still holding her.

"I'm fine," she replied, the satisfaction clearly audible in her voice. "How are you? How are the wounds from the thorns?"

"They're fine."

"Good." Jordan said, too deep in Reece's gaze to say more.

Reece spun them around, their faces just inches apart as they moved across the floor. When the music stopped, they stood locked in each other's arms for a moment, seemingly unable to let go.

"Thank you for the dance," Reece said at last.

"You're welcome," Jordan said softly.

"How is the article coming?"

"I've been busy finishing other things, but I'll get a rough draft knocked out this week. Do you want to look it over?" Jordan asked.

"No. I trust you not to shoot me in the foot." Reece gave a wry smile. "I told you the story, now you make something out of it."

The music started again with a fast song, one neither Reece nor Jordan wanted to attempt.

"Thanks again, Jordan," Reece said, starting off the floor. Jordan instinctively followed her to the bar.

"Do you mind if I sit with you?" Jordan asked cautiously.

"Help yourself." Reece pointed to two stools. "What would you like to drink?"

"Margarita, frozen, no salt."

Reece ordered Jordan's drink and signaled the bartender she wanted another one of what she had been drinking. The bartender set Jordan's drink in front of her and a double shot glass in front of Reece.

"What is that?" Jordan asked, studying the nearly colorless liquid. "It looks like water."

"Try it," Reece said, sliding it over in front of her. Jordan took a tentative sip.

"That is smooth," she said, after an initial grimace. "Tequila?"

"Yes. Patron," Reece replied and took a sip herself.

"I thought you had to have salt and a lime to drink tequila like that."

"Not this. You don't need training wheels for Patron. It stands alone." Reece signaled the bartender to bring Jordan one.

"That's okay. I'll drink my tequila in a margarita."

"That isn't tequila. This is tequila," Reece said, pushing Jordan's drink back and pointing to the double shot glass the bartender set in front of her. Jordan took a sip.

"I don't know much about liquor. A connoisseur I'm not."

"What are you doing here? I didn't know you frequented this place."

"I don't. Hope and her friends invited me to join them for a birthday party. This is only the second time I've been here," Jordan reported.

"I remember the other time," Reece chuckled.

"Me too. I was so embarrassed about that."

"The way you played pool?"

"No, the way you left. I didn't mean to hurt your feelings. I truly didn't, Reece." Jordan touched her arm.

"No biggy. It happens all the time." Reece took another sip.

"I wish I could change that for you," Jordan said softly, continuing to sip her drink.

Reece looked over at her.

"So, how's work?" Reece asked.

"Busy. You know how journalism is. I've got interns who can't spell and don't know what a margin is, computer glitches, last-minute changes, photo releases I can't finalize. Same old stuff."

"Are you understaffed?" Reece asked. She discreetly raised two fingers to the bartender and pointed to Jordan's glass.

"It isn't so much understaffed as it is missed communication. If everyone would do their job, mine would be easier. Did you ever have that trouble?"

"Only all the time. The bigger the operation, the more room

for stupidity. I had a cameraman who couldn't read. He was a junior high school dropout. He couldn't read a road map or a contract."

"Really? How did you work with that?"

"I thought about firing him."

"That would have been justified, I guess," Jordan agreed, working on another double shot of Patron.

"But he was a damn good cameraman. He knew his craft. He knew how to get the shot without shadows or glare. So I hired a tutor for him."

"That was sweet, Reece. What a nice thing to do," Jordan said, touching her arm tenderly.

"I did it for me. I hated breaking in new cameramen," Reece replied.

"I'm sure he appreciated your help."

"Would you like to dance again?" Kelly asked, touching Jordan on the shoulder and smiling at her.

"No. Thank you, though," Jordan replied.

"Go ahead. I certainly don't mind," Reece said, downing the last of her drink then placing her hand over it when the bartender asked if she wanted another.

"Thank you, Kelly. Maybe another time," Jordan said politely but leaving no doubt she wasn't interested. Kelly shrugged and walked away.

"Hey, you better take her up on it while you can. She's quite a looker and I think she thought the same about you," Reece said.

"I think I'm old enough to pick my own dance partners," Jordan replied, giving a disapproving glare.

"I was just trying to help," Reece said.

"Well, I don't need that kind of help from you." A warm tequila glow had begun to settle over Jordan. "I can do that for myself."

"I know you can," Reece replied.

"I can do everything. Almost everything," she said, a tear welling up in her eye without warning. "I can do everything except—" she started, her chin beginning to quiver.

"Except what, Jordan?" Reece asked, reaching out to support Jordan's arm as she began to weave back and forth on the stool.

"Everything except make you love me," she said in a shaky voice, tears trailing down her face. Jordan stood up, stumbling a bit as she found her sea legs.

"I think you need to sit down before you fall down," Reece said, trying to calm her.

"How dare you try to fix me up with someone else? How dare you do that to me?" Jordan turned and hurried toward the door, knocking over the bar stool as she left. Hope saw her rush out and was on her way to see what was wrong when Reece stopped her at the front door.

"I'll go," Reece said. "I think I said something to upset her. I'll take care of it."

"What did you say to her?" Hope asked, giving Reece a cold stare. "I don't want to see my cousin hurt, lady. She loves you, you know."

"I know." Reece's jaw rippled as she looked out the door. She pushed past Hope and went to find Jordan. Reece trotted down the sidewalk toward the parking lot, scanning the dark rows of cars for Jordan. She couldn't see her but she could hear the faint sounds of someone crying. Reece squatted down and looked under the cars. She could see someone sitting next to a car in the back corner.

"Jordan?" she called, striding down the row. "Jordan?"

"Go away," Jordan replied through her sobs.

"There you are," Reece said, looking down at her.

"Leave me alone, Ms. McAllister," Jordan said, sitting on the ground between two cars.

"Why are you sitting in the parking lot?" Reece asked, squatting in front of her, brushing the hair from her eyes.

"Because."

"Because why?"

"Because I can't remember where I parked my car." Jordan looked down, fiddling with the cuff on her slacks. She hiccupped.

"Do you have your keys?"

"I don't know." She looked up, her eyes having trouble focusing.

"Come on, Ms. Griffin. I'm taking you home," Reece announced, pulling her to her feet. "Hope will take care of your stuff."

"I can't leave. I'm supposed to be having fun tonight. Hope told me I was supposed to get out and socialize." Jordan's words were slurred.

"I think you have had about all the fun you can handle for one night." Reece wrapped an arm around her to keep her from falling.

"Did I have fun, Reece?" she asked, a silly grin on her face.

"Sure you did. Come on, now. Let's get you home." Reece tried to walk Jordan down the row to her truck but her knees were like rubber. Jordan stumbled over her own feet, giggling at each step. Finally, Reece picked her up and threw her over her shoulder. Jordan didn't seem to notice she was being carried like a sack of potatoes. She continued to giggle and sing as Reece unlocked her truck and propped her in the passenger seat, buckling her in to keep her from tipping over.

"Where are we going?" Jordan asked, trying to make sense of where she was.

"Home," Reece replied as she pulled out of the parking lot.

"Oh, good," Jordan said, leaning her head on the window and closing her eyes.

Reece gently pulled her head back against the head rest and let her sleep.

Chapter 22

Jordan's mouth felt like someone had emptied a lint trap in it. Her eyes refused to open and there was a loud pounding in her head. She groaned and tried to roll over but she was stuck on her stomach, her arm hanging over the side of the bed. She could feel a cool breeze blowing across her face and it felt good on her skin. She groaned again and opened one eye. The window was open next to the bed, the curtains floating in and out with the breeze. The sun was already up and streaming in the room. She closed her eye again, hoping the pounding in her head would stop. She suddenly opened her eyes. She just remembered she didn't have a window next to her bed. It was across the room and unless someone rearranged her furniture, she wasn't in her own bed. She stared at the wall, trying to gather her senses. For a brief moment she didn't remember what had happened last night, but it came to her in ragged pieces—the birthday party at the Garage, dancing with Reece, drinking doubles of tequila. She rolled over and sat up with a jolt, grabbing her head as it throbbed even harder.

"Damn," she gasped, as her head felt like it would explode. She fell back on the pillow and covered her eyes as the light of day sent daggers into her brain. She reached down and pulled the covers up around her chin, the cool morning breeze chilling her, making her nipples pop. She lifted up the sheet and looked under it, noticing she was completely naked. She quickly locked the sheet under her chin and tried desperately to remember what had happened. Had she gone home with a complete stranger and had wild sex? Had she swung from the chandelier and performed lewd acts in front of a crowd of spectators? She had no idea. She scanned the room, looking for a clue as to where she was and what she might have done. She saw her slacks hanging over a chair with her panties and bra in a pile on the floor. Her blouse was hooked over the door-knob. One shoe was on the dresser and the other was wedged under the bedside table. There were no pictures on the walls that told Jordan where she was. There was one small, framed picture on the dresser of a bird in flight. It looked familiar but she couldn't be sure. Everything was still a blur. She climbed out of bed and wrapped the sheet around her then opened the bedroom door. She peeked out into the darkened hallway. There was no sound, not even the sound of a ticking clock. She tiptoed down the hall and peered around the corner into the living room. No one in sight. She moved through the living room to the dining room and into the kitchen, dragging the sheet behind her as she searched the apartment for signs of life.

"Hello?" she called tentatively, not sure if she really wanted to get anyone's attention or not.

"You're up," Reece said, coming up behind Jordan and scaring her into a scream.

Jordan grabbed her head and moaned, her scream blasting a siren in her head. "Where am I?" Jordan asked, her eyes lowered since the sunlight streaming in the windows compounded her headache.

"My apartment," Reece replied. "Where did you think you were?"

"I have no idea. How did I get here?" Jordan started back for the bedroom where she knew her clothes were.

"I brought you. Don't you remember last night? You were at the Garage with Hope. Something about a birthday party." Reece followed, trying to avoid stepping on the dragging sheet.

"Oh, yes. I remember," Jordan said, sitting down on the edge of the bed, holding her head. "You got me drunk," she said suddenly, staring up at Reece.

"I did not. You got yourself drunk. No one poured that stuff in your mouth."

"How much did I have? A quart and a half?" Jordan moaned and rocked back and forth.

"I don't know how many margaritas you had but you had three double shots of Patron, all in about thirty minutes."

"I don't drink, you know. I've never had that much liquor in one sitting in my life. I'm a glass of wine-type person."

"I see that." Reece controlled a chuckle. "Do you need some aspirin?"

"Yes, a whole bottle of them." Jordan flopped back on the bed.

Reece went into the kitchen and returned with a glass of juice and two aspirin.

"Here," she said, sitting down on the bed next to her.

"I can't sit up. Leave them on the nightstand."

"Come on, Ms. Griffin." Reece pulled Jordan up to a sitting position and held her there while she took the aspirin. "You'll feel better soon."

"When?"

"In three or four days," Reece replied, not able to refrain from teasing her.

"Thank you for your concern," she groaned and tried to lie back down but Reece held her up.

"You need to stay upright for a while. It'll help with the hangover." Reece propped her against the headboard of the bed.

"By the way, how did I get—" she asked, looking under the sheet.

"Naked?" Reece asked.

252

"Yes. Did I do it myself?"

"No. Not exactly."

"You did it?" Jordan asked, totally embarrassed about what she might have done while intoxicated.

"Let's say I helped you. You tried to take your pants off over your head."

"Oh no. I didn't, did I?" She pulled the sheet up to cover her face.

"You were sure you could get your bra off without taking off your blouse first. I'm not sure if all the buttons survived."

"Is that all?" Jordan asked, without looking out from under the sheet.

"Almost," Reece replied sarcastically.

"What else? Tell me what I did so I can be embarrassed all at once."

"Let's just say it involved a long-stemmed red rose and a flash-light."

"Oh, my God. I didn't," Jordan declared, peeking out from under the sheet.

Reece laughed and shook her head.

"No, you didn't. Anyway, not that last thing. Although last night might have been the night for it." She continued to laugh.

Jordan glared at her for making her think she had done something stupid.

"I have to ask," Jordan said quietly after a long silence. "Did we—" She didn't finish. Reece was already shaking her head.

"No, we didn't," she said softly. "I don't take advantage of women like that." Reece stood up and walked out of the room.

"Reece, wait a minute." Jordan climbed out of bed and followed her into the living room, the sheet still in tow. "I didn't mean you would do that. I just meant maybe we might have done something once we got in bed. You know, in the throes of passion or something. I didn't mean you would have taken advantage of me."

"What makes you think we slept together?" Reece asked, looking back at her.

"I just assumed we did. Didn't we?"

"No. I slept in there," Reece said, pointing to the guest bedroom on the other side of the apartment. "I only brought you here because you didn't have your keys so I couldn't get you in your apartment. I called the Garage and told Hope where you were and she said she would take your car home for you. When you get finished assuming I did something sinister with you while you were drunk, you can get dressed and I'll take you home." Reece was defensive at Jordan's insinuations.

"I didn't mean you did."

"It's after nine. Aren't you a working girl?" Reece said, checking her watch.

"Nine?" Jordan's eyes got big. "It's Tuesday. No, no, no. I'm late for the editorial meeting," she muttered, rushing back into the bedroom and scrambling into her clothes. "Do you happen to have a spare toothbrush?" she asked, running her fingers through her hair as she tucked her blouse in her slacks.

"I set out a toothbrush, hairbrush and some makeup for you in the guest bathroom. Help yourself," Reece called from the living room.

"Thanks," she said, hurrying into the bathroom.

"I've made you some coffee and there's Danish for breakfast," Reece added.

"I don't have time for breakfast. I'll have you drop me off at the office. I can ride the bus home later." Jordan was frantic to get herself ready for work as quickly as possible.

"Fine with me," Reece said, looking over the front page of the newspaper. "Do you have your purse and keys with you?" Reece knew good and well she didn't.

Jordan stuck her head out the bathroom door with a disappointed look on her face.

"No, I don't have anything with me, do I?" she asked.

Reece smiled and kept reading the paper.

"Nope, I don't think you do." She finally folded the paper and put it down. She stood up and went to the telephone and dialed *Northwest Living*. "Hello. Yes, I need to get a message to Mark

Bergman, the managing editor. Would you tell him Jordan Griffin has had some car trouble and she'll be a little late this morning? Yes, she had to have someone else drive it. I have no idea. Ignition or something. I'm just relaying the message. Thank you." Reece hung up and nodded decisively toward Jordan. "It's a small lie, so you'll have to come up with whatever explanation works best."

"Thank you, I think."

"Come on, I'll take you home." Reece waited by the front door, tossing her keys in the air and catching them. "Hope said she put your keys in the ashtray of your car."

"Tell me something, Reece." Jordan stood in front of her and stared into her eyes.

"What's that?"

"Why did you let me do that last night?" she asked quietly. "Why did you let me drink myself into a stupor like that? You could have stopped me. You could have told me not to drink anymore. I was vulnerable last night. You know I would have listened to you. Why didn't you?"

"I don't know. I guess I thought you needed it. I guess I thought you could make your own decisions."

"Do you really care so little what happens to me?" Jordan asked, a pained look in her eyes.

Reece didn't say anything. Jordan hesitated, her posture stiffening as she waited for an answer from Reece.

"We better go," Reece said finally, holding the door for Jordan.

Jordan heaved a disgusted sigh and went to the truck. She was too mad to ask anything else.

Chapter 23

Jordan sat at her desk, staring at her computer monitor. Her face was emotionless and pale. She hadn't moved a muscle in several minutes as she read and reread the information she had compiled. It was as if the data was too surprising to accept all at once. As a reporter, she had done her job. She had found out what happened to Pella Frann. She knew where she was and why. She knew what she had done to Reece. She knew every detail and it wasn't pretty. She almost wished she hadn't dug so deep and so well. Jordan slowly reached up and closed the file then sat silently in her chair, staring at the blank screen.

Reece had lied to her. The scar wasn't the result of an accident. It had been an attack, a cold-blooded, vicious attack driven by jealousy and rage. Pella Frann had done it. Pella had picked up a knife and slashed Reece's face, leaving her permanently scarred, both physically and emotionally.

Jordan closed her eyes as a single tear rolled down her cheek.

She wasn't sure what she wanted to do more, call Reece and ask why she lied to her about how she got the scar or delete the entire story and tell Susan there is nothing to print about the elusive Reece McAllister. Reece obviously had her reasons to keep the truth hidden. That fact Jordan was sure of. But now she had to decide if this information should be used to tell Reece's true story. Jordan also had to decide how much her own feelings for Reece would influence what she would ultimately write.

A knock on Jordan's office door brought her back. She quickly wiped the tear from her cheek and straightened her posture. She cleared her throat and took a deep breath before acknowledging the knock.

"Come in," she announced, mustering a smile.

"Hi, Jordy," Hope said, sticking her head in the door.

"Hi, honey," Jordan said, moving to hug Hope. When she did, she could not contain her emotions any longer. She held Hope in a long embrace and fought her tears.

"Jordy, what is it?" Hope said, hugging her tightly. "Are you all right?" She held Jordan for a long minute, listening to her battle with tears.

Jordan nodded, unable to speak. Hope patted her back and continued to hold her until she was finished.

"Okay, what is going on?" Hope finally said, plucking a tissue from the box on Jordan's desk and dabbing at her tears.

"I'm sorry, honey," Jordan replied, drying her eyes and reestablishing her composure. "I guess I'm a little stressed today."

"Does this have anything to do with you and Reece at the Garage the other night? You had way too much to drink and she knew it."

"No, not really." Jordan returned to her desk chair and blew her nose.

"Be honest, Jordy. Does it have anything to do with Reece?" Hope asked deliberately.

Jordan hesitated then nodded slightly.

"What is it?" Hope asked, pulling a chair up to the desk.

"I found out what really happened to Reece, how she got the scar. I should never have done it but I found out about Reece's past with Pella." Jordan looked down and sighed. "I did my job as a reporter and I'm not proud of it."

"It wasn't an accident that caused the scar?"

"No. She was attacked with a knife and then she fell through a patio door." Jordan looked up at Hope with a pained expression. "Pella attacked her with a butcher knife. She has two scars. The one down her back is from the broken glass. The long one across her face, neck and chest, Pella did that."

"Oh, my God," Hope mouthed the words, her eyes wide with shock. "How did you find out?"

"I called the police department and asked about an emergency call to the house Reece used to have in Redmond. All emergency response calls are printed in the newspaper."

"Who called the police?"

"Pella did. When the police pulled up, she was standing in the front yard, waving the bloody knife and screaming. The officer said she was saying things like she didn't mean it. She loved her. She was the ugly one, not Reece."

"Sounds like Pella had lost it," Hope said.

"The policeman said Reece was lying on the kitchen floor, holding a towel to her face and neck. He said there was a pool of blood as big as a bathtub. The knife cut the carotid artery in her neck. If Pella hadn't called the ambulance, Reece would have bled to death in another few minutes. The police took Pella into custody but Reece wouldn't press charges against her. She said Pella wasn't responsible for her actions. The DA agreed to set aside any charges against her, so long as she got professional help. Pella wasn't able to accept her looks as she got older. When she started losing modeling jobs, being overlooked for younger girls, she became jealous of Reece's attractive looks. Her on-air time didn't help. Reece tried to do less in front of the camera and more behind the scenes. She even tried to ease out of journalism altogether, but Pella thought it was only out of pity."

"Where is Pella now? In a mental institution?"

"She was. She's in a halfway house now, trying to learn to cope with society again. It has been hard for her."

"Do you know where, exactly?" Hope asked carefully.

Jordan nodded discreetly.

"She is in Portland. Pella Frann's real name is Frances Pellagrino. She was originally from Boston."

"And Reece didn't want you to know, right?" Hope added.

"I think she was protecting her back then and I think she still is. She hasn't seen her in three years but she doesn't want to expose Pella to public ridicule."

"Sounds like a very devoted, caring person, even if she isn't still in a relationship with Pella."

"I spoke with the counselor at the halfway house. Pella may never be able to live independently again. She has never been able to adjust to getting older. She is several years older than Reece but she isn't able to even enjoy a birthday party. She tried to commit suicide on each of her last two birthdays."

"Jordan, I am so sorry for Reece. She must have loved Pella very much."

"Pella took away more than Reece's looks." Jordan looked away, her eyes scanning the room for relief. "She took away Reece's ability to trust love."

"I can see why."

"She won't let her heart be broken again."

"You are a good reporter, Jordy. You got the story you wanted." Hope patted Jordan's hand.

"Yippee for me," Jordan replied, lowering her eyes. "But I wish I hadn't."

"You couldn't do any less, honey. You are too conscientious not to get the whole truth. That is who you are. Now, what are you going to do with it?"

Jordan slowly looked up but didn't reply.

Hope read her face then stood up.

"You have a tough decision to make, Jordy," she said as she went to the door.

"By the way, what did you want when you came up here?" Jordan tried to smile herself into a better mood.

"I was going to ask you out to lunch, but I get the feeling you'd turn me down."

"Maybe we can have lunch in a day or two. I'll call you." Jordan walked Hope to the elevator. "Thanks for listening, honey."

"Trust you senses, Jordy. Don't be influenced by anything else. Trust them." Hope stepped into the elevator and left Jordan with the hardest journalistic decision she ever had to make.

Jordan had no sooner returned to her desk than her telephone rang. It was Susan and her tone was not friendly.

"Jordan, where is it? Where is my article about Reece McAllister?" she asked sternly.

"I'm working on it. I do have other things to do, you know. It isn't the only story I am working on." Jordan didn't want to admit she was having trouble with the story.

"Jordan, what are you waiting for? You usually don't take this long to get the copy to me. You had the story on the port authority knocked out in two days. What's with you? I need this before you go to Spokane for the conference on Wednesday." Susan sounded disgusted and arrogant.

Jordan didn't need Susan's attitude. It was hard enough deciding how much of Reece's past she wanted to include in the article without Susan hounding her about it.

"Can you have something for me by tomorrow?" Susan asked. "We've got three days before we go to press, Jordan."

"Yes, Susan. I'll have it for you tomorrow. Don't worry."

"Is there a problem with it? Is that why you are taking so long?"

"No. No problem. I just need to verify a few facts."

"Are you worried about a lawsuit?" Susan snapped.

"I don't think so but I need to double-check a couple things." Jordan didn't mean to fib but this stall tactic seemed to be the only way to get Susan off her back.

"Jordan, are you going native on this one? Are you getting too involved with this woman to do the story?" Susan asked.

"No," Jordan insisted.

"Don't give me that. You would never have trekked off into the wilds to interview Reece McAllister unless you were intrigued with her. And you would never have taken so long to knock out this story if you weren't torn over what to include. I wasn't born yesterday, Jordan."

"I'm a writer, a reporter. I'm doing my job. You sent me on this story and I'm perfectly capable of delivering the goods without becoming personally involved," Jordan said defensively. She wished it were true but as professional as she tried to be, she *had* become personally involved, more so than she cared to admit.

"Then do it. Get off the dime and do it," Susan replied gruffly. "I'll be looking for it tomorrow. Don't disappoint me, Jordan." Susan hung up, leaving Jordan frustrated and angry.

She filled her coffee cup then closed her office door, hoping to find privacy. She was ready to devote the rest of the day to finishing the story, in spite of Susan's nagging. Once she got into her groove, Jordan was oblivious to the hours that ticked away. She worked through lunch and through dinner, transforming her computer files of notes, photographs and interviews into an eight-page article, sprinkled with facts and sidebars about Reece's life and career. Just after eight o'clock, long after everyone else had left for the day, she read it over one last time before closing it and turning off the desk lamp. She heaved a deep, resolute sigh, satisfied she had treated Reece's story with journalist professionalism—in spite of her feelings for her.

"There's your article, Susan," Jordan muttered, leaning back in her chair and watching her monitor fade to black.

She collected her things and went home, looking forward to a long soak in a hot bath. She poured herself a glass of white wine, lit several candles and put on some soothing music. Usually, she took a notepad or her voice-activated recorder into the bathroom when she took a long bath, but tonight she didn't want to think about work. Tonight she didn't want to think about anything. She wanted to lose herself in the amber glow of candles and serenity. Jordan slipped into the tub and closed her eyes, hoping even the memory of her evenings with Reece could somehow float away but it wasn't to be. She could almost feel Reece's soft touch and passionate kisses drifting toward her through the dim light of the bathroom.

"Jordan, Jordan," Reece's voice seemed to whisper, wafting through the strains of music. "Jordan."

Jordan opened her eyes and sat up in the tub.

"Reece?" she called. "Are you there?" The lilting melody was the only reply. She leaned back in the tub and closed her eyes, hoping she could put Reece out of her mind. "What happened to us?" she whispered.

Chapter 24

The sound of breakers crashing against the shore broke the silence of the gray misty dawn. A single person walked the edge of the tide, leaving footprints in the wet sand. Seagulls floated on the wind, effortlessly gliding above the white curl of the waves. Reece strolled the beach, her hands buried in the pockets of her jacket. She occasionally stopped to watch one of the waves build and roll ashore. It was not yet six o'clock but she had been up for hours working in the dark room. She collected a handful of pebbles and tossed them into the surf. This was the first time in years she had walked the beach near the cabin at Greysome Point without a camera. Usually she was gauging exposure, trying new angles or just snapping shots to be snapping shots. This morning was different. As much as she didn't want to, Reece knew she would spend the day thinking about Jordan. She didn't want the nagging heartache to occupy another moment of her serenity but she knew it would as sure as she knew she would welcome it. Jordan Griffin was not only in her thoughts—she was in her soul and in her heart. Reece wanted desperately to change that. She wanted Jordan to move past her attachment to her. And Reece wanted that fact to stop hurting so damn bad.

The cell phone rang. Reece pulled it from her pocket and looked at the caller's name.

"Hey, Tony. What's up with you? Are you still in London?"

"Hi, Reece," a man's voice said. "Nope. I'm back in the states. Miami, if you can believe that."

"Don't tell me. The weather is warm and sunny, right?" she teased.

"You bet. Eighty degrees, soft onshore breeze, not a cloud in the sky." Tony chuckled wickedly.

"We've got an onshore breeze today." She didn't tell him the skies looked like they would open up and pour at any moment.

"How's the showing coming along?"

"Good, I guess. The gallery owner said there are only eight pieces left on the wall. Either she is selling them or using them in the bottom of her cat's litter box." Reece sat down on a log that had floated ashore and was embedded into the sand.

"That's great. I told you your stuff is good. Now, what is this about you going to Europe?" he asked. "I thought you had given up your globe-trotting. You said Washington had all the nature you needed for your photography."

"I know I said that three years ago but I've changed my mind." Reece hesitated a moment. "I want to spend some time away from here." Her voice drifted off. "I need to get away."

"What's up, Reece? What's going on?"

"Nothing. I just want to do some traveling overseas. I thought northern Italy, maybe Switzerland. I've never been to Iceland. Maybe I could give that country a look-see." Reece sounded distant.

"Sounds like you want someplace remote."

"I just don't want to be accessible," she replied cautiously.

"Why not try Antarctica then. I hear that is remote," he teased.

"You're my business manager, Tony. I just need you to handle things while I'm gone. I'll give your number to the gallery owner. She can call you when the showing is over and you can make arrangements to have the photos stored or sent to you. I don't care."

"I'll be glad to take care of things for you but I'd like to think I am your friend too. I get the feeling you aren't telling me something, Reece. I get the feeling you aren't going *to* something but running *away* from something. As a friend, I'd like to help. You can trust me enough to tell me what is going on, can't you?" Tony sounded genuinely sympathetic, something Reece hadn't expected.

She sat on the log, staring out over the ocean, squinting at the horizon.

"I'm still here, Reece," he added.

"I know."

"Is it a woman?" he asked finally.

"Yeah," she muttered.

"And you are running away from her?"

"No. I'm letting her go. If I stay here, I won't be able to do that," she said, the words sticking in her throat.

"Why are you letting her go? Is she not worth the effort?"

"Oh, Tony. She is so worth the effort. But it isn't fair to her."

"Why? Because of your face?" he asked, not pulling any punches.

There was a silence, filled with the sound of waves crashing ashore.

"Reece?"

"I can't do that to her, Tony. I just can't. And I won't do it to myself again, either." Reece stood up and continued up the beach. "Hell, I got her drunk the other night just so she'd have to go home with me instead of anyone else. I can't stay here where she is."

"I don't know what to say to you, Reece. I love you like a sister but you have to make the decisions you can live with. But if this girl is worth it, why not give her a chance? Maybe she can deal with it. Maybe this time it will be different."

"I know what is going to happen and I can't go through that

again." She straightened her posture and took a deep breath. "So, I can count on you to handle things here?"

"Sure. I'll handle them. Have your mail forwarded to me. How long will you be gone? A couple weeks?" he asked.

"Couple months, maybe more. Who knows? I may find a nice little place in Tuscany I like and move permanently." She sounded confident and resigned to the trip.

"When are you leaving?"

"In a week, maybe. Before I go I want to see the new issue of the magazine that is doing a story on me."

"Call me before you leave, okay?" he stated.

"I will. Thanks," she said and hung up.

Reece walked out into the tide, the water lapping up around her ankles. She didn't seem to notice the cold temperature or the fact the water was wicking up her pant legs. She stood in the surf, her hands in her jacket pockets, staring out to sea as tears streamed down her face.

"Good-bye, Jordan Griffin," she whispered, every word agony for her to say.

She turned around and ran back up the beach.

Chapter 25

The elevator opened and Reece stormed out, her long strides purposeful as she entered the lobby of *Northwest Living Magazine*. She glared down at the woman behind the reception desk, her nostrils flaring.

"Where is Jordan Griffin?" she demanded, barely able to contain her anger.

"Ms. Griffin isn't in. Can I help you?"

"When will she be in?" Reece tapped her knuckles on the counter.

"I'm not sure. Is there something we can do for you?" the receptionist asked, trying to pacify Reece's growing anger.

"Susan Mackey. Is she here?" Reece continued.

"Yes, Susan is here but she is in a meeting. Could you give me your name and I'll let her know you're here?"

"Don't give me that meeting shit. She's in her office drinking coffee and doesn't want to be bothered. You buzz her and tell her she has company," Reece said, her eyes narrowed.

"Ms. Mackey really is in a meeting with Mr. Bergman, our managing editor," she replied defiantly.

"That's even better." Reece headed down the hall toward Mark's office, ignoring the receptionist's calls to wait.

"You can't go down there." The receptionist was ready to rush down the hall to stop her when the telephone rang, bringing her back to her desk.

Reece threw open Mark's office door without knocking and strode inside. Susan and Mark looked up with surprise as Reece tossed the new issue of the magazine on the conference table, letting it slide across and stop in front of Mark.

"I beg your pardon," Mark scoffed. "We're in a meeting here."

"Your meeting can wait." Reece fired a stare at him.

"Hello, Ms. McAllister," Susan said, smiling an artificial smile at her. "It's nice to see you again."

"You won't think so when I am finished with you," Reece announced.

Mark closed the folder he was working on and pushed it aside.

"Okay. What is all this about, Ms. McAllister? Why are you bursting into our staff meeting and throwing the magazine on the table like this?" he asked, looking up at her.

"Who edited the story?" she asked abruptly.

"What story?" he asked.

"Don't get cute with me. You know damn well what story I mean. The one titled 'Reece McAllister, Reporter Without a Future.' That's the one I mean." Reece opened the magazine and pointed to the full page photograph of herself, her scar larger than life.

Mark stared down at the article, his forehead wrinkled as he scanned it.

"What the—" he started, looking over at Susan.

"It's Jordan's story. The one you wanted her to get, remember?" Susan nodded at him, trying to jog his memory. "She got it in just under the wire so we went ahead and ran it. I made the decision at the last minute to pull the article about the city parks and go with it. After all, you asked her to do it."

Mark pulled the magazine closer and scanned it, his forehead becoming more furrowed as he read.

"Did you give Jordan this information, Ms. McAllister?" he asked, as he turned the page and continued reading.

"Yes, part of it. She got some of it on her own. You sons-of-bitches double-crossed me. There is information in there that will cause real harm to some people. You had no right to do that. I told her information about Pella Frann was off-limits. I told her she was not to be mentioned."

Mark reread a paragraph then looked up at Reece.

"If Pella Frann caused your scar and you told Jordan that, how can you expect her not to mention her name?"

"I did not tell her that. I don't know where she got it but that is not what I told her." Reece turned the page and pointed to a paragraph. "Read that."

"Pella Frann, world famous fashion model, lived for two years behind the locked windows and doors of the Oregon State Mental Institution under her given name, Francis Pellagrino, after agreeing to psychiatric help to avoid being prosecuted for assault on her lesbian partner of several years, Reece McAllister. Ms. McAllister refused to press charges in spite of the vicious attack that left her so disfigured that her days as a top television journalist are all behind her. Pella, a one-time glamour model for many notable publications, now spends her days watching soap operas and making potholders at a halfway house while under constant supervision because of repeated suicide attempts. Having slashed her own face and body in repeated self-inflicted attacks, Ms. Pellagrino is barely recognizable as the former supermodel."

Mark studied the photograph of a group of women sitting around a table eating a meal from foam plates and plastic forks. The woman at the end of the table had thinning gray hair and her face showed the deep wrinkles of age. She was overweight and had a vacant stare in her eyes visible even in the grainy photograph. Her face and arms were littered with scabs and tiny scars.

"Where did this picture come from?" Mark asked gruffly, reading the photo credit along the edge.

"I think it was a stock picture from the Oregon Resource Department," Susan said.

"I don't give a shit who took it." Reece's voice was steeped with resentment. "You had no right to print any picture of her. I told Jordan that was strictly off-limits. I gave her all she needed to know about Pella and me. She promised to respect that restriction. I would never have agreed to doing the story if I knew you were going to print that picture and give out that information. Do you know how damaging that would be? Raking up the past would only drive Pella deeper into herself."

"Ms. McAllister, I assure you *Northwest Living* had no intention of hurting anyone or violating anyone's privacy. I will get to the bottom of this, I promise you that." Mark looked up at Reece.

"Oh, I promise you, you will, too," Reece added, crossing her arms.

"Where is Jordan?" Mark snapped in Susan's direction, his jaw muscles twitching.

"She's in Boise doing a story on an anthrax scare. She'll be back tomorrow morning."

Mark came to his feet and offered his hand to Reece.

"I want to apologize if there has been any inconvenience, Ms. McAllister. It isn't our policy to print this kind of article. We leave sensationalized journalism to the rags and tabloids. We like to think we are more sensitive than this." He looked over at Susan. "We will print a public apology."

"NO!" Reece said, her arms still crossed. "That would just draw more attention to it. The damage is done."

"Let me talk with Jordan," he said quietly, handing Reece her magazine.

"You have not heard the last from me," Reece said, her stare trained on Susan.

She took the magazine and headed for the door. As she passed a wastebasket, she slammed it in then strode down the hall for the elevator.

"How the hell did this happen, Susan?" Mark asked as he watched Reece disappear down the hall and out the front door. "We don't print this kind of shit."

"Jordan thought it must have been important. She did the research and wrote the story. She seemed to have a good relationship with Ms. McAllister. She must have thought it was newsworthy."

"First of all, Jordan should have known better. She's no rookie. I can't imagine she would be so insensitive. It isn't like her. I have to think you might have stopped this, Susan," Mark said as she was about to leave. He gave her a long look. "It's called discretion. I thought you could differentiate between printable material and trash."

Susan didn't say anything. Before Mark left for the day, he placed a copy of the magazine on Jordan's desk, opened to the article about Reece. He didn't want her to say she hadn't seen it.

When Mark entered the lobby the next morning, Jordan was already standing in her office, staring at the article, her eyes wide and her face pinched with anger.

"Jordan, can I have a word with you?" he asked, noticing her light was on.

"Not now, Mark. Please," she said, still reading the article, her blood pressure rising by the second.

"Jordan, this is important," he added, coming in her office and closing the door behind him. "It's about that article."

"Who put this article in the magazine?" she asked, trying to remain calm as she looked at the picture of Pella.

"You did and that is the problem. Ms. McAllister was here yesterday."

Jordan looked at him, shock and regret on her face.

"She is not happy about it," he continued. "She said she told you Pella Frann was off-limits in the article. All you were supposed

271

to use was what she told you. I have to agree with her. I wouldn't have used that crap about the mental institution and the suicide attempts either, if that's what she requested. That's the kind of shit they put in grocery store rags. We are not that kind of publication, Jordan. I thought you knew that. We trusted you to do the right thing."

"I didn't put this in my article," Jordan declared loudly, pointing to the picture of Pella. "I did not write this." She looked up at Mark, flames veritably shooting from her eyes. "I don't know who did, but I did *not* write this."

"You didn't write it?" He raised his voice as well. "Who the hell got the information then?"

"I did, but I didn't write this." She heaved a deep sigh, knowing she sounded confused. "I got the information on what really happened, what really caused Reece's scar. Once I started, it just snowballed on me. One piece of information led to another. Before I knew it, I had the whole ugly truth. But I realized I couldn't use it. I promised Reece I would respect her wishes and only use what she told me. I knew she had her reasons for protecting Pella and I respected that. I have a pretty good idea who wrote this story, though," she said, her eyes narrowed.

"Who?" Mark asked.

Jordan just crossed her arms and stared at him.

"Susan?" he asked in disbelief.

"She got into my computer and read my files." Jordan pushed past Mark and headed down the hall.

Jordan whacked the rolled up magazine against her hand as she strode down the hall to Susan's office, her eyes straight ahead like piercing daggers. She didn't bother to knock. She burst into the office and glared at Susan as she was sitting at her desk, talking on the telephone. It was all Jordan could do not to grab the receiver from her hand and slam it down.

"Jordan," Susan said, scowling up at her. "I'm on the phone here. Can this wait?"

"No Susan. This can't wait." She tossed the magazine on the desk. It disrupted a pile of papers, scattering them across the desk. Susan frowned at her, catching a folder as it slid to the edge.

"I'll call you back?" Susan said then hung up. "I must say, Jordan. That was very rude." She straightened her desk, ignoring the angry stare on Jordan's face.

"Why did you print that story?" Jordan asked, barely in control of her anger.

"What story?" Susan replied, trying to act nonchalant.

Jordan snatched up the magazine and ripped through the pages to find the article about Reece.

"This story. This one right here with my byline on it." She held it up for Susan to see. "This story right here that I did not write. That's what story, Susan." She flopped it on the desk.

"I have no idea why you are acting so huffy. I printed your story. You wrote it. That's what we do here. We publish articles about newsworthy information."

"I did *not* write that story. I gave you the story to use in the magazine. This is nothing like what I gave you. I never included that information about Pella Frann. It was never part of the story I gave you. You had no right to use that."

"I beg your pardon," Susan said, looking up at her with a scowl. "I am the senior editor here. I most certainly do have a right to use anything I think is important." She gave Jordan a cutting stare.

"You took that information off my computer. You pirated my files without asking me. If I wanted that information in my story, I would have put it there. I had a very good reason not to use it. You don't know anything about these people. You don't know how much damage that could have done."

"You are way too emotionally involved with this story. You are infatuated with this Reece McAllister and you let that influence your journalist logic. You obviously couldn't make an objective decision about what was important so I had to make that decision for you. This is a good article. It has all the elements of superior journalism. If Reece McAllister was a good reporter she'd agree with me. She would say how important it is to tell the whole story, not just part of it."

"You have no idea what you did. Pella Frann is a troubled woman with a fragile existence. Printing this garbage couldn't possibly help her. My decision not to expose her history was done out of sensitivity and compassion, something you have none of."

"I don't think we need to lower this discussion to a personal level, Jordan."

"You did that, Susan. When you went behind my back and took that information off my computer you reduced this to a very personal level. Yes, I know any information on a company computer is legally accessible, but I never thought you'd do this. I never thought you'd do something so irresponsible and hateful."

It suddenly became clear why Susan had done it. Jordan knew it was Susan's jealousy that drove her to write such a vicious and revealing attack, cutting Reece's life bare to the bone. Susan had done it because Jordan refused to date her.

"You obviously don't understand the publishing business, Ms. Griffin." Susan sat up straight, summoning her authoritative look. "This decision was made for the good of the magazine. This story will sell copies."

Jordan leaned over, placed her hands on Susan's desk and narrowed her eyes.

"If this is the publishing business, I don't want to know anything about it. I'd rather flip hamburgers." Jordan reached over and closed the magazine. "I quit."

"Suit yourself, but don't expect a favorable recommendation from me."

Jordan turned to leave then looked back at Susan.

"I am only sorry I couldn't stay around long enough for your next invitation for a date," she said with a shy smile.

"Really?" Susan seemed to widen her eyes in expectation.

"Yes. I'd love to have you prosecuted for sexual harassment." Jordan slammed the office door on her way out.

She stopped at her office long enough to collect her things and delete all personal information on her computer. She contemplated deleting the three stories she was working on, but e-mailed them to Diane instead, knowing someone would have to complete them. She turned out the desk light and dropped her key on the reception desk just as Mark came rushing out of his office.

"Wait, Jordan. Don't leave. Let's talk about this," he said, hurrying up to her. "Susan told me about your argument with her. I'm sure we can work this out."

Jordan continued toward the elevator, Mark following. She pushed the button then looked over at him, a caustic look in her eyes.

"Mark, I don't need to talk about anything with you. The only person I need to talk with is Reece McAllister and hope she will accept my sincere apology for this. I don't expect her to but I will try. I promised I would treat her story with dignity and compassion. Now I can't say that." Jordan gave a small chuckle. "She told me not to shoot her in the foot."

"Not to do what?" Mark asked.

"Shoot her in the foot. That's what she said happens when too much information is given and a reporter doesn't handle it well. I hope she doesn't bleed to death before I can get to her. Tell me, Mark. What am I supposed to tell Ms. McAllister? How am I supposed to explain why we did this to her?"

Mark stood staring at her as the elevator door opened. He didn't know what to say. Jordan gave him one last look then strode into the elevator. She stood facing the glass wall as the door closed.

Chapter 26

Jordan headed home, her mind too consumed with her anger over the article to think about the fact she was now unemployed. That didn't seem to be as important as finding Reece and apologizing to her. She called Reece's apartment in Seattle but the number had been disconnected. She tried her cell phone number but it immediately rang to her message service, telling Jordan it was turned off. She called the gallery where Reece's work was on display but the owner hadn't heard from her in over a week. She pulled off Highway 5 and headed for Reece's apartment. Even if she wasn't home, perhaps her neighbor might know where she was. Jordan knocked on the door and Gloria invited her in, remembering their previous conversation.

"I haven't seen Reece in nearly a week. She might have been there a couple of nights ago but I'm not sure. I think she had her phone and cable turned off. I saw the service truck parked in front and the man unhooking something on the pole," Gloria said. "Is something wrong?"

"No, I'm just trying to get a hold of her."

"She's probably at her cabin in Greysome Point," Gloria offered. "She likes to go there when something is bothering her. She said there is a place in the woods not far from her cabin. She goes there to think. She told me she found it by accident. It is on the side of a steep hill. It has a stream and a lovely view. I hope someday I can see it," she said dreamily. "It sounds like a heavenly place to me. Anyway, she told me it was secluded and she could think more clearly up there. She sometimes goes there and camps for days just to be alone. And I'm sure she is a bit upset."

"Upset about—" Jordan asked, as if she didn't know.

"That article, of course. Did you see it? It was in this month's issue of *Northwest Living*. That Griffin woman didn't do Reece any favors printing those pictures or saying what she did. I saw Reece when she took it out of the mailbox. You should have seen the look on her face when she opened it. It looked like someone stabbed her right in the heart. Yes, sirree, right in the heart. I can't be sure, Reece is so private and all, but I think I saw tears in her eyes as she read that terrible story." Gloria shook her head sympathetically. "Poor thing. You'd think she has been through enough."

"Ms. Griffin may not be responsible for the article," Jordan offered.

"I don't know why not. If she didn't do it, you can blame the magazine for printing it. Either way, I canceled my subscription."

"I'm sorry to hear that. I hear Ms. Griffin isn't working there anymore."

"Well, the magazine still shouldn't have printed that article. You'd think they had editors to stop stuff like that. If that is the kind of publication it is, I don't want it in my house."

"Reece is very lucky to have you for a friend," Jordan said, patting Gloria's hand then going to the door.

"I wish I could help but I just don't know where she is, honey. By the way, I don't remember your name," she said, following her to the door.

"Jordan. If you see her, please tell her Jordan needs to talk to her."

"Jordan?" the woman asked as if waiting for a last name.

"She'll know who it is."

Jordan headed home to pack. She would be on the ferry to Kingston and hopefully in Greysome Point by four o'clock, if she hurried. She tried Reece's cell phone every few minutes without results. She dropped her suitcase in the trunk, pushing over the backpack she hadn't yet returned to Hope. She gassed the car and headed for Edmonds. The water was choppy and the wind was chilly as she stood at the railing of the ferry watching a tanker entering Seattle's harbor. She paced the deck nervously, waiting for the ride to bring her closer to Reece and her explanation. She could only guess how mad and hurt Reece must be over the article. Even if she didn't want anything to do with Jordan personally, she hoped she would be allowed to explain and apologize. She knew she had betrayed a trust. Even if she hadn't done it herself, she knew she should never have dug for information Reece asked her to ignore. And leaving it on her computer was as unprofessional as she could get. She knew better.

Jordan pulled into Reece's private drive and eased past the NO TRESPASSING signs. She was sure if there was ever a time Reece would call the sheriff on a trespasser, this would be it. She sped along the path, scraping branches and rolling over potholes. She pulled up to the back door of the cabin next to Reece's pickup truck. She knocked on the door but no one answered. She checked the front door but it was locked as well and there were no sounds of life. Jordan peered in the window, hoping to see Reece sitting on the couch, ignoring her. But there were no lights on and no one in sight. She could see a pair of suitcases standing at the end of the couch as if they were waiting for a trip. Jordan squinted through the window. She could see something else on the table. It was a photograph, an eight-by-ten framed picture of Jordan, apparently taken while on the camping trip. Jordan didn't remember Reece taking any pictures of her.

"Reece?" she called, banging on the door. "Are you here?" Jordan finally gave up and accepted she wasn't there.

She remembered what Gloria had said. Reece had a remote place she liked to go and it was near the cabin. Perhaps she was there, deep in the woods, looking for solace and escape. Jordan again squinted in the window, looking toward the corner where Reece kept her backpack. It wasn't there. Jordan quickly pulled the pack from her trunk and slipped it over her shoulders. She had no idea which way to go but she knew she had to at least try to find Reece and explain.

There was a narrow path that ran along the edge of the cabin then disappeared into the forest. Jordan followed it, hurrying along the darkened route as it ducked in and out of the trees on its way down one hill and up the next. Jordan crossed a stream, carefully balancing on the boulders that were littered across the rushing waters. Once she was on the other side, the path forked. One side meandered down toward the dense valley below and the other side ran up a steep hill. Jordan examined both sides of the path, trying to decide which looked like it had been more recently traveled. The leaves and moss looked more matted on the steep incline so she started up the hill, groaning her way up to the top. Jordan leaned back against a tree to catch her breath, watching the gathering clouds. It had been raining almost all day, heavy at times. She knew the momentary dry spell would soon end as the distant sound of thunder rumbled through the forest. Jordan hoped she would find Reece soon. She hated to be in the forest alone in the rain. She continued up the path, her eyes searching for any signs of a campsite. She wanted to call out to her but she was afraid she would only send Reece deeper into the woods to escape being found.

A gentle rain began to fall and Jordan quickened her pace. She tucked her hands under the shoulder straps and trotted down the hill. The rain fell harder, soaking her hair and her clothes. She couldn't believe she was so stupid as to forget her raincoat. She pushed her hair back from her face and trudged onward. She tried to ignore the idea that she might become lost in the woods. She was going to find Reece. She may tie Jordan to a tree and leave her for the animals to consume but she was going to find her. Jordan trotted down and up another slope, winding her way deeper and deeper into the woods. The rain eased a bit as she came upon a clearing. She stopped, leaning over and resting her hands on her knees as she caught her breath. She wanted to take off her backpack and rest awhile, but she knew if she did, it would be harder to put it back on. She stood staring at the ground, gasping for breath, wondering how far she had come. As she looked up, she could see something orange through the trees. She had seen that color before. It was the same color as Reece's tent.

"Reece," Jordan called as she weaved her way through the trees. "Reece McAllister."

Jordan felt a deep sense of relief to find Reece's tent and her pack resting against a tree. There was a small pile of ashes smoldering in the campfire ring, Reece's empty water pan resting on a rock nearby. Her sleeping bag was spread neatly inside the tent, her hiking boots just inside the tent flap. Jordan knew that meant she was nearby, probably wearing her camp slippers, the ones that made X-shaped marks in the dirt when she walked. Jordan removed her pack and began searching the rain-soaked ground around the campfire and the tent for telltale signs of her rubber slippers.

"Ah-ha," she muttered, noticing a line of Xs leading into the woods toward a cliff. "Reece, where are you? You can't hide from me forever." Jordan called, certain Reece was just out of sight and fully aware she had been found. "Reece!" she called louder. Suddenly she felt the ground move beneath her feet. Jordan screamed and jumped back as a chunk of earth disappeared over the edge of the cliff.

"Get back," Reece called, her voice rising up from over the edge of the cliff.

"Reece, it's Jordan. Where are you?"

"Down here."

"Oh, my God," Jordan gasped, realizing Reece was in danger. "What happened?"

"The cliff gave way with me on it. I'm stuck on a ledge about thirty feet down," Reece called.

Jordan wasn't sure what to do. She prowled the edge of the cliff, frantically trying to find a place where she could see over the side.

"I'll help you," Jordan yelled. She didn't realize it but pieces of dirt and mud were being dislodged by her pacing.

"No," Reece yelled angrily. "Get back. The ground isn't safe. It'll give way any minute and you'll be down here with me. Go back. Hike out of here right now before it gets any darker. Go get help."

"I'm not leaving you," Jordan declared. She tested her footing as she tried to peer over the edge.

"You can't help me here, Jordan. Now go on." Reece was struggling to free herself from the deep mud and fallen trees that encased her.

"Do you have any rope in your pack?" Jordan asked, deciding how she could lower herself down the cliff, but still have an escape route.

"No, not enough to reach down here. And it isn't climbing rope, anyway. Just twine for hanging stuff in the trees. Now go on, please."

"If I leave, I'll probably get lost, you know that. I only found your camp by accident. I'll never get out of here before dark. Then we'd have two stranded people instead of one. Now shut up about me leaving. We're going to figure this out together. So help me decide what to do." Jordan's voice was adamant.

Reece didn't reply. She was busy trying to free at least one of her legs, but they were both hopelessly stuck in the thick mud.

"Reece, are you there?" Jordan said, leaning out to see her.

"Yes, I'm still right here," she replied sarcastically.

"Tell me what to do. You're the person with the experience in the outdoors," Jordan demanded.

Reece grabbed a nearby branch and pulled with all her strength, hoping to free herself. The branch was too thin and snapped off, releasing the rest of the small tree to roll down the embankment. Reece noticed a small hole in the side of the cliff where the tree had been. It was the size of a fireplace opening and just as dark. She couldn't be sure but it looked like a deep hole, one that disappeared into the hillside. She stabbed the tree branch at the top of the opening, expecting it to collapse and fill in with dirt. But it didn't. Instead, the opening enlarged.

"I heard something," Jordan called anxiously. "Are you okay? What happened?"

"I'm all right. A tree slid down the hill." Reece kept stabbing the branch at the hole, curious about how big it was. She struggled against her entrapment, gasping and groaning with every stab.

"What are you doing? I can hear you groaning," Jordan said, trying to find a place where she could see over the side.

"There is a hole in the side of the hill. I'm trying to see how big it is."

"What kind of hole?"

"It might be the opening of a cave."

Jordan shuddered, the thought of a cave bringing a cold chill over her body.

"Is it?" she asked, almost afraid of what Reece would report.

"I can't tell but it is about three feet in diameter and it looks like it goes straight in like a tunnel." Reece threw some rocks at the opening, checking to see if she could raise any animal that might be sleeping inside the cave. Nothing came out.

"This isn't helping me get you out, Reece. How am I going to get down there? Are you sure you don't have any rope in your pack? I could lower myself over the edge."

"I didn't bring enough heavy rope to do that. Besides, the hillside is too unstable. It will just come falling down on me." Just as she said that, a chunk of soil broke free from under Jordan's feet and slid down the side, spraying Reece with dirt. "Get back," she yelled.

Jordan jumped back, screaming at what she had caused.

"Are you all right? Oh God, Reece. Talk to me."

"I'm all right. Stay back from the edge," she advised, spitting dirt.

Jordan tried again to get a signal on her cell phone but there was none.

"My cell phone is useless out here," she muttered angrily. "Shit," she whispered, looking up as a gentle rain started to fall. She knew it meant more mud and more danger to the already fragile hillside.

"It's raining again, isn't it," Reece asked, brushing the dirt from her face and hair.

"Yes," Jordan said, sorry to have to admit it.

"I'm not sure how much more water that hill can take before it comes down on me. Please, Jordan. Hike out. I don't want you getting stuck here."

"Don't say another word about it. I am not leaving you." Jordan's voice was shaky at best. The rain fell heavier. Streams of water ran over the edge of the cliff like a dozen small waterfalls. Jordan was drenched to the skin but she refused to leave the edge of the cliff. She knew Reece was down below, covered with mud, probably sinking deeper into the quagmire.

"Do you have any ideas?" Jordan asked, scanning the ground around her for something to use to rescue Reece.

Reece was muttering something but she couldn't understand her.

"What did you say? I can't hear you," Jordan asked, straining to listen.

"Nothing. I just said maybe this cave goes through to the other side of the hill." Reece replied, resting her head against a tree branch, trying to catch her breath.

"The other side of what hill?"

"There was a slope that led down to the stream. As you came up the trail it would have been on the right side. There is a thick stand of trees against the hillside."

"You think it might come out over there?" Jordan asked, feeling a spark of relief that Reece might have thought of a way out.

"Could be. There are a lot of caves in this area. I stayed in one once during a lightning storm. It could just be a sinkhole but those don't usually run horizontally. They are vertical shafts." Reece's voice was growing weak, as she struggled against the sucking action of the mud that threatened to pull her deeper.

"Let me go look. I'll be right back, sweetheart. It'll only take me a few minutes. You hold on, okay?"

"I'll be right here," Reece muttered.

Jordan retraced her steps and found the spot where the stream crossed the path. Just as Reece had said, there was a grove of trees growing against a hill. The pines were intermingled with scrubby looking Madrona trees, their tangled branches hiding the hillside behind them. Jordan fought her way through the trees to the embankment and sure enough, a small opening was covered by weeds and fallen branches. She pushed them aside and peered into the opening.

"Damn, I should have brought a flashlight," she muttered, squinting inside the cave. "Reece, can you hear me?" she called, cupping her hands to her mouth and yelling. "Reece!"

There was no reply. She hurried back up the path to the edge of the cliff, out of breath from the run.

"Reece, I think I found the other end of the cave. It is right where you said it was. Do you think you can get through it?" Jordan asked, excited at the prospect that Reece would soon be free and rescued.

Reece didn't answer.

"Reece? Did you hear me?" Jordan repeated, yelling loudly over the edge.

"I heard you, Jordan," Reece replied hesitantly.

"What's wrong? I can go down there and shine a flashlight in the opening and you can crawl through to safety. It was a great idea. I'm glad you thought of it."

"Jordan, I can't. I'm too embedded in the mud to get my legs free. I'm trapped up to my chest in mud and tree branches. I can't get free by myself. That's why I wanted you to go for help."

"Did you bring a shovel with you? Something to dig yourself free?" Jordan asked tentatively, her mind already reconciling what she would have to do.

"No, I didn't. Only that little plastic trowel in my pack."

It was Jordan's turn to fall silent, her mind wrestling with the cold, hard truth. Reece was trapped and her only escape was through a tiny opening into a subterranean tunnel, a tunnel big enough for Jordan to crawl through but little else. The weather was making time an important factor, the rain-soaked earth weakening with every passing moment and ready to drop tons of mud on top of Reece, burying her alive.

"It's not too late to try hiking out, Jordan. You can't do anything here."

There was something in Reece's voice, something that told Jordan she was holding something back. Jordan had a pretty good idea what it was too. Reece knew Jordan had claustrophobia and she refused to ask her to crawl through the cave to help her.

"Reece, if I was going to crawl through the tunnel and come out where you are, about how long do you think it would take me to get there?" she asked, her voice riddled with doubt. "How far do you think it is?"

"You can't do that, Jordan. Forget it."

"I don't see we have any other choice here. And I don't think we have the luxury of wasting time discussing it. It is raining harder and it's just a matter of time before the rest of the cliff goes sliding down the side of the mountain." She stopped herself as a lump rose in her throat. The consequences of what might happen if the cliff did slide down the hillside were too much to think about. "I'm coming to get you out, Reece. So please, tell me what I should bring with me."

"Jordan, I can't let you go in that cave. It might not go anywhere at all. It might narrow to little more than a few inches wide. I have no idea what is in there or where it goes. I was only guessing that it came out on the other side. We'll think of something else."

Jordan could hear Reece thrashing among the tree branches, trying to extricate herself.

"Reece, I'm going to do it." She swallowed hard. "I'm coming through the tunnel to get you. Now, for God's sake, tell me what to bring," Jordan demanded, digging deep inside herself for the courage she so desperately needed.

"Are you sure?" Reece asked tentatively.

"Yes," she replied decisively. "Yes, I am."

Reece hesitated, as if accepting this was her only chance to be rescued.

"Bring a flashlight, some drinking water, the plastic trowel from my pack and the hank of lightweight rope in the outside pouch. Maybe we can use it to pull some of these tree branches away. Also, there is a headlamp in the top of my pack. Slip it on your head like a miner's light. If you brought gloves, wear them. The inside of the cave may be dangerous. It could have rocks or sharp edges poking out."

"Anything else?" Jordan asked, trying to concentrate on what she needed to bring rather than where she was going.

"No, I can't think of anything else." Reece hesitated a moment. "Jordan, I'll understand if you can't do this. I know what I'm asking of you."

"You aren't asking me to do anything, Reece. I'm doing this because I want to. That's all you have to know." Jordan turned and ran to camp to collect what she needed. She emptied Reece's small tote bag and filled it with the flashlight and the other items. She added some granola bars, knowing Reece had probably been down there for hours and would be weak from hunger. She scribbled a note explaining where she was going and where Reece was and pinned it to the tent flap in case anyone happened by. She then rushed down the path to the opening of the tunnel. It was smaller than she remembered it being when she first looked at it. She cleaned away the debris, making it easier to find, hung her jacket conspicuously over a branch and tightened the pack over her shoulder. She turned on the headlamp and adjusted the beam to show where she was going. The cave was dark and musty, the smell of rotting leaves and stagnant water filling her nostrils. She crouched at the mouth of the tunnel, coming to terms with what she had to do. Her heart was pounding in her throat and her eyes were as big as saucers as she stuck her head inside the opening, her gloved hands sinking into the muck on the floor of the tunnel. Her hair brushed against the top of the cave, dirt sifting down and settling in her eyes. She quickly backed out, shaking her head and blinking away the silt. She took a deep breath and tried again, crouching lower as she entered the opening. She paused with her hands and head inside the cave, her feet still out in the open air, waiting for her courage to propel her forward. She could hear her heart pounding in her ears, her breathing short and labored as she remained frozen in the mouth of the cave.

"I'm coming, Reece. I'm coming," she whispered, tears filling her eyes. "Please, God. Please help me do this. I have to do this." She rocked back and forth, as if trying to unstick herself from fly-paper. A crack of thunder sent a shiver up her back, making her gasp for breath. She adjusted the headlamp down, shining on the floor of the tunnel instead of the dark expanse ahead of her. "*Un, deux, trois, quatre, cinq,*" she started, enunciating the French numbers carefully as she crawled forward a few feet. She felt the urge to look back at the daylight behind her, but she knew it would only make it more difficult to go forward. "*Six, sept, huit,*" she continued counting, her voice shaky but loud. "*Neuf, dix,* oh yuck. What is that?" she groaned, looking down at her hand that was wrist deep in a slimy sludge. "I don't think I want to know," she muttered, continuing to count in French as she crawled along the tunnel. She kept her eyes down, refusing to look more than a few feet ahead. She was up to ninety-three when the walls of the tunnel began to narrow, rubbing against her shoulders as she crawled along. Her upper lip beaded with sweat and her heart raced as she tried to stay centered in the tunnel. The muddy walls and soggy floor reminded Jordan that the rain had seeped through the ground, possibly weakening the integrity of the tunnel. She forced that thought out of her mind.

The tunnel made a gentle bend to the right. Jordan hesitated, unable to resist the urge to look back to see how far she had come. When she did, she was surprised to see only blackness. She could no longer see the light of day outside. The tunnel had gradually turned, trapping her in a dark void. Jordan reached up to adjust her headlamp again. As she did, she touched the switch and the light went out. She screamed, gasping for breath as if the oxygen had gone out of the air. The world around her had gone completely black. She couldn't tell if her eyes were open or closed. She fumbled with the headlamp, turning it back on. She quickly crawled forward, putting her mind back to the task of getting through the tunnel and rescuing Reece. She couldn't remember where she stopped in her counting, so she began again with one.

As the cave began to widen again, Jordan noticed it was also running downhill at a gentle slope. When she got to the bottom of the incline, she found herself crawling through several inches of water. She shone her headlamp into the water, expecting it to be green and slimy. But it was brown and it didn't smell like the other stagnant water she had crawled through.

"This is rain water. This is water from the outside. It is coming in from somewhere." She continued on, clawing her way back up another slope. Jordan recited a poem in French as she moved along the tunnel, trying to distract her fear. She knew she was deeper into the side of the mountain than she wanted to think about.

Jordan was covered with mud and slime. She was also cold and wet. The farther she went, the more she was forced to face the possibility the tunnel might not come out anywhere near where Reece was stuck. Or even come out at all. She may be crawling toward a dead end.

"I should be there by now. I've been crawling forever. Where are you, Reece?" she muttered, afraid her tears would overtake her. "Where are you? Where is the opening?"

She blinked the tears from her eyes and continued on, her arms and legs seeming to move without her knowing it. Suddenly she heard a loud clap of thunder, the reflection of lightning glowing in the tunnel ahead of her. Jordan scrambled toward the light. Her head popped out into the light of day. Reece was straining to see the opening to the cave over her shoulder.

"There you are," Reece announced, a broad grin on her face. There was an unmistakable quiver to Reece's chin as she saw Jordan's face. "You did it, baby. I'm very proud of you."

"Hello," Jordan said happily, the relief at seeing Reece's face so great it brought tears to her eyes. She pulled herself out of the tunnel, crawled over to Reece and hugged her neck. "I don't know how I did it, but here I am." Jordan opened her tote bag and handed Reece a bottle of water and a granola bar. "You eat this, you hear me. You look tired and hungry. You eat while I pull some of these branches away."

"Yes, ma'am." Reece smiled at her, grateful for the food and water.

Jordan began removing the branches and tossing them down the hill.

"How long have you been down here?" she asked as she worked feverishly to clear the area around where Reece was embedded.

"It was right after breakfast," Reece said, trying to help. "What time is it?"

"I don't know. I lost my watch somewhere in the tunnel. About six thirty, I think."

Jordan dug a trench around Reece, using the plastic trowel until it broke. She then used her hands to pull away the heavy mud. Reece helped as best she could, pushing the dirt back as far as she could reach, finally able to pull first one leg free then the other. By the time Reece was released from her muddy entrapment, they both were covered with mud from head to toe.

"Are you all right?" Jordan asked, hugging Reece with relief. They stood in the rain, the downpour matting their already mud-caked hair.

"Yes, I'm all right. Are you?" She smiled at Jordan, brushing a clump of mud from her face. They looked like mud wrestlers. As they laughed at each other's look, another clap of thunder split the darkness, rumbling across the sky. Just then a huge section of the cliff above broke away and began sliding down the hillside. Reece pulled Jordan out of the way as it settled down the slope, filling in the hole where Reece had been trapped.

"Reece, that would have been right on top of you," Jordan said, hugging her again.

"I think we need to get out of here before more comes down."

Reece took Jordan by the hand and led her back to the tunnel opening. She crawled inside, using the flashlight to guide her route. She allowed Jordan to keep the headlamp for security.

"I don't suppose there is any other way for us to get out of here, is there?" Jordan asked, waiting for her turn to enter the opening.

"Not unless you can fly," Reece said, leading the way. Jordan took a deep breath and followed, glad Reece was moving at a fast pace. Reece also kept up a nearly constant chatter as they crawled back through the tunnel, seeming to know it helped Jordan not think about where she was.

Chapter 27

Once they were out of the tunnel and back in camp, Jordan collapsed onto a stump, tears rolling down her muddy cheeks. Reece took her in her arms and held her while she cried. It didn't matter if it was for Reece's return to safety or for the monstrous fear she had to overcome to crawl through a tunnel. Whatever the reason, Jordan needed to cry, so Reece let her.

"You're covered with mud, Ms. McAllister," Jordan said, smiling through her tears.

"You're no bathing beauty yourself, Ms. Griffin," Reece replied, picking at Jordan's mud-plastered hair.

"We can't hike out tonight. It's almost dark. Maybe we should heat some water over the campfire to wash with," Jordan suggested, looking down at her clothes. The rain had stopped but it didn't matter. They couldn't be any wetter.

"Come on," Reece said, stoking the campfire to get it going. She then took Jordan by the hand.

"Where are we going?"

"To the stream while there is a little bit of daylight left." Reece stopped at her backpack and pulled out her towel and two silver emergency space blankets. "Did you bring a change of clothes?"

"I don't think so. I just grabbed the backpack from the trunk. "I have no idea what is in it."

"Then you'll have to wear one of these things while your clothes dry. We'll wash them out in the stream and hang them near the campfire. Come on," she said, pulling her along.

"That water will be freezing cold, Reece," Jordan said, pulling back.

"I can't help it. We have no choice. You can't stay covered with that smelly, stinking mud all night. Who knows what kind of diseases we crawled through in that cave. It has to come off."

"I still like the idea of heating water over the campfire," Jordan argued.

"It would take all night to heat enough for that."

"But Reece, I'm a city girl. I've never taken a bath in the woods before. I don't think I can do this," she pleaded.

"You said last time you deserved a chance to learn to enjoy camping. This is your chance."

"Yes, I know. But can't I do it gradually? Maybe wash my face in the stream?"

"Nope, it's all or nothing. You had the courage to crawl through that tunnel. You can take a bath in a mountain stream." Reece pulled Jordan along the path.

When they arrived at the bank of the stream, Jordan's eyes widened at the rain-swollen waters rushing along over rocks and boulders, churning and bubbling on its way to the ocean.

"Reece, I don't think I can do this," she said, backing up and staring at the icy waters. Reece had already begun taking off her clothes, draping them over a log.

"You take off your clothes or I will, Jordan." Reece scowled at her. "You can wear your boots. They'll protect your feet from the rocks. But those foul smelling clothes have got to come off."

"Okay, but if I freeze to death, it will be on your conscience." Jordan began pulling off her filthy clothes and piling them on the bank. When she was finished, Reece took her hand and together they stepped into the cold stream, first to their ankles then their knees. Jordan squealed and sucked air, standing on her tiptoes as long as she could to avoid the chilly water. Reece stepped in deeper, bobbing up and down, rinsing off the mud and scum.

"Come on in. The water's fine," she teased, splashing a handful at Jordan.

"Stop that, you brat. I'm dying over here." Jordan folded her arms over her chest as if they would keep her warm. She could feel her nipples growing hard. Her skin was pure white. She daintily washed a spot here and there while Reece bobbed and splashed her way to clean. Jordan ventured out a bit further, her knees now covered.

"It would be much easier if you just come out here and do it all at once. You are just prolonging the agony, Jordan," Reece said then went under, washing the mud from her hair.

"I have to do this. I have to do this," Jordan muttered as she stepped further into the current.

"That's it. Come on," Reece said encouragingly.

"Is this what they call roughing it?" she asked, her chin quivering involuntarily.

"You bet. Come out here where I am. It's a little deeper but the current isn't as strong."

Jordan took a cautious step in that direction.

"Carefully," Reece advised. "There's a rock right in front of you. Don't trip over it."

Jordan shuffled her feet along the rocky bottom, searching for secure footing. Without warning, she suddenly hooked her toe under a submerged log and stumbled, sliding beneath the surface of the fast-moving water. The shocking temperature took her breath away. She struggled to keep her face above the water as the current pushed her downstream. Reece lunged for her as she floated past. She grabbed for Jordan and pulled her into her arms, holding her in a secure embrace. Jordan coughed and sputtered to catch her breath from the dunking, her eyes huge and glazed.

"Are you all right?" Reece asked fearfully.

Jordan was too shocked and cold to reply. She gasped and held tight to Reece's neck. She continued to choke and struggle for breath, pulling herself onto her toes as if to climb out of the cold waters.

"I've got you," Reece said, holding her tight and kissing her check. "I've got you. You're okay."

It took Jordan several minutes to regain her senses. Reece never released her reassuring hold on her, stroking her hair and kissing her cheek as her breath returned to normal and her eyes cleared.

"That's one way of getting the mud off, Surianna," Reece teased, trying to ease her own concern for Jordan's safety.

"I bet you think I'm a real twit, don't you?" Jordan asked, too embarrassed to look at Reece.

"Absolutely not," Reece stated emphatically, brushing the hair from Jordan's face. "I'm just glad you weren't hurt."

"I don't seem to be able to do anything right," Jordan said, her voice cracking and tears welling up in her eyes. Once again she had proved she wasn't at home in the outdoors. She hated it. She desperately wanted to show Reece she was learning to handle herself in the wild. "I'm sorry I'm such a big klutz."

"You are *not* a klutz," Reece replied, smiling softly at her. "You are wonderful. You are the bravest person I have ever met. Don't you forget it."

Reece took Jordan's face in her hands and kissed her tenderly. Jordan was surprised at Reece's sudden display of affection. It was the first time they had touched since that night Reece had denied her feelings for Jordan. The kiss was short but Reece continued to hold Jordan's face in her hands, looking deep into her eyes, their lips just inches apart. They stood waist deep in the stream, their naked bodies glistening in the last light of day.

Reece smiled then slowly kissed Jordan again, closing her eyes and drinking in her taste. Jordan leaned into the kiss, her heart pounding in her throat. She suddenly didn't feel the cold water flowing around her. All she could feel was Reece's lips against hers. It was electrifying, sending tingles down her body. Jordan slipped her arms around Reece's neck and pulled herself tighter against her. She had forgotten her crawl through the cave, the cold stream water and her dunking. She couldn't remember anything but the fact that she loved Reece with every fiber of her being. Jordan could feel herself throb as Reece kissed her. She wanted to place Reece's hand between her legs and press against it. When Reece's hand floated over her thigh, Jordan thought the cold stream water had suddenly heated to boiling, burning the tender skin of her womanhood. Jordan slid her hands down Reece's back and cupped them at her bottom, pulling her hips up to hers.

"We better get out of the water before we get hypothermia," Reece said, suddenly breaking their embrace and stepping back. "Come on." She climbed out of the stream, helping Jordan onto the bank.

Reece's change of mood was as surprising as Jordan's cold dip in the stream. Jordan suddenly felt cold again, Reece's body no longer warming her. Reece handed Jordan the towel then went to work rinsing their clothes in the stream. Jordan wrapped one of the space blankets around herself, shivering uncontrollably. Reece finally wrapped the other blanket around herself and carried the clothes over her shoulder.

"Let's go up to camp and get warm by the fire."

Reece arranged the wet clothes over branches near the fire, stoking it to a full blaze inside the fire ring. Jordan rolled a log to the edge of the fire and sat down, her teeth still chattering. Reece wore her space blanket like a toga, busying herself with camp chores. She heated some water and made hot cocoa for them. She also made Jordan some tomato soup, hoping it would help warm her.

"Here, eat this. It will help." Reece handed Jordan a cup of soup.

Jordan took it but she was so cold, her hands had trouble holding the handle. Reece molded Jordan's hands around the cup then adjusted her blanket around her shoulders.

"I'm sorry you had to do that," Reece offered. "But it really was important to get that nasty stuff off of us. I wouldn't want you to get sick."

"I know. It is just hard when you go under for the first time," Jordan replied with a shudder.

"I have news for you. It is hard every time you do that." Reece warmed her hands against her cup and smiled across at Jordan.

"At least you are safe. I'd jump in the creek again right now if I could have kept you from being trapped like that." Jordan stared back at her, huddling inside her space blanket.

"Believe me, Jordan. I know how hard it was for you to crawl through that tunnel. I will always remember you did that for me. You are a strong woman. You can do anything you put your mind to."

"Yeah, well, sometimes it can jump up and bite me in the ass." Jordan smirked at herself, knowing it was her unwavering curiosity that kept her on Pella's trail until she found what she wanted to know.

"I assume you are talking about the article."

Jordan nodded, slurping the last of her soup.

"I am so, so sorry about that, Reece. You have to believe me. I never meant for that information about Pella to be in the article. I had no idea Susan was going to use it. She pirated it from my files and rewrote the story without asking me."

"I know."

"You do?"

"Sure. I knew you didn't write that. It wasn't your style. I've read your articles. I know how you write. I could tell the first part was your work, but the part about Pella was written by someone else. The sentence structure was different. The story lost its compassion."

"It wasn't all Susan's doing. I have to admit, I did the research. I talked to the sheriff and the counselor. I got the truth and wrote it down. It was my fault for leaving it on the computer for her to find. I should never have done that. You asked me not to include Pella in the story and I didn't respect that. I should never have dug into that part of your past. It was none of my business. I am so sorry." Jordan gazed over at Reece, trying to express her deepest regret.

"Jordan, you did your job. You used your journalistic curiosity to get the story. You did what any good reporter would do. You saw something more to the story and you followed it. That is what you are supposed to do. That is what I would have done. And you did the benevolent thing with that information. You respected Pella enough to withhold it." Reece offered a small smile.

"I am sorry for you and for her. Is there anything I can do to fix this?"

"Yes," Reece said at once. "You can rewrite the story."

"I would love to, but the damage is done. The issue has already hit the newsstands and has been sent to subscribers. And besides," Jordan said then hesitated. "I don't work for *Northwest Living* any longer. I quit."

"Why? You are a damn good reporter."

"I can't work for Susan," Jordan said stiffly.

"I don't blame you," she chuckled. "I probably couldn't either. But when I said rewrite the story, I meant rewrite and clarify Pella's story. She is—or was—a beautiful woman but she had problems, problems that contributed to what she did. There is a story there, a story about abused children and what it can lead to. She wasn't sexually abused, but she might as well have been. Her parents were obsessed with how she looked. They convinced her she had to be beautiful or no one would love her. Her mother spent thousands of dollars on plastic surgery to improve her looks. They had her groomed and schooled to believe that the way she looked was the only key to success. She couldn't accept that she would ever grow old and lose those looks. I couldn't convince her she was still a beautiful person inside."

"Like you," Jordan said softly. "You are a beautiful person inside, Reece. And outside as well."

"We aren't talking about me. We are talking about Pella and the story you should write about her."

"I told you, I don't work there anymore."

"Would you take a job with *Northwest Living* if one was available?" Reece asked.

"I don't think so. Susan and I have too much history. I can't go back there. I don't regret anything I said to her. I'd be a hypocrite if I apologized to her."

"I have news for you. Susan Mackey doesn't work for *Northwest Living*, either. She was fired by the board of directors effective today. There is an opening for senior editor. Are you interested?"

"How did you know that?" Jordan asked skeptically.

Reece took the last sip of cocoa and placed the cup on a rock.

"Because I am on the board of directors of *Northwest Living*," she said, looking up. "I am actually on the board of the blind consortium that owns that magazine and two others, three newspapers and a television station. I bought into the syndicate years ago as an investment. I thought I could ease out of television journalism so Pella and I could spend more time together, travel, see the world. But she didn't see it that way. She thought I was doing it out of pity for her."

"Are you telling me, the three years I worked for *Northwest Living*, I was really working for you?" Jordan's eyes widened.

"Yes."

"And you didn't tell me?"

"No one knew. That's why I insisted it was a blind consortium. My business manager handled it for me."

"All this time, while I was interviewing you and camping with you and dating you, I was one of your employees?"

"Yes. But not directly. I didn't actually write your paycheck."

"Reece McAllister, you should have told me." Jordan suddenly remembered what she had told Susan, that she never dated at work. She chuckled to herself.

"By the way, how did you know I'd be up here?"

"I asked your neighbor Gloria. She told me you had a place in the woods you liked to go when you were upset. And she was sure you were upset about the article. She said she saw you looking at it when the mailman brought it. She is very protective of you. And she doesn't like that terrible reporter who wrote the story about you. She was very happy Ms. Griffin doesn't work for *Northwest Living* anymore." Jordan smiled as she remembered the woman's concern for Reece.

"So you came to Greysome Point to find me and tell me you quit the magazine?"

"That and to apologize."

"I have to say, I'm glad you are still a good reporter. I don't think anyone else would have found me in time."

"I don't even want to think about it," Jordan said, heaving a deep sigh. "I noticed some suitcases in the living room of the cabin. I looked in the window." Jordan looked at Reece, hoping she would dismiss them as nothing.

"I'm going on a trip," Reece offered casually.

"Where are you going?"

"Italy, Switzerland, maybe Spain. I haven't decided yet."

"You have your suitcases packed and you don't know where you are going?"

"I'm starting in Vienna then I'll play it by ear."

"When will you be back?" Jordan asked, desperate for Reece to explain.

"I don't know. Couple months. Maybe longer. I have a one-way ticket." Reece began fueling the fire as if she needed a diversion. "I want to take some pictures of the Alps."

"Couple months? Reece, why are you going to Europe?" Jordan had a worried look on her face.

"I didn't know I had to check with you before I went on a trip," Reece replied, a cocky look on her face.

"You don't. But I think this is far more than just a picture-taking expedition. I think you are running away." Jordan searched Reece's face for understanding.

"Running away from what?" she chuckled. "You?"

"Yes, and yourself," Jordan said softly.

"That's ridiculous," Reece said, then went back to loading the fire.

"Is it? I first thought you might be avoiding me. You said you thought I should date someone. But then you cut in when I was dancing with Kelly. You didn't do that just to ask how the article was going. You did that because you didn't want me to be with anyone else."

"Hey, I'm sorry I got you drunk that night. I shouldn't have done that."

Jordan smiled coyly.

"I know why you did it."

"Why?" Reece frowned.

"Because you didn't want me to end up with anyone else. You love me, Reece. I know you do." Jordan smiled over at her. "You just refuse to let yourself."

Reece was staring at the ground, pretending she needed to rearrange the rocks around the fire.

"Think you're pretty smart, don't you?" Reece replied without looking up.

"I'm a reporter. I'm supposed to figure this stuff out, even when the subject won't cooperate." Jordan pulled her space blanket around herself and walked on her knees to where Reece was sitting. She knelt in front of her and looked up at her, a gentle smile on her face. "I love you, sweetheart. Why won't you let yourself love me back? I am not Pella. I have seen both sides of you. And I don't mean both sides of your face. I mean both sides of your heart. You are a compassionate, caring person. You are intelligent and resourceful. You are tender and loving. Please, I beg you not to judge me by someone else. Let yourself love me for who I am. Not who you are afraid I might be." Jordan touched Reece's face, tracing her fingers down the scar then across Reece's lips. Jordan's eyes were full of love, swimming deep in Reece's gaze. "You kissed me a few minutes ago like you would never let me go. I'm in your soul, Reece. I'm in your heart so deep you can't ignore me. Let me show you how much I love you. Please."

"Jordan, you don't understand." Reece held desperately to her emotions. "Look at this." She turned her face to Jordan and pointed to the scar, exposing it to the light of the fire. "I can't hide this from you. It's there. It'll always be there and I know what will happen. Maybe not today, maybe not tomorrow. But someday. Someday I will see it in your eyes. You will hate it. You will be disgusted by it. I am saving you from that. I am saving me from that, as well." Reece pushed Jordan's hands back into her lap.

"All right then. I'll make us the same," she said smugly.

Jordan quickly stood up and rushed to her backpack, digging out a pocketknife. She returned to the campfire and sat down in front of Reece, opening the knife.

"I'll give myself a scar. Then we'll both have marks on our faces." She held the knife up to her face. "Is this what it takes for you to love me?"

"Are you crazy?" Reece yelled, grabbing the knife from her hand. She threw it into the woods as far as she could heave it. "Jordan, what the hell are you doing?"

"I want a scar like you," Jordan said, looking up at Reece.

"The hell you do." Reece scoffed, looking genuinely angry at Jordan for the first time. She grabbed Jordan by the shoulders and pulled her to her feet, shaking her. "Don't ever talk like that again. Do you hear me? I don't want you to go through what I went through, ever." She hugged Jordan tight in a protective embrace. "You don't have to have a scar for me to love you," Reece declared, tears welling up in her eyes. It was the first time she had admitted she loved Jordan and it opened the floodgates. There was no taking it back. Reece couldn't hide the love she felt for Jordan any longer. She smothered Jordan's face with kisses. Jordan wrapped her arms around Reece, cradling her as she began to cry.

"I love you, Jordan. I do. I can't help it. I love you with all my heart," Reece said, falling to her knees and sobbing as Jordan held her in her arms.

For the first time in three years, Reece allowed herself to *feel*. Jordan stroked her face and rocked her as Reece cried the tears of pain, the tears of rebirth and the tears of love. Reece had found herself once again. And they had found each other.

Publications from
BELLA BOOKS, INC.
The best in contemporary lesbian fiction

P.O. Box 10543, Tallahassee, FL 32302
Phone: 800-729-4992
www.bellabooks.com

OUT OF THE FIRE by Beth Moore. Author Ann Covington feels at the top of the world when told her book is being made into a movie. Then in walks Casey Duncan the actress who is playing the lead in her movie. Will Casey turn Ann's world upside down?
1-59493-088-0 $13.95

STAKE THROUGH THE HEART: NEW EXPLOITS OF TWILIGHT LESBIANS by Karin Kallmaker, Julia Watts, Barbara Johnson and Therese Szymanski. The playful quartet that penned the acclaimed *Once Upon A Dyke* are dimming the lights for journeys into worlds of breathless seduction.
1-59493-071-6 $15.95

THE HOUSE ON SANDSTONE by KG MacGregor. Carly Griffin returns home to Leland and finds that her old high school friend Justice is awakening more than just old memories.
1-59493-076-7 $13.95

WILD NIGHTS: MOSTLY TRUE STORIES OF WOMEN LOVING WOMEN edited by Therese Szymanski. 264 pp. 23 new stories from today's hottest erotic writers are sure to give you your wildest night ever!
1-59493-069-4 $15.95

COYOTE SKY by Gerri Hill. 248 pp. Sheriff Lee Foxx is trying to cope with the realization that she has fallen in love for the first time. And fallen for author Kate Winters, who is technically unavailable. Will Lee fight to keep Kate in Coyote?
1-59493-065-1 $13.95

VOICES OF THE HEART by Frankie J. Jones. 264 pp. A series of events force Erin to swear off love as she tries to break away from the woman of her dreams. Will Erin ever find the key to her future happiness?
1-59493-068-6 $13.95

SHELTER FROM THE STORM by Peggy J. Herring. 296 pp. A story about family and getting reacquainted with one's past that shows that sometimes you don't appreciate what you have until you almost lose it.
1-59493-064-3 $13.95

WRITING MY LOVE by Claire McNab. 192 pp. Romance writer Vonny Smith believes she will be able to woo her editor Diana through her writing . . .
1-59493-063-5 $13.95

PAID IN FULL by Ann Roberts. 200 pp. Ari Adams will need to choose between the debts of the past and the promise of a happy future.
1-59493-059-7 $13.95

ROMANCING THE ZONE by Kenna White. 272 pp. Liz's world begins to crumble when a secret from her past returns to Ashton . . .
1-59493-060-0 $13.95

SIGN ON THE LINE by Jaime Clevenger. 204 pp. Alexis Getty, a flirtatious delivery driver is committed to finding the rightful owner of a mysterious package.
1-59493-052-X $13.95

END OF WATCH by Clare Baxter. 256 pp. LAPD Lieutenant L.A Franco Frank follows the lone clue down the unlit steps of memory to a final, unthinkable resolution.
1-59493-064-4 $13.95

BEHIND THE PINE CURTAIN by Gerri Hill. 280 pp. Jacqueline returns home after her father's death and comes face-to-face with her first crush.   1-59493-057-0 $13.95

PIPELINE by Brenda Adcock. 240 pp. Joanna faces a lost love returning and pulling her into a seamy underground corporation that kills for money.   1-59493-062-7 $13.95

18TH & CASTRO by Karin Kallmaker. 200 pp. First-time couplings and couples who know how to mix lust and love make 18th & Castro the hottest address in the city by the bay.
1-59493-066-X $13.95

JUST THIS ONCE by KG MacGregor. 200 pp. Mindful of the obligations back home that she must honor, Wynne Connelly struggles to resist the fascination and allure that a particular woman she meets on her business trip represents.   1-59493-087-2 $13.95

ANTICIPATION by Terri Breneman. 240 pp. Two women struggle to remain professional as they work together to find a serial killer.   1-59493-055-4 $13.95

OBSESSION by Jackie Calhoun. 240 pp. Lindsey's life is turned upside down when Sarah comes into the family nursery in search of perennials.   1-59493-058-9 $13.95

BENEATH THE WILLOW by Kenna White. 240 pp. A torch that still burns brightly even after twenty-five years threatens to consume two childhood friends.
1-59493-053-8 $13.95

SISTER LOST, SISTER FOUND by Jeanne G'fellers. 224 pp. The highly anticipated sequel to No Sister of Mine.   1-59493-056-2 $13.95

THE WEEKEND VISITOR by Jessica Thomas. 240 pp. In this latest Alex Peres mystery, Alex is asked to investigate an assault on a local woman but finds that her client may have more secrets than she lets on.   1-59493-054-6 $13.95

THE KILLING ROOM by Gerri Hill. 392 pp. How can two women forget and go their separate ways?   1-59493-050-3 $12.95

PASSIONATE KISSES by Megan Carter. 240 pp. Will two old friends run from love?
1-59493-051-1 $12.95

ALWAYS AND FOREVER by Lyn Denison. 224 pp. The girl next door turns Shannon's world upside down.   1-59493-049-X $12.95

BACK TALK by Saxon Bennett. 200 pp. Can a talk show host find love after heartbreak?
1-59493-028-7 $12.95

THE PERFECT VALENTINE: EROTIC LESBIAN VALENTINE STORIES edited by Barbara Johnson and Therese Szymanski—from Bella After Dark. 328 pp. Stories from the hottest writers around.   1-59493-061-9 $14.95

MURDER AT RANDOM by Claire McNab. 200 pp. The Sixth Denise Cleever Thriller. Denise realizes the fate of thousands is in her hands.   1-59493-047-3 $12.95

THE TIDES OF PASSION by Diana Tremain Braund. 240 pp. Will Susan be able to hold it all together and find the one woman who touches her soul?   1-59493-048-1 $12.95

JUST LIKE THAT by Karin Kallmaker. 240 pp. Disliking each other—and everything they stand for—even before they meet, Toni and Syrah find feelings can change, just like that.
1-59493-025-2 $12.95

WHEN FIRST WE PRACTICE by Therese Szymanski. 200 pp. Brett and Allie are once again caught in the middle of murder and intrigue. 1-59493-045-7 $12.95

REUNION by Jane Frances. 240 pp. Cathy Braithwaite seems to have it all: good looks, money and a thriving accounting practice . . . 1-59493-046-5 $12.95

BELL, BOOK & DYKE: NEW EXPLOITS OF MAGICAL LESBIANS by Kallmaker, Watts, Johnson and Szymanski. 360 pp. Reluctant witches, tempting spells and skyclad beauties—delve into the mysteries of love, lust and power in this quartet of novellas.
1-59493-023-6 $14.95

ARTIST'S DREAM by Gerri Hill. 320 pp. When Cassie meets Luke Winston, she can no longer deny her attraction to women . . . 1-59493-042-2 $12.95

NO EVIDENCE by Nancy Sanra. 240 pp. Private Investigator Tally McGinnis once again returns to the horror-filled world of a serial killer. 1-59493-043-04 $12.95

WHEN LOVE FINDS A HOME by Megan Carter. 280 pp. What will it take for Anna and Rona to find their way back to each other again? 1-59493-041-4 $12.95

MEMORIES TO DIE FOR by Adrian Gold. 240 pp. Rachel attempts to avoid her attraction to the charms of Anna Sigurdson . . . 1-59493-038-4 $12.95

SILENT HEART by Claire McNab. 280 pp. Exotic lesbian romance.

1-59493-044-9 $12.95

MIDNIGHT RAIN by Peggy J. Herring. 240 pp. Bridget McBee is determined to find the woman who saved her life. 1-59493-021-X $12.95

THE MISSING PAGE A Brenda Strange Mystery by Patty G. Henderson. 240 pp. Brenda investigates her client's murder . . . 1-59493-004-X $12.95

WHISPERS ON THE WIND by Frankie J. Jones. 240 pp. Dixon thinks she and her best friend, Elizabeth Colter, would make the perfect couple . . . 1-59493-037-6 $12.95

CALL OF THE DARK: EROTIC LESBIAN TALES OF THE SUPERNATURAL edited by Therese Szymanski—from Bella After Dark. 320 pp. 1-59493-040-6 $14.95

A TIME TO CAST AWAY A Helen Black Mystery by Pat Welch. 240 pp. Helen stops by Alice's apartment—only to find the woman dead . . . 1-59493-036-8 $12.95

DESERT OF THE HEART by Jane Rule. 224 pp. The book that launched the most popular lesbian movie of all time is back. 1-1-59493-035-X $12.95

THE NEXT WORLD by Ursula Steck. 240 pp. Anna's friend Mido is threatened and eventually disappears . . . 1-59493-024-4 $12.95

CALL SHOTGUN by Jaime Clevenger. 240 pp. Kelly gets pulled back into the world of private investigation . . . 1-59493-016-3 $12.95

52 PICKUP by Bonnie J. Morris and E.B. Casey. 240 pp. 52 hot, romantic tales—one for every Saturday night of the year. 1-59493-026-0 $12.95

GOLD FEVER by Lyn Denison. 240 pp. Kate's first love, Ashley, returns to their home town, where Kate now lives . . . 1-1-59493-039-2 $12.95

RISKY INVESTMENT by Beth Moore. 240 pp. Lynn's best friend and roommate needs her to pretend Chris is his fiancé. But nothing is ever easy. 1-59493-019-8 $12.95

HUNTER'S WAY by Gerri Hill. 240 pp. Homicide detective Tori Hunter is forced to team up with the hot-tempered Samantha Kennedy. 1-59493-018-X $12.95

CAR POOL by Karin Kallmaker. 240 pp. Soft shoulders, merging traffic and slippery when wet . . . Anthea and Shay find love in the car pool.   1-59493-013-9 $12.95

NO SISTER OF MINE by Jeanne G'Fellers. 240 pp. Telepathic women fight to coexist with a patriarchal society that wishes their eradication.   ISBN 1-59493-017-1 $12.95

ON THE WINGS OF LOVE by Megan Carter. 240 pp. Stacie's reporting career is on the rocks. She has to interview bestselling author Cheryl, or else! ISBN 1-59493-027-9 $12.95

WICKED GOOD TIME by Diana Tremain Braund. 224 pp. Does Christina need Miki as a protector . . . or want her as a lover?   ISBN 1-59493-031-7 $12.95

THOSE WHO WAIT by Peggy J. Herring. 240 pp. Two brilliant sisters—in love with the same woman!   ISBN 1-59493-032-5 $12.95

ABBY'S PASSION by Jackie Calhoun. 240 pp. Abby's bipolar sister helps turn her world upside down, so she must decide what's most important.   ISBN 1-59493-014-7 $12.95

PICTURE PERFECT by Jane Vollbrecht. 240 pp. Kate is reintroduced to Casey, the daughter of an old friend. Can they withstand Kate's career? ISBN 1-59493-015-5 $12.95

PAPERBACK ROMANCE by Karin Kallmaker. 240 pp. Carolyn falls for tall, dark and . . . female . . . in this classic lesbian romance.   ISBN 1-59493-033-3 $12.95

DAWN OF CHANGE by Gerri Hill. 240 pp. Susan ran away to find peace in remote Kings Canyon—then she met Shawn . . .   ISBN 1-59493-011-2 $12.95

DOWN THE RABBIT HOLE by Lynne Jamneck. 240 pp. Is a killer holding a grudge against FBI Agent Samantha Skellar?   ISBN 1-59493-012-0 $12.95

SEASONS OF THE HEART by Jackie Calhoun. 240 pp. Overwhelmed, Sara saw only one way out—leaving . . .   ISBN 1-59493-030-9 $12.95

TURNING THE TABLES by Jessica Thomas. 240 pp. The 2nd Alex Peres Mystery. *From ghosties and ghoulies and long leggity beasties . . .*   ISBN 1-59493-009-0 $12.95

FOR EVERY SEASON by Frankie Jones. 240 pp. Andi, who is investigating a 65-year-old murder, meets Janice, a charming district attorney . . .   ISBN 1-59493-010-4 $12.95

LOVE ON THE LINE by Laura DeHart Young. 240 pp. Kay leaves a younger woman behind to go on a mission to Alaska . . . will she regret it?   ISBN 1-59493-008-2 $12.95

UNDER THE SOUTHERN CROSS by Claire McNab. 200 pp. Lee, an American travel agent, goes down under and meets Australian Alex, and the sparks fly under the Southern Cross.   ISBN 1-59493-029-5 $12.95

SUGAR by Karin Kallmaker. 240 pp. Three women want sugar from Sugar, who can't make up her mind.   ISBN 1-59493-001-5 $12.95

FALL GUY by Claire McNab. 200 pp. 16th Detective Inspector Carol Ashton Mystery.
ISBN 1-59493-000-7 $12.95

ONE SUMMER NIGHT by Gerri Hill. 232 pp. Johanna swore to never fall in love again— but then she met the charming Kelly . . .   ISBN 1-59493-007-4 $12.95

TALK OF THE TOWN TOO by Saxon Bennett. 181 pp. Second in the series about wild and fun loving friends.   ISBN 1-931513-77-5 $12.95

LOVE SPEAKS HER NAME by Laura DeHart Young. 170 pp. Love and friendship, desire and intrigue, spark this exciting sequel to *Forever and the Night.*
ISBN 1-59493-002-3 $12.95

TO HAVE AND TO HOLD by Peggy J. Herring. 184 pp. By finally letting down her defenses, will Dorian be opening herself to a devastating betrayal?
ISBN 1-59493-005-8 $12.95

WILD THINGS by Karin Kallmaker. 228 pp. Dutiful daughter Faith has met the perfect man. There's just one problem: she's in love with his sister.   ISBN 1-931513-64-3 $12.95

SHARED WINDS by Kenna White. 216 pp. Can Emma rebuild more than just Lanny's marina?   ISBN 1-59493-006-6 $12.95

THE UNKNOWN MILE by Jaime Clevenger. 253 pp. Kelly's world is getting more and more complicated every moment.   ISBN 1-931513-57-0 $12.95

TREASURED PAST by Linda Hill. 189 pp. A shared passion for antiques leads to love.
ISBN 1-59493-003-1 $12.95

SIERRA CITY by Gerri Hill. 284 pp. Chris and Jesse cannot deny their growing attraction . . .   ISBN 1-931513-98-8 $12.95

ALL THE WRONG PLACES by Karin Kallmaker. 174 pp. Sex and the single girl—Brandy is looking for love and usually she finds it. Karin Kallmaker's first *After Dark* erotic novel.
ISBN 1-931513-76-7 $12.95

WHEN THE CORPSE LIES A Motor City Thriller by Therese Szymanski. 328 pp. Butch bad-girl Brett Higgins is used to waking up next to beautiful women she hardly knows. Problem is, this one's dead.   ISBN 1-931513-74-0 $12.95

GUARDED HEARTS by Hannah Rickard. 240 pp. Someone's reminding Alyssa about her secret past, and then she becomes the suspect in a series of burglaries.
ISBN 1-931513-99-6 $12.95

ONCE MORE WITH FEELING by Peggy J. Herring. 184 pp. Lighthearted, loving, romantic adventure.   ISBN 1-931513-60-0 $12.95

TANGLED AND DARK A Brenda Strange Mystery by Patty G. Henderson. 240 pp. When investigating a local death, Brenda finds two possible killers—one diagnosed with Multiple Personality Disorder.   ISBN 1-931513-75-9 $12.95

WHITE LACE AND PROMISES by Peggy J. Herring. 240 pp. Maxine and Betina realize sex may not be the most important thing in their lives.   ISBN 1-931513-73-2 $12.95

UNFORGETTABLE by Karin Kallmaker. 288 pp. Can Rett find love with the cheerleader who broke her heart so many years ago?   ISBN 1-931513-63-5 $12.95

HIGHER GROUND by Saxon Bennett. 280 pp. A delightfully complex reflection of the successful, high society lives of a small group of women.   ISBN 1-931513-69-4 $12.95

LAST CALL A Detective Franco Mystery by Baxter Clare. 240 pp. Frank overlooks all else to try to solve a cold case of two murdered children . . .   ISBN 1-931513-70-8 $12.95

ONCE UPON A DYKE: NEW EXPLOITS OF FAIRY-TALE LESBIANS by Karin Kallmaker, Julia Watts, Barbara Johnson & Therese Szymanski. 320 pp. You've never read fairy tales like these before! From Bella After Dark.   ISBN 1-931513-71-6 $14.95

FINEST KIND OF LOVE by Diana Tremain Braund. 224 pp. Can Molly and Carolyn stop clashing long enough to see beyond their differences?   ISBN 1-931513-68-6 $12.95

DREAM LOVER by Lyn Denison. 188 pp. A soft, sensuous, romantic fantasy.
ISBN 1-931513-96-1 $12.95

NEVER SAY NEVER by Linda Hill. 224 pp. A classic love story . . . where rules aren't the only things broken.   ISBN 1-931513-67-8 $12.95